HIS WOMAN, HIS WIFE, HIS WIDOW

HIS WOMAN, HIS WIFE, HIS WIDOW

JANICE JONES

www.urbanchristianonline.net

Urban Books
1199 Straight Path
West Babylon, NY 11704

ISBN- 13: 978-1-60162-995-1
ISBN- 10: 1-60162-995-8

First Printing July 2009
Printed in the United States of America

10   9   8   7   6   5   4   3   2

*This is a work of fiction. Any references or similarities to actual
events, real people, living, or dead, or to real locales are intended to
give the novel a sense of reality. Any similarity in other names,
characters, places, and incidents is entirely coincidental.*

Distributed by Kensington Corp.
Submit Wholesale Orders to:
Kensington Publishing Corp.
C/O Penguin Group (USA) Inc.
Attention: Order Processing
405 Murray Hill Parkway
East Rutherford, NJ 07073-2316
Phone: 1-800-526-0275
Fax: 1-800-227-9604

DEDICATION

I dedicate *His Woman, His Wife, His Widow* to two people who are no longer here with me in this earthly realm, but still reside deep within my heart.

To my mother, Valerie Bumpers. Mama, I miss you so much. Your support and unconditional love has gotten me to this point in my life. You have always made me feel like I could do anything. Of course, I selfishly wish you were here to celebrate the realization of a dream, but knowing that you now live with the Lord gives me consolation. The strong mother figure in this novel is definitely patterned after you. Whenever I wrote about Lindsay's mom, I would ask myself, what would my mother say? What would my mother do? Thank you for giving so much to me in so many different ways. I will always love you.

To Wilbert Eugene Franklin, Jr., affectionately known to all as Junior. You were a great friend, and you applauded my efforts with your support and enthusiasm. You let me into a place where few were allowed to tread, and I appreciated our special relationship. It tears at my heart that you did not live long enough to see this project to its completion, but I am strengthened knowing that you have gone on to be with King Jesus. I remember you in every old school song that no one else around me appreciates, every time I light my grill all by myself, and every time a butterfly comes near. I miss you and I love you.

ACKNOWLEDGMENTS

First and foremost, I have to acknowledge and give thanks to God, my Father, Jesus Christ, my Savior, and the Holy Spirit, my ever present help. Lord, without you, there would be no me; therefore, no *His Woman, His Wife, His Widow*. Father, I thank you for each and every chapter, paragraph, sentence, word, syllable, and letter of this project. I thank you, Father, for the gift of written communication, and I thank you for the ability to hear from you so that I may walk in the purpose you have given me. It is my honor and my pleasure to serve you.

To Jerrick & Derrick, Mommy loves you two so very much. You are my inspiration in everything I do. I pray that I have given to you as much as you have given to me. Prayerfully you are as proud of me as I am of you. To Jevon, my grandbaby, Granny is working hard to leave a legacy of greatness for you.

I would like to say thank you to my daddy, Harold Bumpers. You have always been supportive of me in all of my endeavors and have always had my back through all of my messes. Thank you, Daddy, for loving me unconditionally.

To Denise and Monique: Oh my goodness. You two have been very instrumental in helping me to get this project from chapter one to completion. You have read and read, reinvented, read some more, and given me your invaluable support. You have forced me to write when I did not feel like it, and your honest feedback has helped me to make this novel great. You two are the best friends a writer can have, but even more importantly, a woman can have.

Darrius, Darrin (Main), Darnella, Sherrie, and Linda: I thank God that you all are my siblings. You are always proud of me, and you go out of your way to be there for me no matter what. You all are the bomb. Thank you for all of my nieces, nephews and godchildren.

To my childhood homies, Wendy and Curtrise: You two are just like family. We have had our ups and downs, but NOTHING has been able to break our bond. Curtrise, you taught me so much about writing and a lot of my style in this novel came from you. Wendy, trust me when I say your experience helped me to write this novel as well (smile).

To Lawanda and Sonya, my new friends here in Arizona: You ladies have helped make my transition so much easier. You have supported me as if I have known you my entire life, and you have been great encouragers and cheerleaders. God was surely in charge of our divine connecting.

To my agent, Janell Walden Agyeman of Marie Brown & Associates, another divine connection: Thank you for taking me on even though you had absolutely no room left on your plate. Your expertise and advice has been superior, and I look forward to working with you for a long, long time.

To the Urban Christian family, I would like to first thank Vanessa Miller. You offered to read my manuscript and did not know me from Adam. Then you called me at 6:00 A.M. to give your praises. That was one of the most blessed days of my life. Joylynn, the day you called me ranks up there as well. Thank you for believing in me and for your wonderful eye and ear. Carl Weber, you write the best drama in the world. You inspired me from afar with your special brand of talent.

To my favorite authors, Victoria Christopher Murray and Beverly Jenkins, I pray that I will touch readers the way you two have touched me. I have read everything you have written, and I stalk the bookstores and websites, relentlessly awaiting your next releases. Sista Souljah, *The Coldest Winter Ever* is my all time favorite book. I can honestly say, after reading that book I, too, wanted to write a novel. I pray that Lindsay will be as well received by readers as Winter.

To the ladies of the Women's CSI class of First Institutional Baptist Church, Charmaine, Erica, Lisa, Beverly, Sherrie, Karen, Mrs. Coleman, Kim, and Tawanda. I want to use this opportunity to say thank you for your unwavering support during one of the most difficult periods of my life. You embraced me and loved me just as God has called us to do in His Word. You all did the Lord proud.

To my readers: I thank you for choosing this book, and I pray that you were not disappointed. Thank you for giving me the opportunity to entertain and hopefully enlighten you. It is my desire that you are looking forward to more and more and more . . .

HIS WOMAN, HIS WIFE, HIS WIDOW

Prologue

Iknew in my limited thirty-year-old wisdom, if it were not for God on my side, I would never make it through this day without having a nervous breakdown. I knew I had abandoned God on numerous occasions, yet I expected Him not to handle me in the same manner. Thankfully, God was not like man. So I prayed all morning for the strength to handle Shaun's funeral.

The event played as if that fool had planned the whole circus himself, full of glitz glamour and drama. However, it was his mother, queen of ignorant shenanigans, who was responsible for putting together today's sideshow, never once bothering to ask for my input. I mean, after all, was I not his wife? Patricia even went as far as making the seating arrangements for the two limousines that followed the hearse.

A white-diamond Bentley style Rolls Royce carried the casket. The two limos that followed were of the same style and color. Shaun's mother, his grandmother, his two sisters, Francine, and Tameeka, along with Francine's two children and Uncle Bobby, all rode in the first car. The second limousine held myself and my two children, Shauntae and Lil' Shaun. Also along for the ride were Shaun's son, Kevaun, and his mother, Keva, Shaun's daughter, Shawna, and her mother, Tawanda, and Shaun's oldest son, Sha'Ron, who was being raised by Patricia. I dubbed our vehicle The Baby Mama Car.

The limo was a little crowded, but the atmosphere was thick with uneasiness. Like I said . . . drama! The entire ride to the church was completed in total silence. Not even the children uttered a sound. I guess they too could feel the discomforting tension overflowing inside the automobile.

One of my children sat in my lap and the other by my side. Tawanda sat next to us with her two-month-old child sound asleep in her lap. Keva sat across from us with her son sitting next to her. Throughout the ride, I noticed that Kevaun continually stared at Shauntae with very disbelieving eyes. He probably could not understand why she looked so much like him. Sha'Ron sat next to Kevaun.

When the two limos pulled to a stop at the church, we all made our exit and headed to the front entrance of the church. For the thousandth time since I had learned about the funeral arrangements, I wondered how his mother was able to secure one of Detroit's most prominent churches for this funeral. I knew the she-devil herself never attended church, and I was pretty sure she didn't know or associate with anyone who did. She was a true spawn of Lucifer.

As I passed the crowd gathered outside the church while holding onto my babies' hands, I could hear jeers and snickers emanating from the female "mourners," pointing and letting those who were unaware know that I was wifey.

I scanned the crowd and one lone face stood out prominently. Although she looked very familiar, I could not quite put together the exact nature of our acquaintance. It was obvious that she recognized me as well, and from the heat radiating from her stare, I could tell our previous encounter had been none too pleasant. I ignored the gawker for the time being, making my way into the service.

The immediate family was ushered to the front of the church where the casket lay to view the body of my husband. Now I believe proper etiquette dictated that my children and I say our goodbyes first. However, Shaun's mother very boldly nudged me out of the way and went ahead of us.

Hate-Tricia . . . did I say that? I meant, Patricia stood there in her big purple and black hat, that ugly purple dress, and her fake boobs speaking to her dead son as if he were the world's most precious gift. She wailed as if Shaun's death was the greatest crime ever committed in the city of Detroit. Please! She knew better than most that this punk was no earthly good.

After a very dramatic performance, Patricia finally stepped away from the casket. She stopped in front of me, and after we exchanged rolling eyes, she moved away. I took the children to the casket to say our final farewells.

Standing there in front of his eternal cage, I stared at Shaun's heavily made-up face. He even had on a light shade of lipstick. The paints of presentation drastically altered his appearance. He didn't look a thing like his former self. I felt as if I owed the make-up artist a huge dept of gratitude, because I never wanted to see him again. I hated this man. Yet I somehow managed to keep from wearing my inner turmoil as an accessory to my bereavement outfit because I didn't want our children to feel my animosity. Shauntae and Lil' Shaun both shed silent tears, and they waved goodbye to their daddy.

When we were done, the remaining family said their goodbyes. We were then all seated on the first two pews of the church as the rest of the gatherers were allowed a final viewing of the body. As they passed by us, several people stopped to say nice or comforting things to Shaun's mom. A few of them had some words of encouragement for me. However, most of them just passed by me, choosing to only speak to his mother and sisters. I got very little respect as the *grieving widow*.

When I looked toward the casket, the mysterious woman I saw in the crowd earlier was standing there. She looked truly miserable as she hovered a little longer than the rest of the people. As she stepped away, the familiar stranger came and began talking to Patricia. Before she could complete her first sentence, she broke down and cried.

"I am . . . so sorry . . . for . . . not . . . coming . . . around like . . . I should have. I swear, Mama Pat, I'm gonna do better . . . now that Sha'Ron's daddy is gone," she wept.

Patricia kissed the woman's face and invited her to sit next to her. All this was done while I added and multiplied the words my virtual stranger spoke, my calculations equaling one startling conclusion: the stranger was Rhonda, the mother of Shaun's oldest son. A woman who used to hate me the way I now hated Shaun.

I had not seen Rhonda in quite a few years. I assumed that she kept in touch with my in-laws since Patricia was raising her son. Rhonda was a lot heavier than I remembered which is probably why I had such a hard time recognizing her right away. Her eyes, however, were still the same. She still cradled the same sadness in them as the very first time I saw her. It was her eyes that triggered that flicker of acknowledgment in me. I am sure she knew who I was at first glance.

I turned my head to sneak another peak at her just before the minister began the program for the service. I simply wanted to get another look, but Rhonda must have felt me starring because she lifted her head from Patricia's shoulder and shot me a look filled with putrid loathing. I turned away quickly, confused by her malice. I hoped she didn't still hold a grudge after all these years. Moreover, I really hoped she didn't have any designs on trying to jump bad again. Surely she didn't want an encore performance of the last time she tried that crap.

If she did get any stupid ideas, this would be the best place for her to try to do something. That way they could funeralize her with the simple so-and-so that caused her to get beat down the first time she tried me. I would go for straight up murder and take my chances with a *not guilty on the grounds of self defense* plea.

I let those thoughts slip from my mind as I refocused on what the minister was saying. Those bad events happened more than thirteen years ago. Better to bury them with the man that caused them.

The funeral services concluded without too much commotion. A few of the females in the church threw hissy fits during the preacher's eulogy, but other than that, it was a peaceful affair. Even poor grieving Tawanda, Shaun's latest baby mama, held onto her composure. She acted out something terrible when the funeral directors attempted to close the lid on the casket. That crazy woman actually tried to crawl in there, baby and all, with him.

We left the church in an orderly fashion and all proceeded to their awaiting vehicles for the processional to the cemetery. The seating arrangements for the immediate family remained the same for the ride from the church to the cemetery with one exception. Rhonda now rode in the car with Patricia.

At the cemetery, only six chairs were available for the funeral participants. Each of those was positioned in front of where the casket lay. The chairs represented places of prestige in the life of the deceased. The rest of the mourners were to stand during the gravesite commencement. These accessible seats posed a dilemma. There were only six seats for nine adults who considered themselves prominent figures in this fool's life.

While at the church, I let Patricia get away with bullying

me out of my position as head female in Shaun's life. However, here, I pulled rank. I sat myself in one of those chairs and positioned my children so they stood right near me. After I took my seat, the others stood around looking puzzled for a moment.

After a few seconds, his grandmother insisted on sitting because she was old and her feet were hurting. She then insisted that Patricia take the seat next to her. Uncle Bobby graciously decided to stand and let the women get comfortable. Yet the problem still remained. There were now only three seats unoccupied with five women still standing.

His two sisters subtly bum-rushed two of the seats and Tawanda took the last, leaving Rhonda and Keva standing with much attitude. They both decided to settle in behind the row of chairs. Rhonda positioned herself much too closely to my kids and me for my comfort, but I decided not to say anything as long as she didn't get to acting funky. The other two children stood behind the chairs with their mothers, and the rest of the mourners gathered in various positions around the casket and the hole in the ground that was to be Shaun's final resting place.

Once everyone appeared settled, the minister came over to give his final words. At some point during his second sentence, Keva started muttering audibly under her breath. I could only make out a few of the choice words she spoke, but those I recognized were quite unpleasant.

Apparently Patricia heard them also. "Girl, shut your mouth. All that fussing and carrying on ain't even necessary. This preacher is trying to lay my son to rest."

Keva got downright indignant then. "You don't tell me to shut up, you evil cow. I am a grown woman; one of the women responsible for giving your sorry behind a grandchild. You have been orchestrating and ordering people around all morning and I am sick of it. You hunted me down and insisted I come to this pitiful charade of a funeral; talking about your grandbaby deserved to see his daddy for the final time."

Keva was pissed off and very animated by now. She stomped around, arms flailing, words scattered as she continued to rant. "Why wasn't it important for your grandbaby to see his daddy while that dirt bag was still alive? Why didn't you care enough to see my son before now? You know what? Forget it. It doesn't even matter. I am so tired of all this fake mess that my head is about to explode. I'm getting outta here before I hurt somebody. Come on, Kevaun, let's go."

As Keva grabbed her son and made her exit, my daughter leaned over and asked, "Mommy, why did that lady say that my daddy was her son's daddy too? I don't know him. My only brothers are Lil' Shaun and Sha'Ron, right?"

Instead of giving Shauntae a direct answer, I decided to try to assuage her curiosity for the time being. Just as I turned to her to buy some time, a crushing blow landed on the other side of my face, blinding me for a moment. I fell out of my chair and landed on top of my purse. I tried to get up and regain my composure, but the punch was so brutal I stumbled back down, barely missing the hole dug for the casket. I looked up to find Rhonda standing over me screaming like a crazed lunatic.

"I've waited for too many years to get with you again. What makes you so special he had to marry you? Why do you think you are so much better than me? I was with Shaun when he didn't have a dime to his name. I am the one that carried his first child!"

That fool kicked and stomped at my prostrate body while she yelled her fury at me. "For years, every time you saw me, you turned your nose up at me. The only reason you got the best of me the last time we fought was because Shaun stood there with you. But now he's gone. Now he's not here to save you. I hate you, witch. I have always hated you and I will hate you until the day I die."

Rhonda had truly lost her mind. She was doing her best to inflict upon my physical body the same pain she suffered internally. Her emotional sadness powered her hands and feet as she came after me. While I rolled around on the ground doing my best to dodge her filthy feet and the hole dug for Shaun's casket, I clutched my purse, making sure it never left my hands. My children were crying, swinging wildly at Rhonda and screaming for her to leave their mommy alone. Everyone else stood stark still, seemingly enjoying the performance. Not even the minister intervened.

During the commotion, Shauntae frantically picked up the metal chair that I sat in and swung it at Rhonda. She connected with her back after several swings, momentarily slowing down my rival. Rhonda turned and looked in the direction of my baby still swinging the chair. She ceased in her pursuit of me and lunged for Shauntae, but the metal between them made it hard for her to get within arms reach of her.

In a moment of unbalanced momentum, Shauntae lost her footing and stumbled violently. Rhonda used this opportunity to take the chair. She threw it to the ground and grabbed my baby by her hair, then raised her fist to punch her. However, before the blow could land, a loud explosion rocked the air. The noise sounded again. Then Rhonda landed face first, eyes wide open, at Shauntae's feet.

All movement stopped; all noises ceased. The motionless quiet in the air allowed me to actually hear Rhonda take her last breath.

Finally, I stood up with the still smoking gun in my hand. I didn't know Rhonda's spiritual affiliation, so I could only wonder if she would end up in heaven with my Jesus. I wondered if the hate she felt for me, the hate that cost her life, the hate she said she would feel for me until her dying day, went with her into the ever after.

PART I

AND IN THE BEGINNING . . .

Chapter One

March—1993

For the life of me I will never understand why my mama makes me walk all the way to this silly store to do her shopping instead of getting in her car and driving herself here. It takes me twenty to thirty minutes to walk there and back. In her car, the whole ordeal could be done and over in about five minutes. This is just an example of her laziness and a total abuse of power.

An even better idea would be for her to let me drive to the store. Her excuse for not doing that is I don't have my driver's license yet. Oh, big woo! I'm already sixteen, and I do have my learner's permit. She knows I'm a good driver because she has been teaching me since I was fourteen. The only thing standing in the way of my being a legal driver is taking the actual road test, which I am scheduled to do in the next month. But she is sticking to her principles and not letting me drive alone until then. She always has to be so technical under the guise of being a good Christian.

I can't wait to get my driver's license. Once I get that little piece of paper in my hot little hands, I, Lindsay Renee West-brook, will never walk anywhere again. Not unless I have to do so in an effort to lose weight or something like that. I mean, I'm not fat or anything right now, but looking at Mama, I know the genetic potential for middle-age spread is there. Heck, for that reason alone, her balloon butt should be the one walking to the store. Not me.

Mama and I argue all the time because she says I think that I am so cute and petite. "Beauty fades with time, Lil' Miss Thang. As the years go by, gravity will grab a hold of that tight little butt of yours and send it north, south, east, and west. Mark my words, Nay-Nay, you are not always going to have that thin body and that cute face," Mama says.

Then I constantly remind her that if a person takes care of themselves with exercise, they can outrun gravity for a long, long time. If I have my way, I'll always be as fly as the legendary Dianne Carroll. It doesn't seem as if she is the least bit afraid of gravity, so there is no need for her to run. I, like Ms. Carroll, will remain beautiful up to and through my seventies. Once I turn eighty, I don't think I'll care much about how I look anymore.

It's not as if my mother is jealous of me or anything like that. She just thinks she knows everything because she has the advantage of age on her side. She also thinks her funk don't stink because she is raising me and my little brother without the aid of a man or the welfare system. My mother is a homeowner, not a renter, and we don't live in the ghetto. Now if you ask me, the neighborhood we live in is only a stone's throw from the ghetto. But hey, that's the type of stuff she likes to brag about.

Don't get me wrong. For the most part, my mama and I are pretty tight. I love the fact that she is not always in my face about silly little things. Mama talks to me and not at me, and I appreciate that. We have a big sister-little sister type of relationship most of the time. But trust me, she can pull rank and become all Mama when she deems it necessary.

My mother was only seventeen and a senior in high school when she got pregnant with me. She and my so-called dad married the week after they graduated. I guess one could call their nuptials a reverse version of the shotgun wedding. My father's mother forced him to do the "right" thing. I was born two months after the wedding.

My parents stayed together long enough to have me, then three years later, my little brother, Kevin Jr.; K.J. for short. Soon after Kevin started walking, my pops *walked* away, never to look back. We have not heard a word from him since he left over twelve years ago. I still speak to his mother sporadically throughout the year.

Mama was always the breadwinner in our family. She was blessed to obtain the job as an assembly worker at Ford Motor Company. My father was only able to secure odd jobs here and there, never staying at any one position for too long.

Once my father left, Granny, my mother's mother, came to live with us for a little while. Mama needed someone to sit with us and help her around the house while she worked.

My granny is so cool. She has this special knack for being on the side of both the plaintiff, which is usually my mother, and the defendant, my brother or me, at the same time. I don't know how she does it, but she always manages to make both sides in an argument feel good. Granny moved out and into a great senior's complex when I became old enough to babysit my brother. During the time she lived with us, she was frequently on my mother's case about finding herself another husband.

"Child of mine, these children need a daddy and you need a man. You young modern-day women kill me. You all are always talking about how well you can take care of yourselves or about how you pay your own bills. Well, let me tell you something, Ms. I-Got-My-Own; money does not keep you warm when you are all alone in that big bed of yours. And no amount of money is going to teach your son how to be a man." This was the speech I heard repeatedly while Granny lived with us.

My mother used to counter Granny's complaint with, "Just because I don't have a man smiling in my face twenty-four-seven, does not mean I don't know where to go when I need the chill taken off, if you know what I mean." That is what she would say before she became born again. Now she says, "When God is ready for me to have a man, He'll send me one."

Personally, I think things are cool just the way they are in our household. The last thing I need is for some man to invade our lives and start changing things in our home. I'm not crazy about all of my mother's current rules, but I do realize things could be worse.

One of my mother's rules includes my brother Kevin and me attending church every Sunday with her. During the services, I usually just sit there, bored out of my mind. However, every now and then something will be said or something will happen that catches my attention and I find myself enjoying my time in church. I definitely believe in God, Jesus, and the Holy Spirit, but from what I have learned thus far, I think the latter of the three has missed me.

In all honesty, going to church is not that bad. I actually enjoy the Lenten Journey and the Easter services. When I was younger, that time was always special because I could look forward to getting a pretty new outfit. Now it is about so much more. I get into church during this time because of how special I feel when I hear and learn about what Jesus did for me. I personalize Jesus' death on the cross, realizing that He made such an extraordinary sacrifice for someone like me. That's the kind of love I can get into.

There's another rule of my mother's that I don't particularly enjoy. That rule is my midnight curfew. I constantly try to convince Mama that I'm old enough and responsible enough to stay out until one A.M., but she is not even trying to hear it. That's a perfect example of when she is all Mama.

Another example of how my mother pulls rank is by making me walk to this store. This is no short little jaunt. We live on Pierson, just two blocks north of the infamous Seven Mile Road in Detroit. The grocery store is on Evergreen and Seven Mile. Evergreen is about one-half mile from Pierson. So to and from the store is at least a one-mile walk. Can you tell how much I hate having to do this?

Living near Seven Mile is the best part of our neighborhood for me. Hanging out on the "Mile" is an adventure all its own. Shyanne Kennedy, my best friend, and I have had some of the best times on Seven Mile.

Shyanne and I have been friends forever; nine years, actually. We met in school on our first day of second grade. Shyanne and her family had just moved into the neighborhood and this was her first day at McKinney Elementary School. She and her mom were at the school awaiting the doors to open so they could enter the building. I was with Granny who wanted to meet Mrs. Green, my new teacher. While standing and waiting for the morning bell to ring, Shyanne and I made eye contact. Then I looked down at her hands to find that she carried the exact same Barbie book bag that I owned. This girl had taste.

When we finally entered the building, I noticed that we all were headed in the same direction, and eventually to the same classroom. My grandmother and I entered the classroom first, and while Granny helped me to find a seat and make myself comfortable, Shyanne and her mom talked to Mrs. Green. When they were done talking, Shyanne sought me out and plopped into the seat next to mine, commenting on our identical book bags. We have been as thick as thieves since that moment. Shyanne lives four blocks from my home on Fielding Street. I know for a fact that no matter what goes down, she has my back and she knows that I have hers.

Whenever we end up outside of our neighborhood or around people we don't know, we tell people that we are cousins. Folks usually believe us without too much convincing because we kind of look alike.

I am considered light-skinned by most people, and Shyanne is about two shades lighter than I am; her pigmentation courtesy of her Caucasian maternal grandmother. Shyanne has beautiful gray eyes and medium length reddish brown hair with natural blond highlights. I know females who would pay top dollar to have their hair streaked like that. Shyanne is about five feet seven inches tall and weighs approximately one hundred thirty pounds. She is an absolute beauty.

I'm not so bad either, even if I do say so myself. I own a caramel brown complexion, long jet-black hair, and honey brown eyes. My eyes often change to hazel depending on the season. I am about five feet four inches in stature and also weigh in at one hundred thirty pounds. My hips and butt are thicker and rounder than Shyanne's, courtesy of my big behined maternal grandmother.

What Shyanne is lacking in her lower region, also a gift of her granny, she more than makes up for it on the top half of her body. Shyanne carries a solid D-cup. I barely need my B-cup bra.

Shyanne and I are both juniors at Henry Ford High School. Though we may not be amongst the best dressed or the most liked females, we definitely rank in the top five of the prettiest girls in school. The fact that we don't curse and we do our best to act like ladies also adds points to our appeal. It separates us from the females who want to act hard and tough.

Now we do have a reputation for getting ghetto when provoked by jealous females. We may be Christians, but people shouldn't test us because they will lose. The guys find these multi facets to our personalities intriguing. They are on us like black on tar.

Neither of us have a man right now, but we are regrettably no longer virgins. I lost my virginity halfway through freshman year while I dated this knucklehead named Byron. We went together for six months before we had sex, and the relationship only lasted one month beyond that. I've had a few other boyfriends since then, but I have not been with anyone else sexually.

Shyanne's initial sexual experience came during the first month of our sophomore year. Her lover's name was Troy. She met him the summer before their sexual encounter at a backyard party we attended on the east side of town, which is a pretty jaunt from where we live. This is why it was easy for Shyanne to start and maintain another relationship that she began three months after she met Troy.

My girl had it going on for a while until Troy decided to surprise Shyanne with a visit and busted her kissing her secret lover goodbye on her front porch. Needless to say, she's not with either of those guys anymore. Guys just aren't as forgiving about infidelity as we girls are.

I don't think that Shy will be single too much longer though. There is this senior named Antonio she is interested in and the brother is a cutie. He's six feet three inches tall, has skin the color of a Hershey Bar, and short silky black hair. His brush waves are beautiful. He's also the star forward for the Henry Ford Trojans' basketball team. The problem is Antonio's girlfriend.

What had happened was, Tony stepped to Shyanne about a week ago at McDonald's trying to holla at her. Tony told Shyanne that he had seen her around school and he thought she was really pretty. He sounded as sweet and sincere as an aspiring politician. Couple that with the fact that brother man was fine, and Shyanne found herself almost duty bound to exchange phone numbers with him.

A couple of days later, Shyanne and Tony were standing in the hallway at school between classes talking and were accosted by this chick. Homegirl got between the two of them and started yelling at Shyanne.

"Who are you; smiling all up in my man's face? I'll whoop your skinny, high yellow tail like it ain't ever been whooped before!" She screamed so loud that everyone in the hallway turned to see where the commotion came from.

I quickly made my way down the hall to make sure the tail being whooped that day did not belong to my girl. She had so little tail to spare. Shy has a very quick temper, so I knew it wouldn't be long before blows were exchanged. When I arrived on the scene, Shyanne already had her finger wagging and her neck rolling.

"You better back up off me, and quit spitting in my face. I don't know anything about this guy being your man. That's between you and him. So if you have a problem, it's with him, not me!"

"Who are you frontin' on, tramp?" the girl yelled, and then took an open handed swing at Shyanne. She was unaware, however, that I was standing behind her, and before the blow could land, I was able to grab her arm. That gave Shyanne the opportunity to punch the girl square in the face. The fight was on.

We beat and dragged that girl up one side of the hallway and down the other until one of the teachers came to break it up. During the scuffle, not one person came to her aid, not even her so-called man.

All three of us received a three-day suspension for the fight. Shyanne and I also received a verbal warning that if we were involved in any more disciplinary incidents, we would be expelled for good. That was the second time this semester that we had beat a girl down. Jealousy can be very contagious.

After school that day, Tony stood outside waiting for Shyanne. He explained that Tracey (the cow we beat up) and he used to talk on occasion, but they were never boyfriend and girlfriend. He apologized to Shyanne for his part in the ugly incident and asked if he could still call her.

"If Tracey was not your woman, you should have said something before the fight started," Shy told him. "I'll call you if and when I decide you are worth the effort."

I knew all along she would definitely call him again. Shyanne was just spitting game. I ended up grounded for an entire week. In addition, Mama made both Shyanne and I start attending the weekly Bible Study class for teens at our church. She said spending a little more time with the Lord would help us to calm our spirits and drive out the devilish, violent impulses.

My punishment probably also has something to do with my mother enforcing this slave labor on me. Now that I've finally made it to this funky store, I am in a hurry to get in, get her crap, and get back to my long hike home. I have a Donald Goines novel on my bed calling my name. But little did I know I'd find myself in no hurry at all once I saw what was waiting inside for me.

Chapter Two

"Hello, sexy. Are you with your man, or are you roaming through this big old store all by your lonesome?"

I turned away from the shelf that housed the tomato sauce my mama sent me in search of and into the face of a totally stunning male. I swear 'foe cheese and biscuits; I cannot remember ever seeing anything more beautiful than this man in my whole entire life.

He was tall, about six feet two inches. His perfect skin was the color of melted caramel, and his curly jet black hair was flawlessly faded and tapered. In stark contrast, his eyes were emerald green. He smelled like an angel. His mother and father worked overtime putting this gorgeous brother together.

"What's the matter, cutie? Can't you talk?"

I miraculously found my voice. "I'm here by myself. Why do you ask?"

"May I ask your name?"

"My name is Lindsay, but everybody calls me Nay or Nay-Nay, short for Renee which is my middle name. I hate my first name." I could not believe I actually told him my given name. I never divulge that information to anyone at an initial meeting other than school officials. This guy's looks had me all discombobulated.

"Well, since everyone else calls you by a nickname, I think I will stick to calling you Lindsay. That way you will always think of me differently. My name is Shaun and everyone calls me Shaun. So if you want to be different on my behalf, you will have to think of your own manly nickname for me. How old are you, sexy?"

I was so focused on his beautiful, smooth lips that I barely heard his question. Eventually I regained my composure and uttered a barely audible answer. "I'm sixteen."

"Sixteen! Wow! I thought you were a little older. No offense, but you have this maturity about yourself that betrays your actual age."

I knew he was just spitting game. I hadn't said enough to him for him to make that judgment. But I liked the fact he was interested. In an effort to live up to his impression of my maturity, I did my best to uphold my end of the conversation. "How old do I need to be, Shaun?"

This time before he answered, he rewarded me with a breathtaking smile. "Listen to you sounding like you're about nineteen or twenty. I asked because I'm nineteen and I'm interested in you having dinner with me sometime. I just wanted to be sure that we were age compatible. Some might say there is a big difference between sixteen and nineteen. I think it depends on the individuals."

He sounded very mature and intelligent, and I was becoming more and more impressed with this wonderfully handsome guy with each word he spoke. Heck, as fine as he was, I could fall in love with him if he just stood in front of me and never opened his mouth.

"Do you think we are age compatible?" I asked.

"Would you like to have dinner with me?"

"Aren't you capable of answering my question directly? I hope you are not always so evasive."

Shaun cocked his eyebrow in surprise, then said, "Evasive! That's not a word I've heard anyone use to describe me before. Another sign of your maturity. In answer to your question, yes! I do think we are age compatible."

"Then my answer is yes. I would like to have dinner with you." I was so glad I loved to read. My mother says an avid reader is privy to words that non-readers may not normally use. She says a person never knows when they may have to put that knowledge to use.

"Cool. What day would be good for you? Since you are only sixteen, I'm sure you're still in school. I'm guessing this weekend would be the first time you would have available."

Now how do I tell this guy who thinks I am so mature that I am grounded this weekend? I hope being straightforward works. "I can't go out with you this weekend. Being that I am only sixteen, I sometimes still find myself on punishment. This weekend happens to be one of those times."

"Oh, I see. What did you do to cause your parents to ill out on you?" As he spoke this time, he moved closer to me and positioned his hand just above my head on the shelf in the aisle. I got another whiff of his cologne, and my knees almost buckled. To make sure I didn't fall on my face, I stood a little straighter and folded my arms in front of me.

"I was excluded from school for fighting." As soon as the words left my mouth, I was totally embarrassed. I felt like such a kid. He probably went from thinking I was mature to thinking I was some ghetto street fighter.

"Whoa! Hold up, sexy. I know you're not telling me that you had an actual fistfight, are you? You are far too fine and sophisticated for that kind of stuff."

My initial feelings of inadequacy flew right out the window at his words. Shaun had a way of making me feel special, and I found this fact both fascinating and intimidating. How could I let someone I've known for less than five minutes have any effect on me at all? Even though I felt less awkward about my fight, I still wanted Shaun to understand the circumstances.

"Well, I was actually helping my best friend. It was her fight. But our motto has always been if one of us is swinging, then both of us are swinging."

"I know how that can be. I've been in that position on occasion myself, but we must work harder at avoiding those types of encounters at all cost. We have to make sure we keep that face beautiful. I would not be able to stand it if some crazy female intentionally set out to destroy your beauty. I'm sure there are a lot of jealous ladies out there just waiting for the opportunity to do something evil like that. Promise me you will be careful, okay?"

This brother was so cool that even M & M's didn't melt in his mouth. I didn't even bother giving voice to his question. I was too busy standing there grinning.

The last thing Shaun had to worry about was me being taken down by some jealous female. I had never lost a fight in my life. Though I had not actually kept a record of the number of scuffles I had been in, I liked to brag that I was thirty and zero. My mother hates to hear me talk that way. She says that Christian young ladies should not be fighting. Jesus wants us to love our neighbors as we love ourselves. I say she should tell that to all the haters in the world. Thinking about my mother brought me back to my appointed task.

"I really need to grab this stuff for my mom and get home so she can finish cooking. I have been gone a while now and the last thing I need is to make her any angrier at me than she already is."

"I understand. Did you drive here to the grocery store or do you live in walking distance?" he asked as he followed me to the checkout counter.

"Neither! I don't have my driver's license so my mom won't let me drive. I live about a half-mile away, but she still made me walk," I whined, again hoping he had not reversed his initial opinion of me as I crooned about my predicament like a baby.

Shaun giggled a little. "Why don't you let me drive you home? That way, I'll know where you live when it's time for me to pick you up for our dinner date. We can also get to know each other a little more during the ride." He then flashed that perfect smile again. Was there no end to this guy's great qualities?

I had to seriously think about riding home with him, beautiful face, smile and smell aside. Mama told me not to get in cars with guys I barely know. She knew I had a fascination for guys with nice rides. "I don't know if that is a good idea. I really don't know you, and riding in a car with a complete stranger could be hazardous to my health."

"What do you think I'm going to do to you?" Shaun sounded a little offended.

"To be totally honest, it's not you that I'm worried about. It's my mother that would cause all the damage. She hates for me to get in cars with people I barely know."

"Does your mother have to know we just met? You could tell her that I'm someone you have known for a while, and we ran into each other at the store."

I was very tempted to go along with him and his lie for more than one reason. One, he was *very* interesting to talk to. Two, he was *very* fine, and three, I hated the idea of walking all the way back home *very* much. As if he read my mind, he spoke again.

"Come on, cutie, I know you don't want to walk if you don't have to. Besides, I want to get to know you better. Me driving you home, and I do mean straight home, will afford us the opportunity to talk a little more." Then he smiled again, and my mind became *very* made up.

As we walked to the parking lot I couldn't help smiling at the fact Shaun insisted on paying for my mother's groceries.

She only had a few things, but I thought it was so cool of him to make the offer. I wonder if Mama would classify this as an unexpected blessing from God. Too bad she could never know about it.

Shaun led me to his beautiful, candy apple red convertible Trans Am. It was almost as gorgeous as he was. The leather interior and the drop top were both tan, and the tires housed an extraordinary set of silver rims. This car was stunning.

Shaun walked me to the passenger side door and held it open for me. Once I was seated, he reached inside, pulled my seat belt into place and snapped it. He lingered there, staring as if he noticed something disturbing about me for the very first time. Before I knew what was happening, he leaned into the car and kissed me on my nose. He smiled, closed my door, then sauntered over to the driver's side. As soon as he was settled into his seat, I questioned him.

"So why are we stealing kisses? I rarely let anybody kiss me, especially someone I have known for all of ten minutes."

"I was wrong for that, Lindsay. I apologize. I got caught up staring into those beautiful eyes and I was unable to resist. Actually, you should consider yourself lucky I only landed one on the tip of your nose. I should have aimed straight for your lips," he replied smoothly.

"Well then I guess *you* should be glad you went with your better judgment. My natural reflexes would have probably led me to smack you."

Shaun laughed hard and long. I thought he would never stop, and I became very irritated. It was as if he didn't believe I would hit him. Believe you me I would have. I don't care how fine he is. Kissing is reserved only for guys I am really into.

Once the laughter finally died down, Shaun looked at me and noticed I was a little upset. "You were serious, weren't you? Oh, I forgot. You're a fighter." Before I had a chance to respond, he continued. "Okay, Ms. Mike Tyson, which way to your house?"

My annoyance subsided with his joke, and I even smiled a little when I gave him directions.

"So Lindsay, when can we go out? How long has your mother got you on lock down?" Hearing him continuously call me by my first name grated on my nerves, even from lips as sexy as his.

"I'm only grounded until the end of this week, so anytime next week will be cool. Shaun, can I please get you to call me Nay? I really hate my first name."

"Does anybody else call you Lindsay?"

"Only my grandmother on my father's side, but I only see her once or twice a year, so it doesn't bother me as much."

"Then I'm sorry, but I have to decline your request. Just think about it this way; whenever you hear your name, you will always know it's me speaking even if you don't see me."

I didn't know whether to be mad or flattered. I guess I was actually grateful because I took what he said to mean he planned on seeing me often. I decided to give up my fight for preserving the right to be called what I wanted and got used to the fact that I'll have to hear my ugly name coming from such beautiful lips.

"So tell me something about yourself. I know you're sixteen, you hate your name, and you like to hit people. What else makes up Miss Lindsay Renee?"

Okay! Now enough is enough. Just as I make up my mind to allow this fool to call me by my first name, he goes and gets all kinds of crazy on me.

"Oh no you didn't use both my first and middle names together? Now that is taking it too far. My mother is the only person who gets away with that. And even she only does it when she's upset with me," I told him a little loudly.

Shaun looked at me as if I had lost all my marbles. He threw up his hands in mock surrender and began pleading for my pardon. "Okay! Okay! Calm down! I apologize. Please don't hit me. If you forgive me, I promise I'll never call you anything but Lindsay from here on."

He looked so sorry that I felt bad for going off the way I did, so I gave him a smile. "All right, you're forgiven this time, but watch it, buddy," I said pointing my index finger in his face. Then I proceeded to give him some info. "I go to Henry Ford High School, I have a little brother named Kevin, and we both live at home with our mother. No father to speak of anymore. I don't have any sisters, but my friend Shyanne and I are closer than most biological sisters I know."

"Do you have a man right now?"

"Nope." Then a thought ran rapidly through my mind. A guy this fine probably has about six or seven girls laying claim to him. "What about you? Do you have a woman?"

Shaun didn't say anything right away, and his hesitation made me a little nervous. The last thing I needed was to be seen hanging out with somebody's man and end up in a situation like the one I just went through with Shyanne. I had always made it my policy to never step to someone else's man because I wouldn't want anyone stepping to mine. Granny always says what goes around comes around. I try never to intentionally hurt anyone. I want people to treat me with respect; therefore, I go out of my way to treat others in the same manner. I'm no Bible scholar, but I'm pretty sure that concept is in there.

"Well, to be totally honest with you, Lindsay, I just got out of a relationship a few weeks ago. My ex is still having a hard time dealing with the fact that it's over between us. We were together off and on since I was fifteen. And in sticking with the honesty theme, I guess I should inform you that I also have a one-year-old son. It wasn't planned, but I don't regret it now that he's here."

I sat bug-eyed and speechless in the passenger seat, amazed at all Shaun had revealed. This guy had a kid *and* a potentially fatal attraction in his life. My instincts told me I should put a halt to any further discussions of hooking up with him. A guy this good-looking usually does come with a lot of baggage, and he had just hauled two steamer trunks into our conversation. I guess he could feel my paranoia because he tried making me understand why he dropped those big bombs on me.

"I realize I said a lot about myself in a short time. I'm not usually that open with too many people. I just feel connected to you, and you are so easy to talk to. I also see us spending a lot of time together, and I didn't want you to get caught off guard. I can already tell that you are a special young lady, someone I want to get to know a lot better. But if what I have said to you is too much for you to handle, I'll understand. I'll drop you off at home and try to forget I ever met you." Shaun's conversation then took on a mocking tone. "It'll be hard, but I don't want to inconvenience you with my load."

It was definitely true. Shaun did have a few strikes against him. Dating a man with kids was a no-no in my book. The fatal attraction thing was a big deal as well. Yet he did have a few pluses in his column too: great looking, cool car, and intellect. Everything that came out of his mouth sounded so sincere and grown-up.

"You do seem to lead a very busy life for someone who is only nineteen. I don't know anyone in my age group who has been in a relationship for four years. That's a long time to stay with someone unless you plan on getting married. Why did you two break up?" I asked.

"It's hard to explain. To start with, Rhonda, my ex, is a year younger than I am, but the age difference seems so much greater most times, especially since our son was born. I don't feel like we have anything in common any longer. Rhonda is still into things that no longer interest me. I can't think of anything specific right now, but the bottom line is I don't feel the same way about her that I used to. It may seem cold to say that after she's had my baby, but she is stuck in the same fourteen-year-old frame of mind as when we met. I guess you could say I have outgrown her. I may not seem very prince-like right now, but like I said, I have to be honest with you."

This was the second time in our short acquaintance that Shaun spoke aloud what was on my mind. I was sitting there thinking that perhaps he became uninterested in her after she had his baby. That happened to a few females I knew after they had their babies.

Shaun nearly drove by my street while I sat silently mus-ing. I had to pull myself from my thoughts to tell him where to turn. "Shaun, I live right here on Pierson. Turn right, and my house is in the second block."

"Dang, lady! That was a short ride," Shaun announced as he parked after I directed him to our house. "Seriously, Lind-say, I hope I haven't overwhelmed you. I really want to see you again; spend some more time getting to know you per-sonally. I've already started by telling you a lot of personal things about me, and I hope it hasn't scared you off."

"It's true you've said a little more than a mouthful in the short time we've been talking. The average dude would have me saying, ohhhhh no. But you seem able enough to handle yourself and your current situation, so I won't hold it against you. If you have a piece of paper and a pen, I'll write my phone number down for you. Please don't call me before Sunday because my punishment excludes me from using the tele-phone. We can discuss our dinner plans when you call be-cause I want to get out of this car before my mama looks out the window and comes out here embarrassing me." I looked toward the house to see if I could see Mama peeping out of the windows.

Shaun handed me a matchbook and pen, and I wrote down the number, then handed the matchbook back to him.

"I'll keep the pen just in case you meet anymore cute, mature young ladies that may not be grounded. You won't have anything to write their numbers down with." I got out of the car and closed the door. I ran up the steps to the front porch of my house, turning around to see Shaun sitting there laughing at me.

I planned on adding a little something extra to my prayers tonight. I needed God to bless our potential union.

I hated that Sunday was a whole three days away.

Chapter Three

Today I was up and out of the house early, skipping break-fast and heading straight to Shyanne's house so that we could walk to school together and to give her the scoop on my Prince Charming. I hardly slept last night in anticipation of sharing my news with my best friend. Shyanne was also grounded as a result of the exclusion from school, so using the telephone for either of us was out of the question. I had to get to her and dish my news in person. Our daily trek to school was the only freedom allowed in our prison terms.

When I arrived at Shyanne's house, Mama T (that is what I call Shyanne's mother, Tonya. Shayanne calls my mother Mommy S for Sherrie) answered the door, surprised to see me on her doorstop early for a change.

"Well look who's here already. I can't remember the last time you showed up this early on your way to school. I hope you at least took the time to pray before you left the house. I don't ever want you girls to be too anxious to talk to God first thing in the morning."

"Yes, Mama T. I never leave the house in the morning without asking God for His covering for the day."

Mama T and Shyanne attended the same church as my family. Mr. Kennedy, Shyanne's father, was also a member, but he only attended on days that the service didn't interfere with some sporting event he was watching on television. He was a good Christian leader for his family. He would often remind Shyanne and me about holding on to the values and lessons we learned in church.

I took the stairs to Shyanne's room two at a time and burst into her bedroom, neglecting to first knock on her door. Between my sprint over to the house and my Olympic run up the stairs, I was worn out. I flopped down on Shyanne's bed the moment I entered the room.

"Girl, what's up? It's hardly like you to make it someplace on time. This early thing has totally thrown me for a loop. What happened? Did your mama win the lottery or something? What the heck has got you so excited?" Shyanne asked all at once.

"If you stop coming at me with twenty questions, I can tell you what's up?" That is the way Shyanne talked; very fast. She sometimes spoke as if there were a time limit, and she wanted to make sure she got all of her words out before her deadline.

"No, Mama didn't hit the lottery, but I feel like I did. I met this cute guy at the grocery store yesterday. His name is Shaun, he drives a red convertible Trans Am, and he's nineteen years old. Ooh Wee! Baby boy is beautiful," I blurted in her normal vernacular.

"Did you say he was nineteen? He is hardly a baby. That man is grown. Did you tell him how old you were?" Shy asked a little confused.

"I was straight up with him. After we talked for a while, Shaun said he thought I was mature." I gave her the rundown on my and Shaun's entire conversation while she finished getting dressed. By the time I was done filling her in, we were heading out the door on our way to school. "So what do you think about him having a baby and a potentially crazy baby mama?" I asked as we walked.

"Come on, Nay-Nay. I thought we both agreed we wouldn't get involved with guys that had kids. The drama that comes with it is always negative. We shouldn't have to deal with that at our age. Leave that stuff to the old folks over twenty-one."

"I know what we said, Shy, but there was something about him that made me want to break all the rules. Without even thinking about it, I broke three or four of them between the time he first spoke to me and the time he dropped me off at home."

"Girl, what's happened to you? I don't remember you acting this dizzy over any guy; not even that dude, Byron. And I know he had your nose wide open because he was the guy you let take your virginity. You didn't have sex with this Shaun guy yesterday, did you?" she asked jokingly.

"Maybe it's because he's older, but Shaun is really something else. I mean, forget the fact that he is prettier than most women, he really has his game tight too," I said, trying to defend my insanity.

"I don't know about his game being all that tight since he has a baby and an ignorant baby mama. If his stuff was so together, brotha would have avoided that whole scene," Shyanne said doubtfully.

Shy had a way of making me pause. Whenever I get too excited about a situation, she always makes me stop and seriously think about it. The only time she is not so level headed is when we are about to get involved in a physical confrontation. For a few moments, as we walked, I thought about what my girl said. A guy with a child was some serious stuff. Baby Mama drama is something I wouldn't wish on one of my enemies.

Shyanne noticed I was somberly searching inside my mind, so she tried to ease the tension in my thoughts. "Listen, Nay; I am not trying to make you feel stupid or anything like that. You know that, right?" Before I could answer she kept talking. "I just have never seen you this excited over a dude. I guess my protective instincts are naturally kicking in. You know I love you like a sister, and I just want to make sure you're always all right.

"But if you think this guy is all that, then I'm sure he is. You don't usually have bad judgment when it comes to boys, so I guess that makes you pretty smart. Just remember to pray and ask God to guide your decisions." Shy also always reminded me to keep my relationship with God tight.

I stopped walking and turned to give my best friend in the whole world a big hug. Shyanne hugged me back, then we hurriedly let go and started laughing. We didn't want anybody to think we were lesbians.

Shyanne and I were not lucky enough to have any classes together, so the only time we saw each other during the school day was at lunch and between classes because we shared a locker. During our entire lunch period and between *every* class, I talked her ear off about Shaun. I'm sure she wanted to tell me to shut my face, but she's my girl so she patiently listened to me go on and on.

At the end of the school day, Shyanne and I met outside at our usual spot on the corner of Evergreen and Trojan. Being that this was our first day back to school since the exclusion, Shyanne started talking about all the homework she had to catch up on before we went to our Youth Bible Study class this evening.

"Girl do you have two million pages of make-up work also, or do my teachers simply hate me?" I barely heard her question because my mind was on a certain green-eyed someone. "Nay-Nay, are you listening to me?"

"I'm sorry, Shy. You know where my mind is. I can't help

it. I haven't been able to stop thinking about him since . . ." My throat suddenly locked and my speech came to a complete standstill. Just as we started to cross the intersection, a red Trans Am made a hard left from Evergreen and halted our procession.

"Girl, what's wrong with you?" Shyanne asked before she noticed the car.

Shaun put the car in park, got out and came around to us on the sidewalk.

"Hello, Lindsay," he said, smiling that breathtaking smile.

Shyanne looked at him for a few awkward seconds. Then she came to the realization that the gentleman in front of us must be Shaun. It is a good thing she spoke first because my brain was stuck on straight stupid. I couldn't believe he was standing in front of me. If my life depended on it that very moment, I would not have been able to utter a word.

"So you must be Shaun. I've heard a lot about you these past seven hours," Shyanne said, embarrassing the heck out of me.

"And you must be Shyanne. While I have yet to spend seven hours in Lindsay's company, she did tell me a lot about you during our short conversation. I don't know how the men in this school can handle being around young ladies as beautiful as you two all day." I could tell Shyanne was impressed with Shaun.

"Thank you Shaun. Whenever Nay-Nay, or should I say *Lindsay*, can speak again, I'm sure she would like to say hi."

I was seriously hating her for the way she exaggerated my name. I neglected to tell her about that part of my and Shaun's conversation.

"Hello, Shaun. Please excuse my friend. She sometimes has a problem controlling the things that come out of her mouth," I said to Shaun after I finally found my voice. "So do you make a habit of just popping up on people, or are you here to see someone who is expecting you?" I asked Shaun with a little attitude.

"And you say Shyanne has a problem controlling her mouth. Why is it you always have something flip to say?"

Flip was a word I had only heard Granny use to describe my smart mouth. This guy was old even for his age.

"I'm not trying to be flip. I just don't like people sneaking up on me. I wasn't expecting to hear from you again until Sunday." I was doing my best to make him believe I was irritated. I stood there with my hand on my hip, patting my foot.

"You sound as if you're disappointed to see me," Shaun said apologetically. "Look, please don't be mad. I've been thinking about you a lot since yesterday. I figured it might be a good idea to meet you after school so I could see you for a little while. I hoped you wouldn't mind. I planned to be here tomorrow as well and perhaps give you a ride home. This way we could spend some time together and get to know each other better by Sunday. If it's a problem, I promise I won't be here again." He sounded rejected.

Shyanne stood listening to our conversation as if she'd never heard a male and female talk before. Her look said it all. *'Yes, Shaun is the man!'* I could tell her earlier doubts about him were disappearing as quickly as mine had.

"Shaun, I told you yesterday how my mama felt about me riding with people I don't know. Regardless of what we've told each other, I still don't know you from Adam."

"Nay, please. What your mother doesn't know won't hurt her. Besides, she don't even get home from work until after five. I'm sure Shaun will have *us* home before then. Right, Shaun?" Shyanne walked toward the car as if the deal had already been sealed.

"Looks like you're out voted, Lindsay. Baby, I promise I won't bite, and I'll drive very carefully. If you see anyone you know, you can duck in the seat and hide."

I gave them both the crazy look as I walked over to get in

the car. It was all an act though. After Shaun called me baby, I would have done anything he wanted me to.

"Shaun, what kind of job do you have that lets you afford to drive a smooth ride like this? This baby is pretty," Shyanne said, admiring the interior of Shaun's car.

Shaun looked at me kind of sideways before he answered the question. It was as if he thought I put her up to asking it. In all honesty, I never thought about how he could afford his car. I felt silly now for not at least wondering.

"I work for my uncle doing odd jobs at his collision shop and run errands. Because we are family, I get paid in cash, no taxes taken out of my earnings. Since I still live with mom, I don't have any bills other than the car and my insurance. My son lives with us too, but he doesn't require much financially since he's only a year old."

Whoa! That last piece of information shook me. Shaun didn't tell me his shorty lived with him. In most cases the baby mama always ends up stuck with the kid. I made a mental note to definitely find out more about it. Shyanne was also surprised, but she didn't bother waiting until later to voice her opinion on the subject.

"Dang, Shaun, you're a full time daddy? That's not something you hear about too often. Most dudes get the chick pregnant, and then the girl hardly hears from him again. I guess it's cool that you always have your son."

After hearing my girl give him such props, I felt pretty good that a guy like this was digging me. Shyanne made Shaun sound like a candidate for the Father of the Year Award. I sat there beaming as if he were my baby's daddy. I still had a few questions though.

Shaun got directions from Shyanne to her house, and we dropped her off. I told her I would try to sneak and call her before my mama got home, and then she got out. As soon as we pulled away from Shyanne's house, I began my interrogation.

"Shaun, you didn't tell me your son lived with you and your mom. How did you end up with custody of the baby instead of his mother?"

Shaun fumbled with the radio until he found a station worth listening to. I interpreted his actions as a stall tactic. When he did begin speaking, his stalling continued.

"Well, it's a long story, Lindsay, and I don't think I'll have time to tell it all before we reach your house. Why don't we hold—"

"Oh, it's cool. My mama does not usually get home from work until after five, so we can talk for a little while." His hesitation only served to make me more anxious. At this point, I was so curious, I was willing to risk bodily harm from my mama to get the details of this story.

Shaun continued to take his time about answering my question. As a matter of fact, he didn't utter another sound until we parked in front of my house. "You're sure it's okay for us to sit out here and talk? I would not want any nosey neighbors to tell your mom."

I thought about it for a moment because Ms. Trina across the street might just peek her big nose out the window. It wouldn't have been the first time she told on my brother or me. My curiosity got the best of me though, so I told him it was cool.

His stall tactics were really getting on my nerves. First he acts like he couldn't wait to spend time with me, so he shows up at my school out of nowhere. Now he wants to act like he can't wait to get away from me. This story must be a real doozie.

"All right, Ms. Lindsay; here goes. But again I must be honest. This story does not paint a very flattering picture of what our relationship was like at the end." He took a deep breath and proceeded to spill his guts. "When Rhonda told her mom she was pregnant, she put her out. She was really pissed at Rhonda for getting pregnant at seventeen, but I think she was more upset that I was the father. Rhonda's mother didn't like me at all. Given the fact that the mother of my child was virtually homeless, I figured I had to do something to fix the situation. I spoke with my mother, told her our predicament and asked if Rhonda could come and stay with us. My mother agreed, and we became an instant family; no benefit of marriage, just the bond of impending parenthood sealing our commitment."

Shoot! I knew this was going to be a heck of a story and Shaun had just gotten started. A live-in girlfriend at his age? I sat in my seat with my eyes bulging so far from the sockets that Shaun probably assumed they would fall out of my head. He chuckled a bit and continued with his story.

"During the pregnancy, things were cool between Rhonda and me. I went with her to the doctors' visits, those prebirthing classes, and the whole nine. She and I were behaving like an old married couple going about the whole situation like it was the most normal thing in the world. In reality, I was really scared. I kept my fears to myself though, determined to be there for my child no matter what. I refused to be a punk like my old man and run out on my responsibilities."

I could see the mention of his dad kind of upset him. At first I thought he would stop talking, but he took a few deep breaths and continued.

"My dad left my mom when she was still pregnant with me. She was only fifteen years old. Then she met my sister's father. As soon as she got pregnant with her, that bum was out like a light too. My youngest sister's pop stuck around for a little while, but he used to hit my mom. I was glad to see him leave when he finally did. The father figures in my life didn't offer the best examples of parenthood, and because of them, I put my heart and soul into doing it differently and vowed to always be around for my child no matter what."

I grew to admire this guy more and more every time we

talked. He looked my way to see how I was absorbing all that he told me. I reached over to hold his hand, hopefully conveying that I understood the betrayal of his father-figures. "I can relate to your resentment. My brother and I have the same dad, but he didn't stay around long after my brother was born. We haven't seen or heard from him since he left. I can't imagine ever doing anything like that to my own child either."

"Yeah, that's some pretty messed up stuff." I could tell this was a delicate topic for Shaun, but he continued to tell me what happened. "Around the time Sha'Ron was six or seven months old, I realized my relationship with Rhonda was changing. She got too comfortable being there with my mom taking care of the baby. Rhonda barely lifted a finger to do anything for him. When I would suggest that she needed to change the baby or that the baby needed feeding, she would get an attitude and tell me to do it. It was starting to piss me off royally.

"Rhonda also gained a lot of weight during the pregnancy and seemed content with her new size. She just lay around the house talking on the phone to her girlfriends, telling them how cool it was to live with her man. She even quit going to school after the baby was born. I told her she needed to get a job and at least help take care of the baby financially. Then the crazy ho—"

I stopped Shaun's vile attack on Rhonda with a look before it got out of hand. I hated when guys called females out of their names like that. He noticed my disapproval of his language.

"I'm sorry, baby. I shouldn't have disrespected you or her like that. But I'm telling you honestly, I was very upset with her." I acknowledged his apology and the story rolled on. "Like I was saying, Rhonda said she didn't think she needed a job because we weren't paying any bills at the house. She said that if I were a man, I would handle my responsibility to take care of her and the baby."

His baby's mama seemed trifling to me. In listening to Shaun's side of the story, Rhonda believed that Shaun got her pregnant all by himself, and she held no responsibility whatsoever for their son's conception. I didn't voice my opinion, and he continued with the tale.

"One evening, when Sha'Ron was eight months old, I lost my temper with Rhonda. I told her it was time for her to go. I called her a bunch of ugly names, told her to take her fat, lazy butt back to her mother's house and to leave my son right where he was. I packed her stuff, took her home and told her mother that I would be going to court to get full legal custody of our baby first thing in the morning. Neither of them gave me an argument. Rhonda wasn't much of a mother, and her own mother had not bothered to contact Rhonda or see the baby since he was born. I don't think being a grandmother was high on her list of things she was anxious to do."

Shaun had certainly said more than a mouthful. Under the circumstances, I understood him putting Rhonda out. But I was still a little confused. "Did you and Rhonda get back together after you made her leave?" Earlier he told me they only broke up a few weeks ago.

"Yeah, but it was never the same. I felt bad for the way I talked to her, so after her constant begging and promising that things would be different, I gave in and let her come back after about a week. I also hoped Rhonda would have missed the baby and once she came back she would become a better mother. She came back and began working on our relationship wholeheartedly. She stopped gossiping with her girlfriends, she began studying for her GED, and she became more helpful with the housework, but Sha'Ron still was not a priority. Eventually I ended it for good, telling her that she didn't have to worry about caring for either of us. We would be fine without her."

"And that was just a couple of weeks ago," I stated more than asked. "Did you guys ever work out any type of custody and visitation arrangement?"

I wanted to know exactly where Rhonda now stood in his life and how often he saw the wench. Even though I had only known Shaun a day, I started feeling extremely possessive of him and more than a little jealous of his ex-girlfriend. I needed to know if Shaun still carried any feelings for Rhonda in his heart. I didn't state any of those questions out loud. I just hoped it would come across in his answers.

"I never made good on my threat to go to court to get full custody of my son. He has just remained with me since I put Rhonda out. She comes by three or four times a week claiming she is there to see Sha'Ron, but she spends very little time with him. She somehow manages to end up in my face saying we need to get back together and be a family again."

Shaun was frowning. I hoped that meant the idea of getting back together with her made him sick. But I had to give it to home girl. I can understand why it would be difficult giving up on a man like Shaun.

"Listen, Lindsay. I am not trying to get you involved in something you can't handle or lead you into a relationship filled with lies. I'm being very straightforward with you because I like you," Shaun said very softly and convincingly.

"The truth of the matter is Rhonda will always be a part of my life because she is the mother of my son. But that is all I want her to be. I know how she feels about me and I can't help that, but trust me when I say the feelings are not reciprocated. I respect her, and I try not to be mean when she comes around. But I'm always firm with her when I tell her we are not getting back together." Shaun must have had a connection to my mind. He seemed to always know what I was thinking and had answered just the way I wanted him to.

When I looked at the clock on the dash of Shaun's car, it read four-twelve. I couldn't believe we had been talking for an hour. My mother was likely to be home any minute. She normally doesn't get off work until four-thirty, but she had been known to pull an early showing when I was grounded to make sure I wasn't breaking the conditions of my punishment. That would be all I needed right now. I couldn't stand it if she grounded me for any longer. I was so anxious to go out with Shaun.

"Thanks, Shaun, for telling me about your breakup with Rhonda. I know it is a lot of personal information to share with someone you hardly know. I appreciate your honesty." I opened the door to exit the car. "I really need to get in the house before my mama calls or even worse, comes home early."

"I understand, beautiful. Thank you for the ear and for not openly judging me. I'm sure you will have a mouthful to share with your girl, Shyanne." He smiled. "Can I swing by after school tomorrow and pick you ladies up?"

I forgot he mentioned that earlier. "I would love it. I look forward to spending time with you at every available opportunity." I could not believe I said that even though it was exactly how I felt. I guess this honesty thing he was always talking about was rubbing off on me too. Perhaps I should credit Bible Study and my mother too.

"Now that's the way I like to hear my future woman talking. By the way, Lindsay, what's your last name?"

I barely heard his question because I was still stuck on the future woman remark. Now that's the way I like to hear him talking. I'm already crazy about this guy.

"Lindsay, did you hear me? I asked you your last name."

"Oh! I'm sorry. I was daydreaming a little. My last name is Westbrook. What's yours?"

"Taylor. My full name is Shaun Robert Taylor."

Lindsay Taylor. That has a pretty cool ring to it. "Well, Mr. Taylor, I have to get in the house before I get into some serious trouble. I'll see you tomorrow."

"Until tomorrow beautiful."

Then he was gone.

Chapter Four

"Heavenly Father, I come to you this morning thanking you for waking me this morning. I thank you, God, for a peaceful night's rest. I thank you for my family and my best friend's family. I thank you that we are healthy and clothed in our right minds. And Father, I ask in special prayer that my date with Shaun today goes well and that we start a relationship that is filled with love and trust and respect. This I pray in Jesus' name. Amen."

Today Shaun and I were to go on our first official date. Even though I had managed to see him every day since we met, I am as nervous as if this were a complete blind date. I can't get my thoughts together. I can't remember what he looks like, what he smells like, or a single thing we have talked about over the last four days. No guy has ever given me the flux like this.

Shaun called me bright and early this morning, telling me how excited he was that we would finally be able to spend some time together without sneaking around. He informed me that he would pick me up around four-thirty and we would have the dinner he promised me when we first met. We would play the rest of the evening by ear.

I had been looking for something suitable to wear since I got off the phone with Shaun. Here it was three hours later, and I have not decided on a thing. This is ridiculous.

"Nay-Nay, girl, you are going to have to pull yourself together and get back to your usual totally-in-control-of-the-situation self. You can't let this guy know he has you sweating like this. I'm sure Shaun is not sitting at home with a headache, running around like a chicken with his head cut off for this date," I spoke aloud to myself. I figured it was time to hit my knees again and get God's help on getting me *to* this date, not just through it.

"God, I come back again in just a short time needing your peace and your assurance. Lord, I need you to calm me and to give me confidence so that I can prepare myself for my date. Again I pray in Jesus, name. Amen." Just after I prayed a thought came to mind.

Never let a man know he has the upper hand in your relationship. At least not in the beginning. Never be the first one to say I love you, and until he makes a formal attempt at a commitment, always act like he is just one of the many guys you deal with. That was advice Granny started giving me when I was ten years old. She had repeated it many times over the years.

"Thank you for bringing that to my memory, God. Okay, Granny! I won't let you down. I will pull myself together and act like I date guys as fine and as grown up as Shaun all the time."

I checked the weather report on the news and the funny looking guy on channel four said it would be warm for March; temperatures reaching into the high sixties. So I will wear my peach denim pants with the matching jacket. I will add to it my yellow tank top and my yellow Nikes.

"See, girl, look at you. You made a decision without sweating and second-guessing yourself. If you can just hang on to this attitude until after church, you will be just fine when he picks you up this afternoon."

Well I'll be a funky duck! (One of Granny's sayings). My calm attitude went right out the freaking window. I just realized I had not asked Mama if it was cool for me to even go on this date. How could I forget such an important piece of the puzzle? All I needed was for her to trip and say I couldn't go. And even if she did let me go, she was going to give me the third degree about Shaun. She was going to have a fit about his age and the kind of car he drives.

Okay! Okay! Okay! God shall supply all my needs. And what I need right now is a miracle. Okay! There is nothing I can do about that right now. Mama will be ready to leave for church in five minutes. Hopefully while we are in service, God will give me the advice I need to get Mama's permission to go on this date.

Service today was pretty much the same as always. No lightning bolts. No rain of fire. No advice to help with my predicament. Prayerfully God spoke to Mama's heart and she was prepared to be receptive.

Well, I might as well go on and get it over with. That way if she does say no, Shaun will have plenty of time to make others plans for his day. No sense having him wait until the last minute for me to tell him I can't go.

I entered the kitchen and found my brother there eating what was probably his fifth bowl of cereal for the day. "K.J., where's Mama?"

K.J. is the spitting image of our dad. I only remember what my father looks like from the pictures Mama has of him in our photo albums. They have the same tall, slim build, the same tan brown coloring, and the same sandy brown hair.

The only thing he got from our mother is his eyes. We all have the hazel brown eyes.

Whenever Mama gets mad at K.J. she yells at him to get out of her face. She says he looks so much like our dad she can't stand the sight of him. For that reason, the boy has hardly ever gotten a spanking. I think she's afraid once she starts to hit him she will take out all of her frustrations at Daddy on Kevin Jr. Too bad I don't look like our father because she has never had a problem whacking me around when she felt I needed it. I look like Mama.

"She's in the basement washing clothes," Kevin said through a mouthful of Fruit Loops. After chewing and swallowing he added, "Who were you on the phone with before church this morning? It wouldn't happen to be a certain guy who drives a red Trans Am would it?" he asked with this stupid grin on his face.

"Boy, what are you talking about? What do you know 'bout a guy in a red Trans Am?" I tried to pretend I was clueless.

"Nay, you can give up the innocent act. I saw y'all sitting in front of the house on Thursday and Friday. You were so busy smiling up in his face, you didn't even notice me when I got home from school. I could have been Mama and you wouldn't have noticed over that big ole grin on your face." K.J. was cracking up laughing at me.

He was right. I must have been seriously slipping not to notice Kevin on either day. More proof that I needed to stop letting Shaun have this much control over me. "Shut up, boy, before your mother hears you. You didn't happen to say anything to her did you?"

"If I had told Mama, don't you think she would have said something to you? I *could* use a little hush-hush money though. Being thirteen can be expensive," Kevin whispered and laughed again.

I'm pretty sure my little brother would not tell on me. He never had before. We watched out for each other like that. But I told him I would hook him up when I got my allowance because he didn't tell. I then went to the basement, which also doubled as our family room, to find Mama. She sat on the sofa folding towels and watching television.

"What's up, Mama! You need some help?" I asked as I flopped down next to her. I picked up a towel and started folding.

"What's up with you, Nay-Nay? And don't even come down here with that can I help you mess," Mama said as she snatched the towel out of my hand. "What do you want, child? And before you answer that question, try answering this one. Who was calling my house at the crack of dawn this morning? Your behind just got off punishment today, so whoever it was must have been waiting by the phone to call you since the day I grounded you. I know it was not Shyanne because that child doesn't even get out of bed until ten minutes before she absolutely has to."

Dang, did everybody on the block hear the phone ring when Shaun called this morning? "That's what I wanted to talk to you about, Mommy." My mother rolled her eyes at me because I only call her Mommy when I want something big.

"Talk, Nay-Nay, and quit all this butt-kissing. Something tells me this is going to be good."

Okay, the best way to handle her straightforward attitude was to just go for it. "Can I go on a date today?"

Mama stopped in mid fold and looked at me like I was crazy. That was a bad sign. "A date with who, Ms. Thang? Is that who called my house this morning, some boy wanting to take you out?"

The more Mama talked, the quicker I could see my date with Shaun becoming less and less of a reality. "His name is Shaun, Mama. I met him the last time you sent me to the grocery store. I told him I was grounded until today, so I guess he was kind of anxious to talk since we haven't talked since we met." I hated lying to my mother, and it was something I rarely did. But what was I supposed to say, we had been kicking it everyday while she was at work? NOT!

"Well, since you have only met Mr. Shaun once, why are you trying to go on a date with him so fast? What do you know about the rock-head boy besides absolutely nothing? He couldn't have told you that much over the phone this morning. What has gotten into you, Nay-Nay?"

I might as well call Shaun and tell him it was nice knowing him because I didn't know how long he would be willing to wait for my mama to say I have known him long enough to go out with him. But she still hadn't said no, so there was still some hope.

"Ma, listen. I know I haven't known Shaun long, but he seems like a very mature guy. When we met, he didn't act like the guys my age act when they meet someone they might like." Oh snap! I can't believe I let that slip.

It took Mama a minute to realize what I said, but as soon as she realized it, she zeroed right in on it. "Well, just how old is Mr. Rock-head?"

Why does she keep calling him Rock-head? She has formed a negative opinion about him without having met him yet. And if that were the case, when I told her his age, it would only go down hill from there. I wondered if I should lie to her again. Naw, if I did she would have a royal fit when and if she ever learned the truth.

"Shaun is nineteen, Mama," I said as matter-of-factly as I could, trying to make it sound like it was no big deal.

"Lindsay Renee Westbrook, did you say this boy was nineteen? Don't you think that's a little too old for you?" At that moment I was almost sure my date was as good as a dead issue, but I was still not ready to give up.

"Not really, Mama. It's only three years. Would it be so bad if he were twenty and I was seventeen?"

"Yes it would," Mama said rather sharply.

"Okay, what if we were twenty-one and eighteen?" I knew I was pushing it, but I couldn't help it. Until she said no, I felt I still had a fighting chance.

"At eighteen, honey, you are a grown woman, dating a grown man. Right now you are a sixteen year-old child *trying* to date a grown man."

"Aw, Mama, come on. I'm not a baby, and I think I'm a pretty good judge of character. Shaun is really cool. He's not some child molester or something." I pleaded my case, throwing in a little extra whining.

"Again, I ask you, how would you know how cool he is? You have only had two brief conversations with the rockhead boy."

Man! She was making me mad. She was sitting there talking about how I didn't really know anything about him. She didn't know him at all, yet she had given the man an ugly nickname.

"Listen, Nay. Most nineteen-year-old boys are not interested in sixteen-year-old girls. They don't usually date girls still in high school. They prefer college-aged females like themselves. Is Shaun attending college somewhere? Does he attend church?"

Okay. She caught me off guard with those questions. I never even thought to ask him, and he surely didn't volunteer the information. But aside from that, what did she know about who dated whom? The only person she ever dated at my age was her sorry husband, and we see how that turned out. Now would probably not be the best time to bring that to her attention, however. I was still trying to win this argument and be given permission to go on this date. I needed to use a tone of voice that said I understood my mother's concerns, but there was still room to compromise. I had to use what Shaun found so attractive about me; my maturity and intellect.

"Like you said, Mommy, I have only had a couple conversations with Shaun, so I don't know whether or not he attends college. We also didn't discuss whether or not he went to church, but he knows I attend because I told him I was getting ready to go when he called me this morning.

"Shaun thinks I'm mature, Mama. He was impressed with my vocabulary, the one you said I have because of my love of reading." Giving Mama her props was definitely a plus at a time like this. "Before you pass judgment, why don't you meet him first and see what you think? After that, if you say I should not go out with him, I won't bother you with it again."

Mama looked to the sky, then took a long deep breath, letting it out in a sigh. That meant she was seriously thinking about giving in to me. If she were going to say no, she usually just says it.

"What time is he supposed to pick you up?"

Yes! She was caving. "Around four-thirty." I could hardly contain my smile, but I didn't want to seem over confident so I held it.

"When he gets here, I want him to come in and have a seat in my living room. I would like to have a conversation with him. And I'm telling you, Nay, if there is anything about him at all that strikes me as not right, I'll tell him to his face that he is never to contact you again. Do you understand me?"

"Yes, Mama."

I needed Shaun to put on the charm because I wasn't trying to have my mama embarrass either one of us.

Four-fifty-five and Shaun hasn't gotten here nor has he called. I hope everything is fine. On the two days Shaun picked me up from school, he was right on time, and I don't even remember giving him my schedule, so I'm not used to him being late. His tardiness was not winning any brownie points with Mama either.

Poor Shaun. He doesn't even know what he's in for. It could be likened to a police interrogation. When Mama wants to know something, she doesn't hold back. She's straightforward with her questioning no matter how stupid the questions sound or how embarrassing they can be.

Oh snap! What if Mama found out Shaun has a kid? Shoot! I forgot all about that. "Please God, don't let Mama take it there," I prayed out loud. That is a fact about Shaun I want to keep hidden as long a possible.

Shaun rang the doorbell at exactly five o'clock. When I went to let him in, terror dominated my features. He could have seen it even if he had been a blind man. I guess he assumed I looked this crazy because he was late.

"I'm sorry I'm a little late, Lindsay. Something came up at the last minute that I had to handle. I didn't realize it would take me as long as it did or I would have called you. I'll make it up to you, I promise. Please just wipe that angry look from your beautiful face," he said sympathetically.

"Listen, Shaun, this look has nothing to do with you being late," I tried to explain quickly. "My mother wants to meet and talk with you before we go out. I want to make sure you don't—" Before I could finish my sentence, Mama walked up behind me to introduce herself. She stepped around me and started talking.

"Hello, young man. I'm Mrs. Westbrook, Nay-Nay's mother. How are you today?" she asked in her sugary sweet voice.

"Hello, ma'am. My name is Shaun Taylor. I'm fine today and yourself?" Shaun extended his hand for Mama to shake. Mama accepted his hand and led him toward the living room.

"I am blessed, Shaun. And you don't have to call me ma'am. Mrs. Westbrook will be fine."

I am glad that I am a praying child because I was sure doing some heavy silent praying, asking God to let Shaun tap into his uncanny ability to read my mind. If my mother finds out he's a dad, she will probably denounce her Christianity and cuss him out for even trying to take me out on a date.

It's kind of ironic though. Shaun is older than both my parents were when they had me. Although I don't think it would make a'am (Granny's word which she says means less than na'am) bit of difference if Mama found out. Instead of worry about the negative, I decided to concentrate on the fact that Mama was at least polite to Shaun for now. I also found relief that she had not called him Rock-head.

"If you don't mind, I would like you to have a seat, Shaun, so that we can talk for a moment or two."

Shaun obliged my mother's wishes and sat in the chair by the window. Mama and I sat on the sofa. As soon as we were all settled, my mother started shooting straight from the hip. "I'm a little concerned about the age difference between you and my daughter. I realize Nay-Nay can act like a very mature young lady at times, but the fact remains that she is only sixteen years old."

Dang! What did she mean act? Mama made it sound as if my maturity was a front or something. I knew this was going to be embarrassing.

"I must also admit that the fact that the two of you have only met once bothers me somewhat. What could she possibly know about you after only two brief conversations?"

Shaun positioned himself in the chair like he was on the witness stand. He sat very straight, looking at Mama like she was a Supreme Court judge. "I understand both of your issues, Mrs. Westbrook. If you don't mind, I would like to address the one concerning our age difference first. It is true most guys my age are not looking to go out with young ladies still in high school. I found out when we met, however, that Lindsay isn't your typical sixteen-year-old. She has an extraordinary vocabulary. I was actually rather surprised to find out she was only sixteen."

Mama looked at me, and I could read the expression on her face like an open book. She couldn't believe I told Shaun my real name and allowed him to call me by it. I looked away and stared at the dust on the coffee table to avoid having to give an explanation right then and there.

"I would also like to say Lindsay was hesitant about talking to me once she found out my age." He looked over at me and smiled. Mom didn't seem overly impressed with his little show of affection, but I was ready to melt. I do so love his smile.

While not overwhelmed by his smile, I could tell she was warming to his personality. Shaun talked to my mom as if he had his speech rehearsed. Of course she was not going to let him off that easily. Mama still had some things she wanted to discuss. "Shaun, do you and/or your family attend church regularly?"

I don't know why this question worried me so much, but it did. Mama loved the Lord, and it was her opinion that everyone else on the planet should also. Although she was not a preachy person, she would certainly not hesitate to tell anyone willing to listen how good God had been to her and her family. I appreciate how well we have been taken care of in spite of my disappearing dad, and I credit God for the blessing too. But I understood that there were a lot of people who may not feel so obligated to praise God because they were not properly taught about His goodness. What bothered me about Mama's question, I guess, was I didn't know how Shaun felt about God, or even if he were a believer.

"Well, ma'am, I mean Mrs. Westbrook, I can't honestly say that me or my family are members of a church. Unfortunately, we only seem to visit actual church buildings when we are attending a funeral. But I will say that I do believe in God, and I do feel that I have a spiritual connection with Him. I'm certainly not against stepping up my church attendance. Perhaps I could join you and your family as a guest one Sunday morning. That is if you allow me to see your daughter beyond today."

His answer left me still a little nervous. I didn't know how Mama was going to react to him not going to church on a regular basis. Her facial expression gave away nothing. She remained unmoved and went on with her questioning.

"Are you currently attending college or a university?" Mama sounded like a judge trying to get information for a pre-sentence report. In a sense, this entire scene could be viewed that way. My mother was sizing Shaun up to see if he should be given "time" to spend with her daughter. I chuckled to myself at my own joke as Shaun answered my mother.

"Again the answer to that question is no, at least not at this moment. Presently I work for my Uncle Robert at his collision shop. I attended Wayne State University the semester after I graduated high school and stayed in school for two semesters before I left. During that time my mother was diagnosed with breast cancer. I thought it best that I let it go for a while so I could help at home with paying the bills and taking care of my two younger sisters."

Wow! I suddenly felt very bad for Shaun and his mom. A glance at Mama, and I could see that she was concerned as well. Shyanne had an aunt that died last year from breast cancer. I surely hoped that his mother wasn't going to die.

"I'm very sorry to hear that, Shaun. How is she doing now?" My mother asked, expressing her concern.

I, too, was very anxious to hear the answer to that question. I was suddenly so worried I almost cried. I said a silent prayer, asking God to please let his mother be okay.

"She is doing much better now. Thank you. Luckily they caught her cancer early. She had a mastectomy to remove one breast, then a few rounds of chemotherapy. It's been a year and a half, and so far, none of the cancer has resurfaced."

Mama looked visibly relieved. I didn't even realize I was holding my breath until after he finished speaking and I exhaled in relief myself.

"That is wonderful news, dear. I'll say a prayer for your entire family tonight. But I want to say something to you right now. The fact that your mother's cancer was diagnosed early and she is now doing fine has nothing to do with luck. What your mother and your family experienced was a first-hand blessing from God. Even though we may not all acknowledge Him and His goodness, He loves us all the same. And what He will do for one, He will do for another. God is no respecter of persons." Then Mama smiled for the first time since we sat down. That gave me so much hope.

"Listen to me carefully, Shaun. I am going to go against my initial qualms about you dating my daughter. You seem like a pretty decent young man. I'm impressed with your obligation and your responsibility to your family. A lot of nineteen-year-old men are selfish. I don't see that in you. So I give you permission to take Nay-Nay out tonight. I am also going to hold you to the offer you extended of joining us in church soon." Mama then turned and gave me instructions.

"As far as you, Nay-Nay, since this is your first day off punishment and your first date with this young man, I am going to impose a ten o'clock curfew instead of your normal eleven o'clock school night curfew. I don't want you to come in this house a minute later, is that understood?"

It took everything in me not to jump up and start dancing

when my mama said it was cool for us to go out. Instead I just smiled coolly and agreed to her jacked up curfew. I also thought about my granny's rules, and I didn't want Shaun to realize how important her saying yes was to me. It was probably not a good idea for him to know that it was the best thing that happened to me in a long time. At least, not just yet.

Chapter Five

Shaun and I had dinner at TGI Friday's restaurant in South-field. When our meals arrived, I grabbed Shaun's hand and said my customary blessing of the food out loud. Shaun seemed a little uncomfortable by my actions, but he didn't say anything about it. He gave me an awkward smile, then began to dig in to his dinner.

While eating, we talked a lot about his family. I discovered the names and ages of his two sisters: Francine, seventeen and Tameeka, fifteen. The older sister had a four-month-old son. Even though she had a kid, Shaun made sure Francine continued her education. She was due to graduate with her class in June. He also told me about his Uncle Robert, a.k.a. Bobby. Shaun's middle name was Robert after his uncle, and they were very close. He was the father he never had.

Shaun said he started working for his uncle after he left Wayne State. He was extremely grateful to Uncle Bobby for giving him an opportunity to earn some money and provide for his family during his mother's illness. Shaun was ac-cepted at Wayne State on a full academic scholarship. He said he always enjoyed school and most people were then, and are still amazed at how intelligent he is. It was also during his first semester that he found out Rhonda was pregnant and moved her into his house.

I guess you could color me guilty of short-changing Shaun's intelligence because of his looks. I remembered how surprise I was that he spoke so maturely when we first met. When I think of an honor roll student, my mind conjures up a picture of Steve Urkel from the television show, *Family Matters*, not the rapper, LL Cool J. Shaun looked more like a male supermodel than a bookworm.

After dinner, as we walked through the parking lot, Shaun asked me if I wanted to drive his car. I was so excited I almost screamed. I loved the thought of getting behind the wheel of his beautiful machine. I settled myself in comfortably, adjusting the seat, steering wheel, and the mirrors. Shaun's next statement almost deflated my mood as quickly as the invitation to drive his car inflated it.

"Why don't we go by my house? I want you to meet my son and the rest of my family if they're around," he said.

Shaun's suggestion totally surprised me. My hands gripped the steering wheel in a death grasp. "Shaun, I'm not sure I'm ready to meet your son just yet. This is only our first date. Just thinking about it makes me nervous. And what if Rhonda is at your house? I am sure that she and I are not ready to get acquainted." I wanted my first date with Shaun to be perfect. I think being involved in a confrontation with his baby's mama would surely put a damper on an otherwise good time.

Shaun pulled one of my hands from the steering wheel and kissed the back of it, then looked directly into my eyes. "Listen, Lindsay. I want you to know how much I'm enjoying our time together. I can't remember the last time I felt this relaxed and natural being with anyone. I know it's kind of soon to introduce you to my family. But because of the way you make me feel, I already know I want you to be a very special part of my life. I want to share you with the other people in my life that are special to me. Lindsay, I want you to be my woman."

Oh my goodness. Did he just say what I think he said? My eyes grew big as saucers, and my mouth suddenly became very dry. I was so shocked I couldn't have spoken one word if my life depended on it. I couldn't even breathe without thinking about it first. Earlier in the week when he said something about me being his future woman, I had no idea he meant today; this near in the future.

Shaun realized that I was stunned and he took full advantage of my open mouth by planting a very wet kiss on my lips. He gently placed his lips on mine and his tongue inside my mouth. I was not a very experienced kisser, so I was a little slow in responding, but after a few seconds of his slow coaxing, I was putty in his hands. By the time the kiss ended, Shaun could have offered to take me straight to the moon, and I would not have had the will to object.

Shaun informed me that he lived near the Southfield Freeway and Joy Road on Piedmont Street. I pulled from the parking lot and headed to his house. I had never driven any vehicle other than my mama's Ford Taurus, so I was a little nervous behind the wheel of this beautiful car. I drove about ten miles below the speed limit. When Shaun noticed my paranoia he put on a jazz CD.

"This will help mellow you out while you're driving. Just pretend you're driving your mother's car. There really isn't much difference. I want you to get used to being behind the wheel of my ride. My plan is for us to spend a lot of time together, and I may not always feel like driving." He smiled. I smiled right back. And at that point, I could have driven his car to California and back without needing a break.

I had never heard the music playing on the CD player, but I found myself enjoying it. "Shaun, whose CD is playing?"

"Kenny G. He's a jazz saxophonist. I love his stuff. Whenever things get too heavy for me, I just hop in my ride, pop in Kenny, and all is right with the world again."

I made a mental note to go through my mother's music collection when I got home to see if she owned any Kenny G. Jazz is about the only music other than Gospel that she really listens to these days.

We jumped on the John C. Lodge freeway heading south to the Southfield Freeway, exiting on Joy Road. Shaun's house was about eight miles from the restaurant, so by the time I pulled into his driveway, I felt pretty relaxed. For the duration of the drive, Shaun kept complimenting me on how pretty I looked and how everyone in his family was going to love me.

Shaun got out of the car and came around to the driver's side door to let me out. A few days ago, he instructed me that I was never to open a door for myself while I was in his presence. He felt it was a man's job to open doors for his lady.

We held hands as we walked up the steps to the front porch. He kissed me lightly on the cheek, then used his key to unlock the front door. Once we entered the house, we were standing directly in his living room, unlike our house where we have a vestibule. The living room was furnished with startling loud lemon yellow colored leather furniture. I had never seen furniture that color before. The walls were painted dull blue so the contrast was shocking. The color scheme of this living room was somewhat unsettling, and the relaxation I achieved on the ride over was gone. I was now twice as nervous as I was before.

Shaun's mother was sitting on the sofa watching a very large screened television. His son sat comfortably in her lap. I could have picked this little boy out of a room full of one-year-olds. Sha'Ron was the spitting image of his father.

Shaun began making the introductions. "Hey, Ma. I want

you to meet Lindsay. She would prefer you to call her Nay-Nay. She doesn't like her first name, so calling her by it is a privilege reserved only for me. I want you to get used to seeing this lovely face because I plan to spend a great deal of time with this young lady. Lindsay, this is my mother, Patricia Taylor."

Shaun's mother was pretty. She was very light-skinned and she owned the same green eyes and jet black hair as Shaun. She wore her hair in a ponytail that reached to the middle of her back. Unlike Shaun, his mother appeared to be short and had a tiny build. Patricia also looked rather young. If I could remember correctly, I think Shaun told me she was only fifteen when he was born, but she barely looked twenty five. She also looked to be bi-racial, but Shaun had never mentioned it.

Ms. Taylor raised her eyes and gave me a very casual once over, making me feel as though meeting Shaun's girlfriends was an everyday experience for her. My nervousness tripled.

"Hi, Nay-Nay. It's nice to meet you," she said without ever changing her facial expression. No smile, no frown, nothing. Patricia looked me straight in my face, shook my hand, and returned to her television program.

I had so many butterflies in my stomach my voice cracked when I began speaking, so I had to clear my throat. "Hello, Ms. Taylor; it's nice to meet you too," I lied as politely as I could.

Patricia's vibe was saying *I don't appreciate you trying to take Rhonda's place.* I silently prayed it was just paranoia on my part, but my gut told me this woman was not going to like me. Shaun had one more introduction to make.

"And this here is my little man, Sha'Ron." He picked his son up from his mother's lap and tickled him under the chin. The baby giggled, and then held a steady smile as he looked at his dad. I put my finger inside the baby's hand and he began to squeeze it.

"Hello, Sha'Ron. You are so cute. You look just like your daddy." For that I was rewarded with a big four-toothed grin.

"Hey, little man, don't be grinning at my woman like that. You're going to make your daddy jealous." Patricia coughed as he called me his woman, and I turned to look at her. She cocked one eyebrow then rolled her eyes at the comment.

While looking at Patricia, I noticed that she only had one breast. Like I said, she was a petite sized woman, but the remaining breast was at least a C cup, making the missing lump even easier to detect. I tried very hard to concentrate on something else so I wouldn't get caught staring. Sha'Ron provided me with the perfect diversion when he pulled my hair, then extended his arms, reaching for me to take him from Shaun. I graciously pulled the baby into my arms, ecstatic at his timing.

"Ma, are Francine and Tameeka home? I want them to meet Lindsay," Shaun asked.

"Francine and the baby are in the back bedroom, but I haven't seen that fast-tailed Tameeka since early this morning. You're going to have to talk to her, Shaun, 'cause I don't want no more babies brought in this house. That heifer think she grown," his mother said.

At that moment, Patricia looked at me and frowned as if I somehow left a bad taste in her mouth. I quickly looked away and continued to play with the baby, pretending not to notice. However, I was now sure I was not just paranoid. Shaun's mother didn't like me.

"We'll talk about it later, Ma," Shaun replied, then yelled for his other sister. "Francine, can you come out here a minute?" His sister appeared a few seconds later carrying a little bundle wrapped in a bath towel. "Francine, I want you to meet my new girlfriend, Lindsay. Please call her Nay-Nay. Lindsay, this is my sister, Francine and her son, Daiquan."

Shaun's sister looked like a younger version of his mom. She was petite in height (about two inches shorter than me) and had the same long, jet-black ponytail as her mom. But Francine's eyes were brown instead of green.

"Hi, Nay-Nay," his sister answered quickly. She then started talking to Shaun before I had a chance to reply. "Shaun, can I talk to you in my room for a minute?" Without another word, Francine made haste to turn and exit toward her bedroom. She was visibly annoyed.

"Lindsay, please excuse me while I talk to my sister. Have a seat and make yourself comfortable. I'll be right back." Shaun followed his sister.

I walked over, sat on the chair and put the baby in my lap. Shaun asked me to make myself comfortable and I sat there wondering how that was going to be possible when his mother was sitting there hating me like I stole her favorite piece of jewelry. Patricia kept looking at me like she wanted me to disappear, or even worse; like she thought I was going to purposely do something to harm her grandson.

While I played with the baby I heard approaching voices on the front porch. My senses went on automatic alert, and my heart jumped right into my throat. I just knew it was Rhonda coming to visit her son. And here I sat holding him as if I gave birth to the child.

Before anyone had the opportunity to enter, Patricia got up from the couch, snatched the baby out of my arms, and yanked the door open. I guess she knew it was Rhonda too, and she didn't want any part of her coming in and catching me holding her baby.

"Tameeka, where has your fast tail been all day?" Patricia yelled through the screen. "Get your stupid self in this house and off my front porch talking to that nappy headed boy."

When Tameeka stomped into the house, I found she didn't look like anyone in Shaun's family I had met so far. She was tall like Shaun, but that is where the similarities ended. She was a shade or two darker than I. She wore her hair swept up into some wild looking ponytail in a variety of about five different colors. Unlike her mother and sister, Tameeka's hair was chemically straightened, not naturally straight like theirs and not as long. While she wasn't as pretty as they were, she wasn't unattractive.

As she came in and slammed the door behind her, Tameeka started yelling back at Patricia. "Dang, Ma! Why do you always gotta make a scene and embarrass me in front of my friends? You don't do that mess to Francine when Daiquan's daddy comes around here." Tameeka pointed her finger in Patricia's face and Sha'Ron began wailing, probably responding to the tension between mother and daughter.

"Wench, I know you best lower your voice and quit wagging that bony finger in my face before I knock your black tail back through that door!" Patricia sat the howling baby on the floor, then got in Tameeka's face like she was going to hit her. Before anything could go down, Shaun was making his way to the living room.

"What is going on? Why are y'all screaming like lunatics out here?" Shaun said as he ran down the short hallway. He then stepped between his mother and sister. "Y'all act like you don't hear my son hollering or that we have company right here in the living room." He leaned over to pick up his crying child.

"Forget that, Shaun!" his mother yelled as she tried to get around him. "Under no circumstances does this wench get away with screaming and pointing her finger in my face like I'm some child. I'll kick her black behind all over this house. I don't give a hoot who's here. That goes for you, your girlfriend, or Jesus Christ. Ain't no child of mine gon' ever disrespect me inside of my own house. This heifer here ain't but fifteen years old. She won't run around here acting like she grown." Then she directed her rampage at Tameeka. "And you better not bring your dumb butt up in here pregnant. I ain't putting up with this no more, do you understand me?"

Tameeka didn't even bother responding to her mother.

She stormed from the living room and headed to what I guessed was the basement, mumbling inaudibly under her breath. During the whole scene, I sat there not knowing whether I should get up and leave or what. But I was positively clear about one thing: how relieved I was that it was Tameeka at the front door and not Shaun's baby's mama. In my mind, the blow-up between his mother and his sister was mild compared to what might have unfolded if his ex had shown up.

Shaun sat the baby on the couch and looked at me for the first time since returning to the living room; his embarrassment evident. He ran his hand across his beautiful face, then bent down in front of my chair, grabbing my hands in his. "Lindsay, I'm so sorry you had to witness that ugly scene. Please accept my apology on behalf of them both. Here, sweetie." Shaun reached into his front pants pocket. "Take my keys and wait for me in the car. Turn on the CD player, and I promise I'll be out in less than five minutes."

I got up from my seat and headed toward the front door. I turned long enough to say goodbye to Shaun's mother. "Goodnight, Ms. Taylor. It was nice meeting you."

"Goodnight, Nay-Nay," was all she said. She then rolled her eyes, went to pick up Sha'Ron and left the room.

I left the house and sat in the car for no more than three or four minutes before Shaun came out and got behind the wheel. He took a few moments to collect himself before pulling out of the driveway, backing the car out slowly and driving me home. He was obviously still upset, so I tried to break the uncomfortable silence between us.

"Shaun, don't worry about what happened back there. Mothers and daughters have disagreements all the time. I'm sure they will work things out."

Shaun reached over and kissed the back of my hand, then gave me one of his prize winning smiles. "I'm not worried about my mother or my sister. They'll be fine, just like you said. I just hate you had to witness them acting so silly. Some first impression, huh?"

Since he mentioned first impressions, I decided then would be a good time to talk to him about his mother's attitude toward me. Shaun had this crazy idea earlier that his whole family would like me instantly, but when I thought about it, none of them seemed too friendly toward me. I felt like they really resented me being his new girlfriend.

"Shaun, it was definitely not what I expected. The whole time I was there I got the feeling your mom couldn't stand me. I'm not sure, but I think it's because she didn't want me taking Rhonda's place. Francine didn't seem too pleased to meet me either. Tameeka didn't really get a chance to give her opinion one way or the other."

"Don't worry about Francine, Lindsay. I know for a fact her attitude had nothing to do with you. She was upset with Daiquan's dad. She took me in the back room to explain that she needed money for the baby because his deadbeat daddy wasn't responding to any of her phone calls or pages. My mother was probably just stressed and in a bad mood because of the stunts my little sister has been pulling lately. Don't sweat it, baby. It was the timing, that's all. Nothing personal," he said, trying to reassure me.

I was not totally convinced. The explanation about his sister was believable, but his mom definitely made me feel like it was me she had a problem with in addition to her daughter. As a matter of fact, I believe she yelled at Tameeka the way she did because she was so disturbed by me. I didn't discuss it any further with Shaun because I didn't want to upset him any more than he already was. We rode the rest of the way to my house not talking, just listening to Kenny G.

When we arrived, Shaun came around and opened my door as usual and walked me to my front door. I looked at my Timex and saw that I was five minutes earlier than my curfew.

"Well, Ms. Lindsay, I hope you still want to be my lady after all you witnessed at my house today. If not, please at least consider going out with me again so I can make it up to you." Shaun's face wore a cute little puppy dog expression. I knew he was kidding, but I played along.

"Well, I'll have to do some serious thinking on the subject, Mr. Taylor. I'll call you as soon as I get home from school tomorrow to let you know my decision." I then broke into the silliest grin.

"What do you mean you will call me when you get home? I don't think that will be necessary. I will be waiting right outside the school just as I have since we met. That will be an everyday thing, Lindsay. My woman doesn't have to walk anywhere anymore, so get used to seeing me everyday after school."

Alrighty. He made it one hundred percent official. We are a bona fide couple. I didn't have to bother putting on my game front any longer. I could just be open with my wonderful new man. Shaun made his commitment to me, and now it was time for me to let him know how wonderful I felt about it.

"I love it when you call me your woman and I look forward to seeing you everyday." Then I did something I have never done before. I initiated our goodnight kiss. I usually wait for the guy to make the first move, and it usually takes place after knowing him a lot longer. But with Shaun, I felt bolder and more grown up. So I just went for it. The kiss lasted a little while, and I was more aroused than I had ever been in my entire life. I didn't even realize that my body had the ability to react in such a way.

When we finally parted I used my index finger and thumb to seductively clean my lip gloss from Shaun's chin before unlocking my front door and stepping inside. I turned around, said goodbye to him and told him I would see him tomorrow after school.

I closed the door with him still standing on my front porch, leaned against it and let my body revel in the tingly sensations. When I finally went to my bedroom, I knew as sure as my name was Lindsay Renee Westbrook that I was totally in love with Shaun Robert Taylor.

Chapter Six

August 1993

Shaun and I have been seeing each other constantly and consistently for four months. Things have been going wonderfully. Or should I say the relationship has been going wonderfully. We have had some things come up against us, some of them easier to deal with than others.

In the beginning of our relationship, my grades slipped a little bit, and Mama was none too pleased with my report card. She told me if she didn't see some immediate improvement, I would have to discontinue my relationship with Shaun. She also said I would not be allowed to take the road test for my driver's license until my eighteenth birthday. This was back in April.

She used the straight up big guns on me. I knew I had to get my stuff together quick. Not being able to see Shaun was the equivalent of not being allowed to eat. Not getting my driver's license was only a little less severe. So I put together a game plan that would allow me to continue to see my man and help me bring my grades back to normal.

First I went to each of my teachers individually and asked if they would issue me a progress report that showed how I did in class at the end of each week. Then I started staying up late at night doing extra credit work and studying. That way I didn't have to lessen the time I spent with Shaun each day. There were a few occasions when I fell asleep while we were on our dates, but Shaun understood because he knew the plan.

Today my grades are even better than before, and I received my license the Friday before Mother's Day. That was one bridge we crossed successfully.

Bridge number two came back in June, on the evening Shyanne attended her boyfriend's Senior Prom with him. That day started out badly. The night before the prom, after Shaun and I hung out, I dropped him off at home so I could keep his car overnight. I initially told Shaun that Shyanne and I needed him to drive us around to run some last minute errands for her prom date if he didn't mind. That's when he offered to let me keep the car to do what needed to be done. He said he could find another way to work, but I had to be sure to pick him up when he got off that evening.

When I woke up the morning of the prom and began getting ready for school, I ran into Mama in the hallway while she was getting ready for work. I noticed she looked angry, and I wondered what I had done. "Good morning, Mama."

"Good morning to you, Ms. Lindsay Renee Westbrook." Oh snap! I must be in some serious trouble. "Why is Shaun's car parked in my driveway? I know he didn't spend the night here last night. I know you aren't that crazy, girl," she yelled at me.

Well, if that's what had her so upset, I had nothing to worry about. "No, Mama. I kept Shaun's car last night so I would be able to help Shyanne get ready for her prom date tonight," I replied, not stopping to think for a moment she would have a problem with that.

"Oh, so how many times have you driven Mr. Shaun's car alone?"

My mother had been getting on my case about being so serious with Shaun. She thought I was too young to be tied down to one guy. As a matter of fact, she even tried to get me to go out with her co-worker's son. I couldn't believe my mama was actually trying to hook me up. There was no way I would go out with anyone other than my boo. Even though we had not said the words to each other, I loved him, and I knew he loved me back.

"This is the first time, Mama. Why are you making such a big issue over this? I do have a driver's license." I had begun to get a little attitude of my own. I simply wasn't feeling her frustration.

"Nay-Nay, you are sixteen! Not eighteen, not twenty-one and not twenty-five. You are sixteen and sixteen-year-old girls should not be driving their boyfriend's car. Sixteen-year-olds should not even have boyfriends who own their own cars. Their boyfriend should still drive their parents' car." She spoke loudly as she put one hand on her hip and let her finger go to wagging with the other.

"When I said you could go out with Shaun in the beginning, I figured the two of you would go out a couple of times and discover you didn't have much in common because of your age difference. But this whole thing has gotten way out of control. You are spending entirely too much time together, and frankly, I don't think it's healthy for a girl your age to be so involved with just one boy. Or should I say one *man*."

I couldn't believe she was giving me that speech again. I had explained to her that my seeing Shaun should give her no cause for worry. I assured her we were not sexually intimate, and I let her know that he was in no way leading me into any trouble. I neglected to inform her that I had skipped Bible Study on a few occasions to spend time with him, but I didn't think she needed to know *all* of my business.

But that day I had had enough. I let her know we were serious, and she had no reason to have a problem with it. "Mama, why is the time I spend with Shaun such a big deal? I have never stayed out past curfew. He has never been disrespectful to you or to me. My grades are better, and Shaun wouldn't have it any other way." I paused to see if my words were having any effect on her. After noticing they didn't, I became angry.

"Shaun is my one and only, Mama, which means we are going to spend time together. I am sixteen, not fourteen, or twelve or ten." I knew I was being flip by mocking her, but I couldn't help myself. I thought she was being ridiculous.

"Don't get smart with me. I'm not in the mood to play with you. I will slap you with the permission and strength God gave me." Her tone was deadly calm. "I don't care what you say; sixteen is too young to settle down with one boy. You just began to date, and you are far too inexperienced to think you are ready to make a commitment."

"Listen, Mama, I'm sure your negative feelings are a result of what you went through in your relationship with daddy. What you fail to realize is everybody is not daddy. Why should Shaun and I have to pay for the mistakes the two of you made?" I knew I was hitting below the belt, but I had to get my point across. With or without her consent, I was going to continue to see Shaun.

"What I am saying to you has nothing to do with me and your sorry daddy. What I am talking about is life and men in general. Nothing teaches you about life better than experience; bad experiences are the best teachers in the world. Learning from someone else's experience is far better than having to endure the heartache yourself." Mama was on her soapbox now.

"Now, Ms. Thang, I am not going to stop you from seeing that boy yet. You are right; at this point I don't really have a good reason to do so. But I want you to hear me and hear me good. You are still just a sixteen-year-old child. *My* child. I won't sit idly by and let anyone hurt you intentionally or unintentionally. So when I feel this thing with Shaun has gone too far, I'll put a stop to it, and there is nothing you can do about it. As long as you live under my roof, you will do exactly as I say. That is all I have to say right now because I'm late for work and you're late for school." Mama finished and started toward her bedroom.

"Oh! I'm sorry. There's one more thing," she said as she turned around. "Do not park Shaun's or anybody else's car at my house until you are at least eighteen. You are not old enough to be responsible, and I refuse to take responsibility for any damages that may occur." She then left without giving me a chance to rebut.

And that was just the beginning of that day. Midway through, it got much worse.

Shyanne and I were running the last of our errands when we ended up not too far from Shaun's house. The beauty supply store where we stopped was right next door to the McDonald's in Shaun's neighborhood. I was hungry so I decided to stop in and grab a Big Mac to go. The drive-thru line was ridiculous so I went inside. Shyanne declined the offer for any food because she didn't want to ruin her appetite for dinner.

As soon as I got in line, someone approached me from behind and tapped me on the shoulder. It was Shaun's youngest sister Tameeka.

"What's up, Tameeka?" I greeted.

"What up, Nay-Nay? I see you sporting my brother's car. I bet you think you all that, don't you?" she grinned.

Tameeka and I got along pretty well. Wish I could say that about the other females in Shaun's family. His mother still barely had two words for me. Francine always seemed to be in a bad mood because she was angry at her son's father.

"Can you take me home since you bouncing the Trans? Save a girl some miles on these new sneaks my brother just bought me." She twisted her foot to model her new shoes.

Their house was only about four or five blocks from McDonald's, so her statement of the 'miles' was a big exaggeration, which was typical Tameeka. But I didn't have a problem hooking her up with a ride since it was so close, and it would not interfere with our schedule.

"No problem, Meek-Meek. Just let me get my food, and we can be on our way."

I looked at the gym shoes Tameeka wore as an afterthought. She was sporting the Air Jordan's that had just come out. Those shoes were at least $100. Shaun was always buying things like that for Tameeka, and according to her, she was the best dressed girl at Cody High School.

When we returned to the car, I made the introductions between Shyanne and Tameeka, then headed to Shaun's house. I wished he were home so I could at least get a glimpse of his beautiful face.

Tameeka talked a mile a minute about some dude at her school who apparently had a crush on her. Tameeka thought all the boys in the neighborhood, all the boys at school, all the boys in the universe were jockeying her because she was so cute and she dressed so fly.

"Nay, the guy is cute, but he dresses like a nerd. He doesn't wear any designer clothes and to me that is plain not cool," she said in her exaggerated nasal voice.

Shyanne sat in her seat, looking like she prayed Tameeka would shut up soon. To be honest, she was hard to take sometimes. Every time I saw her, she was bragging about some new outfit she got or some boy who liked her. If she weren't Shaun's sister, I probably would have told home girl that she was not all that, even in her Guess jeans and Gucci gym shoes.

While Tameeka was running her mouth, I tuned her out,

focusing instead for the thousandth time since we started dating on my curiosity about exactly how much money Shaun made working for his uncle. He gave his baby sister anything she asked for, and he was always giving Francine money to help her take care of her baby. Whenever we went out, which was pretty often, he always had large wads of money on him. His mother was still unemployed, so he supported the entire household. He didn't work a lot of overtime at the collision shop because he still picked me up from school everyday, and we managed to spend a lot of time together.

That was the day I regrettably came to the conclusion that Shaun's job at the collision shop was not his only hustle. I hated thinking about it, and I was definitely not prepared to hear him say it to me out loud. During that time I went against every moral and spiritual nagging in my being and pretended not to worry about whether or not my boyfriend was dealing drugs. I rationalized that there had to be some other explanation. And as long as whatever he was into didn't affect me directly, I decided to just not say anything about it.

"Nay-Nay, you about to pass my house, girl. You must be seriously daydreaming about my brother 'cause I called your name twice and you were not even hearing me," Tameeka said with a silly laugh.

I had to screech to a stop in order to not drive by their house. "Sorry about that, Meeka. I was definitely thinking about something too hard."

"Well, you better not tear up Shaun's ride or he gon' be mad," Tameeka said as she exited the car and ran toward her house.

I waited for her to get inside before I pulled away. Before she could make it inside someone else came outside. I didn't take time to find out exactly who it was because I assumed it was Patricia coming to yell at Tameeka like she usually did. I turned to look across the street and pretended I was engrossed in the beauty of the neighbor's flower garden. I was not interest in seeing Ms. Taylor leering at me with her customary frown.

"Nay, is the big girl coming toward the car Shaun's other sister?" Shyanne asked. I turned to look in the direction Shyanne was speaking of. There came a female I had never seen before stomping toward the car.

"No, Shy. That is not Francine. I have no idea who she is."

The girl walked in front of the car, came over to the driver's side and knocked on the window with much attitude; like I didn't see her big butt standing there. She was evidently mad about something. Her anger poured from her eyes like hot sauce from the bottle of a fat man.

I didn't know this wench from Adam, so my first instinct was to ignore her and drive off. I could see Shyanne in my peripheral vision going into defense mode, first taking off her earring, then her seat belt. Shyanne and the Boy Scouts shared the same motto: *Always be prepared.*

"Excuse me. Can I talk to you for a minute?" the thick stranger asked in a huff. I had the air conditioning on in the car and I still had not bothered to roll down the window, but I could hear her loud and clear. She didn't yell, but her voice was laced with venom.

"Who is that, Nay-Nay?" Shyanne asked loudly.

"I don't even know."

"Well, let down the window because I'm curious." Shyanne opened her door, got out and leaned on the hood of the car.

The stranger stood so close to my side of the car it would have been impossible for me to open the door without hitting her with it, which was exactly what I was about to do.

"Rhonda, come back in this house now. Don't make me come out there and get you," Ms. Taylor yelled as she walked off the porch and stood in front of the house.

Rhonda! The name exploded in my brain like a cannon. I snapped my head away from Patricia and back to Shaun's ex so quickly I almost got whiplash; my emotions going through every possible phase. I was shocked, angry, scared and glad all at once. Glad to finally know what she looked like; shocked because she had the dirty nerve to approach the car the way she did; angry because she was confronting me in such a rude manner and scared the hussy was going to cause us to whoop her tail and make us late getting Shyanne ready for the prom.

Shyanne was just as surprised. She nearly banged her head as she leaned back inside the car, asking me what I wanted to do. Before I could answer, Ms. Taylor spoke.

"No, no, Ms. Lady. Just get yourself back in the car and you and Nay-Nay go on about your business. It ain't gon' be no mess out here in my yard unless I'm the one dishing it out," she said as she came toward the car.

I thought Patricia was going to approach Shyanne and perhaps confront her, so I put my hand on the door handle preparing to knock Fatso across the street with the car door. However, Ms. Taylor continued past Shyanne and came to lead Rhonda back to the house.

Shaun's mother gently grabbed Rhonda's arm, trying to lightly steer her back inside the house. Rhonda stood frozen, looking like she was going to ignore her initially, then decided to do as she was told. She slowly walked away, never taking her eyes off me for a second. It wasn't until they reached the front porch that Shyanne climbed back in the car.

"Nay-Nay, you and your friend can leave now. Like I said, ain't nothing going down at my house that I didn't start," Ms. Taylor said with her ghetto self. She continued to hold Rhonda's arm as if she didn't trust her not to come off the porch.

I sat there for a few seconds, just hoping she would jerk herself loose and come after me. Then for the first time since arriving at his house, I thought about Shaun and how he would feel about the scene. I would have hated to face him later and explain that not only did I have to beat down his baby's mama, but his own mama also got caught in the melee and had to take a licking as well. I wasn't sure what he would have said or done, but I was positive he wouldn't have been too happy about it.

I turned the car into the driveway across the street to back out and turn around. Once I got the car pointed in the opposite direction, I took one last look at Humpty Dumpty then pulled away. As I sped away from Shaun's house, the last sound I heard was Tameeka's irritating laughter.

That was a couple of months ago and we have still had other obstacles to climb in our relationship. Yet despite the issues, Shaun has been nothing but good to me. He is attentive, generous, respectful, honest and so darn cute. I truly love him. So much so that yes, I have become sexually intimate with him since the argument I spoke about between Mama and me. I didn't lie to her on that day, but by that evening, things had taken a dramatic turn.

As we prepared Shyanne for the prom that evening, she and I talked about the stereotypical expectations of the after-prom experience. We assumed Antonio would expect Shyanne to have sex with him that night.

"Shyanne, do you think you're ready to have sex with Antonio? You can be pretty sure he's going to want to go there tonight." I brought up the subject while we pinned up Shyanne's hair.

"I've thought about this ever since Antonio asked me to go to the prom with him. He's never put any pressure on me about sex, but he has asked me about it. I've kept him at arms length by trying to explain my reservations about having sex while not being married. At the same time, I haven't been sure of myself. I mean, I don't know if I want to wait until I'm married to have sex. I sometimes wonder if that's a realistic goal, especially since I've already done it before."

"Does Tony know that?"

"Yes. He asked me and I didn't want to lie to him. I really like Antonio. I don't think it would be so bad if we made love. Besides, I don't want to risk losing him to a female willing to have sex with him while I hold out on him."

I could completely relate to Shyanne's spiritual and emotional war within herself. I'd had the same debate with myself since meeting and falling in love with Shaun. "How do you think God really feels about us engaging in sex before we get married? What I mean to say is do you think He will be really mad at us if we do it?"

"Well, we've already done it, and I believe He has forgiven us. I guess I can only hope that Antonio and I will be together forever and eventually end up married." After a short pause, Shyanne continued.

"You know what, Nay? Last night I prayed that if Tony and I did have sex, that it would be enjoyable for both of us. Does that make me demonic to ask God to bless my sin?"

"No. You're definitely not demonic. Look, we're still young and nobody knows us better than God. God understands that we're going to make mistakes. He'll forgive us. Why don't we pray right now together?"

Shyanne agreed and I led us in prayer. "Dear God. Thank you for this wonderful day. Thank you for helping us to avoid what could have been an ugly scene with Rhonda, and I thank you, Lord, for all the people who love me and Shyanne; especially Tony and Shaun. God, we know that you don't want us to have sex before we get married, but I also know you are a God who forgives us. I am certain that Shaun is going to be my husband one day, and Shyanne feels the same way about Antonio. So we ask you right now, Lord, to forgive us for our indiscretions. We are in love, God. Thank you for all of your blessings. In the name of Jesus, I pray this prayer. Amen."

Later that night, I found myself in need of God's grace and mercy as Shaun and I made love for the first time.

That evening, Shaun treated me to a very special evening. He said he didn't want me to feel left out because I wasn't going to the prom with Shyanne. We ate dinner at Andiamo's, an upscale Italian restaurant in Farmington. We then went to a Tyler Perry play at the Fox Theater in downtown Detroit and ended our evening by spending a few hours in a hotel suite that Shaun rented for the evening at the expensive Athenaeum Hotel not far from the theater.

Shaun understood that I wouldn't be able to spend the night with him, but he did convince me to stay with him until I was due home for curfew. He also informed me that there was no pressure for me to sleep with him. "Lindsay, I want you to know that I didn't rent this room to make you feel obligated to have sex with me. I just wanted us to have a nice place to spend time together after our special evening. I wanted it to be a complete evening for you."

The suite was beautiful. There was a sitting room with beautiful cream and gold furniture. In a separate room was the bedroom. The bed was draped with a sheer canopy that enclosed the entire bed, which was covered by a rich cream colored comforter with matching pillow cases and accented with smaller gold throw pillows.

The bathroom was just off the bedroom, which was as big as my mother's bedroom. The sink and shower stall faucets were accented with the same cream and gold coloring as the rest of the suite. But the tub was the showstopper in this room. It was almost as big as a swimming pool. Shaun said it was a Jacuzzi. I can't remember visiting anyone's home that was as nicely decorated as this suite.

"Shaun, this is so beautiful. I can't believe how big it is."

"Well, my lady only deserves the best," he replied as he walked up to me and wrapped his arms around me from behind.

His statement temporarily brought back to mind how Shaun could afford such an expensive room. Momentarily, I worried again about what he did to make his money. His next words made me forget all about my worries.

"Lindsay, I know I have never told you this before, but I think you already know it to be true. I love you. I think I fell in love with you on our first date."

Shaun was correct. I did know he loved me, but hearing him actually declare it out loud seemed to change my life in that very moment. It was as if in the small amount of time it took for him to utter those three words, I metamorphosed into another being. I quickly forgot about my mama, my brother, my granny, Shyanne, and even God. Shaun became my world; 'world' being the operative word. All I wanted to do was seal our love by sharing myself with the man who meant everything to me. That night, after I reiterated my love for him verbally, I reciprocated my feelings by giving him my body, my heart, and my soul.

That was two months ago and as I said, our relationship has been beautiful. Beautiful with one exception. With his declaration of love came his admission of his true occupation.

Chapter Seven

"Of course I'll marry you, Shaun, and I'll spend the rest of my life making you the happiest man on earth."

"Ugghh. You sound too stupid for words."

I can't believe he said that to me. I thought he loved me as much as I loved him. What was going on?

"Girl, wake up and stop dreaming about that fool." Now that didn't sound like Shaun's voice. It sounded more like . . .

"Kevin, what are you doing in my bedroom?" I shouted as I suddenly realized I was not actually talking to Shaun. Instead, my blockhead brother had invaded my space and shaken me out of a wonderful dream.

"Mama sent me in here to wake you up, sleepy head. Granny is on the way here, and she wants you to be ready before she gets here so we can go to breakfast." He exited my room, then he turned around like he forgot something. I was annoyed with K.J. and also a little embarrassed he heard me talking in my sleep. I snapped at him when he didn't immediately leave my bedroom.

"What do you want now, boy? I'm already mad at you for barging into my room without knocking."

"For your information, Ms. Attitude, I did knock, but you were too busy dreaming about your boyfriend to hear me. I only came back to say happy birthday, grouch." He left, closing the door behind him.

Now I really felt stupid. First I got caught having my favorite dream, then I bit my little brother's head off for wanting to wish me a happy birthday. I hope this wasn't an indication of how my day was going to go.

"Nay-Nay, Shaun is on the phone," my mother called from the kitchen. I smiled as I walked into the kitchen to grab the phone, realizing my day had improved just that quickly.

"Don't stay on there all morning because I want to leave here in about twenty minutes," Mama told me as I entered the kitchen and reached for the phone. "By the way, happy birthday, baby." She kissed me on the cheek, then walked away. I took the cordless phone back into my bedroom.

"Hello."

"Happy birthday, Lindsay. I know it's kind of early in the morning to be ringing the phone at your mother's house, but I wanted to be the first to wish my baby a happy 17th birthday."

"I'm sorry, but both my mama and my brother beat you to the punch, but I forgive you. It's hard to compete with the folks that live right here in the house with me."

"Well, we only have one more year to wait and then you and I will get a place of our own, right?"

Shaun and I have been talking a lot about our futures since the night he told me he loved me. We decided after I graduate high school and turned eighteen, we were going to get an apartment together.

My desire used to be to attend an out-of-state university, preferably Clark Atlanta University or Florida A&M. I couldn't wait to get away from the Michigan winters. But since I met Shaun, I knew I would be attending either the University of Detroit or Wayne State University right here in the city.

Shaun assured me that our life together would be great. He didn't mention marriage, but I knew we would get around to that eventually. He promised that in a year's time he would be in a position to handle our living expenses and my tuition.

On the night he told me about his occupation, Shaun explained how he first began working in Uncle Bobby's organization.

"Lindsay, when I told you and your mom that I began working with my uncle after my mother was diagnosed with breast cancer, I was telling the truth. However, Uncle Bobby's collision shop is a front for his very elaborate drug business. When I began working for him, I only operated within the collision shop, serving as office manager because I had no knowledge whatsoever of how to repair cars. But after a few short months, my uncle recognized my intellect and my skills as a leader. He asked if I wanted to take a risk and earn three to four times what he paid me as his office manager. I told him yes and he has been training me in the drug game ever since. Because I'm family and because I was smarter than his average worker, Uncle Bobby put me in charge of three houses he had here on the west side. The territory I run has since doubled, and my uncle is continuing to groom me so that I'll one day be his partner instead of simply his employee."

While Shaun's revelation came as no surprise to me, I was nonetheless disheartened by his admission. I may be a Christian, but I was not naïve. I have lived in Detroit all of my seventeen years, and I knew that what Shaun did, even under the protection of his uncle, was dangerous. I have prayed every night since the night he told me what he does for God to keep him safe until something better comes along.

And something even more dangerous than what Shaun did for a living would be if my mama found it. I could never allow that to happen. Heck, she was still in the dark about Sha'Ron. Shyanne was the only person who knew everything about Shaun.

"Right, Shaun. One year from today we can begin our real life together."

"Well, I just wanted to call to wish you a happy birthday. I know you have plans with your family this morning so I won't hold you any longer. I'll see you around five this evening."

"Okay, I'll see you then. I can't wait to see what you have planned for my birthday. I'll talk to you later."

"I love you, Lindsay."

"I love you too. Bye." As soon as I hung up, the phone rang again. This time it was Shyanne.

"Hey, birthday girl. How does it feel to be getting old?" she joked.

"Whatever, clown. You are only two months younger than me, so just shut up."

Shyanne and her parents were going to breakfast with us this morning. That was the only reason she was up this early. During summer vacation, the only day she gets up before noon is on Sunday, and even then only after her mother practically drags her from the bed for church.

"Are you ready for breakfast? Please don't show up late, because my mama will hurt you and you know it," I said to my slow-poke friend.

"Of course I'm not ready. I just got out of bed right before I called you. But it's only going to take me fifteen minutes to shower, throw on a pair of shorts, and leave the house. It's not like I have to do anything special. We're only meeting you all at Bob Evans," Shyanne said teasingly.

"Since you feel like that about it, you will no longer be invited to my birthday breakfast." I joked right back with her. "Go ahead and get ready. I'll talk to you when I see you." I hung up before she said anything else smart.

As I got out of bed and picked out my outfit for breakfast, someone knocked on my door. I opened it to find my granny standing there with her arms opened wide for a big hug. "Hi, Granny," I said as I stepped into her arms.

"Hi, baby. Uh oh! Maybe I shouldn't call you that anymore since you're just one year away from being a legally grown woman." Granny rocked me back and forth in her arms wrapped in a big bear hug. I love my grandmother so much. She always gives me the best advice, and she never treats me like I'm stupid, even when I make mistakes. I imagine that's how God is. I sometimes equate Granny with God.

She came into my bedroom and closed the door behind her. She sat on my bed and pulled a small box wrapped in pretty dark pink paper topped with a tiny pale pink bow from her purse. "I want you to open my present before we go to breakfast."

I sat down on the bed beside her and tore open the wrapping to get to my present, anxious to see what was inside. I opened the tiny box to find a beautiful gold bracelet with an assortment of gold charms; each representing various things I shared with Granny over the years. There was a pair of roller skates, a small tennis racket, a little key that probably represented her funny attempts at teaching me to drive, a baby doll, a piano that represented my one and only lesson (which I absolutely hated), and a single heart.

"Granny, this is so pretty. These charms are too cute. I have figured out the meaning of all of them except one: the heart. What exactly does that represent?"

"Oh, sweetie, that one should have been the easiest of all to figure out. It represents my unending love for you." There were tears in her eyes. I reached out to Granny for another hug. By the time we parted, we were both balling like three-year-olds.

"Thank you so much for this bracelet, Granny and for everything else you have ever given me; all the advice you have shared with me and for just being my granny. I love you too." Granny smiled at me with a perfect set of white teeth that I'm sure was not all hers.

"Okay, enough of this crying. What did that boyfriend of yours get you for your birthday? I hope it is something big enough to cover all the grief the two of you have been giving your mama. My daughter calls me everyday complaining about how much time you are spending with that rock-head boy. Her words, not mine."

"Granny, I don't know why Mama doesn't like Shaun. Why can't she see we are serious about each other? I am not a baby! I love Shaun and he loves me, but she has a hard time comprehending it. She thinks I am too young to know what love is, and that Shaun is just stringing me along."

Granny nodded her head then gave me her opinion. "Sweetie, listen. Your mama was hurt real bad by your tri-fling daddy. I guess she's afraid of the same thing happening to you. Now your granny understands how you feel because I was about your age when I fell in love with your grand-daddy, God rest his precious soul. We had a wonderful mar-riage all the way up to the day he died. You were two years old when he departed. But times are different now than they were when I was your age. Men are just not as upstanding as your granddaddy. Your mama is just worried about your heart, that's all. Cut her a little slack, okay?"

I don't know how Granny always managed to be on two sides at the same time and never make anyone feel bad. "I'll talk to your mama while you get dressed; see if I can't get her to loosen up on you a little. Now hurry up because I'm hungry. And we better not have to wait for that slow Shyanne."

After breakfast I sat in my bedroom admiring all of my birthday gifts. All of my additional gifts had a return to school theme. Shyanne and her family gave me a beautiful pink sweater and a pair of pink jeans to help kick-start my fall wardrobe for school. Kevin gave me a lovely mint green backpack to hold my books and supplies. Any form of pastel green is my favorite color. My mother gave me a $150 gift certificate to my favorite store, J. L. Hudson's, so that I could add to what the Kennedy's started. Granny's gift was still my favorite thus far. I had yet to receive my present from Shaun.

Today's celebration with my family began and ended with our breakfast outing. They didn't give me a big celebration because I had a major party just last year for my sweet sixteenth birthday and I'm sure Mama plans to go all out next year for my eighteenth birthday.

Now all I had to do was decide on my outfit for my date with Shaun tonight, and then I could just relax and read a good novel while I waited for him to pick me up.

Donald Goines is my favorite author right now. I'm currently reading my fourth book by him entitled *Black Girl Lost*. Mama doesn't particularly care for me reading his type of fiction because of Mr. Goines' graphic and explicit content, but she also recognizes and respects that I have my own taste. She gives me the freedom to have my own forms of interest and expression, trusting that my relationship with God and her parental guidance won't allow me to be shaped by what I see and hear in the world. Mama says as I mature and get closer to God, my likes and dislikes will change.

The phone rang in the kitchen, and I was sure it was Shyanne calling for the third time since breakfast to see if I have figured out what Shaun has planned or what present he has given me for my birthday. It seems she was more interested and anxious than I was.

I heard Kevin outside my bedroom engaged in conversation as he knocked on the door to bring me the cordless telephone. "I can't wait for school to start, Grandma. I'll be a freshman at Henry Ford High School this year," he said as he entered. "Right. That's the same school Lindsay goes to."

When I heard Kevin use my first name I knew he was talking to my father's mother, Nana Westbrook.

"Here's Lindsay, Grandma. I'll talk to you later. I love you too." Kevin handed me the phone, then left my room.

"Hello."

"Hi, Lindsay. Happy birthday, baby."

"Thank you, Nana Westbrook."

I call my paternal grandmother by her last name in order to keep our relationship formal rather than familiar. I regard our relationship as distantly neighborly versus intimate. I rarely see or even talk to her. And with the way my daddy up and left us, I refrain from getting close to her just in case she decides to bail out on us one day also. I realize it may be silly to feel this way since it has been thirteen years since my father left and she's still around, but this has been my strategy to guard my heart since the day I accepted that my father was never coming back.

"Baby, I bought you a nice sweater for your birthday you can wear to school this winter. When Henry comes back from Ohio this weekend, I'm going to have him bring me out to your house so I can visit with you all. I'll bring the sweater with me then."

Henry is my father's brother. He is the one person on that side of the family we see on a regular basis. I like Uncle Henry a lot, but just like Nana Westbrook, I keep my feelings for him in check.

"I look forward to seeing you then, Nana Westbrook. Thank you very much for the sweater. I'm sure I'll love it."

"You're more than welcome, baby. I know it's been a lot of years, but I still feel awful for the way your daddy ran out and left you all. I try to do the best I can to help you all when I can. Saddest thing about Kevin leaving is he hasn't contacted anybody in the family since he ran off. We don't know if my son is dead or alive. It ain't right to just leave and not get in touch with nobody for thirteen years."

This is the main reason I don't like talking to Nana. Every time we talk she brings up my absentee daddy. I would rather not discuss him at all. I realize she must grieve his absence, but I could do without having to be constantly reminded of his desertion. I never have the heart to tell Nana how I feel though. I usually just change the subject or end the conversation.

"Well, Nana Westbrook, I have to go. I'm getting ready to go out with some of my friends for my birthday. Thanks again for the sweater, and I'll see you this weekend."

"Okay, sugar. You go on ahead and enjoy your birthday. You make sure you be good and keep God first, you hear me? I love you, baby."

"Yes, ma'am. I love you too. Goodbye."

I'm always in a funk after every conversation or visit with my Nana. Although I have gotten over my daddy leaving us without so much as a *kiss my butt*, I would rather not be reminded of it when I talk to her. Maybe this weekend I'll tell her how I feel. That way, she just might stop talking to me about him.

I have learned to deal with my daddy's leaving by just pretending I never knew him at all. I pretend he was never here in the first place. Pretending he was dead would mean I might have lots of fond memories of him or miss him. I don't! I was only four years old when my father left. The only nice thing I remember about him, the only memory I have at all of him, is of the day he took me to the supermarket with him. Just inside the building was a coin operated toy pony, and I asked Daddy if I could ride. I remember him sitting me on top of the pony very gently, making sure my feet were properly placed in the stirrups and the lap belt was on correctly. Each ride cost a quarter; my daddy must have spent about a dollar and fifty cents. I was having a royal ball on top of that horse.

Three days later, he was gone. He left without a word, a note, a telephone call. We have remained in the same house since he left, so he knows the address. Never once has he tried to contact us to find out if we were dead or alive.

No, I don't think pretending he's dead is fair. Death implies the possibility of going to heaven and living with Jesus. I don't want that kind of comfort for him; streets paved with gold and angels at his beck and call. I get more satisfaction from just not thinking about him at all. It feels better to pretend he never existed. Someone who was never a part of your life can't leave anything behind. How does one grieve the loss of someone who was never there?

"No, Shyanne. Shaun is not here yet. I don't expect him until seven-thirty. He called me a little while ago to let me know something came up and that he had to change our meeting time. It's only seven-thirteen, Shyanne." Irritation laced my voice.

My girl had been bugging me nonstop trying to find out what Shaun got me for my birthday. That clown actually expected me to receive my gift, give Shaun a big kiss, then call her to tell her what the gift was. She's crazy.

"Girl, what's taking that man so long? It's killing me to know what he bought you. For no reason at all, he gives you lots of cool stuff like gym shoes, purses, clothes and those beautiful earrings. So I know he has something special for your birthday," Shyanne said.

Shyanne was absolutely correct. Shaun had been very generous since we've been going together. At least once a week he gives me a present. I've gotten to the point where I expect something from him whenever I know he's done any shopping for himself or his son. He's spoiling me rotten. My heart tells me that I should feel bad about all the stuff Shaun gives me since I know where his money comes from, but my mind won't allow me to experience any sense of guilt.

"Listen, nosey, as soon as he gets here, we're leaving so I don't know how I'm supposed to call you right away. You might as well calm yourself, and I'll call you with the details in the morning." I was having a good time antagonizing Shyanne, given the fact she's been getting on my nerves about Shaun's present since early morning.

Shyanne was still dating Antonio, and things are cool between them, but I get the feeling she's getting tired of him. If for no other reason, I believe it is because Antonio doesn't have the kind of money Shaun has. It's not that she is jealous of me. Shyanne simply wants what I have. She is always hinting around that she wants me to hook her up with one of Shaun's friends. Then she quickly retracts, saying she was just kidding.

While Shyanne doesn't judge me about my relationship with Shaun, I know she still has qualms about him selling drugs. Yet, I think my best friend is beginning to be open to loosening her standards a little. Slipping by association.

"Nay-Nay, you better quit playing with me. I don't care what Shaun says. Before you go anywhere with him you better let me know what he bought you. Better still, why don't you tell him you need to pick up something from my house? Then you can bring it over here for me to see."

I was cracking up laughing at her silly butt. Then I heard my mama calling me because Shaun was at the front door. Apparently, Shyanne heard her too.

"Okay. Go and see what you got, then call me right back. Don't play with me either, Nay. You know I'll come over there, wait in your room for you to get home, and beat the crap out of you."

Before I had a chance to say anything else, she hung up the phone. I laughed again at my crazy best friend, then took the phone back to the kitchen to put it back in its cradle. I grabbed my purse from the kitchen counter and headed to the living room where Shaun and my mother were having a conversation. This made me kind of nervous considering Mama has not had too many nice things to say about my man lately. She hadn't even followed up on her invitation for Shaun to attend church with us. And Mama usually never misses an opportunity to take somebody to church.

"I see you're driving a different car today, Shaun. Is that your new car?" my mother asked, a little too suspiciously for me.

"No, Mrs. Westbrook. It's actually a used car, and it's not mine. It belongs to a very good friend of mine."

"That car still has a registration tag in the window, so I'm assuming your friend just purchased it. Must be a mighty good friend to let you borrow a car he just bought. Is there something wrong with your car?" she asked with a cockeyed eyebrow.

I couldn't believe she was giving him the third degree, but as usual, Shaun handled himself like the man I had come to adore. He always knows how to speak to her without giving her reason to cause a scene.

"No ma'am, I mean Mrs. Westbrook. My car is fine. My friend needs me to test drive the car and make sure everything is cool with it," he said without batting an eyelash. I'm sure he must have been uncomfortable with the questioning. It was making me nervous, so I decided to speak up; get him out of the line of fire.

"Mama, remember I told you that Shaun works in his uncle's collision shop, so he knows a lot about cars. I'm sure he checks things out for his friends all the time." I told her, then turned to Shaun. "We better leave if we're going to make the movie on time," I lied quickly. I still had no idea what Shaun had planned for us, but I needed a fast escape.

Mama eyed us both then simply said, "I see. Well, you two have a good time. Nay-Nay, you remember your curfew. The rules haven't changed just because you're a year older." She left the living room. We left also, heading in the opposite direction.

The black Ford Thunderbird parked in front of our house

was very nice. Once we got inside, I told Shaun his friend bought himself a clean used car.

"Yeah. This car was definitely a good deal. I hope my friend appreciates it and takes good care of it." He smiled his beautiful smile and said, "By the way, happy birthday, beautiful. Can I get a hug and kiss now that your mama ain't all up in our business?"

Normally I am a little gun shy about kissing Shaun when my mother is within five hundred feet. But today, since it was my birthday, I leaned over in the seat and planted a big wet one on the sexist man in the world.

"I am really sorry about Mama giving you the third degree," I apologized when our lips parted ways. "She has seriously been trippin' on our relationship lately. She is constantly telling me I'm too young to be so involved with just one guy. Most times I ignore her, but every now and then I give her the real, letting her know I'm in love with you and nothing is going to change that."

"Don't let it worry you, baby. And whatever you do, don't piss her off to the point where she flat out forbids you from seeing me. I would hate to have to come up in your mama's house late one night in my army fatigues with dark green paint under my eyes to kidnap you military style." Shaun could be so silly and funny most times. He usually had me cracking up laughing.

"So what do you have planned today, sir?"

"It's your day, baby. What do you want to do?"

We were still parked in front of my house, had not moved an inch, and he still hadn't given me my birthday present. He hadn't even made mention of it. This wasn't like him at all. Shaun was always so anxious to share with me the gifts that he buys me. I guess I needed to drop a hint.

"Shy has been bugging the heck out of me all day trying to find out what you got me for my birthday. She even threatened to beat me up if I didn't let her know immediately after I received it. If you don't mind, I would like to drive by her house and show her *whatever* it is you got me."

My man is no fool. He could tell I was trying to be funny right off the bat. So he played along.

"Okay, cool. We'll drive over to Shy's house and show her your present," he said all nonchalantly. "As a matter of fact, why don't you drive while I fish your present out?"

Shaun got out of the car and came around to the passenger side and opened the door for me. I sat there for a few seconds, confused about him allowing me to drive his friend's car, but I finally got out and went to the driver's side.

"Are you sure your friend won't mind me driving his new car?" I asked as I pulled away from the curb heading toward Shyanne's house.

"It's cool. Don't worry about it. My friend won't mind a bit." He went into the glove compartment and pulled out a white envelope. From the driver's seat I could see the official looking envelope had someone's name on it.

What kind of birthday present came in an envelope like that? It couldn't possibly be jewelry. Maybe it was a gift certificate or cash. If it were either of those, I would have to admit I would be disappointed. Shaun was usually so thoughtful and considerate when picking out trinkets and gifts for me.

Maybe it was airline tickets, and he was planning on taking me on a trip. I didn't know how I was going to swing it if that were indeed the case. Mama barely agreed to let me go to the movies with Shaun. There was no way I would even broach the subject of leaving town with him. Well, I won't worry myself about it until I know for sure. I'll even play it cool and wait until we arrive at Shyanne's to find out what the envelope held.

When I pulled into Shyanne's driveway and parked the

car, Shaun grabbed my hand and kissed it. He then leaned over and gave me a full kiss on the mouth. Next, he presented me with the envelope.

"I hope you enjoy your birthday present, Lindsay. It took me a long time to come up with something special enough for your seventeenth birthday. I love you."

As I took the envelope from his hand, out came my big mouth best friend tugging on the driver's side door.

"I thought I heard somebody pulling into my driveway. When I looked out the window I wasn't sure who it was until I saw y'all smooching. Whose car is this? What did you get for your birthday?" As usual she was talking a hundred miles a minute, not giving me a chance to answer one question before she fired another at me. This time Shaun answered instead.

"Go ahead, Lindsay, open the envelope and tell Shyanne what you got," he said.

"You mean to tell me you don't even know what you got? You got more patience than me, girl. I would have demanded he tell me as soon as he got to my house."

"Shyanne, shut up," I told her as I began opening the envelope. She was truly getting on my nerves.

Inside the envelope was a green piece of paper. As I unfolded it and began to read, I realized it was the title to a car. As a matter of fact, it was the title to the black Thunderbird we were driving. The title indicated Shaun owned the car, not a friend like he originally made me believe. Now I was totally confused. What did any of this have to do with my present?

Shyanne began jumping up and down like a crazed lunatic, and I thought for a moment she was having a seizure or something. Then she started yelling. "I can't believe Shaun bought you a car for your birthday. Oh my goodness. This is the bomb." She was talking so loud and fast it took me a second to understand what she was saying.

Then I looked over at Shaun wearing a big silly grin on his

face, and it hit me. The Thunderbird was my present. "Shaun, is the car mine?"

"Yes, Lindsay. Happy birthday, baby."

I flung myself across the seat and wrapped my arms around him so tight I thought I was going to squeeze him to death. After finally letting go, I got out of the car and started dancing around and screaming with Shyanne.

My man actually bought me a car. This was better than the sweater Nana Westbrook promised me or the book bag or the outfit. It was even better than the bracelet Granny gave me.

I couldn't believe Shaun actually loved me enough to buy me a car. I couldn't wait to tell Mama. This should be all the proof she needed to see how serious Shaun was about me; that we were serious about each other. Maybe she would now understand that we do plan to spend the rest of our lives together.

"Come on, Shy. Lindsay is going to drive us all to dinner to celebrate. Then she and I will have a more personal celebration later," Shaun said with a wink and a smile.

"What do you mean he bought you a car?" Mama yelled at the very tiptop of her lungs.

Okay! This was not going at all as smoothly as I thought it would. I couldn't believe she was reacting this strongly to me getting a car for my birthday. I thought for a minute she was going to slap me after I told her what I presumed to be good news. Mama just stared at me like I'd told her I was pregnant or worse. Then she started screaming at me.

"You are too young to be receiving gifts like that from anyone other than me or your granny. Your grandmother can't afford to buy you a gift like that, and I wouldn't buy a seventeen-year-old a car like that even if I could afford it." Mama was yelling and stomping around the kitchen like a mad crazy woman. What had gotten into her?

"Mama, I don't understand. I thought the fact that Shaun bought me a car would prove to you that he's serious about us. Why are you acting like he has me strung out on drugs or something?" I was confused and angry. I didn't realize it, but I was also yelling.

Mama gave me that stare again, this time with her head cocked to one side and her hands on her hips. She took deep breaths and began speaking to me in her calm but deadly voice. This is the voice that said she was too tired to yell anymore, but still had enough energy to knock me into the middle of next week.

"First of all, you are going to check your tone of voice. I ain't but three seconds off you for being so stupid as it is. Secondly what do either of you know about being serious? This is your first boyfriend. I don't know how many girls Rock-head has screwed around with, but I doubt he has any real experience in relationships either. And third, since you brought up drugs, I have been wondering how can that little pinhead afford to buy you such a nice car? That is a 1991 Ford Thunderbird, Lindsay. Where did he get that kind of money?"

I had no idea Mama suspected Shaun of selling drugs. She was not aware of the large amounts of money he always carried or what he did for his family. I was definitely not about to confirm her suspicions with the truth.

"Mama, I told you Shaun works for his uncle at a collision shop. He works a lot of overtime, and he gets paid under the table so he doesn't pay taxes." My story sounded weak even to myself, but I was sticking to it.

"Whatever, Nay-Nay. You can save that bull for someone who grew up in a pumpkin patch. I was born and raised in these streets, girlfriend. And you know what, it really doesn't matter anyway because from this day forward, you are not allowed to see him anymore. You can just give me the keys to that car and tell me where he *works*. I'll return his property to him myself. Now with that said, there is no need to discuss this any further."

At first it took me a few moments to fully comprehend what Sherrie Ann Westbrook had said. When all the syllables finally sank in, I thought I was going to lose my mind. This possessed woman who had obviously invaded my mama's body was telling me I was not allowed to see Shaun anymore. She was saying that I had to break up with him *and* give him back the car. She wanted me never to be with the person that most made my day worth beginning. The person I loved more than anyone in the world, including her. I mean yes, I loved God, and I appreciated Him for creating me, but I was certain He created me for Shaun. My mama said all of this to me very casual like, then turned her back and faced the kitchen sink to wash dishes as if it were all no big deal. No! I realized at that very moment that it was not I who was losing my mind. It was Mama.

Well, if she thought she was going to have the final say on this matter, she could just think again. There was no way I was going to stop seeing Shaun. I wasn't even willing to start sneaking around with him behind Mama's back.

It was now my turn to deliver my speech, and I would use the same calm but no nonsense manner. "Mama, why in the world would I agree to stop seeing Shaun? I love him."

Mama turned around to face me again. I could tell she was surprised and angry that I was still even discussing the subject. Usually when Mama says no more discussion, I would storm away to my bedroom and pout. I suppose that's what she expected from me this time as well, but this was too important for me to act like a baby. I had to make her understand that I was a grown woman in love.

I continued to talk despite the look on her face that said if I spoke another word she would slap my teeth out. I was fighting for my life here and I had no fear. "Mama, you have been giving me a hard time about my relationship with

Shaun from the very beginning. For the life of me, I cannot understand why. Shaun has been nothing but good to me and polite to you. Why can't you just accept that I love him, and let me make my own decision regarding my relationship? If by some chance Shaun does hurt me, I am the one who has to live with that pain, not you."

Mama chuckled, but I knew she didn't find any humor in our conversation. "You love him, huh? Girl, please. We have already talked about this more than I wanted to, and I am not discussing it anymore." She turned her back to me again.

Now I was truly angry. How dare she keep dismissing me and my man? I was more than one hundred percent sure that all of her grief and stupidity were a result of my daddy leaving her the way he did. Because of her pain, she refused to give Shaun and me a fair chance. But I'll be John Brown if that man's disappearing act was going to be a source of pain for me ever again. Forget that! I walked around to the side of Mama's body and started talking to her profile.

"Mama, as tired as you are of talking about this, I'm just as tired of you treating Shaun as if he has committed some personal crime against you. I'm tired of us having to pay for your failed marriage to Daddy; for his leaving the way he did."

Mama's hands stopped moving in the dishwater and she stood very still, but she didn't say anything so I kept talking.

"Every man is not a low-down dog like Daddy. Just because you have chosen to believe they are and decided to cut yourself off from all of them, does not give you the right to make that decision for me. I am *not* going to stop seeing Shaun. I am *not* giving back my car and I am *not* going to continue to pay for the sins of my dead beat daddy."

I didn't mean to be disrespectful, but I wasn't going to apologize for it either. I was too through with her and her selfish attitude. I felt I had every right to express my views just like she did.

Mama continued to stand at the kitchen sink as quiet and as still as the proverbial church mouse. She didn't even turn to look at me. She just kept staring straight out the kitchen window. I assumed she was praying. I wasn't sure what she was talking to God about, but I knew I was right, so I wasn't concerned about it either. I had to make her understand what she was putting me through. If getting indignant with her was the only way she would listen, then so be it.

The phone started ringing and the side door opened simultaneously. I turned from Mama to see Kevin coming in the house. I said hello to my brother, then walked toward the ringing phone on the wall. Just as my hand lifted the receiver from its cradle, a dinner plate slammed into the side of my head. WHAM! I instantly dropped the phone to the floor and grabbed my head.

Before I could figure out what happened, my mother was on me like white on rice. She grabbed me by the front of my blouse with one hand and slapped the cowboy stew out of me with the other. From her perception, she was probably attempting to literally knock the devil out of me. I lost my balance and stumbled into the stove, but Mama was savagely clutching my blouse, holding me up on my feet, alternating between slapping and punching me.

Next thing I knew, she released my mangled blouse and I fell awkwardly onto the floor between the wall and the stove. My deranged mother was not done with me yet. She kneeled over me with one knee in my chest and her forearm pressed firmly against my neck. I was barely breathing due to both the beating I had just taken and the pressure she was applying to my throat. The side of my head was bleeding steadily where the plate connected. I searched the room frantically for some sort of salvation and rescue. I was so disoriented from the lopsided fight that I didn't have the presence of mind to pray for myself.

I looked over Mama's shoulder to see Kevin standing

there wide eyed and scared. He was unsure as to whether he should run for his own life or do something to try to save his sister from being beaten to death. Thankfully he went with option number two. Kevin came over and put his hand on Mama's shoulder trying to talk to her.

"Mama, please, let her go. You're choking her to death, and her head is bleeding real bad," my little brother pleaded, but it did no good. At first, I didn't think she heard him because she kept her eyes fixated on me. Then she finally spoke to him.

"Kevin, get away from me. If she dies, then she will be getting what she deserves." Then she directed her wrath back at me. "As long as I am alive, you little witch, no child of mine will ever speak to me the way you did. I don't care how old you get, who you *think* you are in love with or how rude or nasty I get.

"Now you have two choices. You can either do what I said and give me the keys to that fool's car, or you can pack your grip and get your grown behind out of my house."

All the while that my mother talked, she continued to apply pressure to my throat. I was only a stone's throw from passing out. I could barely hear her words. I only knew she was speaking because her lips were moving, and in her wrath, she was spitting in my face. However, I understood enough of what she said to know it all boiled down to me making a choice between my mama and my man.

Again my little brother made an attempt to save me by gently pulling on the arm that was lodged deeply under my chin. This time, thank God, his efforts were more successful. Mama slowly removed herself from my body. She stood over me for a few seconds as if she were expecting me to retaliate for the butt kicking I just received. Even as mad and as beat down as I was, I was no fool. I knew there was no way of physically winning against her in her kitchen full of sharp knives and sharp cooking utensils. So an attempt to start fighting with her again was out of the question; even with my bad self.

But emotionally she had not beaten me. My heart still stood with my man. Without saying a word, I went to the bathroom to clean myself up. I did the best I could with the huge cut on the side of my head, thankfully hidden in my hair. I assumed it was going to need stitches to properly fix it. Then I went to my room to pack.

PART II

A BRAND NEW BEGINNING . . .

Chapter Eight

July 1994

Shaun and I had been living together for almost eleven months. Coincidentally, it was he who called the house the night my mother sent that plate crashing into my head. He heard everything going on in our kitchen from the receiver that lay on the floor during the terrible commotion. He headed toward our house to make sure I was okay, and he arrived before I was done packing.

Mama refused to let him in when he knocked on the front door. I could hear her in the living room from my bedroom instructing him to leave her property. She threatened to call the police if he didn't leave immediately, and she promised him she would shoot him on sight if he ever returned again. Then she forcefully slammed the door in his face. Very un-Christian behavior, wouldn't you agree?

After gathering my things as quickly as I could, I left the house in my new car and hurried to find Shaun. I didn't have to look too far because he was parked just on the corner of our block waiting for me. Hearing all of the drama from the phone, he instinctively knew that I would be leaving that evening. That's my man. He knows me better than I know myself.

Shaun followed me to Sinai Hospital where I went to have the gash in my head examined. It took seven stitches to close the wound. The doctor at the hospital asked me what happened, informing me that he was obligated to call the police if a crime had been committed. I was so angry with Mama, that I almost told them that she hit me with the plate maliciously so that she would be arrested. However, my love for her prevailed, and I lied to the doctor, telling them that I had a fight with my little brother and he hit me with the plate. I told them it was a simple case of sibling rivalry and that I didn't want to press charges.

After leaving the emergency room, I followed Shaun to a cozy motel in Redford on Telegraph Avenue. Shaun went in to the front office and checked us in while I sat in the car trying to relax after my stressful evening. When Shaun returned, he informed me that room 117 would be our little love nest for the next seven days. As soon as we were inside the room, I used the telephone to call Shyanne and give her the full lowdown on what happened between my mother and me, and I let her know where I was for the time being.

That initial week was like a honeymoon, minus the benefit of marriage. However, not once during that time did I feel the slightest bit of guilt about shacking with Shaun. I knew in my heart that God was not pleased with our current living situation, but my mind told me that I had no other choice. Shaun was my world, and I just could not go back to living at my mama's if it meant giving him up. I relied heavily on God's grace and mercy during that week.

Our first seven days as common-law husband and wife were perfect. Shaun was allowed to take the entire week off from working with Uncle Bobby. We ate dinner at a fancy restaurant every evening and had breakfast at a nearby diner every morning. During the days, we shopped, went to the movies, and found other entertaining ways to hang out with Shyanne and Antonio. Shaun and I spent each and every moment together. We awoke and fell asleep each day in each other's arms. It was as if we were experiencing our own taste of heaven right here on earth. I felt like God couldn't possibly have been against our arrangement because everything was working out so perfectly.

Reality set in the following week because it was time for me to go back to school. Shaun said I needed someplace more stable to live while I attended school, but he wasn't yet in the financial position to get us our own place. What he said made perfect sense. I felt incredibly stupid for not thinking about my own future with any clarity. I was so happy to be with Shaun, I couldn't think for one second past the second we were in.

When Shaun interjected the reality check, I decided to call Granny. She always understood my relationship with Shaun. However, when I talked to her on the phone about my situation, giving her my side of the story (of course she already had Mama's side) she would not let me move in with her.

"Under the circumstances, Nay, it would be wrong for me to interfere. If I let you stay with me, I would be undermining your mother's authority. I have no right to do that. I could only let you stay here if you agreed not to see Shaun anymore."

I tried explaining that if I agreed to that I may as well go back home. Of course Granny thought that would be the perfect solution.

"Your mama was very upset, but she is still willing to let you come back as long as you do what she says. That is the name of the game. When you live under someone else's roof, you have to follow their rules. Your mama loves you, baby girl. She only wants what's best for you. Is it true that your boyfriend is a drug dealer?"

I didn't bother confirming or denying Granny's question. I simply said, "Granny, I love Shaun. So I can't go back home." Needless to say, I didn't end up at my granny's house.

Staying at Shyanne's entered my mind, but only for a second. I never even bothered to verbalize the thought. I was sure that Mama T and Mr. Kennedy would be of the same opinion as Granny.

Shaun told me that he had a solution, but he was sure I wasn't going to like it. He explained that it was the only thing we could do for the time being. He suggested I move in with him at his mother's house.

I couldn't believe he had the audacity to fix his face to say that to me. At first I thought my mind was playing tricks on me, but when I looked at him I could tell he was dead serious. How could he make such a suggestion? Had he not already had one too many girlfriends live with him at his mother's house? And speaking of his ex, was she not a constant visitor to the house? Oh, and let's not forget the fact I think his mother hates me. How was I supposed to deal with all of that? But as usual, Shaun had everything clearly thought through, as if he had been thinking about it the entire week.

"Lindsay, my mother doesn't hate you. Once the two of you spend some time together, you will learn to be more comfortable around each other. I can't change the fact that Rhonda once lived with me at my mother's house. I can, however, control the time she spends there now. I will work out an arrangement with her that would allow Sha'Ron to visit with her at her home. That way she won't have any legitimate reason to come to our home. I should have done this before, but the necessity was never there. Now it is. I love you, and I want you to be as comfortable as possible."

Once Shaun went over all of his plans in detail, I really had no choice but to go along with him. Shaun had given me no reason to distrust him thus far. Nor did I have any other options for a place to lay my head. So again, I put my faith in my man and let him lead me into my new home.

During our time at Patricia's, Shaun and I lived primarily in the basement. He purchased an inexpensive living room set and added it to the big screen television already there. He also bought an entirely new bedroom outfit and a mini-refrigerator. The only time I had to venture into the upper part of the house was to use the bathroom. Very rarely did we have meals at the house, and when we did, Shaun prepared our food separately from the household and we would eat in the basement.

I did my best not to be a nuisance to his mother and sisters. I would get up an hour earlier than everyone else to get ready for school, making sure I would not be in their way when they got up. I also took a part-time job after school to avoid being there as much as possible. I began working at Mrs. Fields Cookie Shop in Fairlane Mall one week after moving in with Shaun and company.

In the entire time I have lived here, I have had no more than four or five conversations with Ms. Taylor, none being more than ten minutes long. Three days after I moved in, she called me upstairs to lay down the rules of her house.

Rule number one: "You are to address me as Patricia. Not Ms. Taylor and definitely not Mama. Ms. Taylor is my mother, and I don't need any more children than I already have," she said.

Rule number two: "You and Shaun have to get your own telephone line. I don't want your mother calling my house bugging me about how you're doing or talking to me about you at all. I don't want your friends calling my phone. Get your own phone."

Rule number three: "I don't want you running around here

acting like you're Sha'Ron's mama. He has a mama. I don't need no mess started in my house 'cause Rhonda mad about you being around her baby."

Her final and most important rule: "Don't even think about bringing another baby into the house. I ain't trying to be your mama like I said before, so I could care less if you get pregnant or not. You just ain't bringing the baby into this house to live."

Needless to say, we never grew close as Shaun hoped we would. Patricia was more than content with me staying in our dungeon.

Truthfully, I had no problems with any of his mother's rules. Number one: I didn't see her often enough to call her anything. Number two: Shaun had a phone installed in the basement right after I moved in. Number three: I am hardly ever in the house, so I rarely get to see the baby, let alone act like his mother. The only time I see Sha'Ron is when Shaun brings him into the basement to hang out with us. Shaun is home even less than I am, so I don't get to spend enough time with Sha'Ron for Rhonda to get the least bit upset. Most important rule: Being anybody's mother right now is a definite no-no. I have been on the pill since shortly after Shaun and I started having sex, and we used condoms prior to that.

The biggest drawback to Shaun and me living together has been that I see less of Shaun now than I did when I lived with my mother. During the first couple of months, things were cool. When I would get out of school I would go straight to work on the days I was scheduled. Shaun made it his business to come by the cookie store each day. When I would get to the house after work, he would be there waiting to either go out to eat or he would have dinner prepared. On the days I was not scheduled to work, Shaun would insist that I leave the Thunderbird at home and he would drive me to and from school.

Then out of nowhere our time together was cut very

short. One night while we were out, Shaun told me Uncle
Bobby was giving him more responsibility, which would
mean a lot more money. It also meant that a lot more of his
time would be required.

Last month Shaun had to go to Florida for three days to
conduct business on his uncle's behalf. That was the first
time that he left me overnight. It also happened to be the
same weekend of my senior prom. Shaun had explained to
me how important this opportunity was for him and the ad-
vancement of his career with Uncle Bobby. It would mean
big dollars for him. Though he never said exactly how much
money this particular opportunity would generate, he did
say it would go a long way toward us getting our own place.
He then promised me that by my eighteenth birthday we
would have our own fully furnished place together.

Under the circumstances, I was willing to miss my prom.
It was more important for me to get out of Patricia's house
as soon as possible. Shyanne, being the wonderful best
friend that she is, agreed to miss the prom as well. Her rea-
soning was she had the opportunity to attend the prom last
year, and our own prom would not be any fun for her if I
were not there.

Antonio, who by now had started working for Shaun,
found no fault in not having to take Shyanne to the prom. He
used the opportunity to visit his father in Flint. So that left
Shyanne and me without our men for three days. We decided to spend those three days together.

I felt very uncomfortable sleeping in Patricia's house
while Shaun was away so I called Granny to arrange it so
that Shyanne and I could spend the weekend with her. At
first she was leery, but she soon concluded that our visit
would be harmless, no more drama than when I would
spend the night with her while I lived with Mama. She definitely stressed that it could be no longer than the weekend.
Shyanne and I now had to convince her parents to go for it.

Mr. and Mrs. Kennedy were always fond of my granny, but they were too through with me for choosing Shaun, *who was not my husband*, over my mother. Mrs. Kennedy reminded me every time she saw me that the Bible says that we are always to honor our parents, and since my mother was the only parent I had, I should have given her a double portion of honor. I knew Shyanne's parents still loved me, but they had no problem telling me how disappointed they and God were in me with regards to my living with Shaun. While I loved and respected the Kennedys as if they were my own parents, I let them know that Shaun was my life. Ultimately it took Granny to convince the Kennedys to let Shyanne hang out with me for the weekend.

With the exception of missing my man terribly, our weekend was perfect. We ate out every night, we shopped a little, we went to the movies, and we even got Granny to go roller skating with us. It was so cool. My brother joined us at the movies and the skating rink. Though I saw Kevin regularly at school, I still missed his big-headed butt.

At the end of our weekend, as Shyanne and I prepared to leave Granny's apartment, Granny called me into her bedroom for a talk. I was almost positive of what she wanted to talk about, but I went into the room to let her have her say.

"Nay-Nay, I want to start by saying that while I was totally against you leaving your mama's house and moving in with Shaun, I am proud of you for getting yourself a job and staying in school the way you have and maintaining your grades. Most young ladies leave home, quit school and end up pregnant not even ninety days out the door. The way you are handling yourself in those areas is very mature." This was not the speech expected, but I liked where she was going with it.

"But, honey," I should have known there was going to be a but, "I also want you to see things from your mama's point of view. Sherrie raised you and your brother all by herself when your daddy left. For the entire thirteen years after his departure, you listened to her, followed her rules, respected her and turned out just fine without the help of a man. Then in just a matter of months, you threw a great deal of her hard work out the window because of a *man*. Even the behavior I complimented you on is a result of the way your mama raised you. You were raised in a Christian home, and you maintained Christian values until you met Shaun.

"Now I'm not judging you, Nay. The way you are living right now is between you and God. I just want you to try and understand why your mama was so upset by your relationship with Shaun. And I believe I can even touch on why you are so obsessed with Shaun."

I already knew why Mama disagreed with me seeing Shaun. She was still disgruntled about her failed relationship with Daddy. But I figured I would give Granny the benefit of my respect, and listen to her. Besides, I was interested to know why she described my feelings for Shaun as obsession.

"Sherrie was not pleased when your daddy left the way he did, but she wasn't as devastated as everybody thought she was. It really came as no surprise to her when he up and left without a word. Your daddy had not been an active participant in their marriage from day one. My daughter made the money, paid the bills, and took care of the household. Kevin Sr. was simply a part of a romantic fantasy your mother had in her heart. Sherrie wanted the perfect family, the husband and wife, the son and daughter. From the outside looking in, she had it all.

"See, your mama was raised right, just like you were. Your granddaddy and I taught her to be an independent woman. We never wanted her to believe that she had to have a man to be happy. A man was only to be a part of her life if she wanted him to be, not because she *needed* him to be. So the fantasy only remained in her head. In her heart she knew

Kevin was not a good husband. And though he never physically hurt you or your brother, he was not a good father either.

"Sherrie let Kevin Sr. stay as long as she did because she wanted what your granddaddy and I had. She wanted a man she could lean on. Someone she knew would lay down his life for his children. But your daddy, the frog, never turned into her Prince Charming. When your daddy finally did leave, it bought more relief than grief to your mama."

I sat there listening as Granny talked, her words penetrating my skin like grape juice on the white Thanksgiving Day tablecloth. I always assumed that my father's abandonment devastated my mother. While Granny continued, I listened with a whole new curiosity.

"Sweetheart, what I'm trying to say is it's wrong for you to think your mama doesn't want you to be with Shaun because of her failed marriage. Your mama was worried about what the relationship was doing to you.

"Whether you realize it or not, you were becoming too dependent on Shaun to make you happy. You began to lose yourself. Nay-Nay began to disappear. Your mama found out that you would often times skip Bible Study, but she didn't say anything because she didn't want to force God on you. She figured there was enough of the Lord in your heart to make you return to Him on your own. But things just got worse. You hear about this type of thing happening all the time on talk shows and in magazines."

I didn't understand exactly what my granny was talking about when she said *this type of thing* was on all the talk shows. Before I had a chance to voice my confusion, she continued talking.

"Now you have gotten in so deep. Not only are you dependent on him for your happiness, you have become financially dependent on him. What if he decides he doesn't want you anymore? Then what are you going to do? Where will you be then? You know you can't take care of yourself with a part-time job at the mall. You have given Shaun all the power. You have put God somewhere on the back burner and you've made Shaun the most important person in your life. You have made Shaun your god."

Granny words hit me like a bucket of ice cold water. I *had* put all of my faith and trust in Shaun without even thinking about the consequences of my actions. But isn't that what a woman is supposed to do when she loves a man? Isn't she supposed to trust him without question?

"Granny, I heard you loud and clear, but I don't quite understand it all. Doesn't loving Shaun mean I'm supposed to trust him? Didn't you trust granddaddy to take care of you and Mama?"

Granny closed her eyes and took a deep breath as if she were getting exasperated with me. "Nay-Nay, your granddaddy was my husband. God had sanctified and solidified our commitment to one another. Being married to a man gives you favor with God. It also gives you rights and privileges you are not entitled to when you are just shacking up and fornicating."

What Granny said started to make sense now. I began to understand her concern for me. But what she didn't understand was I didn't choose to be in this position with Shaun. I was backed into a corner with the only available option being to give up the man I love, the only man I'll ever love. I was not willing to do that.

"Granny, I appreciate you being worried about me doing things the way I am with Shaun. When I left Mama's house, I was too young to get married, and I know there was no way she was going to give me her permission to marry him. I'll be eighteen in two months, Granny, and Shaun has promised me that we will have our own place by then. I'm sure that we will get married soon afterward. I mean, our relationship is going great, so marriage is the obvious next step."

"While Shaun was promising to continue to keep a roof over your head, did he actually promise to marry you too?"

I didn't answer Granny right away, and knowing me as well as she did, she took that to mean my answer was no.

"Nay-Nay, things are just so messed up these days. The world will have you thinking that God's will is unimportant. And men today are spoiled and pampered. They don't know a thing about responsibility because so many of them are raised in homes run by mothers, and they become accustomed to being taken care of by women. Or they think that if they do go as far as to provide for a woman and move her in, then he is the king of her world, and that should be enough."

I was sure that Granny was wrong about Shaun even though he was raised by a single woman, but I didn't feel like arguing the point with her without any solid promises or commitments to back me up. So I just skipped over this subject and back peddled a little. "Granny, can you explain what you meant when you said this *type of thing* is discussed on television all the time?"

"Sorry, baby. I did get a little off track, didn't I? I'm talking about your dependency on your man. What you feel for Shaun is very typical of what women go through when they are abandoned or never knew their biological fathers," she started explaining. "These women are looking for security as well as love from men in an effort to replace the love they didn't get from the man that was supposed to love them the most: their fathers. Chile, they did a special about this type of dependency disorder on *Oprah* not long after you and your mama fell out. It lasted a whole week."

No way was my granny trying to tell me what I felt for Shaun was the result of my dead-beat daddy leaving my mama, my brother, and me. She couldn't possibly think I was looking for Shaun to be a father figure to me, could she? I thought she understood my feelings for Shaun. She once compared what Shaun and I had to what she shared with my grand-daddy. I couldn't believe my ears. I was very close to tears as I tried to explain that my love for Shaun was genuine.

"Granny, my feelings for Shaun are real. I sincerely love him, and it has nothing to do with my daddy. I don't even miss my daddy. I hardly ever think about him. Mama always made me and K.J. feel loved despite our absent father. So your theory doesn't apply here. I am with Shaun because Shaun is who I want to be with; simple as that." By the time I was done with my explanation, the tears had started to fall.

My granny looked at me with half-believing eyes, then came over and gave me a big hug. "I'm sorry, baby. I didn't mean to upset you. I just wanted you to know the whole story, to give you a few things to think about. You know I think you are the smartest woman alive because I taught you everything you know." Granny released me from the bear hug, smiling at me through watery eyes of her own.

"Listen, Nay-Nay, your graduation ceremony is only a week away. I know you aren't too pleased with your mama right now. I also know that you have not spoken with her since you left last year. But it was your mama who raised you, fed you, clothed you, changed your stinky diapers, and took care of you when you were sick. For seventeen long years, it was your mama you ran to with all of your problems, and it was your mama who helped you solve them. You said so yourself; your mama gave you and your brother the love of two parents when your daddy left." Both Granny and I were bawling now, but she kept on fussing through her tears.

"And while she is a grown woman, she is still my child. I know she is still hurting over the way the two of you fell out that night. You don't even talk to each other anymore. I can't stand by anymore and watch my child be hurt without say-ing something about it.

"Nay, this is what I want you to do. I want you to call your mama and invite her to your graduation. She has more than earned the right to be there."

Granny plopped down on her bed as if she were exhausted from our conversation. She wiped away her tears, staring off into space. I sat on the edge of the bed, lost in my thoughts and Granny's words.

By the time Shyanne and I left, I felt miserable. I was completely silent during the drive from Granny's to Shyanne's house. She could tell I was in no mood to talk, so she just left me to my musings.

I didn't realize how much I truly missed my mama until that day. Mama and I always had a good relationship until I became involved with Shaun. I had always been grateful to her for not always throwing up Daddy's absence in our faces like a lot of single mothers often did. I appreciated the fact that in spite of her having to work a lot of overtime to support us, she never seemed too tired to take us on outings, to prepare our meals or to even just sit and listen. Mama never missed a parent-teacher conference or any school performance I was in. She even volunteered to chaperone a couple of school field trips. And with the exception of this last one, I even appreciated the butt-kickings I received because I knew they were always given with love and for my own good.

When I dropped Shyanne off and we said our goodbyes, I went back to reflecting on all my mother had done for Kevin Jr. and me. Being totally honest with myself, I had to admit I was pretty blessed to have her. I could have gotten stuck with a mother who could care less about what I did, like my friend, Sharay.

Sharay's mom is very pretty. She looks like she is still in her early twenties so she still gets a lot of play from a lot of men. Sharay's mom is always putting her men before Sharay and her older sister, Linda. Every two weeks or so, their mother has a new man in the house.

My mother is still quite attractive as well, but for the life of me, I can't remember her ever introducing us to a man. I can't even remember her leaving the house to go on a date. She hung with the Kennedys or her girlfriends from time to time, but I don't know of any men being involved.

When Mama got saved about eight years ago, the change in her was almost instantaneous. She quit cursing. She started going to church every Sunday and to Bible Study every Tuesday. Mama now seems so much happier and at peace than she did before she became so involved with God. At least she did until I started dating Shaun. I have probably driven her to near alcoholism since I left. Then again, I doubt it. My mama is very strong. She's probably just leaning on God and doing fine.

As I got to the airport terminal where Shaun was arriving, I decided I would call my mama as soon as we got home to invite her to my graduation. I was very nervous about what I would say to Mama when she answered the phone. It had been months since I last spoke to her. Not one word from either of us since the night of my beat down. I never even asked Kevin about her when I saw him in school.

When we got home, Shaun went upstairs to spend some time with Sha'Ron so I could have some privacy. After he left, I found myself wishing he had stuck around for support. It took me forever to talk myself into picking up the phone and dialing my old home phone number. When I did, I dialed the number real fast before I lost my courage. Mama picked up on the second ring just like she always did. I remember our conversation verbatim; like it was just yesterday instead of a month ago.

"Hello," she answered.

"Hi, Mama. It's me, Nay-Nay." I could hear her surprise through the telephone lines.

"Nay-Nay. It has been a long time since I heard from you. Everything is okay isn't it?" I could tell Mama was a little worried by her tone. I almost broke into tears again.

"Yes, Mama. Everything is fine. I'm sorry I haven't called you before now to let you know I was okay. I guess I assumed that Granny would pass along the news that everything was fine." I talked fast because I was both nervous and choked up.

"Your grandmother has kept me informed. I was simply concerned that perhaps something had happened recently. It's good to know you are all right."

"Thanks, Mama. The reason for my call now is to invite you to attend my graduation ceremony." I didn't realize it, but I gripped the phone and held my breath as I waited for her reply. I was so unsure of what she would say. It was at that moment that I realized how very disappointed I would be if she declined my invitation.

"Did your grandmother put you up to this? I know you and Shyanne spent the weekend with her." Mama's question made me think before I answered. It was Granny's idea to invite her, but after our conversation I recognized how much I owed to my mother, how much I wanted her to always be a part of my life. So I told her so.

"Mama, Granny and I did talk. She is the one who suggested I invite you, but it was after our talk that I decided it would be really important to me if you came. I know you don't agree with my relationship with Shaun, but I miss you, Mama. I would really appreciate it if you would agree to be my mother again. I'm not asking to come home or anything like that. I just want to know you will be there for me when I really need you." I fought as hard as I could to hold back the tears. I was winning the fight too until my mother spoke again.

"Lindsay, I would never turn my back on you if you needed me. You are my child. Nobody can change that. I don't have to agree with your lifestyle or the choices you make to support that lifestyle. I don't have to spend every waking moment in your face or in your business. I don't have to like the person you choose to spend your life with. As long as you are committed to your choices and handling your business, then I have no right to interfere in the way you live your life. You are nearly eighteen years old. It is not my place to judge you. As long as you can face God when it is all said and done, then I'm fine.

"But know this: I will always, no matter what, no matter who, no matter where, be there for you when you feel you need me to be there for you. My job was to raise you to be a responsible adult. Just listening to you talk today lets me know I did my job well."

That is when the floodgates came crashing wide open. I boo-hooed like a hungry infant. I cried so hard I didn't think I would be able to utter another word. Yet, I somehow managed to go on.

"It feels so good to hear you say that, Mama. I'm very blessed that you're my mother. Please say you'll come to my graduation ceremony. It's on June eleventh." I gave her all the details through my sobs and tears.

"I would not miss it for the world, baby."

Graduation was three weeks ago. Though our relationship is different now, my mama and I are back to being close again. She doesn't question me about my relationship, and knowing how she feels about Shaun, I don't bother her with our problems. Those I reserve for Shyanne.

Lately her poor ears have been getting worked overtime. My relationship with Shaun is changing so much and so fast. It is like I hardly know him anymore. He's always gone or busy on the phone when he's here. His pager is constantly going off, and there is always some spur of the moment meeting.

The good thing about any of this is I have at least started going back to Bible Study. Shyanne and I now attend the adult class with our mothers.

Shaun is still as romantic as always whenever he has time, but time is our biggest enemy lately. If I get him all to myself one day a week, I have to be grateful. Whenever I complain, he always pacifies me by telling me he is working as hard as he is for us. He continually promises we will have our own place by my eighteenth birthday, which is now less than thirty days away. Maybe things will get back to normal once we have our own apartment . . . maybe.

Chapter Nine

August 1994

True to his word, Shaun and I are moving today, three days before my eighteenth birthday. Shaun signed the lease two days ago, and we have spent the last two weeks picking out furniture.

We are renting a cute two-bedroom townhouse right at Telegraph and the I-96 service drive. It has one and one-half bathrooms, a full kitchen with a nook, a living room, and a small dining area. I love it. I'm the only one in my small crew of friends that has my own crib.

Shaun has given me carte blanche to decorate the townhouse anyway I want, as long as I leave room in the living room for his big screen television. He has been shelling out money like water. Whenever I tell him I want something for the house, he asks how much it costs, then hands me the money in cash, never complaining about the price. I guess this is what he had been working so hard for during those times I barely saw him. Hopefully things can return to normal so I can have my man back.

"When is the furniture supposed to be delivered, Nay?" Shyanne asked.

"I wanted to make sure we were definitely in the place, so I called them and told them to deliver it today. The bedroom furniture and television are on the way here now. Shaun rented a U-Haul truck to bring the things we have at his mother's house."

"Is Shaun bringing the stuff himself or did he hire movers?" This was Shyanne's subtle way of asking if Shaun would be available today to help with the move since he is gone all the time. Like I said, I had spent the last two weeks shopping with Shyanne and she has not seen Shaun once during that time.

"Shaun did hire movers, but he is there with them making sure they don't damage anything. He will be here shortly, Miss Slick."

"I'm not trying to be in your business, Nay, but I've been a little worried about you lately. You've been kind of depressed. I know it's because you're worried about what Shaun is doing while he is away *all the time.*"

I admit I have missed Shaun and the time we used to spend together, but I didn't know I was buggin' to the point of seeming depressed. "Well, I won't have to worry about Shaun, and you won't have to worry about me anymore. Shaun has been working extra hard to get the money needed to move into this place and furnish it. Now that he has accomplished that goal, he will have much more time for us."

"Uh-huh. Okay if you say so. I can't wait to see how this place shapes up once the furniture is put in place. And remember—" I cut Shyanne off mid sentence. I wanted her to explain what she meant by *if I say so.* She acted as if she knew something and wasn't telling me what it was.

Shyanne was always worried about whether or not her boyfriend was cheating on her. For some crazy reason, she was convinced that Antonio couldn't be trusted. This is something we discuss, then argue about quite often. Now, however, her distrust is seemingly being put upon Shaun.

"What's up with the suspicions, Shy? Why do you always imply that something is not right?"

"Look, girl; you know I love you. I love Shaun too, but if you want me to be honest with you, here goes. You said yourself that Shaun is hardly home. When he finally does stumble in, it's usually after one or two in the morning. I know you think he's working, Nay, but come on. Let's get real. What could Shaun be doing in the streets from ten or eleven in the morning until the wee hours of the following morning? Antonio is in the same business as Shaun. Yet he has a regular shift. He has to be at his spot from nine in the morning until seven in the evening. Then someone else comes in and relieves him."

Shyanne is always so convinced that someone is cheating. She is so paranoid it is ridiculous. Perhaps it was because she was unfaithful in her previous relationship. Now it's one thing for her to trip about her man, but now she's buggin' on mine. I didn't like it one bit.

"What makes you think Antonio and Shaun are doing the same thing? There is a world of difference between what they do. Shaun is in *charge* of the house Tony works in, along with several other houses. Antonio is a small player in a big man's game. Shaun is on his way to being the man-next-to-the-man." I didn't have to be so vicious, but she pissed me off.

"Secondly, Shy, why are you so insistent that our men are dogs? You haven't given me one shred of credible evidence to prove that Antonio is cheating on you. I know for a fact I haven't said anything to make you believe that Shaun is cheating on me. Shaun loves me. This I know with every bone in my body. So, Shy, from this point on, I don't want to hear you say or insinuate anything else negative about my man unless you have solid evidence of him being with some-body else."

"Fine, Nay. If you want to live in a dream world, go right ahead. I won't say another word about Shaun one way or the other." She threw her hands in the air and turned her back to me.

I let the conversation drop, but I was still a little upset with her. It was really hard for me to understand her views on relationships. Her parents are still together after more than twenty years and very much in love. Because of that, it seems she would have a better outlook on love. Considering the fact that my father is a runaway, I should be the skeptic, not her.

The U-Haul truck and the furniture store delivery truck arrived at the townhouse simultaneously. I ran from the house to find Shaun, but I didn't see his car anywhere. So I assumed he rode in the U-Haul. I walked over to the truck to find him

"Excuse me, where's Shaun?" I asked the driver.

"He gave us directions, then got in his car and left," the driver responded. I assumed he was on his way here. Do you know where this stuff goes?"

He must be on his way. I showed the U-Haul driver where to put the things and asked Shyanne to show the furniture store gentlemen the same.

Two hours later, both trucks were emptied and everything put in the proper places, but there was still no sign of Shaun. I was surprised he hadn't bothered to show up or at least call. I began to get worried so I paged him. It wasn't until I keyed in our new phone number that I realized he probably had not called because he couldn't remember the number.

"Who you calling?"

I knew Shyanne already knew the answer to her question, but I responded anyway. "I paged Shaun and don't start with me, Shy. He probably hasn't called because he couldn't remember the new phone number."

"Whatever you say." Before I had a chance to start arguing with her again, the phone rang. I picked up assuming it was Shaun.

"Shaun, where are you?"

"Hello to you too, Lindsay."

"Sorry. I'm just worried about you. Why didn't you come with the movers? The driver said you were on your way."

"I never told the driver I was on my way to the townhouse. I gave him the address and directions and told him to tell you Uncle Bobby paged me 911 from the collision shop. So I headed straight there."

"How long will it be before you come home?" I watched Shyanne while Shaun and I talked. She was doing her best not to seem interested in what I was saying, but I knew her too well. She was all into our conversation.

"Lindsay, I've explained this over and over to you. I don't punch a time clock. My business can call me anytime, all times of day and night. Since I'm trying to come up and make a name for myself, I have to work twice as hard as the next guy. My uncle doesn't play favorites. Now I have two meetings, then I need to pick up some money. I should get there no later than eight this evening."

I really hated when Shaun talked to me like I was a child with comprehension issues. I understood the demands on his time when he was working toward us getting this place, but I didn't see the need for him to continue the crazy hours now that we had moved.

"Shaun, I thought you could cut back now that we have our place. I see you so rarely, I'm forgetting what you look like."

"Lindsay, hustling is what I do for a living. It is not some part-time job at Mickey D's where I can ask the supervisor to change my schedule to accommodate my whining woman. What makes you think I can cut back now anyway? I have only paid the first month's rent and a deposit on the town-house. We still have to pay rent, utilities, buy food, and other necessities. Do you think we can afford to do that with your cookie store paycheck?"

I couldn't believe he was snapping at me. All I tried to do was tell him that I missed him. Fine! Let him stay gone. And while he is out, I'll just go and spend some more of the hard earned money he is so fond of making.

"Sorry to be a whining woman, Shaun. I'll talk to you whenever you get here." I hung up the phone before he could say anything else. And before Shyanne had a chance to question me, I said, "Let's go shopping. I just thought of a few more things this place could use."

The last three days have been strange. Shaun, as usual, has hardly been home. Even when he is here, we have barely spoken to each other. He was really upset that I hung up on him the other day, and I am still upset about the way he spoke to me. This was the first time in our seventeen-month relationship that we have been angry with each other. I have been upset and disappointed with his work schedule, but never angry.

However, today is my eighteenth birthday. Despite the fact that he is a little pissed with me, and he left this morning without wishing me happy birthday, I know my boo is going to do something special for me. That's just the kind of man I have.

I said a special prayer this morning when I woke up. I'm sure God is none too pleased with me right now; especially since Shaun and I are continuing to live and sleep together without being married. Even still, I prayed intensely, asking God to forgive my indiscretion. I asked Him to have patience with me.

"Dear God, I come this morning giving you thanks for allowing me to live to see my eighteenth birthday. I realize that I am now an adult and responsible for my own actions. I also know that you are not pleased with my living arrangement. But God, I know that you love me and I ask that you forgive me. I know my church attendance has not been great, but I'm still attending Bible Study regularly. And I'll get back in church and I'll even try to get Shaun to come with me. I pray for your patience, God. This is my prayer in Jesus' name. Amen." My prayer had made me feel better as always.

This morning I did the breakfast thing with Mama, Granny, K.J. and the Kennedys. We had a blast. We ate, we talked, and I received great presents as usual. Granny presented me with a pair of small gold and diamond earrings and a matching necklace. K.J. gave me a cute pair of pink and white Nike gym shoes. The Kennedys gave me a gorgeous black leather jacket, and Mama gave me an application to a local bank for a checking account along with a check for $350 as my opening deposit. The money replaced what she might have spent on a birthday party she would have thrown me if I were still living at home.

"I thought it would be wrong for me to give you a birthday party and not allow your boyfriend to attend," she said. Shaun was no longer allowed in my mother's home. "I want you to make sure you always keep some mad money stashed, Nay-Nay, just in case you find yourself in a position to have to strike out on your own. And remember that my door is always open to you," Mama said. Both Granny and Mama had been saying that to me since my high school graduation. Think they were trying to tell me something?

After breakfast, I went back to Mama's to spend some time with her, Granny and K.J. before going home. When I did arrive at our house, Shaun was also just getting there from wherever he spent his morning. We approached the front door at the same time, and Shaun used his key to open the door. Once we were inside, Shaun began apologizing and explaining his behavior of late.

"Happy birthday, Lindsay," he said as he kissed my cheek. I thanked him and he continued. "I want to apologize for the way things have been between us lately. I know I haven't been around a lot, but you have to know that I have missed you as much as you have missed me."

Shaun took me by the hand and led me to our sofa. "I've been putting in work with my uncle for over two years now, and he is finally starting to trust me with bigger things. I know you would prefer if I didn't go into detail, so I won't, but just know I am not some petty hustler who sits and sells dope out of a drug house or on a street corner. I'm working very closely with my uncle to make big things happen."

Shaun and I have had this conversation before. I was aggravated that he felt the need to even repeat it. All I wanted to hear was that his new position in Uncle Bobby's organization had allotted him the opportunity for us to spend more time together. However, that is not what he said next.

"Lindsay, once I have accomplished the goal of being Uncle Bobby's partner and not just his employee, there will be plenty of time and money for us to do everything we want to. See, baby, I'm doing this for us and our future. I want you to live like a queen because that's what you deserve. I love you. Being in a position to give you anything you want will make me the happiest man alive. All I am asking of you is a little patience."

Didn't I just have a similar conversation with God this morning?

How could I be mad at him for wanting us to have the best of everything? I already had more than any of my friends. My own house, my own car, and money always at my disposal. All I had to do was ask. Here it is that Shaun was working very hard to put things together for our future, and I was complaining about the here and now like always.

"Shaun, I'm the one who should apologize. I have a hard time focusing on the future sometimes, but I'm an adult now, and you are right. We should make plans for the future. But I still miss you."

"Well, in honor of your birthday, I told my uncle I was taking the whole day off and devoting it to you. I spent the morning making plans and picking out your present. I have a wonderful evening planned for you."

I was so excited, I threw myself across the sofa kissing and hugging him like it was the last time I was ever going to see him. Next thing I knew we were on our way upstairs to our bedroom to get the celebration started a little early.

Shaun and I ate dinner at TGI Friday's in Southfield. He thought it would be special since this is where we had our first date. I would have preferred to go to Edmonds, the upscale soul food restaurant downtown, but I was impressed with his thoughtfulness.

Before we left home for the restaurant, he gave me one of my birthday presents: a Marshall Field's department store credit card with a $2,500 limit. I was ecstatic. Shaun knew that Marshall Field's was my favorite store. If he didn't give me anything else, it would have been all right with me.

When we arrived at the restaurant, Shaun removed a large, beautifully wrapped package from the trunk of his car, but he insisted that I not open it until after we ate dinner. I asked for hints several times, but he wouldn't even give me a clue. It was only after we finished our meals and the waiters came to present me with a dozen white roses while singing "Happy Birthday," did he give me the box.

The box was so big and heavy that I had trouble maneuvering it around the table, but once I did, it was on. I tore at the wrapping paper like a five-year-old on Christmas morning. When I finally got all the paper off and the lid removed, I stared bug-eyed at the contents of the box. For a moment I thought I was dreaming. I stood up from the table and continued to stare at it for several moments before I had the nerve to remove it from the box. When I finally took it out, the full-length blue fox fur was even more beautiful than I initially perceived.

The people sitting near our table looked as surprised as I was. I overheard an elderly lady say, "Isn't she too young for such an expensive coat?" I looked at the old bat and rolled my eyes, but I didn't say anything to her. My mother always taught me to respect my elders; otherwise I would have told her to mind her own business.

"Shaun, this is the most beautiful thing I've ever seen. I've seen fur coats in magazines and on television, but I have never been this close to one so pretty. Thank you so much. I love you." I think I was speaking to Shaun when I said the last part, but I could have very well been talking to my new coat.

"I love you too, Lindsay. This time next year, I'll be able to afford mink instead of fox."

For the first time in my life, I wished I was born in the winter months instead of the summer. I wanted to put my coat on so badly, but I would have looked really dumb considering it was seventy-nine degrees, even at nine-thirty in the evening.

When we left the restaurant, we headed downtown to Club Nile to go dancing; something Shaun and I had never done together. In Detroit, you have to be at least twenty-one to be admitted into the nightclubs. Shaun wouldn't be twenty-one until November, but he assured me he had it covered. When we approached the door, a tall bulking figure asked for our identification. Shaun whispered something in his ear, and the gentleman let us enter with a smile.

I had never been inside a nightclub before. I was surprised at how dark it was inside. After being there for a few moments, my eyes began to adjust, and I was able to see through all the smoke and haze. The music blared loudly, and there were wall-to-wall people.

Shaun and I made our way past the dance floor to a roped-off area where the signs on the tables said V.I.P. I couldn't believe my eyes when I saw Shyanne, Antonio, Sharay, and three of Shaun's male friends were already there. They all yelled surprise as we approached the table.

"Do you like your surprise party, boo?" Shaun asked.

"I love it, Shaun, but how did you get my friends in here? None of them are twenty-one."

"Don't worry about it, baby. Just set your mind on having a wonderful eighteenth birthday party."

Before I could get seated, Shyanne attacked me with questions about my birthday present. She and Sharay were speechless when I told them about the coat, but only for a second. Shyanne is never speechless for too much longer than that.

"Girl, are you serious? He gave you a fur coat? That is so cool, Nay," Shyanne said.

"That is cool, but where are you going to wear a fur coat? It ain't like you still go to church. That's the only place I know folks to wear fur coats," Sharay added. She always had something negative to say, which explained why I didn't hang out with her all that much.

"Well, for your information, I promised God just this morning that I would start going back to church regularly. But even if I didn't go to church, I would wear that puppy to bed if I couldn't figure out anywhere else to where it. Trust me when I tell you, it will be worn." The three of us cracked up laughing.

Shaun left the table for a moment to go to the bar. He returned with two bottles of Moet champagne. He and his friend, Leonard, popped the corks on both bottles and filled everyone's glass. Shaun then stood up and gave a very romantic speech.

"I'd like to make a toast to my one and only, Lindsay. Today you are officially a woman in the eyes of the law, but you have never been anything less to me, baby. You are the most intelligent, mature, and definitely the finest lady I have ever met. As long as I have you by my side, there is nothing we can't accomplish together. To you . . . to us . . . forever, baby. Happy birthday."

"Happy birthday, Nay-Nay!" everyone else said in unison, and then we all took a drink of our champagne. That was my first taste of alcohol. I didn't particularly like it. So after the first sip, I didn't bother to have any more. Everyone else seemed to be enjoying theirs, including Shyanne. To my knowledge, this was her first time too.

When Shaun finished his first glass of champagne, we went to the dance floor. Soon everyone else followed suit. We were having a ball dancing and hustling to all the latest jams. Everyone in our crowd was chanting, "Go, Nay-Nay. It's your birthday," and before I knew it, the whole club knew it was my birthday, and they were chanting too. The DJ even announced it on the microphone. I was so excited.

Shaun was ready to leave the dance floor before me, but I followed him back to our table anyway. I was still so pumped and full of energy, I could have danced all night. Everyone else stayed on the floor. When we got back to the table, there was a pretty birthday cake decorated with pink and white icing. It read: *Happy Birthday Lindsay a.k.a. Nay-Nay.*

While I admired my cake, Shaun went to the bathroom. I guess his bladder was a little full from all the champagne he drank. Soon after he walked away, someone tapped me on my shoulder from behind. When I turned to see who it was, she was standing so close we nearly kissed. I had to take a step sideways to bring her face into focus.

"Happy birthday, tramp!"

It had been nearly a year since I last saw her, but I still remembered her jacked up mug. Rhonda stood there with her hand on her fat hip wearing a red dress at least three sizes too small.

"Thank you very much. And by the way, it's your mother that's the tramp," I said and turned back to admire my cake.

Rhonda pushed my shoulder this time more so than tapped it, yelling, "No, yo' mama's a tramp and a slut. I'm about to whip your ugly . . ."

WHAM! Before she could utter another word, I turned and hit her right in the face with my whole cake. She stumbled backward, and I started swinging. She was so caught off guard that she couldn't even raise her arms to defend herself. She couldn't even see me. I beat that cow all the way back toward the restrooms. Before I realized what was happening, someone snatched me into mid-air.

Without taking the time to find out who held me, I turned and began swinging and kicking at them without missing a beat. I assumed it was one of Rhonda's friends coming to her rescue, but it turned out to be Shaun.

"Lindsay! Lindsay, stop kicking me," he yelled.

By now security had gotten in on the act. One guard held onto the screaming, cake-splattered Rhonda, and another one pulled me out of Shaun's arms. It seemed he believed that Shaun and I were fighting each other.

"Let me go! Let me go! I'm gonna kill her!" Rhonda screamed at the top of her lungs. The music had now stopped because of all the commotion, so she could be heard all over the club.

Shyanne forced her way through the large crowd that gathered to get a glimpse of the fight. She immediately went into action, swinging on the guard who held me when she realized I was one of the participants.

"Let her go, punk." She started punching the big security guard in the back, but I doubted he even felt her blows. He was as big as a tree, and soon another one of them appeared and grabbed Shyanne.

Shaun explained to the security guard that I was his girlfriend and that Robert Taylor was his uncle. He then went on to explain that his ex-girlfriend had more than likely attacked me. Security let me and Shyanne go, and we went to sit with the rest of our crowd. Rhonda was still being held by one of the guards, spitting piercing daggers at me with her eyes. She looked a ridiculous mess with cake all over her hair and clothes. Blood dripped from her nose and mouth. She took one of my better beat-downs, if I do say so myself.

When Shaun returned to our table, they were escorting Rhonda to a room in the back to let her get cleaned up. He said security was giving us fifteen minutes to leave the club or they were going to call the police.

"Why do we have to leave, Shaun? She's the one who started it," I moaned.

"I know, baby, but remember, we're not supposed to be in here in the first place. They only let us come in because my uncle arranged it with the promise of no trouble. They just want us all to leave. Once we have left the premises, they will let Rhonda go. They don't want any more fighting. Are you okay?"

Without realizing, I was limply holding onto my right wrist with my left hand, and my knuckles were all scraped and swollen. I was still so angry at the Hungry Hippo for confronting me I didn't even notice the pain.

"My wrist hurts a little, but she never laid a hand on me. So I'm fine otherwise," I reassured Shaun.

"I wish I were here when that fat pig came over. I can't be-

lieve I missed out on another opportunity to kick her butt,"
Shyanne said. She was just as furious as I was.

"I wish I were here too," Sharay said. "That way I might
have been able to stop you from hitting her with your cake.
I'm hungry as a hostage."

We all cracked up laughing and made ready to leave the
club. This was the best birthday party I'd ever had. Kicking
Rhonda's butt was the icing on the cake.

Chapter Ten

March 1996

"Ms. Westbrook, would you like a pillow for your desk in an effort to make you more comfortable?" My math professor squatted by my desk, patting my back trying to wake me during class. When I came fully awake, he was staring me straight in the eyeballs and his ugly mug startled me.

I was so embarrassed. I couldn't believe I fell asleep in class. Whatever he was lecturing about must have been boring as heck, because it knocked me right out. I apologized, pulled myself together, and tried to get back into what he was saying.

I must have slept for quite some time because there were only ten minutes left before class dismissed for the day. Professor Waters is the only instructor I have that holds class every session for the entire ninety minutes. Most of my instructors would dismiss class about ten minutes early, at least some of the time.

It seemed like I was falling asleep at the weirdest times

lately and I didn't know why. I only hung out on the week-ends (still not going to church like I should). During the week, I stayed home studying. I would sometimes fall asleep for the longest before I finally got up to go to bed.

Whatever it was that had me taking extra trips to la-la land, I needed to get a handle on quickly. The last thing I needed was to fail because I was unable to concentrate properly on my studies.

"Class, don't forget we are having an exam during our next session that will count for thirty-three percent of your grade. This will be the last test before the final exam. Class dismissed."

When I started taking classes at Wayne County Community College two semesters ago, my mama was a little disappointed. She'd always wanted me to go to a big university. She was especially hard on me when Shyanne left for Oakland University in Rochester, Michigan, and I had not even applied to any in-state or out-of-state schools.

"What has gotten into you, Lindsay Renee Westbrook?" my mother had scolded. "You don't attend church anymore. You're no longer interested in your education. What is wrong with you? Don't even bother answering because I know exactly what your problem is. It's Mr. Rock-head. He probably won't allow you to go away to school. I see he has made you quit your job," she said. "I can even understand you not leaving the state to go to college because you didn't want to leave him, but you could have at least applied to Wayne State right here in the city."

In actuality, Shaun had very little to do with me ending up in community college. He would have preferred if I had gone to a larger university. It was all my fault. I forgot to get my application in by the assigned deadline. I had so much on my mind during my senior year of high school. I was es-tranged from my mother, I was living with a woman who hated me, and the time between Shaun and me had been dramatically cut. I was doing good to even get through high school during that time. Wayne State was the only application I had, and I let it totally slip my mind because of the stress I was under.

It was Shaun's idea for me to quit my job back then, however. He didn't see the point in me having to work in the evenings when he was more than able to take care of us. Shaun wanted me to get myself in school and concentrate on my classes. I was to let him worry about the money. He even pays my tuition.

Financially, things couldn't have been better for me. I was living in my own fully furnished townhouse, I was driving a brand new Honda Accord, which I got after trading in the Thunderbird, and I had a closet full of clothes. Shaun made good on his promise to purchase me a mink jacket for my nineteenth birthday, and he even stepped it up by buying me a full length mink coat for Christmas that same year.

Socially, things were cool too. Even though Mama was not too happy about my school or living situation, she, Granny and I were as close as ever.

Shyanne stayed on campus at Oakland, but she came home every weekend. I missed her tremendously during the week, but we had a ball when she was at home. We would shop up a storm during the day, my treat most of the time, and we would party like crazy every Friday and Saturday night. Even though we would not be twenty-one for a year and a half, we never had a problem getting into the clubs. All it took was a little something extra for the security guards checking the identification, and we were in like Flynn.

Spiritually, I was lukewarm. Mama would occasionally chastise me about partying so often on the weekends, but not having time for church on Sundays. I would listen to her, feel bad for a while, and then justify my absence from Sunday service by rationalizing that I was still attending the adult Bible Study class every Tuesday. I always promised Mama, myself, and God that I would start showing up on Sundays eventually. The Kennedys were not too happy about Shyanne's party habits either, but they didn't give her too much flack because she always made time for church on Sunday mornings.

Personally, things were just not right. I mean, I still loved Shaun with all my heart, and I know he still loved me. He was as generous as always with his family and with me. However, I started to feel like Shaun thought the material possessions were interchangeable with his time. If it were not somebody's birthday, Christmas, or our anniversary, which we celebrated on the date of our first date, we never spent any quality time together.

Shaun rarely made it home before 3:00 A.M., and he never got out of bed before 1:00 P.M. When he did get up, he would shower, dress and head straight to Patricia's to spend the early part of the day with Sha'Ron. Since Rhonda was adamant about her son not being allowed anywhere near me, I only got to see him on Christmas and Shaun's birthday. Those were the only two occasions I would visit his mother's house. On Thursdays, Tameeka and I had a class together, so I would drop her off at home after school, but I never went inside the house.

Shaun would stay at Patricia's house until 4:00 or 5:00 P.M., and then he would head out to handle his business. I'm sure he spent some time hanging out with his friends while he claimed to be working, but I never doubted that he was faithful to our relationship. Shaun knew how much he meant to me and how much I sacrificed to be with him. I couldn't imagine him ever doing anything like that to hurt me.

Shyanne thought I was crazy. She and I argued constantly about how naïve she thought I was. She broke up with Antonio about eight months ago because she busted him cheating. Now her attitude toward men and relationships was worse than ever. It didn't stop her from dating though. She was now involved with Shaun's friend James, a.k.a. Jamo.

Since Mr. Waters' class was the only one I had today, I decided to go by Granny's house and take her to lunch. Mondays and Wednesdays I only had one class; two on Thursdays. Tuesday was my homework and Bible Study day, and Sundays I caught up on my school related reading. Like I said before, Fridays and Saturdays are reserved for hanging and shopping with Shyanne.

The moment I pulled in front of Granny's house, my stomach did a triple somersault. I found myself suddenly ill, making a mad dash through Granny's house straight to the bathroom. I slammed the bathroom door, barely making it to the toilet before I starting puking my guts out.

Granny was immediately at the door trying to make sure I was okay. "Nay-Nay, girl, are you all right in there?"

"I don't know, Granny. I'll be out in a minute." I hovered over the toilet bowl trying to make sure I had nothing left on my stomach before emerging from the bathroom.

When I opened the door, Granny was all over me, feeling my forehead checking for a fever. "How long have you been sick?"

"I wasn't sick, Granny, until I got to your house. Then I suddenly felt nauseous." Granny gave me a strange look, forcing me to wonder if she knew about some bug or virus going around.

"Chile, when was the last time you had a period?"

Oh my goodness! My granny thought I was pregnant. I couldn't possibly be pregnant. I had been taking the pill for years. I never missed one pill . . . Oh no! I forgot about the time I lost my purse.

Shyanne and I were out clubbing when my purse came up

missing. My birth control prescription for the remainder of
the month was in it. When I called the pharmacy, they told
me I couldn't get a replacement for the lost pills. The phar-
macist suggested I use another form of contraceptive. Her
advice came in one ear, parked on my brain for about ten
minutes, and then went out the other ear. I didn't have enough
sense to think of using anything else. That was about eight
weeks ago.

"I can't remember the last time I had a period, Granny.
Ever since I've been on the pill, my periods have been so ir-
regular; they just kind of show up from time to time. But I
can't be pregnant can I, Granny? I've only missed a couple of
pills." Granny's look of skepticism made me sick all over
again.

When I came from the bathroom this time, my grandmother had her jacket on and her purse in her hand. "Come
on, baby, we are going to the clinic right now to see if the
rabbit dies . . ."

Six weeks pregnant! Those words sounded no less
strange when I said them to myself than when the nurse at
the clinic said them to me. It had been two hours since I
heard them the first time, and I still could not believe it.
What in the world was I supposed to do now?

The nurse explained that since my pregnancy was still in
the early stages, I had a few weeks to consider whether or
not I wanted to terminate it. I wished she hadn't said that in
front of Granny. All the way through lunch I had to hear her
moral lecture against abortion.

"Nay-Nay, I know you're still young and unmarried, but
neither of those is a good enough reason to have an abortion. We are Christians, and despite your circumstances, including the fact Shaun already has one son, that baby is a
blessing from God. The sin was in you deciding to have pre-

marital sex, not the conception of your child. Please don't decide to commit another sin by aborting your baby." And on and on she went.

Before I made any decisions, I needed to talk to Shaun. Since this was not something I felt should wait until the wee hours of the morning when he usually crept in, I was on my way to try and catch him at Patricia's house. According to his normal schedule, he should still be there kicking it with Sha'Ron around this time of day. Hopefully they were hanging around the house and not out somewhere together.

I was glad to see his car parked in the driveway when I pulled in front of the house. Shaun was now driving a 1993 candy apple red convertible Corvette. Even though I hated coming to Patricia's house, I was really anxious to have this discussion and find out how Shaun felt about the prospect of having a second child.

I stepped onto the porch, but before I had a chance to knock, the front door flew open. Patricia stood on the other side of the threshold and gave me her usual greeting of plain old silence. However, this time I got the eerie feeling she was a little more agitated than normal by my presence at her home. She kept the front door pulled close to her, indicating that she had no intention of inviting me in for tea. I had to be the mature one as usual when dealing with this hateful woman.

"Hello, Patricia. Is Shaun here?" I tried not to sound as irritated as I felt for just having to talk to her.

"Well, you know he's here because his car is here!" Dang! Must this woman always be a witch?

Before I had a chance to ask her to get him, Shaun appeared at the front door. I actually heard him speaking before I saw him. "Who you talking to out here, Mama?" he said, and then opened the door to see for himself.

Shaun had on his jacket as if he were getting ready to leave. I felt blessed to have gotten there just in time. But feelings of joy were quickly overshadowed by feelings of panic when I saw a very pretty girl standing behind him with her jacket on as well.

The young lady was tall and slim, yet still very shapely. The honey caramel complexion of her skin was beautiful. She had long, jet black hair and jet black eyes, something I had rarely seen. Perhaps she was not solely black, but of biracial heritage. Maybe part Asian.

I could have sworn, when I refocused my attention on Shaun, that he looked guilty for a split second. But he recovered quickly and started to question me. "What are you doing here, Lindsay?"

"Hello to you too, Shaun. Who's your friend?"

"Is everything okay? You don't usually show up at my mom's house like this unannounced," he asked, completely ignoring my question. Patricia stood in the doorway watching our verbal exchange like a tennis match.

"Who . . . ? Is . . . ? Your . . . ? Friend . . . ?" I repeated each word very slowly, very clearly and a little loudly to make sure he heard me this time. However, it was little Ms. Runway Model who spoke first.

"Shaun, I'll take the bus home. I'll talk to you later. Bye, Pat."

She left the house, slightly bumping me as she descended the steps heading toward Joy Road on her way to the bus stop, I assumed. She never once looked back because I stared at her until she was at least two houses away.

Patricia smiled as she left; speaking the only nice words I have ever heard uttered from her lips. "Bye, Keva. You be careful at that bus stop, baby." I guess all of her rudeness is reserved for me. As soon as I turned around, Patricia gave me one last eye-roll then walked away from the door.

"So what's up, Lindsay? Why the sudden visit?" I couldn't believe this fool was playing stupid on me. I was about two seconds from slugging my man for the very first time.

"Shaun, who is Keva, and why was she in your mama's house with you? Don't give me any more of your runaround crap either."

"Runaround? What are you talking about? Look, let me say goodbye to Sha'Ron. Then we can get something to eat and talk about whatever it is that caused this attitude you seem to have."

He turned and walked away before I had a chance to say another word. He reappeared about ten minutes later, leaving me standing on the porch the whole time. I'm sure he was using the time to compose a good lie about Keva. It didn't take that long to tell a four-year-old goodbye.

"All right. Let's go. We'll take your car since it's already warm, but I'll drive. You drive like a bat out of hell."

As soon as we were settled in the car and on our way, I started again with the questions. "Shaun, why are you stalling on answering my question? I've asked you at least three times who Keva is and not once have you bothered to answer me. I want to know, and I want to know right now." The calm in my voice certainly was a betrayal to the rage in my heart.

"I don't know why you keep sweating me about her. She's nobody. Keva is a friend of my sister, Frannie. She came by to see her and decided to wait for her since she wasn't at home. I was just about to give her a ride home when you showed up because she got tired of waiting. Where do you want to eat?"

I sat there processing Shaun's answer. I simply couldn't wrap my arms around it. If Keva was just a friend of Francine's, why did both he and his mother look like they got caught with their hands in the cookie jar when I arrived at the house? I was about to ask him that very question when he started bugging me again about where I wanted to eat.

"Lindsay, I asked you where you want to eat."

"I don't want to eat, Shaun. I am not hungry. I had lunch with my granny right before I came to see you."

"Then why did you say you want to get something to eat?"

"I never said I wanted to eat. Eating was your suggestion. I want to talk about this Keva tramp. If she is not some trick you are cheating on me with, then why did you look like I caught you with your pants around your ankles when you saw me at the door?" Now I was yelling.

"You need to calm down and quit yelling at me. I'm the one who should have an attitude here. I could have still been spending time with my son if you weren't hungry."

No he didn't! No this idiot did not just tell me he should be the one with an attitude. I was getting angrier by the second. Shaun was playing on both my intelligence and my last nerve.

Yelling at the top of my lungs now, I really went off. "I never said I was freaking hungry. I just want you to tell me and tell me right freaking now why it is that you and your stupid mama both looked like you had something to hide when I showed up at the house. Now I know the witch doesn't like me, but she had the dirty nerve to look nervous when she saw me on her porch."

Before Shaun responded, he pulled my car into a Wendy's restaurant parking lot. "Like I said before, Lindsay, you need to calm down before you say something else you might regret. I don't appreciate you disrespecting my mother like that."

"Screw your mother!"

"That's it! If you say one more word I don't like, I'm gonna slap the taste out of your mouth."

WAIT! Wait one minute! Now it was one thing when I felt like punching him on his mother's porch, but it was an entirely different story for him to tell me he was going to hit me. I will be John Brown if I sit still and let anyone get away with threatening me.

"Oh! So you gon' hit me if I say something else, huh? Well, I guess you best get ready to fight. I'm about to say a whole lot of stuff that I'm sure you won't be too happy about, starting with get out of my car."

Shaun and I had only had two major disagreements before now. And never once had I wanted to hit him nor has he ever threatened to hit me. But fight number three was on and in a big way now. I was so angry I was sure I could take him in hand-to-hand combat and win.

I jumped out of the car from the passenger side, ran around to the driver's side and yanked open the door. I started pulling on his arm in an attempt to get him out of my car. The sight of him was making me ill again.

"Get out, Shaun. I want you out of my car and away from me. I know you are lying about your little girlfriend. I don't want to look at your lying face for another minute. I gave up everything for you. I defied my mother. I didn't go away to college. I have even betrayed my God for you. And then you go and cheat on me?"

My fury was increasing with each word I spoke. I pulled his arm so hard I was sure it was going to come off any second.

Shaun rested his head on the steering wheel, taking deep breaths as if he were trying to calm himself. Then he started talking very calmly. "Lindsay, let go of my arm. I apologize for threatening to hit you. I should have never said that because you know I would never do that. Let me go so I can get out of the car."

He was a little too sedate, so I really didn't trust him, but I let him go. I stepped back from the car so he could get out. I was standing in the fight-ready position just in case he tried to pull a sneak attack on me. Shaun got out and threw his hands up in complete surrender. He just shook his head at me.

When I was confident he was not going to hit me, I jumped in my car, slammed and locked the door. I then began my tirade again as I rolled down my window. I yelled at him while I readjusted my seat and mirrors. "You know what? I don't care who Keva is, you liar. I don't care what you were doing with her. All I do care about is my bills and my tuition. And you better continue to pay them. I better not have to ask you for anything twice. I also suggest you keep sleeping with the tramp because I don't want your nasty hands anywhere near me ever again."

I sped away from the parking lot burning rubber. I was enraged. I didn't give Shaun a backward glance nor did I care how he got home.

I guess I didn't care if he knew I was pregnant or not either because in all the commotion, I surely forgot to tell him.

Chapter Eleven

I was still so furious when I got home that it took me at least five minutes to get my key in the lock to open the front door. Once inside, I stomped around, yelling and cursing to myself, punching and throwing sofa pillows around the house. I couldn't believe Shaun was actually cheating on me. After stubbing my toe for the fourth time, I figured it was time to sit down and try to think things through carefully.

Here I sit, pregnant, not even sure if Shaun and I are going to make it. The last thing I need is to have to raise a baby by myself. And even worse, what if I turned out to be hard and cold like Rhonda, not wanting my baby because I didn't have the father? Abortion was still an option because I had time, but I knew I could never go through with it and be able to face God or Granny.

After I sat for a while trying to think, my anger began to subside, the pain started to settle in, and the tears came a flowing. I know I told Shaun I didn't care what he did or who he did, but the reality was I couldn't bear the thought of him being with someone other than me. I have been with Shaun for three years. I could not imagine ever being without him. The pain I felt was horrible. No one could have ever made me believe that my man was capable of causing me this kind of agony.

I tried again to clear my head and think about our relationship, about how much I thought it meant to Shaun. As I tried to rationalize it, the whole thing just became more and more bizarre.

As I sat in our living room wallowing in broken-hearted misery, I went over the scene at Patricia's house again. Thinking things through more clearly, I realized I didn't have any proof Shaun was actually cheating. Everything that led me to my conclusion was based on what all the lawyer dramas call circumstantial evidence.

In all honesty, I had a pretty flimsy case. When using my head instead of my heart, I recognized Shaun's reaction to my showing up on his mother's doorstep made perfect sense. It wasn't like I was a frequent visitor to Patricia's. And why on earth couldn't Keva be Francine's friend that Shaun was simply being nice to by giving her a ride home? But if all that were indeed the case, why did Patricia act so guilty?

My confusion only served to make me more upset. What I needed was solid proof. I needed to talk to Keva directly, just flat out ask her if she and Shaun were having an affair. Okay, so now I had a solution. What I didn't have was any idea how I was supposed to go about instituting my plan. I had no way of knowing how to get in touch with Keva. I could casually ask Tameeka about Keva tomorrow on our way home from school, acting as if I were simply curious about Francine's friend and not trying to find out if she knew anything about her and Shaun seeing each other. But even as dumb as she is, she would get suspicious. Besides, I'm sure Patricia will instruct her to keep her mouth closed after today's incident.

It was times like these when I missed my best friend the

most. I hated that Shyanne was away at school instead of just a hop, skip, and jump away. I knew Shyanne's thought on the prospect of Shaun's cheating, but I still needed her input. Besides, I needed to tell her about the pregnancy. I decided to give her a call.

Shyanne stayed in a dormitory on campus. She didn't have a private telephone in her room, nor did she have a cell phone, so I had to reach her on the pay phone a few doors down from her room. Nine out of every ten times I dialed the number, I got a busy signal because someone else was on the phone. Tonight, however, the phone rang straight away. God knew how much I needed my girl.

"Hello," said the perky voice answering the phone.

"Hello. May I speak with Shyanne Kennedy in room 312, please?"

"Sure. I'll check to see if she's in her room."

Three other females picked up the phone to see if anyone was using it before Shyanne came on the line.

"This is Shy. Talk to me."

The moment I heard her voice I burst into tears again. I couldn't control myself. I began to weep and sob like a baby. I scared poor Shyanne half to death.

"Nay-Nay, what's wrong? Did something happen to your mother or your grandmother? Did something happen to my mother or father? Is Kevin all right?"

As usual, Shyanne was firing the questions a hundred miles a minute, but this time her barrage was warranted. I calmed myself as best I could and then tried to calm her by giving her a complete rundown of today's events. After my explanation, I began to cry again as I waited for Shyanne to go into her I-told-you-so speech. To my surprise, she was patient and extremely comforting.

"It's okay, Nay. You go ahead and cry. Get it all out. Even though I'm not right there, I'll wrap my hands around this phone and we can pretend I'm holding on to you until you are all done crying."

I didn't bother questioning the change in her. I just took advantage of the moment and cried until I felt there were no more tears left. Once the well had run dry, I asked Shyanne for her advice. Again, I was pleasantly surprised by what she had to say.

"Listen, Nay; what you said about jumping to conclusions makes sense to me. You're probably reacting to your hormones. I know I have given you a hard time about trusting in Shaun's fidelity, but you have ignored me. I'm sure you had good reason. You know your man."

Okay, who was this person and what had she done with my best friend? I was so blown back by Shyanne's attitude that I took the phone away from my ear, staring at it like it was some foreign object.

"Shy, are you taking Sensitivity 101 or something?" With that I smiled for the first time all day. Shy chuckled a little too.

"Nay, I want you to know something else also. Even if it turns out that Shaun did cheat, it doesn't have to mean the end of a three-year relationship. You two could work this out. Nobody's perfect. God says we are to forgive. I say it's okay too."

"I don't know if I could do it, Shy. Shaun is away from home too much for me not to be able to trust him totally. Then on the flip side, what if I do forgive him, we have this baby, and he does it again? I'll be stuck raising a baby by myself because I could never forgive him again. I could never even speak to him again."

I don't know where I drew the moisture from, but the tears started to re-fall. This time I was a little more controlled. Shyanne was able to talk over my misery.

"First of all, you would never be stuck raising a baby

alone no matter what happens between you and Shaun. I am always going to be there for you. I'm sure both your mother and your grandmother would too. The baby will never want or need anything. Secondly, what makes you think Shaun wouldn't take care of his baby? He's taking care of Sha'Ron and he and the Hungry Hippo aren't together anymore."

She was silly, but she was absolutely right. Shaun would never abandon any baby he fathered. He had told me that on more than one occasion. I just wished I were as sure about this other part of our dilemma.

"Do you need me to come home tonight?"

"No, that's okay. I'll be all right until you get here on Friday."

"Are you sure? I only have one class tomorrow and one class Friday morning. I could easily make up both of them."

"As much as I appreciate your offer, Shyanne, I can't accept. I don't want you missing classes over what could turn out to be nothing. Besides, I have two classes tomorrow. Unlike you, I can't afford to miss one second of class, let alone a whole session."

Shyanne and I talked for a few more minutes, then I heard Shaun sticking his key in the front door. This was the earliest he had been home in a long time. I guess the scene today really shook him up; either that or Keva put him out early.

"Shy, Shaun is coming in the door right now. I'll talk to you when I see you Friday. I love you." I hung up before she had a chance to reply.

I sat on the couch waiting for Shaun to come in like a child awaiting punishment from a parent after they come home from work. At first I didn't understand why I was so nervous. I was not the one with some explaining to do. Then I realized it was the explanation itself that had me so paranoid. I dreaded the thought of hearing any deception in Shaun's voice.

Shaun came in the house and straight to the couch. He sat down and immediately starting trippin' on me. "Lindsay, what is up with you? Why in the world would you suddenly start accusing me of cheating? Not only that, you just flat out went off on me about my mother. She hadn't done anything to you. Then you leave me stranded, not caring if I made it back to my mother's or not. I know you've had problems with me being gone a lot, but today your actions were way out of line."

"Shaun, I'm pregnant."

Shaun looked at me like I had grown another head. His mouth fell wide open. Then he closed his eyes and began shaking his head like he felt sorry for me. I didn't quite understand his patronizing attitude until he spoke again.

"I can't believe this, Lindsay. You are pulling out the oldest trick in the book. Sweetie, it's not necessary for you to tell me you're pregnant so I'll stick around. I'm not going anywhere."

My first instinct was to go ballistic. Just straight up act a fool on him. But something inside me quelled my anger and I decided to give him the benefit of the doubt. Considering the way I blurted my statement, combined with all the events of the day, he did have reason to think I was trying to trap him.

"Shaun, I'm not playing silly games with you. That is the whole reason I showed up on your mother's doorstep unannounced. In the mix up of everything that happened afterward, I forgot to tell you I was pregnant."

Shaun gave me that two-headed stare again, then suddenly reached across the sofa and pulled me into his arms. This was the first time in quite some time that we shared this kind of closeness between us. Our embrace, again, brought on the tears. I never knew one human was capable of producing so much water.

"Wow! I can't believe my little Lindsay is pregnant."

"Yeah, I'm six weeks along. The nurse at the clinic said I could safely abort up through the entire first trimester, which is up to twelve weeks. I have to be honest with you, Shaun. I was seriously considering doing just that. I was so unsure about what was going on between you and Keva. I didn't want to get stuck raising a baby by myself."

"Well, I'm not going anywhere, lady. And even on the off chance something did happen between us, I can't believe you would think I would not help you support my baby. I'm still taking care of Sha'Ron, right?"

"That's the same thing Shyanne said."

"I guess this has been a true test of our relationship. Look at us; we came through with flying colors. I love you, Lindsay. You are the only woman I want to be with. Although I wasn't expecting to be a father again just now, I'm happy about the baby. So there will be no more talk about abortion, okay?"

I assured Shaun I wouldn't talk about it anymore, but I was speaking more for myself than him. After talking with Shyanne, my grandmother and now Shaun, I knew I wouldn't be alone in raising our child.

But even as he held me now, with all of his reassuring words, I still felt uneasy. For all of his talk of loving the baby and me being his one and only, he never once said he was not cheating on me.

Chapter Twelve

July 1996

“Can you see that, Mrs. Westbrook? It looks like you are going to have a little baby girl in just over four months.” The ultrasound tech was grinning from ear to ear as she announced the gender of my baby. “Did you and your husband want a girl?”

Why do some people always assume you’re married just because you’re pregnant? “It really doesn’t matter as long as the baby is healthy. By the way, it is Miss Westbrook. My *boyfriend* and I are not married.” I knew I was being testy, but I couldn’t help myself. She got on my nerves with her assumption.

The technician was clearly embarrassed. “I’m sorry, dear. I hope I didn’t offend you. At any rate, your daughter is growing right on schedule, and everything looks normal. You can get dressed now. I’m all done here. Just make sure you stop by the reception desk on your way out to make your next appointment with your OB.” She gave me a friendly smile as she left me alone to get dressed.

After making my appointment, I considered looking for the tech to offer her my apology. I had no cause to be nasty with her. I should have actually been flattered that she thought I was responsible enough to be married before getting myself knocked up. Perhaps my spiritual light still shined despite my unethical behavior. The technician could probably still see in me what I had been neglecting for the past few years. And as further evidence of my lack of fellowship with God, I go and take out my frustration with Shaun on an innocent woman. I felt so guilty.

I had come to each of my previous prenatal appointments alone with the exception of my very first one; and it was my mother who accompanied me to that one. Shaun promised me after each visit he missed that he would make it to the next one. But at the last minute, something would always come up. Because he was anxious to find out the sex of our child, I was sure he would move heaven and earth to be present at this ultrasound. Yet, two hours before our scheduled time, Shaun got a call from good old Uncle Bobby.

"Lindsay, honey, I'm so sorry. Uncle Bobby just told me about a meeting with some major players in the game. Now you know I really want to go with you for the ultrasound, but I just can't miss this meeting. It is the opportunity I've been waiting for. This could be the break I need to push my plan of getting out of the game and into a legitimate enterprise ahead that much sooner.

WHATEVER! I had heard the speech about getting out of the drug business and into a legal business more times than I cared to count. I was starting to doubt that Shaun would ever give up his position in his uncle's organization. He loved the power and the money too much. I was pissed at him for putting his work ahead of the baby, and yet again, I had no problem telling him so.

"Shaun, I'm so sick and tired of everything and everybody coming before me and the baby. What I want or need is never a priority with you. No matter what we've planned, if Uncle Bobby calls, all bets are off for us. I'm tired of competing with your family. We have a baby on the way, and you need to start making some hard choices right now about who and what comes first in your life."

But as usual, he tried to turn it around and make it all my fault. "What do you mean, Lindsay? Every hour of work I put in, every deal I'm involved with, and every dollar I clock is done for the benefit of you, Sha'Ron, and my unborn child. I just bought you a brand new Jeep so that you will have more room for you and the baby. Now you have two cars while most of your friends are still riding the forty-seater. Every single weekend, you're out shopping. You have clothes stuffed in every closet of this townhouse. The baby already has more stuff than I have ever owned and he/she hasn't even been born yet. Please don't have me remind you of the *three* jewelry boxes you own. So you tell me, Lindsay; if I'm not doing this for you and the baby, then who am I doing it for?"

After his little tirade, he got angry and left without giving me a chance to tell him how unimportant all the *stuff* was. Yes, I appreciated everything Shaun did for me, but he refused to try and understand how much more he and the baby meant to me. I wanted us to be a family, to spend time together as a family. At the rate things were currently going, Shaun would never get to truly know his daughter.

Well, forget him. I guess the baby's godmother would be the first to know that it's a girl since Daddy Dearest couldn't find the time in his schedule to put us first. Thank goodness Shyanne was home for summer vacation.

"Girl, even though your belly is poking out like a little watermelon, I'm still having a hard time believing you're going to be somebody's mama; me somebody's godmother."

"Well, get used to it, Auntie Shy, because in just four and a half months, we will be on diaper duty," I said as I bit into cheeseburger number two. Shy and I were having lunch at Kerby's Coney Island in Fairlane Mall.

"We? Who said anything about me changing funky diapers?"

"You did, remember? And I quote: 'I will be there for you every step of the way, helping in any way that I can.' That covers everything from two A.M. feedings to college tuition."

"Dang! Me and my big mouth." We both laughed because we already knew Shyanne would almost be as much of a mother to my daughter as I would.

"Well, since I have to put in so much work, I feel I should have a say-so in naming the little brat. What about naming her after her Uncle Kevin and calling her Devin? I think that is so pretty."

"Pump your brakes, home girl. There is no way I would name my daughter after my brother. In case you have forgotten, my brother Kevin is named after our father, so my daughter will not be called Devin, because I wouldn't name a cactus after that man." Suddenly, I was not hungry anymore. The mere mention of my father depleted my appetite. I balled up my napkin and threw it in my plate as I made a disgusted face.

"I'm sorry, Nay-Nay. I wasn't thinking. I didn't mean to upset you." As close as Shyanne and I were, we never ever discussed my father. It was like an unwritten rule. The topic of my dad was off limits. Shyanne never pushed the issue.

"Don't worry about it.You know I don't sweat him not being a part of my life," I said quickly, then I changed the subject. "I like the name Shauntae. I think it's so cute when little girls are named after their fathers. Or I could do a combination thing like Rhonda did when she named Sha'Ron. What do you think about LinShaun or Shaunsay?"

It was now Shyanne's turn to make the crazy face. "I think

you should stick with Shauntae. Let's get out of here. I should beat you unconscious for even letting anything as stupid as those two names leave your lips." We both fell out laughing as I put the money on the table for the bill and made ready to leave.

As I wiggled from behind our booth, I caught a glimpse of one of the waitresses coming on duty. Something about her was very familiar. Then it suddenly hit me who she was. I stopped mid-step.

Shyanne ran right into the back of me and stumbled, nearly losing her balance. "Nay, what's wrong with you? Why did you stop like that?"

"Do you see that waitress over there behind the counter with the long hair? That's Keva."

"Who, the pregnant girl?" I didn't even bother answering Shyanne. I just put my stalled feet in motion and marched right over to the counter where Keva stood.

"Hello, Keva. Do you remember me?" By the time I reached the counter she was bending, putting something away. She lifted her head slightly to look at me then turned away again before she answered.

"No," she said, but it was obvious she was lying.

I had not thought much about Keva since the first time I saw her, but seeing her again today stirred something in my spirit. Seeing her in what looked to be the latter stages of her pregnancy brought back to my memory the day I accused Shaun of cheating with her.

"Oh, but I think you do remember me. Francine's brother Shaun is my man. I want to know if that is his baby you're carrying?" I'd raised my voice at this point. Everyone in the restaurant stared at us bug-eyed after my question, including Shyanne who had made her way to the counter by now.

"Look, stupid little girl, don't come on my job starting mess with me because you can't control your relationship."

She had the dirty nerve to say that and then walk away from me as if there was the slightest possibility I was going to let her get away with it.

I waited for her to come from behind the counter, then I lunged at her. However, before I could make contact, Shyanne grabbed my arm, yanking me backward. "Nay-Nay what is wrong with you? Even if we excuse the fact that this chick is pregnant; did you forget you are too?"

I became more enraged when Shyanne grabbed my arm and started yelling at me. I couldn't believe she wasn't on my side. "Let go of me, Shy. I want to know if she's sleeping with Shaun. She's going to tell me or take a beat down for trying to keep it from me."

While Shyanne and I stood there arguing with each other, Keva took advantage of the distraction and hurled a napkin holder at me, hitting me in the shoulder. I snatched away from Shyanne with all my might and went after Keva again. But again, Shyanne somehow managed to stop me. However, this time my girlfriend went into action. As soon as she had me safely out of arms reach, Shyanne swung around and punched Keva square in the face, knocking her on her butt.

Keva made an attempt to get off the floor, but her big belly made it troublesome. "Listen, tramp. I've stopped her once; I've stopped her twice. If you come after her again, I'm letting her loose, and I promise we will put a beat down unreal on you."

During the commotion, a man I assumed to be the manager came from the back to find out what was going on. The moment he saw Keva on the floor, he immediately started to yell at Shyanne and me.

"Hey, I don't know what happened out here and I don't want to know. I just want you two out of here before I call mall security," he screamed as he helped Keva to her feet.

Shyanne grabbed our bags. Then she grabbed me by the

arm, dragging me out of the restaurant. I was protesting every step of the way though. I still wanted a piece of Ms. Keva.

"Wait, Shy! Let me go! She still hasn't told me whether or not that's Shaun's baby she's pregnant with or if the two of them are sleeping together." Shyanne paid my protest no never mind. She continued to push me out of the restaurant.

"Stop it, Nay. First of all, you are pregnant so you are not about to fight with anybody. Secondly, I'm not about to stand around here and let you get me arrested over some stupid mess. We are in the freaking suburbs now; not Detroit. These white people don't give a hot ham sandwich about who you think your man is sleeping with. All they care about is putting our black behinds in jail."

With that said, I calmed down somewhat and walked out of the restaurant on my own accord. I was still fuming even after we got in the car. I guess Shyanne was too. Before I could back the Jeep out of our parking spot, she let me have it with both barrels.

"What got into you back there? Why would you go off like that without even considering your baby's health? Couldn't you for once think about somebody besides your stupid boyfriend? Do you really think I've got time to spend locked up in a jail cell? What makes you think she's pregnant by Shaun?" She fired the questions typical Shyanne style. When I opened my mouth in an attempt to answer, she cut me off, which was good because I had no idea what I was supposed to say.

"Just shut up, and take me home. I don't even want to hear it."

I pulled from the parking space heading for her house. Not another word was spoken for the entire ride. I had hoped Shyanne would have calmed down by the time we made it to her house. When she attempted to get out of the car without saying anything to me, I knew she was still angry. I realized then that I owed her an apology.

"Shy, wait. I'm sorry about the way I acted at the mall. When I saw Keva in the restaurant all swollen and pregnant, all the hurt I felt the day I first saw the two of them together came rushing back to me. When I looked at her, all I could see was her and Shaun in bed together having sex. I simply lost it." Just sitting there saying it out loud to my best friend brought back the pain, and I started to cry.

Shyanne got back in the car and rubbed my back while I let the tears flow. We sat in the car for about two minutes. "Come in the house, Nay. I'll get you some juice. We can talk some more in my bedroom."

Shyanne still lived at home with her parents. Jamo, her boyfriend, offered to get them a place together, but she declined. She didn't want to live with a man she was not married to. He then offered to get her a place of her own so they could at least spend more time together without all the rules and curfews. Jamo worked pretty closely with Shaun, so he had money like that. But again, she said no. Shyanne refused to be dependent on any man other than her daddy.

I used to wonder if Shyanne was trying to tell me something when she commented on not being dependent on anyone other than Mr. Kennedy. My girlfriend had always been straightforward with me, so I knew that if she had a problem with my living arrangement, she would have said so. Shaun was the only man I could depend on, so I didn't have the same options that she did.

Once we were settled in Shyanne's bedroom, me lying on the bed positioned on my side, her rubbing my back, she got serious on me. I knew it was going to be a critical conversation because she addressed me by my first name.

"Lindsay, listen to me. Hear me out totally before you answer, okay?" I agreed and she began. "You know I love you like a sister. There is no one in the world that I'm closer to than you. For those reasons I feel I can say what needs to be said." Shyanne took a deep breath, then lay down on the bed

beside me. She stared at the ceiling for a few moments before she resumed talking.

"Why are you with Shaun, Nay? Like I said, let me finish
before you attempt to answer. I want you to think about
what I'm saying while I'm talking. I get the feeling you're just
holding onto memories from your beginning with him. I
have never seen you so unhappy. You're always complaining
about him never spending any time with you and about him
always putting everything and everybody ahead of you.
After that horrible scene at the mall, it's obvious you don't
trust him anymore. I mean I thought that whole thing with
him and Keva was resolved between the two of you."

Shyanne then sat and positioned herself Indian style in
the center of her bed, giving the impression of meditating
before she continued to talk. I don't know what they were
teaching my girlfriend in school, but I was definitely noticing a change in her. It was all for the good.

After sitting and thinking for a couple of seconds, she
continued talking. "You seem as if you've lost yourself. You've
revolved your whole life around Shaun. There's no room left
for Nay-Nay. You're about to be a mother, and because
Shaun isn't your husband, the baby has to come first. Yet you
neglected to think about your baby when you wanted to
fight Keva. Nay, I was so disappointed in you."

Shyanne and I always had the type of relationship that allowed us to be no holds barred with one another. Today my
girlfriend was letting loose, straight up no-chaser.

"There used to be a time when I was envious of your relationship. Not jealous because you had it, I just wanted the
same thing you had. But if being in love with someone
makes you act this nutty, you can keep it. My biggest question is this: do you think he still loves you?"

I guess lecturing me tired her out because once she was
done, Shyanne lay back on the bed next to me. I had heard
every word, every syllable my best friend said. While her

words stung my heart, I knew they were only intended to help me. I continued to lay there for a moment, quiet as a church mouse. I had no real clue how to respond to her very sensible questions.

Then as I shifted positions getting ready to sit up, I felt a big thump in my belly. I was unsure of what it was at first, then I felt it again, realizing it was the baby moving and kicking. I became so excited.

"Shy, here; put your hand on my stomach." I grabbed her hand and placed it on my belly. At first there was nothing, but just as we were about to give up, my little girl moved around again. It was then that I knew the answer to Shyanne's question.

"Oh, Shyanne. At first I wasn't even sure I could answer you. I didn't know what to say. Everything you said made so much sense. But when I felt my daughter, *our* daughter moving inside of me, it all became clear." I began crying again before I could go on, but I didn't let that stop me. I had to make Shyanne understand what I was feeling.

"None of this may make sense to you, Shy, because you've never walked in my shoes. You've never been in love. Everyone you've ever dated has been expendable to you. You don't know what it's like to depend on a man for your happiness because you've never had to. Your dad has been all the man you ever needed. He's never left you or deserted you. He has always cherished you the way a father is supposed to cherish his baby girl." I was sobbing now, but I didn't let it deter me.

"I have never had any man care for me in that way. My grandpa died when I was too young to remember him. My own father abandoned Kevin and me like we were nothing. In all the years since my daddy's disappearance, I'd convinced myself that it wasn't important to me, that it didn't bother me one bit because my mom and grandma gave me more than enough love. It wasn't until just now, after hearing you lecture me about my relationship, that I realized how unworthy I have felt all these years."

My eyes burned, my face was red and swollen, and my heart felt as if it would explode. I was now experiencing an emotional pain greater than any I had ever felt.

Shyanne was crying now also. We were both too caught up in our own misery to comfort each other. I calmed myself as best I could and continued to make my point.

"Then Shaun came into my life. He gave me all the love my daddy never gave me. He made me feel like I was supposed to be loved and taken care of by a man. Despite his actions and all the complaining I do about him, I know Shaun still loves me. I know it because I couldn't take it if another man stopped loving me. Even though things aren't great between us, I have to stick this out. I never want my daughter to experience any of what I'm feeling right now. I never want her to have to depend on another man for her happiness because her own father was not around for her."

I was exhausted when I was done explaining myself. I curled up as much as my pregnant belly would allow me to and stared off in space. I lay there wallowing in misery as I thought about the pain my father's disappearance caused; how I never realized it until now.

Shyanne lay down next to me, wrapped her arms around me, and spoke words that I would carry in my heart forever. "Nay, I never knew how badly you hurt over your father's leaving. I'm sorry. I can only imagine how painful that is because if anything ever happened to my daddy, it would tear me apart. But Nay, even though I would never stop missing him, I would eventually stop hurting. I know that because God would make sure of it. He would dry my tears and ease my pain, just like He will do for you if you allow Him to. Now that you have opened up to Him about how much it hurt you for your daddy to leave, just pray about it, and soon it won't hurt anymore."

Shyanne continued to hold me as she made a vow that I knew would be the truest words I would ever hear. "Nay, as long as I'm alive, I promise I will never leave you."

Chapter Thirteen

November 1996

"I wonder how much snow is going to fall before it stops, Mama. We don't usually get this much snow so early in the season. It's still two weeks before Thanksgiving," I said as I stared out the window from Mama's kitchen.

"I know. If it doesn't stop soon, we'll need skis to get you to the hospital if you go into labor," she replied.

I'd been staying with my mother since yesterday. Shaun had to leave town on one of Uncle Bobby's emergencies. For the first time since I've known him, he and Mama actually agreed on something. They both felt I should stay with Mama just in case I went into labor even though my due date was not until the day after Thanksgiving.

"We could always just bounce Blimpo over to the hospital," Kevin added. He had been teasing me about being so big every minute of every hour of every day I had been here. It was just like the days of old when we all actually lived here together. I was really enjoying it.

"Oooooor," I dragged out, "I could climb in one of your

gym shoes. With one good shove, I'd be there in no time you big-foot Bozo," I replied. Mama had to laugh at that one.

"Whatever, Hilda Hippopotamus. When is Shaun coming home? We can't afford to keep feeding you. I'm scared that when we run out of food, you're going to start eating the dishes, Myrna Moose."

"What do you mean *we* can't afford? You ain't got a raggedy dime to your pitiful name, Broke Benny. And I would rather be pregnant and look like a moose than not be pregnant and still look like a one-eyed wildebeest . . . like your girlfriend."

K.J. and I traded insults for a few minutes more. Mama stood in the background laughing at us. I could tell she was getting nostalgic.

"It's so good to have both my children together in my home again. I didn't realize how much I missed you living here until now, Nay-Nay. Since K.J.'s a high school senior, come this time next year he will be away at college." Mama leaned back against the counter at the sink and suddenly started to cry.

Kevin and I looked at each other confused at first, then we smiled as we realized how blessed we were to have a mother that cared so much about us. K.J. helped me up from my seat at the window, and we went to embrace Mama together.

"Don't cry, Mommy. No matter where we are we'll never be more than a phone call away. Besides, isn't this what you've worked so hard for all these years? Now you can finally relax and take care of yourself for a change," I told her as K.J. rubbed her back and I wiped her tears. We finally got her to stop crying. Then we all sat down at the kitchen table.

"Anyway Ma, the likelihood of K.J. actually getting into an out-of-state college is very slim. He's too dumb. We will be lucky if he even graduates high school on time."

Kevin countered with, "When Nay has the baby, you'll

have to start all over again. From the moment the baby gets a look at her ugly mama, she'll start to cry so loudly that Shaun won't be able to stand the noise. They'll have to give the baby to you to raise."

Mama was now crying tears of laughter. "You two are a mess. You're worse than Thelma and J.J. on *Good Times*. Do you remember that show?"

"Yes, and speaking of old shows, guess what I saw on TV the other day? *Child's Play* with Chucky. I love that movie," Kevin reminisced.

"You didn't always love it. I remember the first time we saw it at the movies. You came home and threw away your My Buddy doll and slept in my bed for two days," I reminded him.

"Why you gotta be bringing up old stuff, Nay-Nay?" Kevin said in his Chris Tucker imitation. We all laughed at his silliness.

"Speaking of old stuff, Nay, do you remember your first day of kindergarten? K.J., you were only two so I'm sure you can't recall this, but on your sister's first day of kindergarten, we all walked over to the school together."

"Oh, I remember," I interrupted.

"No, Nay! Let me tell the story. After I was all done talking to your sister's teacher and giving Nay a few last minute instructions, you and I got ready to leave. You yelled to your sister in your little baby voice, 'Come on, Nay. We go bye-bye.' I tried to explain that Nay was staying at school and we would pick her up later. But again you repeated, 'Come on, Nay. We go bye-bye.' I decided to ignore you and explain it more on the way home, but you were not having it. You started hollering at the top of your lungs, refusing to leave without Nay-Nay. You ran over to her desk and threw your arms around her neck. You wouldn't let go."

"Yeah. I probably still have the bruises on my neck," I laughed.

"What happened next?" K.J. asked, wanting to hear the rest of the story.

"Mama tried everything to get you to leave," I said. "She attempted to leave without you, hoping you would follow her, but instead you plopped your little butt in my lap and waved bye. She even threatened to spank you, but you would not budge."

Mama took over. "Finally Nay's teacher decided to let you stay for the day. But little did she know it would end up being three days in a row you would act like that. On the fourth day, I got your granny to come over early and sit with you while I walked Nay to school alone."

"Even then, Granny had to take you to the basement so we could sneak out without you seeing Mama and me leave," I concluded.

K.J. made a goofy face and said, "I can't believe I ever liked you that much. I can't stand you now. Ugh!"

We all got a pretty good laugh out of the story. We sat and went down memory lane with a few other stories from the past for about an hour. Then Mama got that look on her face again. Both K.J. and I started reassuring her that we would never completely leave her. We promised that we would call and visit a hundred times a week just so she would not start crying again.

This time Mama's reason for her solemn look took us totally by surprise. For the first time in a long time since he left, Mama began to talk about Daddy.

"I got a call a little while ago from Grandma Westbrook." Mama looked like she had something unpleasant she needed to say, but was afraid. I was reminded of how I used to behave when I had to tell my mother something I knew would cause me to get a beat down. But what could she tell us about Nana Westbrook or her son that would cause her that kind of distress?

Finally Mama started talking again. "She told me they finally got word about your father. She said they found his body about two days ago down in Louisiana, near Baton Rouge. Kevin Sr. is dead."

K.J. and I looked at each other in stunned silence. I didn't know what my brother felt, but I was ready to bolt from the room. I didn't feel sad, but I was having a hard time accurately describing what I did feel. I just know I wanted to run.

"How did he die?" K.J. asked.

"Does it really matter?" I replied bitterly. "Besides, the peace of death is too good for him. He should have been made to live a long and miserable life, just like the one he thought we would have when his selfish behind walked out on us."

Mama looked surprised that I had such harsh words for her stupid husband. I was shocked that she would be surprised by my outburst. She couldn't possibly expect me to be saddened by his death.

"I think it's time I told you two more about your father's leaving. When Kevin walked away from this family all those years ago, he didn't just up and go without a word like everyone suspects. I asked him to leave."

K.J. and I stared at each other for a moment. Then we stared at Mama silently pleading with our eyes for her to tell us more. She picked up our cue and explained.

"You both know how your daddy couldn't hold down a job for any length of time. I had always been the one who worked hard and supported us all. But there was something you didn't know. I guess you're old enough now to find out the whole truth." Mama took a deep breath, then just blurted her next statement. "Kevin Sr. was a heroin addict. I found out about his drug use about a year before you were born, Nay-Nay, when we were still just seniors in high school. I begged him to get help, but he kept saying he could quit all by himself whenever he got ready. Well, I guess he never got ready because that's what killed him. Your father died of a drug overdose."

Oh my goodness! I could hardly believe my ears. My daddy was a junkie; a miserable freaking dope fiend, just like in one of the Donald Goines novels I had read.

The subject of our father had been off limits for so long now, I had never bothered to ask K.J. how he felt about him. We never talked about Daddy amongst ourselves. I had no idea how the news of his death affected him. Even now I was unwilling to find out how K.J. felt. I was comfortable assuming it really didn't bother him. He was so young when Daddy left, he couldn't possibly remember him.

I was angry, however. I was mad at him for being dead. Death now gave him an excuse for deserting us. I wondered to myself if my thoughts somehow made me warped in some way.

"I know your father isn't a favorite on either of your lists, but I just feel like our look back would be incomplete if we didn't include him in at least one of our memorable stories. I think it's appropriate considering the circumstances. There is a particular happening that I'm sure neither of you remember that I would like to talk about."

Again, K.J. and I gave each other a pained look, but we silently agreed to let her have her say.

"It was the Christmas after you were born, K.J. You were about eight months old. Nay, you were three. Your daddy had been working at a decent paying job for about four months. As a matter of fact, it was the same job he held until the day before he left, which was nine months later. Kevin came home and told me he was fired because he failed a random drug test. At that point I'd had enough. I told him it was time for him to go.

"Anyhow, back to the story. Your daddy insisted on doing

all the Christmas shopping for you two. He made me promise not to purchase a thing for either of you." Mama looked pleased as she told the story. I felt good that she had at least one good memory of her horrible husband.

"Kevin was so excited about buying the presents for you two that he decided to keep it all a secret from me as well. I don't know where he hid everything. On Christmas morning, the living room overflowed with presents. I couldn't believe all the stuff that man bought. There were things that were far too advanced for your age groups, including an expensive train set with an authentic smoke stack. If I'm not mistaken, I think that is the same train set that someone in this room continues to have sitting fully assembled and actively uses in my basement to this day."

K.J. stared bug-eyed for a long moment. "My father bought my train set? I didn't realize it was so old. I always assumed you bought that for me, Mama." You could see in his face that he gained some newfound respect for the runaway now known as our dead father.

I didn't think I could be swayed as easily. Mama apparently read my expression as she continued to talk about that Christmas.

"Nay-Nay, your daddy bought you three or four different baby dolls, a Barbie corvette with a black Barbie doll, and a fourteen carat gold chain with a gold heart-shaped locket. It was far too big for such a young girl, so I held on to it until you were ten years old. It is the same gold necklace I gave you for Christmas that year."

I couldn't believe it. I probably looked as Kevin did when he learned about his train. I sat there speechless. I still had the chain and locket in my jewelry box. I hardly ever wore it when I was younger because I cherished it so. I was afraid I would lose or break it. When I turned fourteen, I told Mama that I would put it away until I had a child of my own.

Daddy's death presented perfect timing. I looked at the necklace not two days before, deciding that I would put my daughter's first picture in the locket.

The three of us sat in the kitchen quiet as mice for quite a while; each absorbed in our own thoughts. Mama was the first to break the long silence.

"No arrangements have been made for Kevin Sr.'s funeral as of yet. It may be a few days before they decide anything because your grandmother has to go to Louisiana to claim the body."

"Wouldn't you be considered his next of kin since you two never divorced, Mama?" Kevin asked.

"Your father and I are divorced K.J. I filed for divorce about a year after he left. I received a default judgment because he never showed up in court."

That just went to show how little we talked about Daddy. I didn't know they were legally divorced either. I was definitely happy to hear about it though. I would have hated for Mama to have to deal with identifying the body and being responsible for his funeral arrangements. As far as I was concerned, they could put him in a plastic bag and dump him in the nearest body of water in Louisiana. Mama obviously had other thoughts.

"As I was saying, so far they have not made any arrangements, but I expect both of you to attend the funeral with me. Nana Westbrook has already decided that she was bringing her son back here to bury him."

"Why, Mama? Why should we be expected to pay respects to a man who cared more about putting poison in his veins than he did about his own children? I don't want to go. I would feel like such a hypocrite sitting there pretending to be sad he was dead when I'm not," I said.

"I don't think you should pretend to feel anything that you don't, Nay. I do, however, think you should go to say goodbye. Use this opportunity to put real closure to Kevin Sr.

being gone." I opened my mouth to protest some more, but Mama cut me off before I could continue.

"Nay-Nay, K.J., listen. I'm not in support of your father's actions. I probably have more cause to be angry with him than anybody. But I'm not. Once I got saved and became born again, I learned to let go of all that hatred and anger. I learned that as the hater, I was only hurting myself. Kevin was going about his life doing what he wanted, and I was sitting here in this house raising two kids, hating the man who was responsible for me having these two kids. It just was not worth it. So I forgave Kevin, and I let go of the anger. God forgives us over and over and over again. He expects us to be forgiving also."

Okay, Mom was hitting below the belt with that. I knew that I lived and depended on God's forgiveness, grace and mercy, especially with my current condition and living arrangements. But I was having a hard time forgiving my father.

"Forgiveness isn't something that's going to happen overnight. It didn't happen that way for me," Mama said as if she read my mind. "I just want you two to go with me and say goodbye. Your healing could begin right there."

I really wanted to tell Mama that her little guilt trip was not going to work, that I was still not going to the funeral. But I couldn't because it really did work. It worked on both Kevin and me. We just shrugged our shoulders as our way of letting her know she'd won and we were going.

Five days later, I sat in a chair in Nana Westbrook's living room watching all these people I didn't know or remember walk past me, their plates piled high with food.

At the funeral, Nana insisted that me, Mama and K.J. sit on the front pew. Personally, I would have much rather stayed in the car. During the viewing of the body, these same strange people kept stopping by talking to us, telling K.J. and I how much we had grown since the last time they saw us. Duh! What did these clowns expect? It had been sixteen years. What irked me the most was when they constantly said how much Kevin looked like our father when he was his age. It didn't seem to bother K.J. though. Never once did he frown or give them a dumb look.

I wore a stupid look on my face during the whole service. The only time I stopped looking hateful was when I would turn around to look at Shyanne, who sat in the pew behind me. Shaun was a no show. I called him on his cell phone to let him know about the death and funeral, but told him he didn't have to wrap up his business early on either account. Though I missed him, I was enjoying staying with my mother and brother. Shaun was due to return the following day.

At the burial site, I managed to slip away from the crowd and stand in the background. I used my pregnancy and the size of my belly as a reason not to stand too close to the hole in the ground prepared for my father. I didn't know what sense my excuse made, but no one wanted to argue with a soon-to-deliver pregnant woman. Shyanne stood back with me, holding my hand.

Several times during the service and again at the burial site, Shyanne asked if I were okay, and I would nod my head affirmatively. I don't think she really believed me, but I was serious. There was no love lost or found with my father's death. I simply resented having to be a part of his *celebration of life*. As far as I was concerned, other than the fact he was part of Kevin's and my creation, there was nothing about his life worth celebrating.

Nana's small house was filled to capacity, overflowing with folks that came by to eat after the funeral. There were so many people in the house I lost track of Mama and Kevin, soon after I found myself a comfortable seat. Shyanne was sticking to me like glue, however. She was only now away from me because she was in the crowded kitchen preparing us both a plate of food.

Nana Westbrook came and sat next to me. From the moment she put her butt in the chair, the baby started kicking and moving around fiercely. I guess she was reacting to the nervous energy that always surrounded my conversations with Nana. I rubbed my stomach to try and calm my daughter. Nana took notice.

"Is the baby kicking, Lindsay?" she asked.

"Yes, ma'am."

"That is such a special feeling, ain't it, baby? Feeling the life of your child moving around inside your belly; knowing that you would do anything in your power to protect that life from all hurt, harm, or danger. Yes indeed. Being a mother is the greatest gift God gives a woman."

Nana wrapped her arms around her waist as if she were holding on to her own unborn child. She was rocking back and forth in the chair, and I realized she was trying hard to keep herself from crying. All day long, folks walked around sad and sorrowful; it amazed me. How could they grieve someone they had no contact with for more than sixteen years?

Nana pulled herself together. As if reading my mind, she started answering the question that I never actually voiced.

"You know, Lindsay, it doesn't matter how grown your children are or what age they get to be, they are gon' always be your children. Losing even a grown child to drugs or the streets is always gon', be hard on a mother. You get this guilt inside of you that makes you wonder if maybe you could have done something different." Again Nana took time to compose herself before she continued talking to me.

Shyanne returned with my food. She sat on the floor at my feet eating and listening to Nana talk. I held my plate in my lap. The baby was still so active I couldn't eat.

"When a child passes away from this life before his parent, it is the most unnatural thing in the world. It's real hard, Lindsay, real, real hard. Your daddy may not have been much of a father to you and Lil' Kevin, or much of a husband to your mama, but even if he wasn't nothing else in this world, he was my child."

Nana was still able to keep the tears from falling, but I could tell she was in a lot of pain. That made me feel sad. Not for my daddy, but for his mother.

"I feel really bad for you, Nana," I said.

"Me too," Shyanne co-signed.

"But you know what? The way I see it, life recycles itself. That baby you're carrying is coming in your daddy's place. She is God's way of taking up the space in the family left vacant by his death." Suddenly all the pain in Nana's face just disappeared. She now wore a huge smile.

It was great to see Nana smiling again, but I didn't like the comparison she made. I didn't want to think of my daughter as a replacement for my dead daddy. I refused to associate anything good with my father. I know what my mama said about forgiveness being what God wanted, but He was going to have to give me a little more time. Instead of spoiling Nana's good intentions, I kept my thoughts to myself.

"Well, I have talked your ear off long enough now. I'm gon' get myself in this kitchen and grab something to eat before all these folks eat it up. You remember what your grandma told you now. Take good care of that child, okay?"

"Yes, Nana. I'll take great care of my daughter. I promise."

I stood up and gave Nana as big a squeeze as my belly allowed, along with a kiss on her cheek. Then I attempted to put my big butt back in the chair. Before I was completely seated, a pain shot through my back and around my stomach that caused my knees to buckle. Shyanne jumped to her feet and grabbed me to keep me from hitting the floor. I couldn't express how great the pain was I felt.

"What's wrong, Nay?" I could hear the fear in poor Shyanne's voice.

"I don't know, Shyanne. I just had this terrible pain in my . . . Oooooh no!"

"I think it's time for my great grandbaby to be born." Nana was grinning from ear to ear.

"It can't be time. I'm not due for another week. Besides, Shaun won't be home until tomorrow. I can't have my baby without Shaun," I whined as I cautiously sat on the edge of the chair. I was too afraid to put my butt completely in the seat. I didn't ever want to feel the pain I did when I initially tried to sit down.

Somebody obviously told Mama I was in distress. She and K.J. came running into the living room.

"Are you in labor, Nay-Nay?" Mama asked.

"Yes!" Both Nana and Shyanne answered at the same time.

I was terrified, praying it wasn't true. I didn't want to have my baby without Shaun in the delivery room. I guess God wasn't listening to that prayer because the next thing I knew, a sticky liquid poured from between my legs onto Nana's nice chair.

"I knew my great grandbaby was gon' come today. I just knew it. That's just why I had that little talk with you about one life recycling itself to make room for another. My God works in mysterious ways." Nana was shouting and lifting her hands to the sky.

I guess you had to be an old lady to get your prayers answered in this house.

Chapter Fourteen

January 1997

I stared at my daughter in the amazed wonder of a mother, marveling at how very pretty she was. She looked so much like her daddy it was frightening. Each and every day of the two months Shauntae Devin (it's all about my brother and my best friend, not my father) Taylor has been here, I have noticed something different and more special about her. She is wonderful, beautiful and perfect. Motherhood made me so sappy.

On the day my daughter was born, Shyanne and Mama stood in as my birthing coaches, getting me through the longest, most agonizingly painful eight hours of my life. I alternated between ear piercing screams with the labor pains and heart wrenching cries because Shaun was not there. It was a mess, but the result was my beautiful daughter.

Along with my daughter came the return of some of my spiritual fervor. I have been praying everyday asking God to make me the best mother possible. I have continually prayed for my child's health and development, and I have been in church each Sunday since the Sunday Shauntae was christened at three weeks old. On that Sunday, Shaun also joined us in church, but on that Sunday only. I have also included in my prayers a desire for Shaun to develop a closer relationship with God.

Though Shaun's relationship with God was not very strong, ours has been pretty close to perfect. He was a no show for the birth of our daughter, but he has been the most attentive dad and boyfriend since coming home from Florida the day after she was born. I have rarely gotten the opportunity to see Shaun interact with his son because of the restrictions put on by Rhonda, so I had no true idea how great a father he was. He has been the bizzy bomb.

Since Shauntae's birth, Shaun hasn't taken one out-of-town trip. He rarely even leaves the house. He feeds her, bathes her, changes her, and he allows me to get my well-needed rest. He has even started ignoring Rhonda. He brings Sha'Ron to our house to spend time with him so he won't have to be away from home everyday. On the few occasions he does leave for business, he is never gone for more than a few hours at a time. He has also promised me that someday in the not too distant future, he is going to give up the drug game for good and invest his money into some legitimate enterprises. I love it, I love it, I love it.

I guess I should be a little envious. I've asked Shaun to cut back and spend more time with me over and over again. My pleas have continually gone unanswered. But the moment 'another woman' enters the picture, he's all in to stay at home. I am only kidding. I think it's so wonderful he's willing to put our daughter first.

As Shauntae lay asleep in my arms, the doorbell rang. I was all the way upstairs in our bedroom, and this was one of the rare occasions Shaun was away from home. I reluctantly put my daughter in her bassinet to go downstairs to answer the ringing doorbell. I gave my baby a peck on the cheek, letting her know I would miss her for the brief moment I would be away. Life was so wonderful right now. God was surely blessing me in a big way.

I knew it was either Mama or Shyanne ringing the bell. Mama had been by practically every day, and Shyanne was here whenever she was home from school. Heck, Mama even put aside her dislike for Shaun just so she could come to our house and spend time with her first grandbaby. Knowing it was one of them, I almost neglected to check the peek hole. But with Shaun in the line of work that he was in, I erred on the side of caution and double checked.

No amount of preparation, time, or forewarning could have prepared me to see the face staring back at me from the other side of the door. I was so stunned I took a second and third look to be sure that my eyes were not playing tricks on me.

In a last ditch effort to reassure myself, I opened the front door. Still there she stood. Keva, it seemed, since she was no longer fat from her pregnancy, was even prettier than the first time I saw her. I was so surprised she was at my house, on my doorstep that I was unable to put two words together. I just stood there staring. Keva was the first to break the thick ice of silence.

"Can I come in and talk to you for a moment please?" she asked in a monotone voice. No passion, no flare, like she showed up on folks' porches and shocked the heck out of them for a living.

"Why?" Hearing her voice gave me back the power of speech.

"It's a very long story. I would appreciate not having to go through it all out here on your front porch."

"How did you know where I lived?" I asked as if I didn't hear her response to my first question.

"Lindsay, look. I would really like to talk to you before Shaun comes home. It would be a lot easier if you just let me in. I promise I'm not here to start anything. I just think there are some things you need to know that I'm sure you don't know."

It was not until she shifted the baby in her arms that I realized that she had it with her. It was cold outside, so I stepped aside and allowed her entrance into my home. As she bent to retrieve the baby's diaper bag, I remembered two other things. She knew Shaun was not at home, and she called me Lindsay.

"Keva, don't call me Lindsay. It's either Nay or Nay-Nay. How did you know Shaun wasn't here?"

"Because he left my house about thirty minutes ago. He said he was going to run by a couple of his spots, then he was going to visit his mom and take Sha'Ron shopping. I figured that would take up the remainder of the afternoon; providing he wasn't lying like he has been lately."

Okay, what the—?

I remained standing while Keva made herself comfortable on my sofa and removed the baby's outerwear. Once the baby was out of the snowsuit, I discovered she had a little boy. He was dressed totally in blue. I walked to the front of the sofa to get a good look at him. He was very handsome, almost as pretty as my daughter. They had the same jet black curly hair, the same green eyes and . . . No! It could not be. Please, God, let it not be so.

I fell more than sat on the couch right next to Keva who was holding the baby in her lap. I got so close to the baby's face that Keva had to pull her son away. "Exactly!" was all she said.

I stared at Keva, my eyes begging for her to say she was joking. I closed my eyes, praying to God to let it be April first and not the middle of January. But when I opened my eyes, she was still sitting in my living room, on my sofa, holding my daughter's half-brother.

"How old is your baby?" I asked.

"Six months."

"How long have you been having sex with my man?" I didn't raise my voice, but my tone was laced with venom and hate. Yes! I hated Keva and her baby for walking into my home, into my life, disrupting the peace and perfection I enjoyed not a full five minutes before she showed up.

"Shaun and I started messing around about two years ago."

I wanted to choke Keva. I wanted to scream at her. Tell her she was lying. There was no way Shaun would do this to me. Not the Shaun I was with now; definitely not the Shaun I was with two years ago. But I couldn't. Keva brought the evidence with her for me to see with my own stupid eyes. Had her son not been with her, I would have beaten the stuffing out of her for causing me all this agony. The hostility was written all over my face. Keva began her explanation with an apology.

"I'm sorry, Lindsay." Before she could utter another word my left eyebrow shot up in warning. She corrected herself. "Sorry about that. Shaun calls you Lindsay, so that is the only name I know."

It burned my ears and my heart to hear that she and Shaun discussed me while they were having their illicit little affair. Suddenly my townhouse became very warm. I moved from the sofa to a chair to put some space between Keva and myself in hopes of getting some much needed air.

"Like I was saying, I'm sorry for coming here like this, but I'm tired of Shaun's lies. He's been lying to me, and he's obviously been lying to you."

"Why did you decide to come to talk to me today? Why didn't you tell me this when I asked you at your job that day? Why would you sleep with him if you knew he was mine?" With each question my voice rose. I was yelling when I asked the last one.

Keva picked up her son as he started to whimper, probably reacting to my anger. It was then that I remembered that my own daughter was sleeping. I decided to remain calm for her sake. I took a few deep breaths, letting my face rest in the palms of my hands for a few seconds. When I again raised my head, Keva restarted her explanation.

"I met Shaun through his sister, Francine, when I was sixteen years old. She and I were friends from high school. I had a crush on him from the moment I first laid eyes on him, back when he and Rhonda were living together in Patricia's house. I didn't let that stop me from flirting with him or begging Frannie to hook me up with him. I was digging him strong, but for the most part, he didn't even realize I was alive."

Keva checked her son and saw that he had fallen asleep. She lay the baby down on the couch before she finished her story. "By the time I found out he and Rhonda were no longer together, he was already with you, so I just gave up. I started dating a guy in our neighborhood named David. Soon after we got together, I moved in with him.

"One night after I had come in from being out with Frannie, David accused me of cheating on him with Shaun. He said I only spent time with Frannie to be close to Shaun. I guess I still had it pretty bad for him and my boyfriend apparently picked up on the vibe.

"In the heat of the argument I told David the truth; I would rather be with Shaun than him. I informed David that I only settled for him because I couldn't have Shaun. I humiliated him, and for that I was rewarded with a major beat down. I left the house immediately after the fight, and ran straight to Frannie's house. Shaun was there, demanding to know who beat me up. After I told him it was David, he, Frannie and I went back to my house to get my things. Shaun confronted David and told him if he ever put his hands on me again, he would kill him"

I was so into Keva's story I almost didn't hear my daughter's cries through the baby monitor in the living room. It was her feeding time. I excused myself to check on Shauntae.

For some reason, I didn't want to take my daughter anywhere near Keva and her son. I couldn't explain it, but I was uncomfortable having Shauntae in the same room with them. My curiosity over Keva and Shaun's relationship overrode the discomfort, however. I went back downstairs, prepared Shauntae's bottle, then went back to the living room to feed her. Once I settled in the chair, Keva came to look at my child. Her reaction to our children's resemblance was pretty close to my own.

"She's a very pretty little girl. They both look just like Shaun." Keva returned to her seat on the sofa and resumed her story.

"Shaun and Frannie took me home to my mother's house. During the drive, he kept telling me I was too pretty to be with any fool who would hit me. He made me promise I would not go back to David no matter how many times he promised he would never hit me again. My teenage crush on Shaun turned into full blown love that night, but it only served to break my heart because I knew he was with you."

How I remained composed and outwardly unmoved by Keva's story was far beyond even my own comprehension. On the inside I was slowly and painfully dying. It killed me to listen to another female sit and talk to me about being so in love with the same man I loved so dearly. I attributed my calmness to having my daughter in my arms. It made me give the institution of motherhood an even deeper level of respect. What I really wanted to do was yank all of Keva's pretty hair out, but I sat quietly feeding, then burping my child and let her finish her story.

"Even though I knew Shaun had a woman, I couldn't help wanting to be with him. So for the next three weeks, I went to see Frannie everyday at the same time, after figuring out the time Shaun would be there visiting Sha'Ron. Frannie realized what was up and she helped me by making it possible for her, her son, Daiquan, Sha'Ron, Shaun, and I to do little things together. I assumed Shaun looked at me like another little sister, so he didn't mind me hanging out with them. I was unconcerned with his feelings for me as long as I was allowed to be near him."

I was not the least bit surprised that Francine would help Shaun cheat on me. From day one, I knew Francine and I would never be friends. I never understood why; I never cared one way or the other. But she was now on my list as public enemy number two. I put her status aside for the time being while I continued to concentrate on number one's explanation.

"After three weeks of us all hanging out and having fun, I discovered I was pregnant by David. Once again I freaked out and ran to Frannie for comfort and advice, but Shaun informed me that she wasn't home. I instead poured out my misery to Shaun, explaining that I was not ready to have a baby, but I couldn't afford to pay for an abortion. Shaun told me not to worry. He said he would pay for the abortion so I wouldn't have to go to David for the money. He and Frannie went with me a couple of days later to have the procedure done."

My already strained heart snapped at that moment, breaking into a million pieces. How could he do such an intimate favor for another woman? I understood at this point in the story no actual cheating had taken place. However, this prelude gave indication that when the cheating did start, it would be more than just a physical affair. I began to get the impression that their liaison would be emotional as well.

The tears that built in my heart sprang into my eyes. The last thing I wanted was for Keva to see me cry. In an effort to shield my eyes, I looked down at my daughter. She had fallen back asleep so I used that as an excuse to leave the room.

"I'm going to lay my daughter down," was all I said. I left the room heading upstairs, the water from my eyes wetting Shauntae's receiving blanket.

After I laid Shauntae down I went into the bathroom and cried for five minutes. I hadn't given Keva any indication that I would return to hear the rest of the painful story. I wasn't honestly sure if I could. I almost hoped she would just leave so I didn't have to hear the rest of the mess. However, I knew I would always wonder how they ended up sleeping together. So I dried my eyes, gathered my courage and went back downstairs. Keva was still there waiting to finish shredding the illusion I had of my wonderful relationship before she showed up on my doorstep.

I sat down with full comprehension that I no longer had Shauntae to act as a buffer, keeping me from attacking Keva when she started to tell the worst parts of the story. I silently prayed for God to give me strength to at least allow her the opportunity to get it all out before I started to choke her.

"Finish," I commanded.

"It was right after the abortion that my relationship with Shaun began to change from big brother-little sister to friends with a mutual attraction. I remember it as if it were yesterday. On the day after the procedure, Shaun called me at my mother's house. He said he just wanted to check on me to make sure I was feeling okay." Keva then began her tour, taking me back to the beginning of her and Shaun's relationship . . .

"After I told him I was okay, he asked if we could hook up sometime, minus Frannie and the kids. I asked about you and he asked me if it bothered him that he had already had a girlfriend." Keva turned her eyes away from me for a second when she said, "I told him that I was only asking to be courteous. If it didn't bother him, it didn't bother me." She looked back at me. "And it was on from there. Shaun and I saw each other practically every day. With each new day I fell more and more in love with him. He made me feel like it was more than just a sex thing because we spent more than a month together hanging out before we ever actually had sex."

Now we were getting to the part I dreaded hearing most. I closed my eyes to block out the images of Shaun and Keva locked in several different sexual positions. Those images obviously managed to enter my brain via some other orifice because they were all I could see.

The two of them had an ongoing relationship for more than two years. They were friends, then lovers, and now the proud parents of a bouncing baby boy. It all happened right under my stupid, naïve nose. I know I had my suspicions, but this was more than I could have imagined. It was now my turn to talk. I needed some flippin' answers.

"Why should I believe anything you've said to me? How do I know you're not making this whole story up?" The questions were dumb even to my own ears, but I didn't know where else to start.

"You know I'm telling the truth. You've suspected it since the first time you saw me. You can see with your own two eyes this is Shaun's son. What logical reason would I have for creating such a story?"

Keva spoke with no animosity in her voice, at least not any toward me. I felt myself relaxing and letting go of some of the hate. After all, I am a rational Christian woman. The person I should fault right now was Shaun, not her, although she did enter into a relationship with him knowing he and I were together.

"Why were you so willing to accept being the other woman? You're a pretty girl. Didn't you think you could get your own man?"

Keva took her time answering this question. I guess I had made her feel inadequate with the implication that she warranted nothing better than second hand love.

"At first it didn't matter to me that I was the other woman. I was so crazy about Shaun I was more than willing to share him. I was happy just to have a piece of him. But as time went on, I stopped thinking about it like that. Like I said, I saw him almost every day. We spent our time together at his mother's house with Sha'Ron. He was there for me whenever I needed him. I started feeling like I was his main woman, and you were the outsider."

Now it was my turn to feel insufficient. I thought Shaun was actually working during the time he spent away from home. I was angry, but I believed Shaun when he said he was out all the time putting things together so he could get out of the business. I was so humiliated by my dumbness, this time I didn't bother checking my tears. I just let them flow. I cried my way right through my next question.

"Has Shaun . . . Has Shaun ever told you . . . he loved you?" I sniffled out.

Again Keva contemplated her answer. For the first time since she entered my house I saw her show sadness. Strangely, this gave me comfort.

"No!"

Keva's answer had opposite effects on both of us. While her reply made me happier than any time since she had been here, she began to cry. This time it was Keva who fought through the tears to continue the story.

"The day I found out I was pregnant by Shaun was the absolute best, yet one of the worst days of my life all rolled into one. I was thrilled to find out I was carrying his child. I knew this information would be all I needed to make him mine for good.

"Normally Shaun would pick me up once he left here going to his mother's house, but I was so exited after learning I was pregnant, I went straight from the clinic to Patricia's house by cab. I called Shaun on his cell phone to let him know he didn't have to come get me. I told him to hurry though because I had a surprise for him."

Her recollection took me back to the day I rushed over to Patricia's house with the same surprise; the first time I saw Keva. At that point she was already seriously involved with my man and pregnant with my daughter's half brother. Hindsight was kicking in like a mug.

"Shaun and I were in the basement where he kept his little apartment at his mother's house. We had just finished having sex, and I was still beaming with my secret I hadn't yet shared with him. I lay there smiling from ear to ear. Shaun, in his arrogance, assumed it was because the sex was so good." Keva then resumed telling me, practically verbatim, her and Shaun's conversation . . .

"Hey, baby! Did daddy do you right or what?"

"You always do. Shaun, do you love me?"

"What? Where did that come from?"

"We've been together for about a year, and we've never said those words to each other. I'm sure you know I love you. Do you love me?"

"Keva, you know I already have a woman. What is with all this love stuff? I thought you realized we were just kicking it with each other."

"I felt as if Shaun punched me in the chest." She sighed heavily. "That's how badly my heart hurt after hearing him say that. I was stunned speechless. I just lay there in bed with my mouth hanging open hoping he would retract his words, but he didn't. He simply explained how he was not willing to leave you for me."

"Look, Special K. I enjoy the time we spend together and everything, but at the end of the day, I go home to Lindsay. We discussed this in the beginning. I don't think I've ever led you to believe anything different."

"What do you mean you have never led me to believe

anything different? How can you expect me to believe that everything is honky-dory with you and Lindsay when you spend almost every day with me, having sex with me, getting me—"

"Shaun cut me off, figuring he knew what I was going to say next, supposedly setting me straight."

"How was I getting you all confused or worked up? I have never said anything negative to you about Lindsay or our relationship. You and I have never even spent the night together. Keva, I like you. If it's cool with you, we can still continue to kick it, but I'm not leaving Lindsay to start a full-blown relationship with you."

"Even though he had hurt me beyond what words could accurately describe, I still loved and wanted to be with him. I realized if I told him about me being pregnant right then, he would probably suggest I have another abortion. There was no way I was getting rid of his baby, so I decided to hold on to the information a while longer, hoping that eventually Shaun's feelings for me would grow deeper, and he wouldn't want me to abort our child."

"I'm sorry, Shaun. I did jump to conclusions. It's just that we always have such a great time together I got ahead of myself. We can definitely continue to kick it."

"I lay there feeling like the biggest dummy, but a dummy holding a trump card." Keva ended that part of the story with a faraway look in her eyes, staring off as if she were viewing the sad scene on the screen of her heart.

I sat in my chair listening as Keva told the cheerless saga of her and Shaun's lopsided love affair. I almost felt sorry for her. How could she allow him to treat her so casually when she was so deeply in love with him? Where was her sense of self-worth?

As much as I hated her and Shaun's betrayal, I still felt I could hold on to some shreds of dignity for two reasons. One, he never told her he loved her. He often said those words to me. Two, he told her he wasn't willing to leave me for her. Yet and still, there were still some unanswered questions, so I prepared myself to hear more of their sordid tale.

"When did you finally get around to telling Shaun you were pregnant?" I asked.

"Would you believe it was the same day you found out you were pregnant?" Keva responded.

My eyes became as big as saucers. All the color drained from my face. My ears were ringing. My head felt like it was in a vice grip. I instantly became a physical and emotional mess. My God! So much happened that day, and I was the recipient of only half the day's events while Shaun and Keva knew everything.

"Tell me what happened," I demanded.

Before she could begin again, Keva's son awoke. She gave him a bottle of infant formula prior to telling me the next phase of this crazy drama. Keva was very gentle with her son. I could tell she adored him the way I adored Shauntae.

"What's his name?" I was almost afraid to ask.

"Kevaun," she replied and spelled it. The name was a combination of her's and Shaun's like Sha'Ron. Keva finished her story while she fed her baby. "I was three and a half months pregnant the day I finally told Shaun. Again, it was after we finished having sex. Shaun made mention of the fact that I was picking up weight. Up to that point, I purposely spent a little less time around Shaun. Francine knew the situation, and she and I would make it our business to be doing something away from the house. I also went out of my way to hide the pregnancy from everyone else as well. The last thing I wanted was for someone like Tameeka or Patricia to bust me with any *looking like you're pregnant* remarks. The fact that my belly had not gotten that big helped a great deal. I concealed my size with big clothes."

She went on to tell me about her and Shaun's conversation that day.

"Keva, what you been eating, girl? You're starting to get a little thick around the stomach and hips," Shaun remarked.

"I haven't been eating anything unusual unless there's something you can eat that causes pregnancy."

"That's not even funny, Keva. Don't play around like that."

"I'm serious, Shaun. I'm three and a half months pregnant."

"I can't believe this. Why would you do something so dumb? What Do you think by laying up here telling me you're pregnant, you're going to make me leave Lindsay?"

"My being pregnant has nothing to do with your girlfriend, Shaun. This is between you and me. This is our baby."

"This is not our anything. I'm not trying to be a daddy again right now. And even if I were, I would be having the next child with my woman, okay. So if you're telling me the truth right now, you're just going to have to have another abortion."

"I'm fifteen weeks pregnant, Shaun. It's too late to safely have an abortion."

"You did this on purpose, didn't you?"

"I went on to explain how I wanted to tell him about it the first day I found out and how I couldn't after our conversation about love. Shaun had never gotten upset with me before, but at that moment, he was pissed."

As I listened to Keva, I remembered the tension that was in the air that day. I correctly assumed at the time that it was all due to Shaun being caught up in something, but I had no clue how much *something* there was until now.

"When you were leaving Patricia's house that day, you and Shaun had just argued about the pregnancy?"

"Yes. Believe it or not, I was glad you showed up when you did. I really needed to get away from Shaun. The last thing I wanted was for him to drive me home and torment me some more about my stupidity or his love for and refusal to leave you."

My emotions were now all over the map. I was angry, confused, hurt, sad, jealous, scared, and even a little proud. I lowered my head to my knees and closed my eyes in an effort to sort through everything Keva had said. I had listened to more than I cared to ever hear. In my heart I knew there were still some things I was unaware of, but needed to know. Keva picked up the story again just as she finished feeding her son.

"I walked to that bus stop, crying all the way there. I cried the whole time I waited for the bus. I cried through the entire ride. I cried for the better part of two days. That's how long it was before I heard from or saw Shaun again. He showed up on my mother's doorstep to talk to me."

"Hey, Special, K. What you been up to? Can I come in?"

"Hello, Shaun. Come on in."

"How you feeling?"

"I've been better, Shaun."

"Look, Keva. I'm sorry if I hurt you the other day. When you told me you were pregnant, I was seriously shocked. As much as I love my son, he was an unexpected baby. Just once, I would like to be in control of if and when I have children. To top it off, Lindsay's pregnant too. She told me when I got home; right after you laid your news on me . . ."

Keva paused to take a breather, then continued on.

"I cried after he told me that too. My plan was falling apart right in my face. I was supposed to have Shaun make a choice; me and our baby, or you. Knowing his feelings about abandoning a child, I figured I would have a good chance of getting him all to myself using the baby as my ace in the hole. But I knew I couldn't win against you and a baby. You made the playing field level without even knowing you were in the game."

Keva was absolutely correct. I had no idea that I was being played like Lotto. Up until the day I initially saw the two of them together, you couldn't have paid me to believe Shaun was cheating on me. I began to feel naive and stupid all over again. Shyanne tried to warn me repeatedly. All the signs were there in plain sight. I was just too much in love to read them.

I got up from my chair and walked to the shelf in our living room. On the shelf was a brand new picture of Shaun and Shauntae. When we took her for pictures at six weeks old, I didn't want to participate because I felt my face was still too fat. I stared at the picture for a long moment, wondering how he could be so dirty and deceitful. Wondering how long he would continue to cheat on me. Wondering how, after everything I learned today, I could still be so much in love with him. I returned to my seat and continued the inquisition.

"So what's going on between you and Shaun now?"

"The only thing between me and Shaun now is a bunch of lies and broken promises. That's why I'm here today. I'm tired of being lied to. I'm tired of me and Kevaun being treated like Shaun's dirty little secret."

"What do you mean dirty little secret? Doesn't his family know about you and Kevaun?"

"Yes, but ever since your daughter was born, Shaun acts as if we don't exist anymore. I used to see Shaun everyday. When Kevaun was born, he got me my own apartment. He even started staying the night with us sometimes. He told me you thought he was out of town on business with Uncle Bobby on those evenings."

Though I was not surprised to find out he lied about being out of town at this point, there was one imaginary trip that concerned me.

"Was Shaun with you or was he really in Florida on the day my daughter was born?" I asked.

"What do you think?" was her simple reply.

AGHH!!! Again I put my head down, trying to alleviate the pounding in my brain. I wished somebody would have warned me that today would be the worst day of my life. I would have stayed in my bed and slept through it. Keva kept on talking through my agony.

"Since you gave birth to your daughter, Shaun has completely ignored me and Kevaun. I can never catch him at his mother's, but he leaves money for me with Frannie. He has only been by my apartment two or three times in the last two months. When he does show up, he only stays long enough to hold the baby for a moment. He then gives me some money and leaves, always promising to return soon," Keva complained.

Wait!!! Now I got it. Everything was certainly becoming very clear. As long as Shaun was willing to see her and sleep with her everyday, she was cool with keeping their *dirty little secret*. Now that he had dissed and dismissed her, Keva was playing the role of the woman scorned, willing to tell it all. I was now back to being pissed and ready to choke her. This cow brought all this grief into my household to hurt me, not to help me. This little visit today was a clear-cut case of misery loving company.

Motherhood must have made me soft because the only two things that kept me from pounding Keva's head into my carpet were my daughter and her son. I'm sure my increased church attendance and renewed relationship with God had something to do with it also. Keva was about to get a verbal beat down, however.

"Let me get this straight, Keva. Shaun has played your sorry behind to the left, so you decide to come to my home and snitch on him, probably hoping I'll kick him to the curb. You waltz all up and through here pretending like you were really concerned about me knowing the truth, when the real truth is your second-string butt is just trying to get my position in the starting line-up."

I stood up walking in slow circles around the couch where Keva and her son sat. I was doing my best to intimidate her, making her think I would start swinging on her at any moment. My little performance obviously achieved its desired effect. While I talked, Keva started putting the baby's coat on and getting her things together.

"Listen, *Special K*. No matter how good you are in bed, no matter how many babies you have, no matter how much his hateful mama likes you, Shaun will never ever leave me for a whore like you. You played yourself like a dollar store toy, and when he was all done having his fun, he put your behind on the shelf. Bet you don't feel so *special* now, do you?"

Keva finished bundling her baby and stood up to leave. She had nothing else to say. She walked to my door, head hanging low, clutching her child like a lifeline. Just as she got ready to open my door, I walked up and stood no more than six inches behind her. She didn't turn around, so I started speaking to her back.

"Shaun has been here every single day and night since our daughter was born. When I told him I was pregnant, I let him know that I was considering having an abortion. He said he was having none of that kind of talk from me. And not one solitary day ever goes by without him telling me how much he loves me. Now get out of my house."

I walked around Keva and snatched the door open. She practically ran through it trying to get away from my verbal abuse. I could feel the misery seeping from her pores. I slammed the door and went back to the sea that held me hostage during Keva's outpouring of pain into my life. I sat there wondering if my last words were said for her humiliation or the benefit of soothing my own broken heart. Keva's misery had a whole lot of company today.

Chapter Fifteen

My heart and soul ached as I held my head and thought about Shaun's betrayal. I searched the Spirit in me; the Spirit I had neglected, for answers. I started making myself believe that since I had been so neglectful to God, perhaps He started neglecting me. I was living in sin, I had a baby out of wedlock, and I was living with a lying, cheating, drug dealer; a perpetual destroyer of human lives. I'd been back in church for six weeks, yet I had virtually walked away from God for over four years. I couldn't blame Him for forgetting about me.

I remained in the chair for more than an hour after Keva left. I sat there crying until I heard my daughter awaken. I went upstairs, changed her, came back down, prepared her bottle and then went back upstairs to feed her. I held my daughter, looking down into her beautiful face, staring at the face that belonged to the man who had broken my heart.

While I loved my daughter with all my heart, I hated looking at her right now. I hated what her face represented. I hated the pain I was in right now because of the face that looked just like hers. It was very hard to be with her at this moment, but I knew Shauntae had to eat. I silently pleaded with her, however, to hurry up, finish and go back to sleep. I needed to be away from her.

Shauntae must have felt my need for space, because she fell right back to sleep as soon as I burped her. However, moments of solitude were not to be had. Shaun came in just as I headed downstairs to wash my daughter's bottle.

He had not even closed the door behind him before I hurled Shauntae's bottle down the stairs right at his head. The plastic bottle connected with a dull thump, making me angry because it was not made of glass.

"What the . . . Lindsay, why are you throwing things at me?" Shaun spat.

I didn't answer his question. Instead I ran down the stairs at top speed and attacked him. I swung my fist with all my might. I didn't even bother aiming. I just swung. It had been a long time since I had actually been in a fistfight, but the way my blows were connecting let me know I had not lost my skill. Truth be told, I was probably only winning the fight because Shaun wasn't fighting back. He was so caught off guard by the whole attack that he just stood there trying to block my punches.

Eventually his defensive nature took over. He grabbed me off my feet in a big bear hug, throwing us on the sofa. Shaun held my arms very tightly to prevent me from hitting him anymore. By then, however, his nose was bleeding, his lip was busted and bleeding, and my knuckles were scrapped and swollen. Oh yes! I whipped his tail, but I still wanted more.

"Let me go!" I started to swear and call him ungodly names. I struggled so hard to get free that we both rolled off the couch onto the floor. On the way down, I bumped my shoulder on the coffee table, yelling in agony. The pain knocked the rest of the fight out of me.

Shaun got off me and lifted me to my feet. He immediately

moved away from me and went to stand behind the chair. Out of breath, he began trying to find out the reason for my attack on him. "What . . . is . . . wrong . . . with . . . you? Are you suffering . . . from postpartum depression? What demon has possessed you?"

"Try Demon Keva and your seven-month-old son!" I yelled while trying to rub away the pain in my shoulder.

Shaun's face instantly turned as white as a ghost's. He looked like he had stopped breathing. He walked around to the front of the chair, literally plopping into it, holding his chest with one hand and shielding his face with the other. Humiliation radiated from his pores, and his leg started twitching nervously. I verbally attacked while he was vulnerable.

"What's the matter, Mack Daddy Shaun? Cat got your tongue? Aren't you even going to deny it like you did the first time I asked you about having a relationship with Keva? Remember that, Shaun? Remember telling me that she was just a friend of Frannie's?" I continued without taking a breath.

"I know what happened. Frannie got Keva pregnant, and since you're such a wonderful man, you decided to take responsibility for the baby the two of them conceived. We all know how you hate to see a child without a daddy." I yelled at the top of my lungs, momentarily forgetting about the baby upstairs. Shaun, however, regained his composure long enough to protect his daughter.

"Can you lower your voice, Lindsay? I know you're angry with me, but Shauntae should not have to suffer because of it."

"I'm surprised you remember her name considering you've got kids running around all over the city." My voice was lowered, but my sarcasm was on full blast.

"Lindsay, I don't know what to say to you right now. I'm sorry seems so weak in the wake of what you found out today."

"I wish you would utter the words I'm sorry right now. I

just wish you would, Shaun. I'll come over there, sore shoulder and all, and beat you again. I swear 'fore cheese and biscuits, I will." I finally sat on the sofa, too drained to fight anymore, no matter what Shaun said next.

Shaun and I sat like that for a long while, each of us brooding in our own thoughts. I was unaware what that slime ball was thinking, but I kept replaying the painful story Keva told over in my head. It was as if the conversation was mentally recorded. I could hear it verbatim in my brain. I was the first to break our silence.

"How could you disrespect me so badly, Shaun? Your other baby's mama came over, waltzing into my home with your child, telling me all about your funky little love affair. I have never felt so bad or been so embarrassed in the entire twenty years I've lived on this earth. How could you hurt me so easily?" I began to cry, and I hated myself for allowing Shaun to see me doing it.

"Lindsay, I know I hurt you, but believe me it wasn't easy," was all he said in reply.

"I've gone through a lot of crap with you in this relationship, Shaun. I should be in Texas, or Atlanta or Alabama in college, but no, I stayed here with you. I quit school altogether to have a baby that you begged me not to abort. I went into that hospital and delivered our daughter without you because you screwing around with baby mama number two; not because you were putting things together for us so you can one day get out of the business. I can't believe that you let me do all I do for you and all I get in return is lies and pain."

I pulled my knees to my chest hugging myself as tightly as I could, figuring I could squeeze away the searing hurt in my heart. My efforts were futile, so I closed my eyes and leaned back against the cushions of the sofa, letting the tears flow freely.

Shaun sat still and quiet in the chair with his head hung low. I had never seen him look so somber. He looked so pitiful I almost felt sorry for him. Almost! What I really felt was the need for answers as to why he would be so deceitful and doggish.

"Just tell me why, Shaun!"

Shaun looked me square in the eye for the first time since I'd busted him. As much as I hated to admit it, my heart softened toward him just a little. I was clueless as to how I could be so weak for this man, and my weakness made me angry. I looked away from him as he began to speak, hoping to recapture some of the animosity I had for him.

"There is no good explanation for what I've done to you, Lindsay. I was selfish, greedy and arrogant. I figured I was a big man because I was bringing in big money, taking good care of you. And because I was so good to you, I had the right to have a little extra fun for myself. I thought as long as I didn't take anything from you, it was all good. I had the right to be a player, therefore an idiot."

Shaun always spoke intelligently no mater what was going on, but his intellect always seemed more prevalent when we argued. I could be angry, screaming, yelling, and acting a royal fool. Shaun would remain his normal calm, clever self. I think he did this consciously, knowing it would remind me of what I loved about him and hopefully make me neglect why I was annoyed.

"The thing with Keva started so innocently," he said. I was trying to be a big brother to her initially, then I found myself physically attracted to her. Since I considered myself the man, I convinced myself that I was entitled to a fling. But I never loved her, Lindsay. My heart always remained with you. I told her that in no uncertain terms."

"How can you say you love me, then disrespect me so badly? You put my life at risk by having unprotected sex with another woman. That's not love, Shaun. What I feel for you is love. True love. I would never consider sharing my body with anyone else."

I was crying again. This was the first time since this whole sordid mess began that I thought about the possibility of a sexually transmitted disease. It made me sick to think that Shaun had so little regard for our life. It was one thing to cheat, it was totally another to be careless about it. I sat there wondering if it made sense to continue to think of Shaun as smart. Maybe I was giving him too much credit.

Shaun came and sat on the sofa with me, putting his arms around me. I didn't want it to, but it felt so good to be wrapped up in him. I wanted him to hug away the pain and misery. I wanted him to tell me this was all a big joke. Nothing I went through today was real. I hugged him back waiting for him to say the words to me. But it was not to be. His next words only gave confirmation to my hurt.

"Plainly stated, Lindsay, I took advantage of your love for me. Baby, it's not to say that I don't love you as much as you love me, because I do. It was a simple case of the old cliché of having my cake and eating it too. As far as being careless, that's another matter. You see, baby, in my arrogance I knew Keva truly cared for me too. I took advantage of her as well. I knew she would never put me at risk by sleeping with anyone else."

It was killing me to hear that the man I loved with all my heart was such a dog. Not only could he hurt me with such callousness, but he had no qualms about hurting another woman as well. I would have never thought Shaun capable of being so selfish. How could I still be in love with him when he was gifted with the art of such cruelty?

My head was screaming, telling me to put an end to this relationship. My heart was reminding me of how much I loved him, telling me to stay because I didn't want to live without him. Stay because I didn't want to raise my daughter without him. Stay because he admitted he was wrong and that he never loved Keva.

But what about Keva's son? Did he love him? How did he plan to handle that situation?

"What am I supposed to do, Shaun? You're now a man with three children and three separate baby mamas. Sha'Ron was one thing because he came along before me. But what about Kevaun? He is no less your child than Shauntae or Sha'Ron. What are you going to do about that?"

"Lindsay, I would never turn my back on any child I fathered, but that doesn't mean I have to be involved with the mother. I am no longer involved with Rhonda, am I?"

"No, but you weren't cheating on me with Rhonda either. How can I be sure this thing with you and Keva is over for good when you continue to see her?"

"It has been over with Keva ever since you came home with Shauntae. I let go of that little fling after I laid eyes on the beautiful daughter you gave me. I knew then there was no way I could go on deceiving you after everything I'd put you through already. I love you, Lindsay. I'll spend the rest of my life making this up to you if you just give me the chance. Give us the chance."

Shaun's affair with Keva was much more than a little fling and we both knew it. What he had with Keva was now an eighteen-year commitment whether he saw it that way or not. I wanted to believe he was truly sorry, that he loved me enough to never do this again. But it was harder than I thought it would be. Everything he had said so far has coincided with everything Keva said today, so I knew he was telling the truth about the affair being over, at least for now.

How was I going to deal with his new child? Every time I saw Kevaun I would be reminded of his betrayal. Or would Keva be like Rhonda, not letting her son anywhere near me?

There were a million and one questions running through my mind. I was getting dizzy thinking about everything. The next words out of Shaun's mouth brought the whole thing into focus instantly.

"Marry me, Lindsay."

Chapter Sixteen

February 2002

"Would you please hurry up, Shyanne? I still have a million things to do before I go home and get ready for my anniversary celebration tonight."

"Stop moaning, Nay. You've been married for five years. You have been with the man for more than nine years. Anniversaries should be no big deal by now, at least not until the tenth. Now what I'm doing is important. I'm buying shoes and that will always be significant, twenty-four hours a day, seven days a week, fifty-two weeks a year, and so on. Isn't that right, Shauntae?"

"Don't you dare try to corrupt my baby, turning her into a shopaholic like you. Shauntae, put on your coat."

I started preparing my daughter to leave Saks Fifth Avenue in Fairlane Mall, where we had spent the better part of ninety minutes in the shoe department. We had been sitting in this store so long, my daughter took her coat off and started playing dress up in the shoes from the clearance racks. I began helping Shauntae back into her coat, hoping it would give Shyanne the hint that we were ready to leave. I still had a million things I needed to do, including dropping Shauntae at Mama's and getting my hair done for tonight.

Shaun and I were married two weeks after he popped the question. We left Shauntae with my mother and eloped to Las Vegas. I was married for two months before I told anyone other than Shyanne. She went with us to Vegas and served as my maid of honor. I was afraid and embarrassed to tell my mother or grandmother I married Shaun because of the incident with Keva and the baby.

I initially turned down Shaun's proposal. I took my baby and left that evening, going to stay with my mother for three days. When I went to my mother's, I was of the mindset that I would never go back to Shaun because I was sure I could never trust him again. So I saw no harm in telling her everything that had transpired with Keva and her child. Mama was ecstatic that I had finally come to my senses and left *Rock-head*.

I never knew it was humanly possible to hurt or miss someone as much as I did while we were apart. Shaun felt it too. He called my cell phone, and when I wouldn't answer it, he would call my mother's house every hour on the hour. He even dared to come by the house on the second day, which was a definite no-no in my mother's book.

On the third day, I gave in to his pleas, flowers, promises, and my own broken heart, and I returned home. Mama was upset, but she said I was a grown woman who had to learn to sleep hard in the bed I made.

Mama's warning has been unwarranted however. For the last five years, the bed I have slept in has been as soft as ostrich feathers. My life as Shaun's wife has been everything but troublesome.

One month after we got married, we moved out of the townhouse and into a beautiful four-bedroom home in

Southfield, a suburb near Detroit. I drive a new BMW and at the beginning of each year, I trade in the old one for the newest year. Shaun buys himself a new Corvette each year as well. We also own a Cadillac Escalade and a Chrysler Town and Country mini van.

In addition to the house and the cars, we have two legitimate business ventures—a party store and a mobile car wash. Everything we own is in my name. This way, if Shaun ever runs into any legal problems, our possessions will be protected.

Shaun is still in the drug business with his uncle, but now as an equal partner. For the most part, all my man does is dictate and delegate. While I can't wait until he gives up this business for good, I'm still proud of his progress.

I still love God, though my actions may state otherwise. I still attend church regularly and Bible Study occasionally. I am also raising my daughter to be a believer. Shauntae, at five years old, can pray as well as teenagers far more advanced in age.

I believe that my marriage being a success is a result of God's blessing the fact that I am no longer living in sin, but I know He is still not pleased that I am married to a drug dealer who has very little interest in developing a better spiritual relationship. Shaun never attends church with us, but he never hinders my and Shauntae's spiritual growth.

Shyanne is employed as vice-president of Westbrook Enterprises, the company that manages the store and the car wash. She graduated with a Business Management degree from Oakland University. Shyanne is compensated very well for her services. She runs the day-to-day operations for both businesses. I am listed on paper as the company President and CEO.

My actual job, though, is to take care of my husband and daughter. I also paid K.J.'s college tuition. He graduates in

May from Wayne State University, also with a Business Management degree. Kevin is also an employee of Westbrook Enterprises. He's the manager of the party store.

Mama hates that K.J. is involved with Shaun's mess in any way. However, she looks at the tuition payment as a community scholarship (Shaun giving back to the community that he is destroying). She doesn't hassle us, but she cautions me about my lifestyle.

And like I said, my lifestyle has been ostrich feathers all the way. I honestly don't have a clue what the day-to-day operations are of either of the businesses that I "own." I trust my husband and business partners, and that is all there is to that. Shaun pays the mortgage, the car notes, and car insurance and handles all the business areas of our lives. I handle the grocery shopping, the clothes shopping, furniture shopping, etcetera, etcetera . . . I love my lifestyle.

Patricia and Shaun's sisters are well taken care of as well. Shaun has offered to get his mother a bigger house, but she prefers to stay in the hood and live ghetto fabulous.

The only sore spot in our marriage are the relationships Shaun has with the mothers of his other children. We've got baby mama drama up to our elbows. Make that our earlobes, considering I had to kick Keva's tail a couple of weeks ago.

Keva has been salty for the entire five years that Shaun and I have been married. When she came to my house and told me about their affair and the baby, she assumed that I would leave Shaun and he would come running to be with her. So you can only imagine how angry she was when she found out that we were husband and wife. The first three months after we got married, Keva refused to let Shaun see his son. That was devastating for my husband.

Then out of the clear blue sky Keva called to say she needed money for Kevaun's first birthday. Shaun was so happy for the opportunity to see his son. He agreed to give her the money as long as she followed one condition; she was to formally invite me to the party. She reluctantly agreed. Needless to say it was an awkward adventure, and that is stating it mildly.

The party started with us getting directions to the wrong place. Our invitation indicated that the party was going to be at the Chuck E. Cheese in Dearborn. However, when we arrived, we were informed there was no party scheduled for a Kevaun Taylor. Shaun called Keva and when he couldn't reach her, he called Patricia on her cell, who told him that the party was at the location in Dearborn Heights, a forty-five minute drive from where we were.

By the time we got to the party, the birthday cake was already cut, and they were opening the last of the presents. We were already furious about intentionally being given the wrong location, but Keva put the icing on the cake when that heifer opened our present for Kevaun.

Shaun purchased a $250 gift certificate to Toys R Us and another $250 certificate to Kids R Us. When Keva opened the envelopes, that dirty low-down cow announced in front of the entire group of guests, "This is so typical of you, Shaun. You are always throwing your money around. You have time to do everything else you want to do, but you can't find time to shop for a proper present for your son's first birthday. I bet Shauntae doesn't get a gift certificate for her first birthday."

Shaun was livid, but he maintained an outward calm. He didn't want to make a scene in front of all the children in attendance. I, on the other hand, was not so level headed. I practically shoved Shauntae into Shaun's arms and went after Keva with the intention of pounding her head into the size of a pepperoni slice.

Shaun handed our daughter to Francine and caught me

just as I was about to stomp a mud hole in Keva. It took everything in me not to break from his hold, but his soothing words worked their magic and I dismissed Keva.

Francine didn't get off as easily. As I snatched my baby from her on our way out the door, I "accidentally" stomped on her foot . . . really hard. "I'm sorry, Frannie. Please excuse me and my big foot," I said with as much sincerity as I could muster. I still had not forgiven her for the part she played in Shaun's affair with Keva.

Keva's next stunt was taking Shaun to court to obtain a formal child support order. Shaun already gave the witch a weekly allowance, which was large enough to support her and Kevaun. She simply wanted to make trouble. So off to court we went.

"Your honor, I am a struggling single mother. Yet Kevaun's father and his wife live lavishly in a big suburban house, they drive fancy cars, and they take expensive vacations. Shaun is a well know drug-dealer in this city and it is his illicit income that allows him to live so luxuriously," Keva said.

I was shocked speechless and scared stiff, which was a good thing. There was no telling what I might have said or done otherwise. I had no idea Keva was going to play so dirty, and even less of an idea how the judge would react to her last statement. I immediately started praying.

Shaun, as usual, was cool. When it was his turn to address the court he said, "Your honor, Ms. Simpson is a petty young lady and a woman scorned. Her allegations have absolutely no merit. I have financial statements that accurately document every dime earned by my wife and me. I also have receipts of all I have paid to the plaintiff for the support of Kevaun. I think that you will find the amounts to be more than sufficient in accordance with our income. However, your honor, what I don't have is proof that I fathered the plaintiff's son. As you can see in her complaint, she and I

were never married nor was there ever a DNA test performed. Therefore, no actual proof of paternity has been established. I would like to go on record at this time petitioning
the court for a DNA test before any other monies are paid to
Ms. Simpson."

I sat there bug-eyed and speechless for the second time
during these proceedings. I never knew that Shaun doubted
Kevaun's paternity. However, after the day's proceedings
were over, everything ended up settled, and we never set
foot in the courtroom again.

Once the judge set a date for the paternity hearing we left
the courtroom. In the hallway Shaun confronted Keva, giving her an ultimatum. "Keva, not for one second do I doubt
that Kevaun is mine, but if you want to play hardball, then
I'll play with you. You know you are only bringing this child
support suit against me to be spiteful. The money I give you
each week is more than enough to support both you and my
son. If you would rather do it through the courts, that's fine
too. But trust me, by the time my lawyers get through doc-
toring up my books and receipts, any amount awarded by
the judge will be substantially less than what you get now.
So I am asking you right here, right now, one answer only.
What do you want to do?" Shaun stood six inches from
Keva's face waiting for an answer. He was so close I thought
he was going to kiss her, but he wasn't that crazy.

"I'll let it go for now, Shaun, but don't you ever try to
screw me or my son," she replied, then stomped off. Those
were the last words spoken about a child support case or a
paternity test.

Keva's little court stunt also earned her a spot on Patricia's hate list. She stopped dealing with Keva altogether and
would only see Kevaun when he was with Shaun or
Francine. No female messed with Patricia Taylor's son and
got away with it. Even though Keva was on the list, I think
the number one spot was still reserved for me.

Next was the incident two weeks ago that led to Keva getting her butt kicked.

Shyanne and I had just come back to my house after a Saturday afternoon of shopping. We were exhausted. Shaun, Shauntae and Kevaun were at Patricia's house for the birthday party of Frannie's two-year-old son, her second child. When I pulled into my circular driveway, Keva was already parked there sitting in her car.

"Why is this heifer sitting in front of my house?" I asked Shyanne.

"There is only one way to find out," she replied. Shyanne grabbed the bags and went into the house. I went to talk to Keva.

She rolled down her window as I approached. "Why are you sitting out here in the cold, Keva?"

"I'm waiting for Shaun to get back with Kevaun. Is that all right with you, *Mrs. Taylor*?"

I could tell by her tone that we weren't going to have a pleasant conversation, and I was too tired for her mess. I spoke my next words very carefully in an effort to not let my frustrations show. I was irritable and my feet hurt. The last thing I wanted to do was stand in the cold trying to reason with one of Shaun's baby's mamas.

"Keva, this is Shaun's weekend to keep Kevaun. He will spend the night here with us, and Shaun will bring him to you tomorrow."

"Well, something just came up. I need to get Kevaun tonight. Shaun will just have to reschedule his time." I couldn't believe she was talking to me like I was getting on her darn nerves. This caused me to go off on her.

"No, Keva. You will have to make other arrangements. I am sick and tired of you pulling these little capers to aggravate my husband. This is Shaun's weekend and he is keeping Kevaun. If there were some real emergency and you just had to have your son, you would be taking this drama to Patricia's house irritating her instead of arguing with me. Now I suggest that you take your hooptie and leave my driveway right now."

Keva pushed the automatic button and rolled up her window while flipping me the bird with her opposite hand. She put her car in gear getting ready to drive away so I ignored her obscene gesture. I was just glad to see her leave.

I guess Keva changed her mind suddenly because as quickly as she put the car into gear, she threw it back into park and got out.

"You know what I'm sick and tired of, Lindsay? I'm sick of you and your husband thinking you can order me around and get away with it. Who do you think you are, telling me that my son is staying here tonight? I'm his mother, not you. If I say Kevaun leaves with me when Shaun gets back, then he leaves with me."

No this trick was not standing in my face, in my driveway, in front of my house, yelling at me. Keva had truly lost her mind. I was no dummy. I knew this was just another of her attempts to get back at Shaun because he dumped her. But my goodness! It had been five years. Shouldn't she have gotten over it by now? Who lives with bitterness, resentment, and jealousy that long? I guess the answer to that would be bitter, resentful, jealous people.

"Keva, leave my driveway now and go get a life. You are a hateful woman who can't stand it that Shaun and I are happy. Every chance you get you throw one of these little fits to get back at him. I'm telling you here and now that I am not going to stand by and let you use Kevaun to try to hurt my husband."

Keva stepped closer to me and began pointing and wagging her finger in my face. "There you go again telling me what you won't let me do. Telling me what I'm going to do. I am not leaving this house without my son, so you can go on about your funky little business and get out of my face, Lindsay."

I think it was the accidental spit that landed in my face after she said my name that sent me over the edge. The next thing I knew I had Keva's neck wrapped between both my hands and I was banging her head against her car door. I mean come on; I let her get away with calling me Lindsay once. Did she think she I was standing for it twice in one day, especially after she served it up the second time with a little spittle?

Keva pulled at my hands to no avail as she slid down the side of her car. I finally let go of her neck and yanked her by her hair with one hand while punching her senseless with the other. She swung back defensively, but I was not feeling anything. I had lost it. I beat her for every little stunt she had pulled in the last five years, including her very first visit to my house. Everything came back to me in one big rush, and I took it all out on her face.

Shyanne saw the fight from inside the house. She came running, waiting for an opening to join in and help me. But I was all over Keva, leaving no room for my girlfriend to get a lick in edgewise. Shyanne opted for kicking Keva while she lay on the ground.

One of the neighbors must have witnessed the beat down and called the police who seemed to arrive immediately. That's the way it was in the suburbs. The police came right away for something as small as a noise disturbance. In the city, you could get mugged, raped, and shot, and the cops would not show up for hours.

The police broke up the fight and asked us who lived in the home. When I told them it was my house, the female officer led Keva to the squad car to question her there. The male officer remained behind to question Shyanne and me.

"Ma'am, can you tell me what started the fight between you and the other woman?" Mr. Officer asked me.

I gave the cop complete details of how the fight began, leading up to the first punch. This is where I embellished just a bit.

"After going back and forth with Keva for several minutes, I finally got fed up. I told her I was going to call the police and have her arrested for trespassing. That's when she jumped from her car and started punching me in the back as I walked toward my house." I prayed that whoever called the police had not gotten a good look at the entire episode; giving the police a different version than mine.

"My best friend came out of the house to help me after she witnessed the attack." I could see Shyanne doing all she could to keep from laughing out loud as she replied.

"That's correct, officer," was all she could sniggle out.

Ms. Officer returned to our little group to report on Keva's story. "Ms Simpson is being quite uncooperative. The only thing I can get out of her is that she came here to get her son. Then Mrs. Taylor and her friend attacked her. When I ask her for any more details, she gets belligerent."

It was now my turn to hold a straight face. I thanked my Heavenly Father that it was not going to be a case of my word against hers with the police having to decide whose story was more credible. Keva made my case for me by being an idiot.

"Well, it looks like Ms. Simpson will be placed under arrest for trespassing and assault. We are going to have to call a tow truck to impound her car. Then we'll be off to the station with her. The District Attorney's office will be in touch with you so that you can make a formal complaint against Ms. Simpson," Mr. Officer said.

When Shaun came home a few hours later, he insisted we go to the police station and drop the charges. He didn't want any vindictive repercussions from Keva. Shaun figured she would now go out of her way to make it hard for him to see Kevaun.

I gave in without too much argument since I did sort of lie to the police to get her arrested in the first place. Besides, I was satisfied with the whooping I put on her. Risking Shaun's relationship with Kevaun by letting her stay in jail would have been over the top.

Nonetheless, here it is exactly two weeks later, and Shaun has not been able to get in touch with Keva or Kevaun. A couple of weeks without contact would usually not seem so abnormal. However, not only was she not responding to his phone calls or answering her door, she had not gotten the money Shaun left for her at her apartment or with Frannie. When the wench wouldn't go for the cash, there was a problem.

Shaun was naturally thinking the worse. He was freaking out. I've tried to assure him that as soon as Keva gets broke enough she would be in touch with him just like every other time. Shaun was really worried though. He thought my kicking her tail and having her arrested was too much for her to take.

Well, tonight my plan is to take Shaun's mind off of this for just a little while. I planned a wonderful anniversary celebration and I didn't want anything to spoil it.

"Look, Shyanne, either you hurry up or you walk home. My husband and I have plans for tonight that don't include being in the mall. I can't wait until you get married so I can mess up your anniversary."

"Never that, cuz Lady Shy is never getting married. I like being a playa, playa. Ain't that right Shauntae Pooh?" she cooed at my daughter.

"Didn't I just tell you about trying to corrupt my daughter?"

"Oh hush up! You sound like an old lady. That's another reason I'm never getting married; all wives turn into nags. Come on, we can be out of here. I don't like any of these shoes anyway."

I tried my very best to make this a special evening for my husband. Shaun was doing his very best to make it difficult to enjoy. He sat brooding and complaining all through dinner at his favorite restaurant. I could only get him to dance with me once at the nightclub. I made a special request to have the DJ play "For You" by Kenny Lattimore. This was the song we were married to. And now as we sat in our family room on a cozy rug in front of a romantic fire, Shaun looked like he had lost his best friend. He was really taking Keva and Kevaun's disappearance hard.

I sat holding him trying to think of something to say or do that would perk him up. I tried all week to convince him that Keva would surface any day now. I tried getting him to see that he had little to worry about because two weeks was not a very long time. Now I was at a loss for words.

Then I remembered we hadn't done our gift exchange. Shaun had always been thrilled with my reactions to the wonderful gifts he gave me, and I was sure he would be pleased with all the thought I put into his gift.

"How about I go upstairs and get your gift, baby?"

"Fine," was all he said.

As I went upstairs to get the gift that I had spent precious, loving time putting together, I thought about how Shaun was getting on my nerves. It was our anniversary for goodness sake. I hoped he would put aside his self-pity for at least this one day. If he simply tried concentrating on having a wonderful celebration with me, he would start to enjoy himself. Shaun had to know that Keva was far too greedy to stay away for much longer. He was expending too much energy moping and whining. If he didn't get his act together by the time I got back downstairs, he was going to get a none too friendly piece of my mind.

When I got downstairs, Shaun was still sitting in the same spot with the same sad look on his face. Once upon a time, his face would melt me like butter. I had always thought he was so fine. Right now I wanted to slug him in that face just to see the expression change.

I sat down next to Shaun, looking around the room expecting to see my beautifully wrapped present. When I didn't see it, I was not too worried. He had been known to give me great gifts small enough to fit in his pockets. I decided to be patient and I gave him his gift first.

Shaun unwrapped the box unceremoniously and removed the leather burgundy binder. On the cover of the binder was an 8 X 10 photo of Shaun and Shauntae's first picture together. The photo album was titled *All of Me, Daddy*, spelled in small 14 karat gold letters. As Shaun opened the album, he found a vast array of pictures of our daughter filed in chronological order. A few of the photos had Shaun or me in them, but the majority was of Shauntae from birth to five years old. There was a caption describing the date and event of each picture. As he reviewed the book, I saw him smile for the first time in many days.

"This is great, Lindsay. It's better than anything you could have purchased for me. I love it. Thank you, baby."

Shaun pulled me into his arms, hugging me passionately. It felt so good to have him hold me like this that I was reluctant to let him release me, but I wanted my present. As he let me go, Shaun reached into his pants pocket, just as I suspected, to retrieve my gift. I could hardly wait to see what he was hiding in there.

When Shaun pulled out his wad of money, I naturally assumed he was moving it aside so he could get to my gift, which had to be jewelry since it could fit in his pocket. I was so excited I could hardly stand it. But when he started counting off one hundred dollar bills, I was speechless. I refused to believe it when he stopped at twenty-five and handed me the money.

"Here, Lindsay. This is for you. Buy yourself something special. I love you."

I took the money from his outstretched hand, staring at it for a long moment. I looked into his face, waiting, hoping, praying that his expression would reveal this was some sort of prank. Never in all the years Shaun and I have been together had he ever given me money as a celebration present. He had always gone out of his way to give me extra special gifts. I was now shocked down to my toes that he was not kidding when he said, *"Buy yourself something special."*

Shaun must have felt my irritation, because the fool had the dirty nerve to ask, "What's wrong, baby?"

"What do you mean buy myself something special? That was your job, Shaun. You were supposed to buy me something special."

"Lindsay, with everything going on with Keva and her disappearance, I just haven't been in the mood to do any shopping. Will you please forgive me this once, baby?"

"No! I won't forgive you. How could you be so thoughtless about our fifth anniversary? Shaun, I am your wife and the mother of your daughter. Yet you discount me because of a problem you are having with your baby's mama. No way am I letting this slide."

Shaun looked at me like I had grown another head, then he gave a slight humorless chuckle. "What do you mean you are not letting it slide? What are you going to do, leave me? Beat me down? Yes, Lindsay, you are my wife. Because you are my wife I expect you, more than anybody, to understand my distress about losing my son; especially since it's probably your fault that he's gone.

My jaw dropped to the floor like an anchor was attached

to it. I never thought Shaun blamed me for Keva taking Kevaun and leaving. I was puzzled as to why he would feel this way.

"How in God's name can you say it's my fault the dizzy broad ran off with your son?"

"You knew Keva was fragile. You knew that she was having a hard time dealing with our marriage and all that we have. But instead of being sympathetic and compassionate, what do you do? You beat the girl down and have her thrown in jail. You humiliated her, Lindsay. Not even the strongest person can be expected to be that forgiving. Somebody as weak as Keva would definitely have a hard time dealing with what you did to her. And you call yourself a Christian. Always running around talking about how God expects us to behave. Do you think He was pleased with the way you behaved, with the way you're behaving now?"

Okay! Okay! Okay! My head was spinning with the thoughts racing around at a hundred miles a minute. How dare he speak to me like this? How dare he call me on the carpet about my Christianity? As far as I was concerned, Shaun didn't have the right to talk about what God expected from anybody. I was choking on the venom lodged in my throat, so I had to let it out. I stood up from the floor and became very animated as I paced from one end of the room to the other, flailing my arms this way and that as I spoke.

"Wait one Mickey and Minnie Mouse minute, Mr. Taylor. Don't you dare question my relationship with God. What you are suggesting is too big for even the biggest saint. You are sitting there telling me that I am supposed to be understanding and sympathetic to your baby mama drama. Baby mama drama, may I remind you, that came about because you were cheating on me. You want me to take into consideration that even though the witch stood in my driveway, yelling and spitting on me, the fact that she was unstable? I was supposed to take that from the tramp that lied to me the first

time I asked her if she were messing with you? The same
funky little tramp that has been pulling stunts and playing
games with you for the past five years? You, my husband,
want me to play nice with your bed buddy?"

I wore myself out. I took a seat in the nearest chair to
catch my breath. How dare this clown tell me I should have
been nicer to his ex-lover? He should be glad I even toler-
ated her considering how she came into my life. Heck, he
should be counting his blessings over the fact I stayed with
him and continued to be nice to him. Fool!

"You are very selfish, you know that, Lindsay? You got
your man, your child, your big house, and you don't care
about anything or anyone else. With the exception of your
mother, grandmother, brother and Shyanne, there is no one
outside of this house you are concerned about."

I was still too tired to speak, so I shot Shaun a look that
said, *You are absolutely correct. What is so wrong with that?*
I guess we had been together long enough that we knew each
other's looks and body language. He answered my unvoiced
question.

"Lindsay, please don't get me wrong. I love Shauntae with
all my heart, but she is not my only child. I also have two
sons, one of which happened to come under some very painful
circumstances. Nevertheless, I love all my children equally. I
expect you, as my wife, to love them too. I am just as much
a father to Sha'Ron and Kevaun as I am to Shauntae. So just
trade places with me for one second. Imagine if someone ran
off with your daughter. How much concern would you have
about an anniversary present?"

Shaun always had a way of turning things around and
making me out to be the bad guy. But this time I wasn't having it. I wasn't about to let him guilt me into feeling bad.

"That was a nice speech, Shaun, but you can save that bait
for another worm 'cause I'm not biting. This is no longer
about an anniversary present. It is about you disrespecting

me and trying to blame me for your mess ups. How can you expect me to love your sons with the same passion that I have for my daughter?" Shaun tried to interrupt but I cut him off.

"I'm not finished. Sha'Ron was born before you met me. However, because you chose to have a relationship with someone as juvenile as Rhonda, I was never allowed to bond with him. I never got the opportunity to learn to love him. As far as Kevaun is concerned, how can you expect me to be overflowing with love for a child that was conceived out of disrespect to me and our relationship?

"Those are your children, Shaun, and yes, you should love them all equally, but you have no right to demand the same from me. I would never try to keep you from doing your best for your boys, nor would I disassociate my daughter from her brothers. But personally, I don't give a hot ham sandwich if I ever see Keva, or for that matter, Kevaun again."

I knew I didn't mean most of what I had just said. I was still very angry. But in all honesty, I had to recognize some truth in them. I truly hoped that Kevaun was fine, but that was the extent of my concern. Keva could rot in hell.

"You evil witch! I can't stand to be around you right now. I don't give a ham sandwich, or whatever you said, if I ever see you again!"

Those were the last words spoken to me on our fifth wedding anniversary. Shaun got up and left the house, slamming the door on the rest of our celebration.

Chapter Seventeen

"Mama it's been three days since my husband left. I have heard nary a word from him."

"You sound just like your grandmother, talking about nary a word. You two are so much alike until it isn't even funny," Mama said, chuckling.

I couldn't believe it. My world was falling apart, and she was sitting here laughing and joking. Okay, Shaun was not one of Mama's favorite people, but I was hoping she could muster up a little sympathy for me.

I had stopped by my mother's house to talk to her about my predicament with Shaun after I picked Shauntae up from school. She fell asleep in the car, so I laid my baby down in my old bedroom, which Mama kept the same as when I lived here.

When Shaun walked out on me the other day, I was so furious I couldn't care less if he ever came back. I remained mad too, until bedtime the following evening. That's when I started to calm down. I began to think about how very much I still loved my husband. Shaun and Shauntae were the most important people in the world to me. The three of us were a team, a package deal. For me there was not one without the other.

In my calmer state I also accepted that Shaun was right about a few things he said that night. If I loved Shaun as much as I claimed I did, I should have been more sensitive to his situation with Keva. When I forgave him five years ago, I should have begun letting go of the animosity I felt for Keva and even their baby. I held on to my resentment just like she held on to her jealousy for all this time. My actions could have possibly cost me my marriage. If it did, it would be entirely my fault.

Shaun may not have had a true relationship with God, but he was absolutely correct for calling me out about my behavior as a Christian. I should have been more supportive of my husband, and I should have tried to get along better with Keva. I was unaware of Keva's spiritual affiliation, but I suspected that she was lacking in the knowledge of God's ways. I'm a Christian and I knew better. Knowing better meant I was supposed to do better. Last night after I prayed for Shaun's return, God set me straight as He spoke to my heart. Now I just wish I knew where my husband was so I could make it up to him.

Yesterday morning, I really became concerned. Shaun hadn't even called to check on Shauntae. He had never gone more than twenty-four hours without talking to our daughter. When he occasionally leaves town for business, he does his best to at least call Shauntae before I put her to bed. I understand that he is upset with me, but I can't believe he would turn his back on Shauntae.

I became so desperate yesterday that I broke down and called Patricia's house looking for Shaun. I never call Patricia. Ever! She still hates me, so I avoid my mother-in-law at all costs. She certainly had no problem reminding me of that very fact when I called.

"Hello, Patricia. This is Nay-Nay. I called to ask if either you or Sha'Ron have seen or heard from Shaun. He left the house a couple of days ago after an argument and that was the last time I spoke to him. I'm starting to get worried about him."

"You know you got some nerve calling here, little girl. If you ain't the most typical, trifling female I know. You don't call here no other time, but as soon things stop going the way you want them to, you reach out to somebody to help you. You know what? Even if I could help your sorry behind I wouldn't. It's a stone mess when a man lets a woman keep him from being a good father to his children. Shaun don't go too many days without seeing or talking to Sha'Ron. My grandbaby has not seen his daddy since the day of your piti-ful wedding anniversary. I don't know what you have said or done to my son, but you're getting just what you deserve if he ran away and left your tail for good." She slammed the phone down so hard it took five minutes for the ringing in my ears to stop.

How one woman can live with so much hostility and anger is beyond me. Then again, Patricia is probably not like that all the time. Perhaps it is only I that brings out the beast in her. What in the world did I do to make this woman hate me so much? Well, I didn't have time to worry about her or her emotional state right now. I was on a mission to find my hus-band. So again I dialed a number that I otherwise never use. I called my sister-in-law, Francine.

Francine and I have not had a decent conversation since I found out she was instrumental in getting Keva and Shaun together. I hated her and she hated me. This was at least a hate I could understand.

"Hello, Frannie, this is Nay-Nay. I was calling to see if you heard from your brother in the last couple of days. We had a fight and he left. I just want to make sure he's all right."

"My name is Francine. Unlike you, I happen to like my name, and I don't mind using it. Besides, only my friends and family are allowed to call me Frannie. You are neither. My mother just called to warn me that you would probably call. She not so subtly said I should cuss you out if you did. But you know what, Nay? I am a bigger person than that. So I'll tell you. No, I have not seen or heard from my brother in about three or four days. It's my hope, though, that he finally went out of his way to find Keva and Kevaun. I hope he and Keva get back together. You don't deserve him."

Click!

It took everything in me not to push the redial button and cuss that heifer out, but I knew it wouldn't end there. We would just end up going back and forth, and before I would be able to stop myself, I would be on her doorstep trying to get in her house to pound her head through a wall. Right now I didn't have that type of time.

My last call of the morning went to Uncle Bobby. This is who I should have called in the first place. It just showed how warped my mind had become since Shaun left. If anybody knew where he was, it would be Uncle Bobby since they worked so closely together. Shaun never neglected his work no matter what.

However, my big idea proved to be just as fruitless as my first two calls. Uncle Bobby didn't even answer his phone. I left him a voicemail message, but I have yet to receive a return phone call.

That was yesterday. Today I sit in my mother's kitchen no closer to finding my husband and seeking a shoulder to cry on. Mama was probably the last person I should expect to help me grieve over the shattering pieces of my marriage. I wouldn't have been surprised at all if she gave me an I-told-you-so speech.

"Mommy, I am so miserable. What am I going to do if Shaun never comes back? What if he did go searching for Keva and the two of them are together living happily ever after? How are Shauntae and I going to survive without him?

I put my head down on the kitchen table and cried. Mama got up from her chair and came to rub my back. She stroked me gently with both her touch and her words.

"Nay-Nay, I think you're making yourself sick for nothing. Honey, all married couples have fights, arguments, and times when they just don't want to be around one another. I'm sure Shaun will be home in no time at all. I may not like your husband, but I know he loves you and Shauntae too much to stay gone for too long."

At that moment, I wasn't sure if I actually believed Mama's words, but just hearing her say them made me feel better. I felt so blessed that she was my mother. She could have easily and rightfully dismissed me and told me to get over it. She could have been a real monster like Patricia was to her daughters. Patricia never seemed to have a nice word for Francine and Tameeka. *Stupid little tramp* was her pet moniker for them both. Yet I had put my mother through so much, especially when it came to my relationship with Shaun, and she was still always there for me. I loved her so much.

"Thank you, Mama, for always having my back."

"Honey, you know that's what good mothers do. And your mama is the bomb." We both smiled and amazingly, I felt quite a bit better; if only for a little while.

"Now that I have gotten a smile out of you, perhaps you can help me with something. Have you heard from your brother? He left yesterday morning, telling me he was going to work. That was the last I heard from him."

I was lost as to why, but for some reason K.J.'s absence set my nerves on edge again. His and Shaun's disappearance had to be purely coincidental, but I suddenly got the feeling the two incidents were somehow connected.

"Mama, is this the first time Kevin has stayed out overnight without calling?"

"Yes. The only other time he stays away from home is

when he spends the night at your place. I realize Kevin is 22, but I don't care if the boy is 71. If he is still living under my roof, then he will follow my rules. Kevin is not allowed to gallop in and out of my home at all hours of the night or day, and he will keep in touch with me to let me know he is safe so I don't worry."

I couldn't blame Mama one bit. I was getting plenty worried myself. My anxiety quickly turned to nausea.

Mama continued to talk while I sat there in a confused daze. "Kevin has somehow changed too, Nay. I have noticed a difference in him the past few weeks. Nothing I can call bad or good or even specifically pinpoint, but there is definitely a difference. Until now I just attributed it to his growing up; becoming more mature."

I knew exactly what Mama was talking about. Shyanne and I were just teasing Kevin about something similar a week ago in the store.

"What is up with you, Kevin? Lately you been walking around here looking and smelling all good. What? Is there some new lady in your life?" I had asked my little brother as we stood in the back office of the party store.

"Yeah. I noticed some changes too, K.J. You've got this little swagger that you have not always had. If you weren't like a little brother to me, I think I would be trying to holla at you myself," Shyanne had chirped in.

"There's nothing different about me. I have always been fine. You two just never took the time to notice before now," Kevin replied, and we all shared a good laugh.

My mother's voice brought me back to the present. "Have you seen his new car?"

"New car? No. Kevin never mentioned anything about buying a new car. I thought he was cool driving your old Taurus. Whenever I ragged on him about how old his car was, he always said, 'That's okay. It's paid for.' What kind of car did he buy?"

"A brand new 2002 black convertible Mustang. What kind of money are you all paying that boy at the store?"

I personally didn't think a Mustang was an extravagant purchase for a 22-year-old who still lived at home rent free. What else did he have to spend his money on?

"I'm not sure what kind of money Kevin makes. I don't get involved with any of the business at the store. Shaun and Shyanne take care of all that. It's really not that strange for Kevin to buy himself a car though. He has no other expenses since he lives here with you."

Even as the words left my lips I wondered if I were repeating them out loud for Mama's benefit or my own. The whole conversation had gotten me so antsy that my nausea finally got the best of me. I ran from the kitchen straight to the bathroom. I made it to the toilet just in time to let lose the contents in my stomach.

Mama was right on my heels, standing outside the bathroom door when I emerged. (Déjà vu??)

"Nay, are you okay, sweetie?"

"I don't know, Mama. I started feeling sick just a few minutes ago. The last time this happened I found out I was pregnant with Shauntae."

"Well, is it possible that you are pregnant again?"

"I guess it's possible, just not the best timing."

"Honey, that's one thing about babies. They come whether you're ready for them or not. For richer or poorer; for better or worse; in sickness and in health. Babies are the only ones these days that actually live up to the wedding vows." Mama laughed at her own silly joke, then announced, "Come on, baby girl, let's make our way to the women's clinic on Seven Mile before they close to see if the rabbit dies. I'll wake up Shauntae and we can drop her off with Shyanne's parents on the way."

Like I said, déjà vu.

* * *

Why? Why? Why? Why do I always find out I am pregnant in the midst of a crisis with Shaun? Why can't I ever have one of those television commercial scenarios where the wife surprises the husband with the news over a romantic candlelight dinner?

According to the nurse at the clinic, "Your new bundle of joy should arrive around mid-September. You're approximately five weeks along. You and your husband are so blessed." I wanted to slap that silly smile off her face.

I also wondered why they didn't speak to me about abortion like they did when I found out I was pregnant with Shauntae? I guess it's silly to even think about it when there was no way I would consider terminating this pregnancy. I knew I couldn't live with myself no matter what happened between Shaun and me.

As I thought about abortion no longer being an option for me, I also thought about God. Today, as I had so many times in the past, I began to feel guilty about letting my relationship with God take a backseat to my relationship with Shaun. I sat and wondered if I had done more to develop my spiritual self, would my marriage, my life, be in better condition. Then this arena of thinking scared me. I was afraid because I knew deep within my bones, if I had let God lead and guide my life as I should have, Shaun would not be a part of it. I just couldn't deal with any thoughts that led me to life without Shaun. I didn't believe I could handle that.

I sat on my sofa in our living room speculating for the millionth time how I could still be so in love and so attracted to Shaun. I had put up with so much of his crap until it was nowhere near funny anymore. Everything and everybody came before me in our relationship. Not only did he cheat, but he had a child with another woman. He was a freaking drug-dealer, something he has been promising me for years he was going to let go of. And now he had walked out on me and was spending time with only God knew who. Yet for the life of me, I could not imagine trying to live my life without him. I wanted him to come back home.

After I left the clinic and took Mama back home, I was so tired that I called Shyanne and asked if she would swing by her parents' home and pick up Shauntae for me. I told her I would come by in a little while to get her. I just needed a little time by myself to think.

As I sat at home alone, the tears started falling. I had gotten so used to weeping over my relationship that I hadn't even noticed I was crying until the doorbell rang. I wiped my eyes and went to the door with as much energy as I could muster. I was so emotionally drained, it took all I had left to walk from the sofa to the door.

I looked through the peep hole to find a stranger standing on my front porch. I was hesitant to open the door for someone I didn't know, but curiosity about the female on my porch got the best of me.

"May I help you?" I said as I swung the door open.

"Shaun sent me. Can I come in?" she replied. I nearly lost my footing at the mention of Shaun's name, but now I was plenty energized. *Please God not again; not another baby mama.*

"Excuse me? What do you mean Shaun sent you? Who are you?"

She placed her hand on her hip and gave me an incredulous look, like I was getting on her doggone nerve. "Look, I'll answer all of your questions if you just let me in. I know you don't know me, but considering I was sent by your husband, I would think you would be a little anxious to hear what I have to say." The huffy stranger sucked her teeth and rolled her eyes. I was ready to punch a hole through the screen door that separated us and slug her right in those same rolling eyes. But she was correct; my curiosity overrode my anger so I opened the screen door and let her into my home.

She waltzed in, went into the living room and sat on my

Queen Anne chair as if it were her personal throne. I stood in the entryway for a few seconds, staring at her, marveling at her attitude. Finally I joined her in the living room and sat across from her on the sofa.

"What is your name and how do you know my husband?" I asked.

"My name is Toni, and I uh . . . work for Shaun."

Toni was about five foot two inches tall. She was light in complexion, had grey eyes, and pretty long black hair pulled back into a tight ponytail. She was quite attractive. My mind again started conjuring up thoughts of this possibly being another of Shaun's lovers. However, since she exuded such confidence, the last thing I wanted to do was come off as jealous and insecure; at least not until I knew for sure what role she played in Shaun's life. I pushed aside my thoughts and continued my interrogation.

"Do you know where Shaun is?" I asked.

"Yeah. He's in jail."

Okay! So much for my composure. I nearly fell off the couch. I grabbed my chest like Fred Sanford during one of his many heart attacks. I opened my mouth several times to say something, but I could not push the words past the lump in my throat.

Again Toni gave me that annoyed look, but she at least managed a little civility. "Are you okay?"

"No, I'm not!" I screamed, finally managing to find my voice. "What do you mean Shaun is in jail? In jail for what?"

"Wait one minute, Lindsay. Don't start yelling at me. I'm just the messenger. Shaun asked me to come here to let you know where he was. He said that he needed you to get in touch with his attorney."

Toni flopped back onto the cushions of the chair, folding her arms, indicating that she was too through with me. Personally, I gave less than a hot ham sandwich how she felt about me. However, I knew I had to calm down so I could get to the bottom of the situation with Shaun . . . Did she just call me Lindsay?

"All right. Let's start over, beginning with this. Don't call me Lindsay. It's Nay, Nay-Nay or *Mrs. Taylor*. Next, do you have any idea why Shaun was arrested?"

"No. All I know is he called my house collect and asked me to make a three-way call to your cell phone because he couldn't reach you on the home phone. When you didn't answer your cell phone, he asked me to come in person. He needs you to contact his attorney and tell him to get down to the sixth precinct in Detroit as soon as possible."

I just realized that I had left my cell phone upstairs on the nightstand when I went to pick up Shauntae from school, and subsequently, to my mother's house. And I was so caught up in my misery and confusion when I got home that I neglected to check the home phone for calls and messages.

Furthermore, I realized I had no idea who Shaun retained as an attorney; let alone how to get in contact with this individual. It embarrassed the heck out of me, but I had to ask Toni if she knew the information.

"It figures you wouldn't know," Toni said, shaking her head. "Shaun gave me his name. He knew you wouldn't know either. Shaun said he couldn't remember the number off-hand, and the police confiscated his cell phone, so I took the liberty of looking it up myself." She reached into her purse, pulled out a piece of paper with the name and number on it and handed to me.

I snatched the paper with a little force. Ms Toni was starting to push her luck. She was certainly willing to be very helpful to my husband. My inquisitiveness about her position in Shaun's life piqued again.

"How did you say you were acquainted with my husband again?"

"I *said* I worked for him."

"How long has Shaun been in jail?"

"Since yesterday morning. Today was the first time the police let him make a phone call."

Okay, that explained where he had been during the second half of his departure. Where did he spend the first day and a half? I wondered if Ms. Toni had anything to do with making sure he had shelter during that time, but I would never give her the satisfaction of letting her know I was suspicious. I would find out all I needed to know when I talked to Shaun. If necessary, I would *deal* with her later.

"Well, I guess you did what you came here to do. I need to make this phone call and get down to the precinct. You can go now." She was dismissed.

Toni stood up, and I walked her to the door. As I opened the door for her she had a parting comment for me.

"You know what? I can't believe you're being so rude. But if what Shaun and Rhonda say about you is true, I really shouldn't be surprised." She walked out before I had a chance to reply.

I spoke with Shaun's attorney and gave him what little information I had available. He listened, then agreed to meet me here at the precinct at 4:30 P.M. It was now 5:00. I called his office three times since my arrival to the precinct. Each time his secretary told me that he had left more than an hour ago and had not yet returned during either of my repeat calls. I could tell she was becoming a little aggravated with me, but who cared?

I was anxious to find out the details surrounding Shaun's arrest. I also wanted to know what he had been up to since he left our house on the night of our anniversary. In particular, who and what role Ms. Toni truly played in his life.

I tried talking to the officers at the precinct, but they were absolutely no help at all. Each one of them—I talked to four—told me the same thing. Shaun was being held on a drug charge, but they couldn't give me any details. When I inquired about seeing him, they said suspects being held at the precincts were not allowed visitors. I either had to wait for him to be released from custody, or transferred downtown to the county jail. Something told me they were all lying. They were probably just giving him a hard time because he refused to talk to them.

The longer I sat waiting on the attorney, the more upset I became with everybody: Shaun, the lawyer, the police and still, Ms. Toni.

A new police officer, or at least one I had not yet spoken to, entered the front door of the precinct. Before I realized it, I was in his face asking him about Shaun.

"Excuse me, officer. My name is Lindsay Taylor. My husband Shaun is being held here—" That was as far as I got before I was interrupted by the second most beautiful man I have ever seen in my life. Shaun, of course, was the first. But the more I stared at this man, the more my brain waged war as to how true that really was.

"Hello, Mrs. Taylor. I'm Cody Vincini, Shaun's attorney." Mr. Vincini held out his hand for me to shake, and on automatic impulse, I lifted my own in return. I certainly don't remember doing it consciously. I stood mesmerized by this man's handsomeness.

He was six foot three inches tall and about one hundred ninety pounds, each ounce strategically placed in just the right areas. His dark olive complexion and his last name led me to believe he was Italian. He had thick black hair with slight waves combed toward the back of his head, but a few stray strands lay untamed across his forehead. He had dark brown eyes and a voice that sounded like it was made for singing sensual love songs. He was a perfect cross between Ben Affleck from the movie *Armageddon* and Benjamin Bratt, the Native American actor from the television series *Law and Order*. Neither actor is Italian, but the comparison is accurate. Woo! Woo! Woo!

"I'm sorry I'm late, Mrs. Taylor. I stopped to speak with one of Shaun's friends to get as many details as possible before I went in with him."

Not five minutes ago I was ranting and raving about his tardiness. Now all I could say was, "Oh, it is perfectly understandable. It was no problem at all."

I couldn't believe I had so little control over my actions. Never before had any white man had this kind of effect on me. I was actually attracted to this man. I had never been attracted to anyone other than Shaun since the first time I laid eyes on him.

"Have they let you see Shaun since you have been here?" he asked me.

Doing my level best to answer without stumbling over my words I said, "No. They told me there was a policy against precinct suspects receiving visitors."

"Well, they're right. But they bend the rules when they want to. They're being especially hard on Shaun because he refuses to cooperate with them. He has maintained his right to remain silent and not be questioned without the presence of his attorney. I'm assuming you haven't seen your brother yet either. Is that correct?"

If dreamy eyed drunk described my fawning over Shaun's attorney, I was now Sober Joe. His words felt like the equivalent of someone throwing hot coffee in my face.

"What do you mean my brother? Why would I be looking for Kevin here?" The questions sounded stupid to me even as they left my mouth, but I needed Mr. Vincini to tell me that he made a mistake; that my brother was in no way involved in the mess with Shaun.

"You mean no one has told you that Kevin was arrested with Shaun?"

"Arrested with Shaun? For what?" I shouted.

Everyone in the front area of the precinct stopped what

he or she was doing. They were now staring at Shaun's lawyer and me. Mr. Vincini gently grabbed my arm and led me to a bench near the front door. I guess he could tell I was on the verge of hysterics. I was torn up enough over Shaun's being in jail. Now I had to deal with both my husband and my brother facing prison time. How in the world was I going to tell Mama that her son, whom she presumed to be just acting disrespectfully, was actually locked up?

Suddenly I became light headed and nauseous. I hadn't thought about my pregnancy since Toni showed up on my doorstep. Now the reminder came at me with a vengeance. I looked around for the nearest restroom, spotting one behind the big desk where the officers were seated. Without warning, I jumped from my seat and bolted toward the bathroom. Shaun's attorney was right on my heels, and the police were yelling that I couldn't go back there, but I was not to be stopped. Unfortunately the door to the restroom was locked. So right there in front of everyone, I puked. The spasms were so violent that I lost control of my bladder, and I peed myself as well. It was the most embarrassing moment of my life.

I stood there with my head hanging low, my clothes wet, and vomit at my feet. I was just as big a mess on the inside. I fell on the floor in the mess I had made, balling like a big baby. Mr. Vincini bravely approached me and helped me up, just as a female officer approached with a washcloth, towel, and some dark blue clothes that looked like a prison uniform.

Cody accepted the things from the officer and said to me, "Why don't you go in the bathroom, clean yourself up and change. When you are done, go home. I'm sure I'm going to be here a while sorting through all of this with your husband and brother. As soon as I'm done, I'll meet you at your house and give you all the details. I promise."

He spoke so calmly and softly that his voice helped me to compose myself. Mr. Vincini acted as if dealing with funky vomiting wives was in his job description.

"But what about bail money?" I asked naively

"Shaun and Kevin will have to go before a judge before any bail can be set. The earliest that can happen is tomorrow morning, so don't worry about it. Just go home and try to rest until I get there, okay?"

I was again overwhelmed by how sexy he was. Immediately, I started to feel a little bit better. I nodded and let the policewoman lead me into the bathroom so I could at least wash away my physical disarray.

Chapter Eighteen

As I drove home from the precinct, I started to miss my daughter. I stopped by Shyanne's condo to get Shauntae and to give her a blow by blow of all that happened so far. Once she knew all the details, she agreed to come and stay with me for the evening. That way she would be there for me if I needed her for support this evening, and she could get Shauntae off to school if I needed to go to court with Kevin and Shaun in the morning. Shyanne said she would meet me at the house after she tidied up behind her goddaughter. I truly loved my best friend.

Once I got home, I put Shauntae down for the night and took a much needed shower. I stood there under the spray of hot water trying to figure out a way to tell Mama about Kevin. I didn't want her to worry anymore when he didn't come home tonight, but telling her he was in jail wasn't something I was excited about either, especially since I was still so fuzzy about the details. I was sure Kevin hadn't called Mama for the same reasons I dreaded having to talk to her. Even though Kevin was twenty-two, Mama would probably still beat him silly.

After I got out of the shower, I decided to bite the bullet and let Mama know as much as I knew. The thought of her imagining anything worse than jail had happened to her baby made me sad.

Wearing my thick velour bathrobe, I went downstairs to the den to make the phone call. That way I would already be downstairs when Mr. Vincini arrived. Shyanne could let herself in with her key.

Mama, against normal procedure of a two ring minimum, answered the phone on the first ring. She was probably sitting on it, hoping to get a call from Kevin letting her know he was all right.

"Hello!" she answered anxiously.

"Hey, Mama."

"Hey, Nay. Have you heard from your brother yet?" That has always been my mama's way. Straight to the point.

"Yes and no, Mama."

"What do you mean yes and no? What's going on with your brother that you're afraid to tell me?" she yelled.

There was no use telling her to calm down so I could explain, so I just gave it to her in her own way, straight up; no chaser. I explained everything I knew, telling her that I would have more details when Mr. Vincini arrived at my house. Afterward I would call her back and let her know what I found out.

"Nay-Nay, I want you to pick me up in the morning. I'm going to the courthouse with you."

"Mama, I don't think that will be necessary. I'm only going to post bail, then your son will be straight home."

"Nay, don't make me hurt you. I said pick me up. I'm going with you."

She also had a few choice words about my husband getting her baby involved in his mess. I expected her to blame it all on Shaun even though Kevin was an adult, and we were still ignorant to all the facts. But I wasn't about to argue that point with her.

Just as I hung up the phone, the doorbell rang. I sprinted to the door, hoping it was Mr. Vincini with good news, or at the very least, some plausible answers. My heart told me that this whole mess was going to get a lot worse before it got any better though. I opened the door to find Mr. Fine standing on my porch with Shyanne pulling up the rear.

Mr. Vincini stepped aside to let Shyanne enter first, then followed her through the door. "Hello again, Mrs. Taylor," he said as the three of us stood in the entranceway.

"Hello, Mr. Vincini. I would prefer if we put aside the formalities and you called me Lindsay. This is my best friend, Shyanne Kennedy." I was unaware of exactly what I said until I saw Shyanne staring at me like I had a big booger in my nose. Then Mr. Vincini drove her point home.

"On one condition, Lindsay; you must call me Cody." I felt it was too late to tell him then how much I hated my first name. For some reason, I didn't feel the need to.

"Why don't we have a seat so I can bring you up to speed with your husband's case?" he suggested.

"I'll leave you two to talk," Shyanne volunteered. She was normally too nosy to make that kind of declaration. Cody's looks must have had an effect on her too.

"No, Shy. Stay. That way I won't have to repeat it to you later."

We all went into the living room and took a seat. Cody and I sat on the sofa. Shyanne sat across from us in the chair. From the way she looked at Cody, I could tell Shyanne was just as impressed with his beauty as I was. This man was dangerously fine.

"Well, ladies, what we're working with is this; just before I left the precinct, Shaun was formally charged with possession with intent to deliver an unspecified amount of cocaine and assault with intent to do great bodily harm. Both charges are felonies that could carry a concurrent sentence of fifteen years to life in prison."

I almost fainted. My head started spinning and the nausea returned. I immediately left the room as to not have an encore to my performance at the police station. Shyanne came in the bathroom with me. She removed my robe so I would not soil it if I had another accident with my bladder. I was lucky this time, only letting loose the bitter bile in my stomach. Then I realized I hadn't eaten anything other than a bag of potato chips and some cookies since Shaun left.

Shyanne gave me a cool washcloth for my face and stayed with me while I thoroughly rinsed my mouth. Then we went back to the living room to hear the rest of Cody's story. Hopefully there was some trace of a silver lining in this sea of endless clouds.

When we took our seats, Cody asked, "Are you okay, Lindsay? This is the second time tonight you have gotten ill. Maybe you should see a doctor. All this stress could be causing you a physical problem that you are not aware of."

"Actually, it's the third time today, Cody. I'm pregnant."

"Oh wow! Shaun didn't tell me that."

"Shaun doesn't know yet. I just found out today myself. Please don't tell him. I'll let him know the first chance I get to see him," I pleaded. I sounded like a weak little girl. This whole situation was wearing on my nerves.

"Of course not. I would never do anything like that." Cody took hold of both my hands and held them for a long moment. "It's not going to be as bad as you're thinking right now; I promise."

His words and his voice were so gentle that I instantly felt calm. In the midst of the possibility of me losing my husband to prison, I was sitting here getting turned on by his attorney. What kind of wife was I?

Shyanne cleared her throat to get our attention and bring

us back to the matter at hand. "What were you saying about Shaun's charges, Mr. Vincini?"

"Please call me Cody, Shyanne. We are all going to be spending a great deal of time together until this thing is resolved. We might as well be casual."

Why did his statement about us spending lots of time together excite me? I was overheating in my heavy bathrobe. Considering I had on nothing but a t-shirt and panties underneath, I had to keep it on and sweat it out. This attorney-client relationship was going to truly be dangerous.

"As I was saying, Shaun's charges carry a heavy sentence. From what he told me, they will be hard to beat."

My emotions were a terrible wreck. It was as if I were riding a huge unbalanced seesaw. I went from being unbelievably distraught over my husband's situation to being turned on by another man and back again. Shyanne saw me stressing and excused herself to get me some juice.

"What exactly did Shaun tell you, Cody?"

"Shaun's explanation is this. He was driving and your brother was riding shotgun in his friend, Jamo's, car. They were pulled over for failing to signal before a left turn. Unbeknownst to Shaun, the blinker in the car was not operating properly."

Shyanne re-entered the room handing me my juice. She cordially brought a glass for Cody too.

"Thanks, Shyanne." Cody took a swallow from his glass and continued with Shaun's story. "The broken blinker turned out to be the least of their problems. The car's license plate was also linked to an assault that took place a few days prior. That gave the police the right to search the car. In the trunk they found a bloody tire iron in the door panels and two kilos of cocaine."

Where is that silver lining? This is getting unbearable. The more Cody talked, the worse things seemed. What happened to his promise? I put my head in my hand and folded

my arm against my waist, taking short breaths to keep myself from crying out loud. Shyanne must have thought I was
hyperventilating because she came over and started rubbing
my back, instructing me to breathe. Cody moved to the side
to make room for her and I felt the absence of his warmth
immediately. There went that seesaw again. Shyanne was
the next to speak.

"Cody, you said Shaun was charged. What happened to
Kevin?"

"Between Shaun and I, we were able to convince the police that Kevin was merely Shaun's brother-in-law catching a
ride home from school. His being a college student and having no prior contact with the police helped too. He was released, and I dropped him off at home on my way here."

Finally! I was beginning to see some traces of silver. I
wasn't going to celebrate that victory too much though. I
was sure there was more to Kevin's story than meets the eye.
For now, I wouldn't worry about it. I would get the low down
from Kevin later. I was just glad he was home with Mama.
There was no need for me to call her now as I promised earlier. I was sure that Kevin was giving her his version of the
day's events. I'm certain she was eating the same cocka-
mamie tale they had fed the police.

"So what now, Cody?" It felt good just to say his name.

"Either tonight or tomorrow morning, Shaun will be transferred downtown to the county jail. He will go before a judge
tomorrow morning for arraignment and bail will be set.
Shaun has no criminal record, but the judge will more than
likely be hard on him due to the seriousness of the charges.
The bail will be quite high. I'm going to request that he be released on a personal bond, but it will be denied."

"So how much money are we talking about?" I asked.

"Anywhere from one hundred thousand to half million
dollars."

"Dang!" Shy exclaimed. I thought she was going to faint and throw up this time.

"The drug charge is what will garner the most attention. Two kilos is a lot of cocaine. But you won't have to post the full amount. Ten percent of the ordered bail will be due. So we are really only talking about ten to fifty thousand dollars. Shaun said it would be no problem."

Shaun was right. The money would not be an issue. We kept much more than that in a safe hidden in the ground of the garage. It always made me nervous when I would see the amounts of cash Shaun kept at our home, but now I was glad it was right at my disposal.

"I'll have the money. Where do I need to show up with it?"

"The arraignment will take place at Thirty-six District Court. However, I don't advise you take the money there. It will be in your best interest if you got a bail bondsman to insure Shaun's bond right after the exam. Look, just meet me downstairs in the lobby of the courthouse at nine A.M. We will handle everything from there." Cody grabbed one of my hands again and smiled. I began to see more traces of silver in his perfect set of pearly white teeth.

"I'll be there. Thank you for everything, Cody. I had no idea what to do about any of this. You have been a tremendous help. I'm glad you're Shaun's attorney." I smiled at him, wondering if my last statement had a double meaning.

Shyanne and I both walked Cody to the door and said goodnight. As soon as he was out the door, Shyanne attacked me in the entranceway.

"What was going on between you and Cody? Since when do you keep secrets from me heifer?"

"What do you mean? There is nothing going on between me and Cody. What secret have I kept from you?"

Shyanne folded her arms across her chest and reduced her eyes to mere slits. She rocked back on the heels of her bare feet, starring at me for long seconds before she said another word. "You mean to tell me you have never met Cody before today?"

"No," was my simple and truthful answer.

"Well, all I can say is, be glad Shaun is locked up and the two of you didn't meet in his presence. There were some serious sparks flying between you and Cody. If there was a gas leak in the house, there would have been a huge explosion."

I walked back into the living room and laid down on the sofa staring at the ceiling. There was no point denying my attraction to Cody. Shyanne knew me better than I knew myself.

My desire for Cody was unreasonable at best. I loved Shaun so much. I never imagined I would ever feel like this about another man. In just a few short hours, Cody's beauty had rearranged the stability of my dysfunctional marriage. While I was *unsure* about why I was so devoted to Shaun with all he had put me through, my actual devotion could never be questioned.

"Well, I'm sure the sparks were only coming from one direction, not passing between us as you suggested. Cody was not thinking about me. He was nothing other than professional and courteous," I explained to Shyanne as she sat Indian style on the floor.

"Please! Professional and courteous my butt. That man was feeling you and feeling on you. All that hand touching. I started to excuse myself so you two could be alone. I was sure you were going to go at it right here on the sofa." Shyanne and I both started laughing.

After we composed ourselves, I asked, "Do you really think Cody was attracted to me too, Shy? The man saw me covered in vomit and urine for goodness sake. How could he be attracted to a pregnant disorderly mess like me?"

"Trust me, *Lindsay*. There was some sexual tension between you two. I couldn't believe you let him call you by your first name." I laughed again. I couldn't believe it either.

"Well it doesn't matter anyway. He is Shaun's attorney and Shaun is my husband. You know better than most how much I love my husband. Anything I feel for Cody is strictly physical. I would never cheat on Shaun or God, especially not for a cheap sexual thrill."

"Okey dokey pokey. I will say this and then I'm going to bed. Please be careful tomorrow around Shaun. Stevie Wonder, Ray Charles, and Blind Mellow Jelly, whoever he is, could see that the two of you were *feeling* something for one another."

Shyanne and I straightened the living room, taking the juice glasses into the kitchen, then made our way upstairs for bed. I stopped suddenly about half way up when a very disturbing thought hit me.

"Oh God! What if we're all together and Cody calls me Lindsay? Shaun knows that privilege is reserved strictly for him."

"Like I said . . . be vewy, vewy carefwul. Huh! Huh! Huh! Huh!" Shyanne said in a poor imitation of Elmer Fudd. Then she ran upstairs to the guest room, laughing her fool head off.

The following morning, I arrived at the courthouse at nine o'clock on the dot. This time Cody wasn't late. He was already there waiting for me, or so I thought. He spotted me as I came into the lobby and he made his way over.

"Hey, Lindsay. Glad to see you made it on time. I've been here since eight this morning. I had to take care of another client."

So much for thinking he made a point of being on time just for me. Part of me wished he was thinking that way. He looked like a god standing there in his crisp navy blue suit, white shirt, and yellow and navy print tie. I wanted to run to the bathroom and check my face to make sure I was not drooling. Hopefully I wouldn't be running to the bathroom for anything else. Morning sickness had kicked in full swing when I got out of bed.

"Hello, Cody. You look nice." Oh no, did I just say that out loud?

"Thank you. So do you," he replied as he blushed. Somehow it made him even more appealing, if that were at all possible.

We stood staring for a few seconds until I found words to break the awkward silence.

"Well, I've got fifty thousand dollars in cash in my purse. I'm very uncomfortable having this much money on my person," I whispered. Big mistake, because it meant I had to stand closer to Cody.

"Don't worry, Lindsay, there's armed security throughout the courthouse. As soon as the judge sets bail, we will go across the street to the bail bondsman. Let's just hope Shaun's case gets called before the judge recesses for lunch." Cody gave me his breathtaking smile, and we headed toward the elevators up to the courtroom where the arraignment was to take place.

The elevator going up was extremely crowded, so Cody and I had to stand body to body all the way to the seventh floor. By the time we reached our destination, I was covered in a thin layer of perspiration and more than a little turned on. Shyanne was right. There was no way Shaun could witness Cody and me together. I was totally out of control.

Thankfully, Shaun's case was called before lunch. The judge set bail at three hundred fifty thousand dollars. Cody informed the judge that Shaun waived his right to a preliminary exam, whatever that meant.

I got a look at Shaun for the first time in more than four days. Even though he was a little rumpled and unshaven, he was still beautiful to me. He searched the courtroom when he entered. I could tell he was looking for me. When he saw me sitting in the second row, he gave me a brief smile. And right then and there I knew that regardless of how sexy I found Cody, Shaun would always be the only man I would ever love. The only man I ever wanted to be with physically, emotionally, and in every way possible.

Right after bail was set, Shaun was led away again. Cody and I rushed from the courtroom to the bail bondsman's office. Cody did all the talking. I just handed over the money.

Now I stood downstairs in the lobby of the county jail, alone thankfully, waiting for Shaun. Cody had to leave to deal with yet another client. He told me to tell Shaun to call him as soon as he got home and settled so they could arrange a meeting to discuss their next move.

"I'll see you later, Lindsay," he said as he left.

I kept my mouth shut tightly and just waved goodbye. I didn't want to get any more dialogue started between us, then have Shaun walk in and see the look that Shyanne said was so obvious.

When Shaun finally entered the lobby, I became nervous. Even though I missed him and was worried sick about him and our relationship, I didn't know what to say to him. The last time I spoke to my husband he told me he didn't care if he ever saw me again. I wondered if he still felt the same way. I stood rooted in my spot until he approached me.

Shaun came to where I stood, placed his soft hands on both sides of my face and smiled. Then he kissed me lightly on the lips and gave me a full hug. As much as I enjoyed Cody's touches, they were nothing compared to what I felt right now. I was sure that even if Cody were right there with us, there would be no more sparks flying.

Shaun released me from the bear hug after several seconds, then stared into my face again and simply said, "Let's get out of here and go home."

I drove home because Shaun was uncomfortable driving my BMW 325i. He said the baby blue coloring on the two-seater made it look like a woman's car. It was a good thing too, because he was asleep before we left the parking lot. He probably hadn't had a decent night's rest since being arrested.

As I drove, I began to wonder how well he slept before he was arrested; more importantly, where he slept before he was arrested, and most importantly, who the heck he slept with. My mind immediately filled with images of the sassy Ms. Toni. I glanced at Shaun's sleeping form, deciding to let him get his rest instead of waking him with my concerns. He was going to need it. There were a million and one questions he needed to answer when he awoke.

Shaun woke up instantly as I pulled into the driveway. He climbed from the car and ran to the door, leaving me alone to put the car in the garage. I knew his urgency. He could not wait to see Shauntae.

I entered the house through the door off the garage and found Shyanne in the kitchen by herself.

"Your man almost knocked me down trying to get up the stairs to find Shauntae. Then your daughter practically deafened me yelling 'Daddy' at the top of her lungs when she saw him. The members of your family are rude." Shyanne is always the clown.

"I offer my sincerest apologies on behalf of my daughter and husband."

"So what happened at court?"

"Nothing much so far. I paid thirty-five thousand dollars to bail him out. Now he's here. He's supposed to call Cody so they can get together to discuss their next course of action."

"Any more fireworks between you and the S.I.A.?"

"S.I.A.? What does that mean?"

"Sexy Italian attorney."

I truly loved my best friend. "No, silly. The moment I saw my husband, his eyes extinguished all those little fires."

Shyanne looked at me like she was not convinced, but I was certain that seesaw ride had ended.

"What did Shaun say when you told him you were pregnant?"

I totally forgot about this pregnancy again. Unless I was puking my guts out, it seemed I couldn't remember I was carrying another child. I guess the look on my face told Shyanne all she needed to know.

"Why didn't you tell him?" she asked.

"I forgot. Besides, the time hasn't been right yet. Shaun fell asleep as soon as we got in the car."

"I see. You're waiting for *just* the right moment. Let me see if I can help you figure out when that might be. Your man is facing up to life in prison, which could begin who knows when. So the stress of that alone will keep him occupied for at least a couple of months." Shyanne had an attitude now, and she was being very sarcastic. "I know. We will just hope for the minimum sentence. Cody said about fifteen years, right? Then you can just tell him when he gets out of jail. *Like you should have done today.*"

I dreaded these moments when Shyanne would get on her soapbox about my marriage. She didn't understand all that went into making things work, especially in a relationship as delicate as Shaun's and mine. Shyanne had never been married. I don't think she has ever really been in love. Yet she felt she was the authority on what was best for me and my man.

"Once again, big mouth, you don't know what you're talking about. I know what is best for me and Shaun, not you. You don't have the right to tell me what to do when it comes to my marriage. Please let me handle this."

Shyanne put her hands on her hips and shook her head at me like I was the biggest dummy in the world. "You just don't get it do you, Nay? This is not about me butting into your relationship. This is about you and the way you have handled your life since the moment you met Shaun. You have carried on with this reckless abandonment. Screw the world and everybody in it. Forget about God even, as long as you have your precious Shaun."

I could tell she was about to go off on one of her tirades. I pulled her into the cold garage so Shaun would not hear us arguing.

"What are you raging about now, Shyanne?" I asked after we were safely out of the kitchen and shivering in the garage.

"Nay, I cannot believe this is where you are in your life. Either you don't see it or you don't care."

Okay now I felt as stupid as the look Shyanne gave me, because I truly had no clue what she was talking about. "Where am I, Shy? I have a husband who loves me. I have a beautiful daughter and another child on the way. I own a beautiful home and profitable businesses. Yes! Shaun and I have issues, but all married couples do. It's not the problems that make or break the marriage. It is the way you handle them. And personally I think Shaun and I have done okay."

Again Shyanne shook her head at me, this time with her arms wrapped around herself. She held onto herself tightly, looking like she was wrestling with herself to keep from choking me. "My God, Nay, you are married to a drug dealer. A drug dealer, I might add, who is faced with possibly spending the rest of his life in prison. You don't see anything wrong with that?"

"Is that what this is all about? Shaun's occupation?"

Shyanne threw her arms up high, rolled her eyes to the ceiling, and gave a chuckle that held no humor. "Occupation! Is that what you call it? Your man is not a doctor or an accountant, Nay. He is a criminal."

"Hold up, Shyanne. You are way out of line." She cut me off before I had a chance to finish my sentence.

"I may be out of line, but am I wrong?"

I ignored her question because I felt it was totally irrelevant. She knew what Shaun did before I married him. Now all of a sudden it's a problem? Today it is a sin; five years ago it was the best thing that could have happened to me.

"Why today, Shy? Why is what Shaun does for a living a crime today? And why don't you have a problem working for that criminal?" I was tired of her sanctimonious attitude. It was time to turn the tables a little bit and give her a taste of her own medicine.

"Nay, it didn't become a crime today. It has always been a crime. However, when you got married, we were twenty years old. Now I don't know about you, but I have aged five years and hopefully I have matured some in those years. Also, when you married Shaun, he promised he would go legit; he would get out of the drug game. He pacified you with the store and the car wash and then got deeper involved in his uncle's organization. Nay, you and I both know that there are only three ways out of this. He either walks away on his own, hopefully to start something prosperous for his family; he goes to prison, the option that is staring him in the face, or he ends up dead."

Shyanne's rationale knocked all the fight out of me. I was broken and she was correct as usual. I stood there shaking, unable to discern whether it was from the cold or the good scolding I just received. As bad as I felt, my best friend was not done with me yet.

"You're right, Nay, I work for Shaun and he pays me well. But my *occupation* is legitimate. If and when he goes to jail, or worse, I'll get another job. I have a college degree. It's a good thing too, because it looks like I'm going to have to be the father figure to your two children eventually, one way or the other."

Shyanne gave me one last look, this one more compassionate than the others, and then returned to the kitchen. I followed behind her after a few seconds with my proverbial tail between my legs. Not even Mama had come at me about Shaun the way Shyanne just did.

Despite the fact that Shyanne always gave it to me straight, I could never get mad at her. Her words would sting and wound deep down to my soul, but I knew they were always uttered from the depths of her heart. I truly loved my best friend. I just wished she would understand my devotion to my husband.

We entered the kitchen just as Shaun did. "Hey, you two. Shauntae is out like a light. What in the world were you doing in the garage?"

"Just having some girl talk," Shy answered and moved past Shaun into the breakfast nook without even glancing his way. She was disappointed in me, but I could tell she was angry at Shaun.

"Is everything all right?" he asked. Shyanne looked at me as if she expected me to tell Shaun right then and there that I wanted a divorce or something. Shaun saw the look, then looked at me too.

"Everything is cool, Shaun. Shy and I are just having one of our moments."

"Okay, cool. I hope you were able to work through it. Shy I need you to keep Shauntae for us tonight. My wife and I have some catching up to do. If you don't mind, we'll drop her off on our way out for the evening."

Shyanne was spitting daggers at him with her eyes, but he was oblivious to her feelings for him at that moment. I stood there silently praying that she would not attack him with what she gave me in the garage.

"No problem, Shaun. I always enjoy spending time with my goddaughter. I'm going home now so I can get some rest. *Our* little girl is a bundle of energy." Then she abruptly left the kitchen to get her things.

"Are you sure everything is cool between you two? Shy seems a little upset."

"We're fine, Shaun. Shy is just concerned about everything that's happened to you with the arrest. She's worried about me, Shauntae, and the baby because we don't know what's going to happen to you in the future." It was as honest as I could be with him about our conversation. Lying to him completely would have been a big mistake. Shaun has mental telepathy when it comes to me. He knows what I'm feeling or thinking all the time, sometimes before I do.

"Hold up, Lindsay. Did you say baby? What baby? Who's pregnant, you or Shyanne?"

I was unaware of my faux pas until Shaun reintroduced it. "I am. I'm about five weeks along."

Shaun wiped down the front of his face with his hand then stood and stared at me for a few brief moments. "Man!"

That one word said a lot, but it was still an incomplete thought. "Are you upset about the pregnancy?"

"I wouldn't say I'm upset, Lindsay. It's just not the best time to have another baby. Cody said he was straight with you about what I'm facing. I may not even be around for a while. We don't need to add another child to this already complicated equation."

"I'm keeping the baby, Shaun, no matter what. It's ours and I want it." I was calm and adamant, and I meant what I said.

"Look, baby, we will talk about it all later. Right now I've got a million phone calls to make, the first one being to Cody. Have you spoken with Kevin since he got out?"

I hadn't even thought about my little brother since Cody told me he was home safe, but I did have some questions for him. "No. I'm going to go over to the store now while Shauntae is napping and you're making your phone calls."

I wanted to ask Shaun how he could let my little brother get caught up in this mess, but I figured I would hear Kevin's side of the story first. I would just add that to the list of things Shaun and I needed to discuss while we were out tonight.

"Cool. We will hook up when you get back. By then I'll have some information from Cody to give to you. I'll see you when you get back. I love you." Shaun gave me a slow passionate kiss, then headed up the stairs through the kitchen. I grabbed my purse and headed out the door, going to the party store we owned. I should be able to catch Kevin at work now.

Chapter Nineteen

"What's up, little brother?" I asked Kevin as I walked into the back office of the store. Kevin sat behind the desk dealing with what looked like a mountain of paper work. I guess things got a little behind while he was out working his *second job*.

"Hey, sis. Have you talked to your best friend today? I tried calling Shyanne at home but she didn't answer. She has instructed me that calling her cell phone is a no-no unless the store is on fire. Since I only have a few questions for her, I wasn't about to make that mistake," he replied.

"Shyanne just left my house a little while ago. She spent the night with me so she could keep Shauntae while I went to bail my husband out of jail. Know anything about that?" I asked sarcastically.

Kevin stopped rumbling through the papers long enough to hang his head and look embarrassed. His reaction said pretty much all I needed to know. Kevin was a willing participant in Shaun's business and not just along for the ride, so to speak.

"Look, Nay," I cut Kevin off with the wave of my hand and

stood looming over him next to the chair he sat in at the desk.

"No, you look, Kevin. What were you thinking? Are you trying to give Mama a heart attack or send her to prison for murdering you? Why did you get involved with Shaun's organization?" I yelled so loud I'm sure I scared away any customers that may have been up front.

"I'm so sorry, Nay-Nay. I wasn't thinking. I saw all that you and Shaun have and I got greedy. So I asked Shaun to put me on. He was hesitant at first, but I kept pestering him, so he gave me a little work."

"I want to know exactly what you did for Shaun."

Kevin's ruddy red skin was tinged an even deeper shade of rouge. It was so good to see that my baby brother was indeed sorry about what he had done. Embarrassment oozed from his skin like cheap cologne.

"Because I was your brother, Shaun said he wouldn't start me at the bottom like he did other new guys. He was also impressed with the job I did here at the store, so he knew I had a good head on my shoulders. So I began my work with him as a sergeant, and my job was to collect the money twice a day from each house."

I walked away from Kevin to put some distance between us. At that moment I felt more like his mother than his big sister. I wanted to whack him over the head with my shoe. I eventually came back and sat down in a chair in front of the desk. The office was small; therefore, I was still actually in striking distance if I decided to take a swing at him. I took some deep breaths to calm myself. It was difficult for me to distinguish which emotion was stronger: anger or sadness.

"Kevin, I hear what you're saying about seeing all that Shaun and I have, but I still don't get it. Doesn't Shaun pay you well for the job you do here? And if you really wanted something that you couldn't afford, all you had to do was ask me. You know that. So again I ask, why?"

"Nay I'm a 22-year-old man. I shouldn't have to ask my big sister to take care of me. I wanted to be able to take care of myself, get things for myself without needing yours or Mama's permission or approval. And look at Shaun. You all have that big house. He owns this store. He drives an SUV and a Corvette. Shaun makes it all look so easy; as if he doesn't have a care in the world other than taking care of you and his kids.

"Yeah, the money I make here is cool, but going about it that way would mean I had to save for quite a while to move and furnish my own place, and I would have had to finance my Mustang. Working with Shaun, my ride is paid for and I had less than thirty days to go before I could have been out of Mama's house and on my own."

I sat in the chair as my emotions became clear. Any trace of anger I possessed drained from my body. I was now sure that all I felt was pain, hard and strong. I couldn't believe it. Everything Shyanne said earlier was true. My life and my relationship with Shaun were costing me more than I even began to realize. My own little brother was willing to risk jail or death just to be like my husband. What was I doing to my family?

I put my head down on the desk and began to silently cry. Kevin came around to comfort me, obviously feeling like he was the cause of my tears. He had no clue that he was a victim in the circle of my life.

"Nay, I apologize. I promise I'll never do anything this stupid again. That one night I spent in a jail cell was more than enough to teach me a lesson. Besides, I also got a good look at what that kind of business entails. There is so much more to it than what I saw Shaun doing on the surface. These are brutal young guys with brutal attitudes. It was scary, Nay. In the short time I worked for Shaun, I met two guys that ended up dead. I don't know the circumstances. All I know is these two dudes were here one day and now they are gone." I looked into Kevin's face and saw shame and fear plastered all over his features.

"I'm sorry you had to witness that, K.J., but I'm glad to know you won't do it again. If anything ever happened to you, I could never forgive myself nor would Mama ever forgive me."

"This was in no way your fault, Nay. Mama can't blame you for my greed and stupidity."

I let the matter drop without elaboration of the real truth since it was over. I now had to figure out what changes I was going to make to protect my family.

"So what's up with Shaun? What's going to happen to him now?" Kevin asked.

"I'm not totally sure yet myself. He's at home now talking to his attorney trying to figure out some sort of strategy."

Kevin went back to his seat behind the desk and stared off into space for a few moments. He looked as if he had something serious on his mind, and it had nothing to do with the mountain of paperwork on his desk.

"What's wrong, Kevin?" He turned his head to look in my direction, but I could tell he was not actually seeing me. It was as if he were looking right through me, trying to see inside of me. His face was again shadowed in fear. His fear terrified me.

"Tell me what's wrong, Kevin. Now!" I shouted

"When those two guys I met got killed, it freaked me out, Lindsay." I knew this was serious because Kevin has never called me by my first name. I didn't comment or correct him however. My brother was dealing with something that was far more menacing than my ugly name. "I didn't know them, and I don't know what really happened to them other than they were found together shot to death in one of their cars. But if I understand correctly, Nay, there is going to be another murder before this whole situation with Shaun is put to rest."

Kevin's words knocked the wind from my lungs. I felt myself getting nauseous again. I fought down the urge to vomit because I was desperate to know why he felt someone else was going to get killed soon.

"What do you know, K.J.?"

Kevin began explaining what happened on the day he and Shaun were arrested. "Shaun asked Jamo if he could use his car to make a run because he had paid some little kids to wash the Vette and the kids weren't done yet. Shaun had no idea the dope was in the car, and he didn't know anything about the car having any defects. Shaun felt Jamo should have let him know what was up. He said because that fool Jamo neglected to handle his business and put him up on the car being hot, he was about to face some serious time in prison. Shaun said he couldn't let that ride."

"Oh my God! Are you sure you heard him correctly, Kevin?"

Kevin stood up and started pacing the floor. "I'm one hundred percent certain. I asked Shaun why he didn't just tell the police the drugs belonged to the person who owned the car, but he wasn't even trying to hear me. He said being a snitch was the worst thing a person in his line of work could be. It would cost him everything. I tried explaining that if he went to prison for life, not telling was going to cost him everything anyway."

I sat there mesmerized by what my brother was telling me. I could not believe how naively I had been living my life for almost nine years. I knew the dope game was vicious, but I neglected to think of my own husband in those terms. Was Shaun capable of murder?

"I truly hope you are wrong, Kevin. I'm on my way home to get ready for a night out with Shaun now. I'll talk to him, and if it is true I will talk him out of it."

Kevin shook his head like he thought my idea was unfeasible, but he said, "I hope so, Nay. I don't want to hear about anybody else I know getting murdered."

"Stay away from this mess, Kevin, do you understand me?" I commanded my little brother.

"Trust me. I am so far away that it isn't even funny. That little bit of time I spent locked up was all the wake up call I needed."

I gathered my things and made ready to leave. I stood looking at my little brother for a few seconds before I headed for the door. I guess he really did look like Daddy. For the first time in more than twenty years, I wished that our father had been a better man and stuck around for us. His leaving us made it easy to blame all the wrongs in my life on him.

One thing I know for sure; Kevin's quick about face in the drug game was not only a result of his short jail bid, but more so an effect of Mama raising us to know and depend on God. Kevin may not have said it, but I'm sure he prayed while he was locked up, promising God he would repent if He got him out of that mess.

I kept my thoughts to myself and gave Kevin a hug. "I love you, K.J." I couldn't remember the last time I said that to him.

"Be careful, Nay. I love you too." Nor the last time he said it to me.

"Baby, it's so good to spend some time together; just you and me. You were all I thought about while they had me in their little cage," Shaun said between bites of his food. We were dining at the Whitney, one of his favorite restaurants, and he was truly enjoying his meal.

I sat barely touching my dinner because I had too much on my mind. When Shaun asked about my appetite, I feigned an upset stomach due to the pregnancy, one of the many items on the agenda Shaun and I needed to discuss tonight. I didn't want to ruin his meal, so I patiently waited until we left the restaurant. We were in the car before I started talking about all of our issues.

"Shaun, what did your attorney say about your case?"

Shaun reached over and grabbed my hand, holding it while he drove. It took him a few moments before he answered. I knew then it wasn't going to be good news. "Cody thinks it's best for me to consider taking a plea bargain with the District Attorney on my case. Under the circumstances, I think he's right. They have me dead to rights on the cocaine possession, and they did find the weapon used in an assault crime in the car I was driving."

"But, Shaun, it wasn't your car. It was Jamo's. Why don't you just tell the police that? The car is registered in his name, right?"

"It is not that simple out here in the streets, Lindsay. Even if I did tell them that, it doesn't automatically prove that the stuff was not mine. It would be Jamo's word against mine. Besides, I'm not about to put on a snitch jacket and live the rest of my life being viewed as a punk.

I was stunned. He was repeating what Kevin told me earlier. I prayed he wouldn't tell me he was going to kill Jamo. I couldn't stand to hear him say it. I diverted to something else before he went there. "Shaun, I understand you not wanting to wear a snitch label, but we are talking about them putting you away for fifteen years or more."

"Not necessarily, sweetheart. If I take the plea and not go to trial, Cody says he can get them to drop the assault charge and change the drug charge from possession with intent to simple possession. Since I don't have a prior record, Cody can probably get the D.A. to agree to a sentence of one to five. I could be out in about three-sixty-five, love."

I squeezed Shaun's hand and closed my eyes. I was so relieved. That was the best news I had heard in the past four days. Then just as quickly as the relief came, the sadness returned. My life had been reduced from being a young, naïve Christian girl, to being a drug-dealer's wife who was happy that her husband would now be a convicted felon who only had to serve a year in prison.

"That would mean I would be locked up when you give birth to the baby, Lindsay. I would miss out on being in the delivery room again. I don't want to do that to you again, baby. I want to be there for you when you go through that again. I really wish you would reconsider your decision to go through with this pregnancy."

How dare he sit here opening up old wounds? I guess he just happened to forget why he missed the delivery of our daughter? I started to go there with him, but I figured it just wasn't worth it. I didn't want to rerun any part of the argument we had on our anniversary. God had already corrected me about that mess. Besides, we had too much else to discuss right now.

I kept my eyes closed, but I pulled my hand from Shaun's and placed it in my lap. When I opened my eyes again, I took a deep breath and reiterated my position on terminating my pregnancy. "I'm keeping this baby, Shaun," I said with the same authority and unwavering firmness as I did when I told him I was pregnant.

Shaun obviously understood that I wasn't changing my mind, so he let the subject drop. We rode in silence the rest of the way home. I used the time to gather the rest of my thoughts regarding everything else we needed to discuss.

When we arrived home, Shaun went into the living room and started a fire in the fireplace. He then went into the kitchen to get some champagne glasses and a bottle of expensive champagne. When he returned, I was sitting on the sofa. Shaun gently pulled me onto the floor with him. He poured champagne into both glasses and then held his up for a toast. I lifted mine as a gesture as well.

"Lindsay, things have been difficult to say the least for the past few days. I want to thank you for keeping your head on straight and for being there for me. I know you must have been frantic not knowing where I was after I walked out on you, but you have handled everything so gracefully. I am happier than you will ever know that you are my wife."

Shaun drank from his glass. I set mine on the table. When he gave me an inquisitive look I simply said, "The baby."

I was moved by his words. God knows I love my husband. It was nice to know he acknowledged and appreciated me. But I was not going to let him woo me with words. Shaun may not think as highly of me by the time we went to bed tonight.

I pulled two throw pillows from the sofa, resting one behind my back as I leaned against the couch and the other under my legs. I made myself comfortable as I prepared to talk about some very uncomfortable topics. One being his *employee*, Toni, and the other his former employee, Kevin.

"Shaun, I want to talk about Toni, the woman you sent here to tell me you were in jail. What is your relationship with her?" I asked in as non-accusatory tone as I could muster.

"Toni is Rhonda's cousin. She works for me as a sergeant. She is someone I can trust to handle pick up money. I told her to make sure she let you know the only relationship she and I had was a working one. Didn't she tell you that?"

"Yes she did, but it wouldn't be the first time you gave me only half the story about your relationship with a female. Keva was just Frannie's friend, remember?" I knew I was pushing the envelope so to speak. There was no way Rhonda would stand for her cousin having any other type of relationship with Shaun and still be cool with her. Toni mentioned that she and Rhonda had talked about me, so I knew they were cordial.

Shaun shifted around on the floor, and his features became uncomfortable. A sadness washed over his face, and I momentarily regretted bringing up Keva. I knew Shaun still missed and worried about Kevaun.

I recovered quickly though. Shaun brought this all on himself. I was getting tired of taking the blame for all of our unhappiness. It was time for him to be accountable for the position he had placed us in right now. I had to go a little Shyanne on him.

"Look, Shaun. You are my husband and I love you with all that I am. From the first day I met you in the grocery store you have been my life. Now the life I have been living has been turned upside down. I don't know whether I'm coming or going. This is not what I signed up for. You have promised me year after year that you were getting out of the street game, and I believed you. Now five years later, here I sit, the mother of one, pregnant with another, and my husband is on his way to prison. I am stepmother to a child born of your infidelity and another child I barely know because his mother hates me."

With each word I had spoken to Shaun, I had become more and more upset. I got up from the floor and moved to the sofa. Shaun got up too, but he moved to the chair. As always he was in tune with my mood, and he knew I wanted some space between us.

Shaun opened his mouth to speak, but I interrupted because I already knew what he was going to say.

"Don't apologize yet, Shaun, because I'm not finished. You see, it's not just me anymore. My children are going to be affected by your selfishness, your greed, and my inability to see beyond the love I have for you. Shaun, I appreciate that you know how much I love you, but it's that same love that could have possibly landed my little brother in prison for twenty years. In turn, my mother would have been crushed. This is affecting my whole family."

Shaun sat quietly, looking at me as if he were seeing me for the first time ever. He looked like I felt after Shyanne said basically the same things to me.

"I see that you are feeling me, Shaun; that you are absorbing and understanding everything I'm saying. I don't give a hot ham sandwich about the money, this house, those cars, nothing. All I care about now is preserving my family and holding onto my sanity. So the ball is now in your court."

I got up from the sofa, leaving Shaun sitting in the living room staring after my retreating back. I headed up the stairs and into our bedroom. I undressed, took a nice long hot shower and put myself to bed snugly under the covers. I felt at ease and peaceful for what seemed like the first time in the nine years I had known my husband.

I meant every word I said to Shaun. It was do or die time for our marriage. He was either going to have to honor the promises he had been making since we married, or he was going to have to leave my life and let me grieve the loss of this relationship. But I promised myself if that indeed became the case, it would be my final loss. I was going to hold onto my children, my brother, my mother, and my best friend from this point on.

Shaun came up about an hour later. He assumed I was sleeping, so he followed my regimen. He undressed, took a shower, and climbed into bed beside me. He wrapped his warm freshly soap scented arms around my body and held on for dear life. When he felt me stir in an effort to get closer to him, he realized I was awake.

"You are so right, Lindsay. I have been selfish and greedy under the guise of doing what's best for my family, including my mother and sisters. We have all enjoyed the benefits of my money without thinking about the consequences my lifestyle brings. I thought I was so careful, so smart by avoiding the police and the D.E.A. Then I got caught on a humble. Somebody else's bad."

Shaun paused and nuzzled the back of my neck with his warm nose. He reached around to hold both my hands in his. "I don't know what's going to happen with my case; if Cody can cut a deal with the Assistant Attorney General or not. But if he can and I can get away with doing a year or less, I want you to wait on me, Lindsay. Once I get home, I promise, I swear, I pledge that I won't go back to the streets. I'll go back to school, I'll get my degree, and I'll legitimatize everything we have. I'll be your husband. I'll be a father to my children, and I will be a son-in-law your mother can be proud of." Shaun knew that would make me laugh.

I turned over to face him and looked into his face to search for sincerity. Our bedroom was dark, but I stared anyway hoping I could find truth in his eyes. Shaun grabbed me and began caressing my body before I had a chance to complete my search. Before I knew it, we were done making love and I fell asleep with just another promise in my heart that I prayed he would keep this time.

Chapter Twenty

The following day, both Shaun and I met with Cody to get more information on his case. I presumed that since I had Shaun back in my life, the original attraction I felt for Cody would not surface. I was so wrong. Several times during our visit, Cody and I made eye contact. I had to look away quickly so I wouldn't get caught staring at his beautiful face.

I sat listening to Cody speak to Shaun, marveling at not only how gorgeous he was, but also how smart, articulate, and very knowledgeable he was about the workings of the law. He could also hold a pretty street savvy conversation as well. Cody and Shaun bantered on and on about the ins and outs of the drug game and how it related to Shaun's current predicament.

"Shaun, I have talked to the assistant Attorney General, Theresa Barnes, twice. She is really trying to give me a hard time. Theresa knows she pretty much has you dead to rights, so getting probation or a suspended sentence is going to be out of the question. However, in order to save the government the cost of a full-scale trial, she is willing to plead you down to simple possession and drop the assault charge since you have no priors."

I fidgeted in my chair as I listened to Cody. While I was concerned about my husband's future, it was the delicious man Shaun chose as his attorney that mesmerized me. Shaun noticed my discomfort.

"Lindsay, are you all right? Are you nauseous, baby?"

"I have a private restroom, Lindsay, if you need to use it," Cody said as a help.

I almost fainted when he casually used my first name in front of Shaun. Big mouth! All I could do was pray that either Shaun paid little attention to it, or he assumed Cody said it because he'd said it.

"Cody, Lindsay prefers to be called either Nay or Nay-Nay. She dislikes her first name. Using it is a privilege reserved just for me," Shaun told him.

Oh please! Oh please! Oh please! Let Cody not push the issue, Lord. My husband's senses were too keen for him not to realize there was an attraction here, especially if Cody said I never informed him of any objection to my name.

"I'm sorry. I think she and Shyanne did mention that the other day. It won't happen again, Nay." Cody said with straight-faced sincerity.

Thank you, God. Cody's apology and explanation seemed so natural. If I didn't know the truth myself, I would swear he was speaking from complete honesty. I guess that is why he's a lawyer that makes the big bucks.

Cody looked at me and smiled, but the gesture never quite reached his eyes. They were saying something I was unable to read. I figured now was as good a time as any to take him up on his invitation to use his restroom. I needed to escape the sudden tension I felt.

"Uh . . . Mr. Vincini, I mean . . . uh, Cody. I probably should use your restroom if you don't mind," I stuttered. I acted like a dork who wanted her husband to know she was physically feigning for his attorney.

"Sure. It's right through that door on the left. The one on the right is my closet. Please don't go in there and throw up." Both Cody and Shaun chuckled at his joke. I got up quickly and made my escape.

Once I was securely inside the bathroom, I leaned against the door and took some deep breaths. I was a little queasy, but I didn't need to vomit. I just needed to get out of the office before Shaun started feeling that I was feeling Cody. Why did he have to be so fine, smart, and even funny? I stayed in the bathroom a few moments to compose myself. I splashed some cold water on my face trying my best to clear my head of visions of Cody and me in a serious lip-lock. *Where did that come from?*

"Lord, please help me here. You came through for me out there with Cody's story about my name. Please stop me from being so attracted to him before I get both of us killed."

"Who are you talking to in there, Lindsay?" Shaun heard me praying and came to the door.

"Uh, I . . . was . . . speaking to the baby. I was asking him or her to um . . . give me a break on the morning sickness," I lied. "I'll be out in a minute."

"Are you sure, baby?"

"Yes, Shaun. I'm cool."

I took a few more deep breaths and tried thinking about something really dull to take my mind off Cody's aura. When I returned to the office, Cody was saying something about federal time versus state time.

"See, Shaun, with state time, you get sentenced from a minimum to a maximum amount of years. With the feds, however, you get a flat sentence. An in-date and an out-date, and you have to do every day of that sentence. No good behavior decreases or anything like that. As long as you stay out of trouble, Nay, here will know exactly what day to pick you up." This man was good. He used my nickname like he had been doing it all his life.

"So give me your best guess on what my sentence could be," Shaun said.

"I would say anywhere between two and five years."

"Five years!" I blurted.

"Calm down, Lindsay. That's just the maximum. I'm sure our boy here will do his best to shave off as much time as possible," Shaun assured me.

"Yes, little lady. Let's think positive here. Shaun's been a model citizen up until now, so we should hope for the best."

But be prepared for the worst, I thought.

"Shaun, I really wish you would have just told the police the drugs and the tire iron belonged to Jamo at the start of this whole mess," I whined as we walked into our home. I was so glad to be away from Cody's office and his beautiful smile.

"That is not the way I roll. I will never wear a snitch jacket."

We both went into the kitchen. I poured myself some juice, and I gave Shaun a glass of water. We sat at the kitchen table and talked more about what our future was going to be like.

"I understand the code of the streets, but this is going to affect our entire lives. You could go to prison for up to five years. How am I supposed to raise two kids alone for that amount of time?"

"I'm sure I won't get the five-year sentence. But even if the worst case scenario prevails, you will have more than enough to stay afloat while I'm gone. Since the properties, the store and the car wash are in your name, you don't have to worry about the FEDs taking them away from us. There is more than enough money stashed in the garage safe to last while I'm gone, even if I have to do the max."

This man had no idea what I was talking about. All he cared about was money. What about his wife and kids? Not once did he mention how we were supposed to get along as a family without a husband and a father.

"What about your children, Shaun? I'm going to have a baby that won't even know you when you come home."

Shaun looked at me cocked eyed and crazy. "I am not going on that guilt trip with you, Lindsay. I gave you the same explanation, but you refused to discuss it with me. You are the one determined to carry this baby full term—" I stopped him with the customary talk to the hand gesture.

"Abortion is not something I am discussing. I am having this baby. It is not his or her fault that you are in the predicament you're in. I have asked and begged you—" It was now his turn to stop me.

"All right, baby. Stop yelling. Let's not go there again. We are where we are. The situation is what it is. We can't change it now. What we have to do is hope for the best outcome and make the best of it for each other. Okay?"

I didn't answer since I felt the question was rhetorical, but reality set in with a raw fierceness. I started to feel pressured and stressed and the nausea returned. I headed to the bathroom without bothering to excuse myself.

I stood over the toilet bowl retching this morning's breakfast. If memory served me correctly, I was not this sick when I carried Shauntae. It worried me. I wondered if the stress of our current situation caused me to throw up so much more often. How was my child going to receive the necessary nourishment if I was unable to hold down any food?

Then I went from being upset to feeling guilty. If I had left Shaun when I found out about Keva and Kevaun, I wouldn't be faced with this mess. However, I would also not be blessed with this baby.

But there was still today. I could walk out right now and make my own way for my children. Shaun's inevitable prison stint could be just the push I needed to take myself out of this lifestyle and start fresh and clean.

Yeah, right. Who was I kidding? Even with everything I had gone through with Shaun, I still loved him as much as I ever did. As far as I was concerned, there was no life without him; locked up or not. I was determined to stand with him through this ordeal just as I had with all the others. I knew once he came home he would keep his promise, and we would begin living normal everyday lives.

I made up my mind right then that I would go back to school and finish my degree in something. There was still time, before the baby came, to enroll and complete at least one semester. By the time Shaun came home, I could get a job and we could be the typical husband and wife, two-income family. Shoot! I could get my degree in Business Administration or Management like Shyanne and Kevin. We could expand on our current business and all work together as one cohesive family unit. I instantly began to feel better now that I had a plan to better my family.

When I returned to the kitchen where Shaun still sat, I was wearing a big grin. I was at peace. Shaun looked perplexed, but decided against questioning my renewed spirit.

"This is the first time you have come out of the bathroom grinning after throwing up. But you know what? I'm not going to even ask why. It is just good to see you smiling and happy for a change." Knowing how well Shaun could read my mind, he probably already knew why I was smiling.

I grabbed hold of his hands and they were ice cold, so much so that the simple touch chilled my whole body. The temperature outside was freezing, but we had been in the house long enough for his hands to have warmed by now. I slowly removed my own hands and rubbed them together to reheat them.

I stared at Shaun, and he gave me an apologetic look as he placed each hand between his thighs. Gazing into Shaun's eyes, I pondered whether or not the frost that settled in my bones was from the cold.

Three months later, as if this ordeal was not painful enough, I had to sit in the court with Patricia, Uncle Bobby, Francine, Tameeka, and of all people, Rhonda, as the judge announced Shaun's fate. Thank goodness Shyanne was with me. There had still been no trace of Keva or Kevaun in the nearly ten months since she left. Shaun was sentenced to serve two years in a minimum-security federal prison in West Virginia. The distance between West Virginia and Detroit could be covered with a seven hour drive or ninety-minute plane ride.

We were allowed a few brief moments to say our good-byes before he was taken into custody. Patricia bum rushed past me and led her crew to the defendants' table first, which was about thirty feet from where we were seated. I started to pull rank, but decided to just let her go first. I stayed in the background as they gave their hugs and kisses. Cody came to where Shyanne and I sat and held my hand while the real live version of the *Adam's Family* said good-bye.

"Don't worry, Lindsay. This time will fly by. Before you know it, you will have your husband back. West Virginia is just a quick plane ride away. You can get a relatively inexpensive flight, visit and be back home in the same day," Cody said as he smiled.

I returned his smile while feeling totally uncomfortable as Cody held my hand. With Shaun being as close as he was, I was certain my husband could feel the heat radiating from my body due to Cody's nearness. Three months had passed, and I was no less attracted to him than the very first day I laid eyes on him.

"Thank you, Cody. I'm sure it was because of your legal expertise that my husband received such a minimal sentence. I appreciate everything you have done for us."

I was amazed at how calm my voice sounded considering my insides were stirring with desire.

Cody placed his free hand on my back and gave it a quick rub. Then he gave my hand a final squeeze. "I'll be in touch." And then he left the courtroom.

My eyes trailed him as he went through the double doors. I didn't even realize I was staring until I saw the last of the idiots walk out a few seconds behind him, and I heard Shaun calling my name. I shook myself from my trance, and Shyanne and I walked to where Shaun stood. Shyanne said goodbye first.

"Take care of yourself in there and don't worry about Nay. I'll take care of her out here." She then directed her words to me. "Nay, I'll meet you outside. I need to go out to the car and check my phone to make sure everything is cool with Kevin at the store. We are expecting a big delivery today of some new stock." Shyanne hugged Shaun quickly then left.

I looked Shaun directly in his eyes to see if I could read exactly what he was feeling. I saw no fear in the green reflection that I loved. Shaun had the nerve to look like going to prison was something he did every day. He has always been so very strong.

"Well, Lindsay. This is it. You're going to be okay, right, baby?" I couldn't answer due to the strong rush of emotions that assaulted me. Before I knew it, I was standing there crying like an infant. "Oh baby, please don't do this. This is hard enough on me. I need you to be strong. Be happy that your man will only be gone a short while. I'll be home in no time. Recognize that we are better off than a lot of other people I know whose family can't visit them. In just six short weeks, you can come up and see me. Keep your head up and know that I love you more than anything in this world."

I pulled myself together and forced myself to be strong like he asked me to. "Okay, Shaun. I'll be a rock for you. I'll hold it down out here. I promise I'll make you proud while you are away. When you come home you will be very grateful I'm the woman you're married to."

"That's my girl. Kiss my baby girl for me." We both decided it was best not to have Shauntae at the proceedings. She spent the night with my mother, who took her to school for us this morning. Shaun sat with her last night and did his best to explain that he would be gone for a while without actually telling her where he was going.

The guards came over just then and informed Shaun it was time to go. They were about to put the handcuffs on him, but he asked for just a few seconds. Before they had a chance to object or consent, Shaun grabbed me and hugged me very tightly. It was the best and the worst hug I ever received from him.

When he released me, the guards put the cuffs on him and led him away. I stood there and just as he was going through the door, I yelled out and told him I loved him. Then I blew him a quick kiss. Just as he disappeared the same chill that ran through my body three months ago in our kitchen reappeared. I recognized it instantly. I knew that my life would forever be changed from this moment on.

I slowly left the courtroom and went to my car where Shyanne was waiting. As I approached the parking lot I could see she was crying. I ran the short distance to the car to find out why.

"What's wrong, Shy? Why are you crying?"

"Jamo's dead, Nay!"

PART III

THE BEGINNING OF THE END

Chapter Twenty-One

October 2002

I thought the second delivery was supposed to be easier than the first. The amount of pain I was in was unbelievable. It's already been six hours, and it looked as if I were going to be in labor longer than I was with Shauntae.

The contractions were darn near killing me, but I flat out refused the epidural Shyanne kept suggesting. The thought of having someone stick a long needle in my back was far more frightening than the pain of the contractions.

"No . . . needles . . . Shy," I yelled. I was right in the middle of a strong contraction. They were now coming every two to three minutes.

"Okay! Fine, Nay. I won't mention the epidural anymore. Just calm down, and try to concentrate on breathing through the contraction."

I really appreciated my best friend being here with me again as I delivered my second child. This time she had to do it alone because Mama and Granny were out of town at a funeral. But Lord help me. If she tried to tell me one more time how to get through this delivery, I was going to slap the taste out of her mouth.

"Stop telling me what to do, Shyanne. I don't want to breathe. I don't want an epidural. I don't want anything other than this baby out," I screamed.

Just as I finished my tirade, my obstetrician appeared. "Did I hear something about an epidural in all that yelling? Well, let's hope we are beyond that stage now. How about we take a look to see where we are."

Dr. Howard seemed to have a permanent smile. That very smile often comforted me during the stress of both my pregnancies. But right now I wanted to smash my I.V. pole into her face just to see if she would still be smiling. What did she mean *we*?

"Just as I thought. We are all ready for delivery. I'm going to get everyone assembled and we will push that little bundle of joy right on out of there."

"Thank God," Shyanne said.

"Shut up, cry baby," I yelled at her.

It has been two and a half hours since they brought my son to me for his feeding. I still haven't been able to put him down. He is just as beautiful as his sister. I may have been shady toward God, but His mercy has been so very prevalent in my life. I knew that it was a blessing from Him that both my children were healthy and gorgeous.

I was so excited when the doctor announced I delivered a boy. I was hoping for a son to complete my set and to name after my husband. Shaun and I decided just before he went away that we didn't want to know the sex of our baby until it was born. We figured the suspense would add some excitement and fun to an otherwise unhappy time in our lives.

In the five months since Shaun's incarceration I have visited him five times, usually on an every-three-week basis. However, it's been four weeks since I last saw him. Dr.

Howard prohibited me from flying during the last month of my pregnancy. Shaun decided that I should not drive to see him either.

Shaun seemed to be handling being in prison a lot better than I was. He says it's really not so bad. As long as he has plenty of money in his account, he would be okay. He spends his time reading and taking prison offered classes. His mother and sisters visit about once a month also. However, we are never there at the same time. Shaun and I talk on the telephone three times a week. The worst part for him is doing the actual time and being away from his family.

My plan is to visit him just after the baby's two-week check up. I won't take either of my children though. Shaun figures it is best for Shauntae to remember him the way he was before he was locked up. Since she's still so young—she turns six next month—he figures she will be better off not knowing about his spending time in prison. We tell her that Daddy is away taking care of family out of town. The baby will only be a little more than a year old when Shaun gets out.

Shyanne has held true to her word as usual. She has been my rock, my coach, my sounding board, and my shoulder to cry on since Shaun has been away. And for a change, I got the chance to be all that for her as well when Jamo was killed. Though Shyanne and Jamo were no longer going together when he died, they remained good friends. She never fell deeply in love with Jamo, but she did care for him a great deal.

Fortunately for me, I never told Shyanne about Kevin's story on Shaun's plan for revenge. Shyanne assumes that Jamo was just another casualty of the street game. That's the only secret I have ever kept from my best friend, and it is one I'll take to my grave.

During the first two weeks after the funeral, I was a wreck for two reasons. One, I was scared, knowing that my very own husband was more than likely responsible for taking another person's life. Secondly the guilt of not telling Shyanne the probable truth tore me apart.

I got over my guilt and fear quickly as I began to settle into life with Shaun in prison. The more I missed him, the more I figured that Jamo got what he deserved. I blamed him for Shaun's arrest and prison time. After all, the dope, the weapon, and the car belonged to him. It was his stupidity that cost my husband this time away from me and our children.

I have not yet made it back to school to complete my degree. My entire pregnancy was difficult, and I remained sick well into the beginning of my last trimester. I had to be hospitalized for dehydration twice. On a couple of occasions, Dr. Howard would caution me about flying to see Shaun, but I ignored her, never telling Shaun about her restrictions. I refused to let anything keep me from my time with Shaun. Whenever he asked about my and the baby's progression, I would tell him everything was normal. And as I look into the precious face of my baby, I can see how blessed I am that everything did turn out well. He looks just like Shaun and Shauntae.

My children are the most important people in this world to me. It's amazing how much I love my son, and I have only known him for a few short hours. I felt the exact same way when Shauntae was born.

When a woman gives birth to a child, after looking into their eyes even that very first time, she knows in that moment that she would die and kill to keep them safe. This overwhelming rush of responsibility and fierce protectiveness took over my whole heart and soul. I would do whatever it takes to make sure they have all they need in this life to succeed. If the possibility existed that I could shield them from ever feeling a moment's pain or heartache by throwing myself in front of a moving train, I would do it without hesitation.

Shyanne would probably disagree that I feel all of this for my children. She believes the only person I love that strongly is my husband. And yes. I do love Shaun with the same intensity, but still it is different. As much as I hate to think about it, and I seriously doubt it would ever happen, I do realize that Shaun could leave me at any given moment. He can walk away, get a divorce, and no longer be my husband. But no one can take my babies from me. No matter what they do or where they go, the fact will always remain that they came from my body. They will always be mine.

In giving it serious thought, I know that about Shyanne too. No matter what we go through or how much we disagree, we will always be there for each other. Our bond is strong and unique because it is not necessarily natural.

As parents, we love our children because we are bound to them by blood and natural instinct. The same could hold true for sibling and all familial love. Even the love between a man and a woman is natural because it has been that way since the beginning of time. But the love of a friend is different. There is no blood to bind us or a physical attraction that blossoms into a passionate love. Shyanne and I have built our love on mutual trust, respect and admiration. It is instinctual out of habit, not nature.

All this brought to mind a very strange question; one that is not so easy to answer. Shaun is my husband and the father of my children, who are the most important people in the world to me. Therefore, if I had to make a choice between my children and my husband, I would choose my children. I described what I felt for Shyanne as being similar to what I feel for my children. So if a situation ever arose and I was forced to choose between my husband and my best friend, whom would I choose?

Wow!

* * *

"I'm here, Old Mother Hubbard; coming to take the little old lady in the shoe home," Shyanne sang as she waltzed into my hospital room.

"I can hardly be compared to the little old lady in the shoe. I only have two kids, Shy."

"Whatever. It's two more than I want."

I just shook my head at her silly butt. She was always popping off about not wanting kids and not wanting to be bothered with them. But every chance she gets, she's spending time with Shauntae. I'm sure she'll be the same way with her godson.

I was anxious to get home myself. Shaun and I hadn't had the opportunity to talk since I gave birth to Lil' Shaun. Shaun is aware that his baby has been born. Shyanne called his mother to inform her, and I'm positive she has since talked to Shaun. Shyanne asked Patricia to make a three way call to my hospital room the next time Shaun called, but I knew the odds of that happening were slim to a snowball's chance in hell.

Dr. Howard came in soon after Shyanne to give me a quick once over and the okay to leave. "Everything looks fine here, Mrs. Taylor. You can get dressed and take your beautiful son on home. I will see you in six weeks." Then she departed with her ever-present smile.

"All right, Shy. Let's be out of here. We can swing by Mama's to pick up Shauntae. I want her to meet her baby brother."

On the ride to Mama's, Shyanne filled me in on what's been going on at the store and about the new guy she's dating that she met at church. She also made other small talk, which is really not Shyanne's style. Knowing my best friend the way I did, I recognized she was babbling to cover something that bothered her.

"What's wrong, Shyanne?"

"What makes you ask that?" Shyanne asked nervously.

"This is me, Shyanne."

"I'll give you all the details when we leave your mother's."

She was silent the remaining quarter of a mile to Mama's house. We stayed with Mama for a short time while she ooh'd and aah'd over her grandson, then we left and headed to my house. With Shauntae now in the car, I decided not to press Shyanne for information, but the moment we got in my house and got the kids settled, I was on her like funk on fish.

"Okay, Shy, what's up?" We were seated in the kitchen and Shyanne was making lunch.

"Two FBI agents came in to the store yesterday asking to see the owner. I told them you were in the hospital, having just given birth to a baby. Then they asked a lot of questions about Shaun and his Uncle Bobby."

"What kinds of questions?"

"They had a picture of Uncle Bobby and asked if I knew him. I told them I did, that he was your husband's uncle. They asked if I had seen him lately and I told them no."

"What did they say about Shaun?"

"They asked if he were co-owner of the business, and I told them you were sole proprietor. They asked if the two of you jointly owned property or any other businesses. I told them that was something they had to discuss with you. They left after that, telling me to let you know they would be in touch soon."

Great! This was all I needed. I was about to become the subject of an FBI investigation because of my husband and his crooked uncle. Why now? Shaun has been in jail for five months. What in the world was I supposed to say to these people? I didn't know a darn thing. Shaun and I never discussed his business. I was clueless to even the mundane matters, such as the location of the titles to the store, the house, or even our vehicles.

"Shy, did they give you any indication when I should expect them to contact me?"

"Nope."

"Thanks a lot, Shy. You are always such a big help," I replied sarcastically.

"Hey! Don't get an attitude with me. I don't know any more about your husband's affairs than you do, so I can't help you with this one, Nay."

"I'm sorry, Shy." My apology was weak because I was too busy trying to sort through this mess. Shoot! I deserved the comfortable lifestyle I had become accustomed to. I have put up with and gone through hell in this relationship. Now the FBI was threatening to take it all away. I sat right there at the kitchen table and began praying, asking God to have Shaun contact me before the FBI did.

The following evening, soon after I put Shauntae to bed, my prayer was answered. I was in the process of placing Lil' Shaun down after his feeding just as the phone rang and the chipper recorded female voice proceeded to ask if I would accept the collect call from a correctional facility. After giving my consent, the call was put through, and I was on the line with my husband.

"Hey, Lindsay. How are you doing? I've missed talking with you so much. How was the delivery? How is my son?" Shaun excitedly quizzed. He sounded like Shyanne.

At the mention of the delivery, my heart sank just a bit. It brought back painful thoughts of Shaun not being there for the birth of either of our children. He was with Rhonda at the birth of Sha'Ron and Keva for Kevaun's birth. I was so jealous. But now was not the time to dwell on those things. I had to work on maintaining my lifestyle for my children and myself. Neither Keva nor Rhonda could say they lived as well as I did.

"I'm fine, honey. Lil' Shaun is gorgeous and healthy. I just finished feeding him, and now he's sleeping soundly in his crib."

"That is the kind of news I like to hear. It is practically killing me that I'm here and not there with you all, but I'm doing my best to work through it. I've only got a short time, so I have to preserve my sanity in order to do the time and not have the time do me."

"That is what I like to hear. Stay positive, baby." I believe that Shaun gave those little pep talks for my benefit as much as his own. He knew I was in a constant state of worry while he was in prison. This was his way of taking some of the edge away.

"Shaun, I really hate to interrupt such a pleasant conversation with other matters, but, honey, we have got a problem. Shyanne said the FBI came to the store the other day asking her questions." I gave Shaun the details just as Shyanne had given them to me and waited for him to tell me what to do.

"Baby, if that's the problem you're speaking about, then there is no problem. When they contact you all you have to do is give them Cody's card. Tell them that any questions they may have can be answered by your attorney. As a matter of fact, first thing tomorrow, give Cody a call. Tell him what you just told me. He'll handle everything, I'm sure."

At the mention of Cody's name, my face became flushed. For the first time since Shaun's incarceration I was glad that he was away and unable to see my reaction. I was in awe that after all this time, Cody still had such a profound effect on my libido. I honestly hadn't thought about him since the last time I saw him. Yet at just the mere mention of his name, my body instantly heated. And I'd just had a baby for goodness sake.

I talked with Shaun for the remainder of the time he had left, then I went to lie down to get some rest before Lil' Shaun's next feeding. While I napped, I dreamt of Cody, seeing his face over and over in my subconscious state. Even though it had been months since I last saw him, I could remember every beautiful contour of his features as clearly as if he were standing in front of me. I remembered his smile, his intellect, his wit, and his touches.

Shyanne insisted there was chemistry between me and the S.I.A. (Sexy Italian Attorney) as she called him, and that it wasn't one-sided as I believed. But after Shaun's incarceration, I never heard from him again. If he were attracted to me, I would think he would have come up with some reason to see me again. I'm sure Shyanne was wrong.

Then again, Cody could simply be acting on ethics and morals. He knows I'm a married woman, so he was doing what's right and keeping it strictly professional. Somehow that thought only served to make me think more fondly of him.

That evening after I had lain down for the night, or at least until the baby woke me up, I dreamt that Cody and I were making love. I awoke for Lil' Shaun's three A.M. feeding, and surprisingly, not a trace of guilt accompanied me in my conscious state. After the feeding I went back to sleep eagerly anticipating making the phone call later in the morning.

"No, I insist. You just came home from the hospital. It would be better if I came to your house."

"Okay, if you insist, Cody. Thanks a lot. I really appreciate you responding so quickly."

"You don't have to thank me for dong my job, Lindsay. I'll see you at about eleven thirty." Then he disconnected the call.

I was surprised and fascinated at how effortlessly he reverted to using my first name. I was so anxious to see him. Eleven thirty gave me ninety minutes to get ready. I ran around the house for the next forty-five minutes making sure everything was spotless. I even cleaned my bedroom and changed my sheets. Uh . . . oh! What was I thinking? It wasn't like his visit was going to end in there. I pulled the reins on my wayward thoughts and decided to call Shyanne to come and act as a chaperone.

After getting Shyanne to agree to come and sit with the Lil' Shaun while I had my meeting with Cody (at least that is the line I fed her) I jumped into the shower. Shyanne would only have the one child to contend with since Shauntae was in school. Once my cleansing was complete, I put on the prettiest fragrance of lotion I had, then attempted to step into a pair of tight fitting Guess jeans. My body said *guess* again. The jeans only came as far as my knees. I *guess* I forgot that I had just given birth four days ago and had gained twenty pounds since I last wore those jeans. Now what was I supposed to do? The last thing I wanted was for Cody to see me looking like Myrna Moose.

I searched my closet again for a cute loose fitting dress, but realized I didn't own anything like that. I finally settled on a pink and blue Nike sweat suit with an elastic waist-band. I was going for the sporty, yet sexy look. I pulled my hair back into a cute ponytail, letting a few loose wisps of hair hang around my face. I applied moisturizer to my skin, and I put dark pink lip-liner and light pink lip-gloss on my lips to give them the pouty look. When I was all done I was pleased with what I saw.

However, I was unsure of what I felt. Here I was going out of my way to look attractive for a man who was not my husband. Never before meeting Cody had I been the least bit interested in any man other than Shaun. But I was wanting Cody and wanting him to want me. What God must be thinking of me now. But in the very next breath, I felt that I had a right to have Cody if only for a little while because of all the crap that Shaun had put me through. I knew God was not in agreement, but my mind was made up.

As I came down the stairs, Shyanne entered the front door. "Don't you look cute!" she exclaimed.

"Thank you," I replied and did a spin move as I reached the bottom of the steps.

I contemplated telling her of my plan to seduce Cody, but I figured I had better wait until I knew for sure Cody would take the bait. Knowing Shyanne, she would probably figure it out on her own.

"Is all this cuteness for the fine Italian attorney that's on his way over here?"

Just as Shyanne uttered the last of her question, in walked Cody through the door that Shyanne left opened behind her. I knew he heard her comment because he wore a slight smirk on his face. I was slightly embarrassed, but I didn't let it worry me too much. I figured I could use it to my advantage at some point.

"Hello, ladies," Cody greeted.

"Hey there, Cody. How have you been?" Shyanne responded. I never said a word. Shyanne and Cody stood in the foyer making small talk. I used the opportunity to walk into the bathroom just down the hall.

I stood in the bathroom and took a deep breath. I looked in the mirror and checked my face, my clothes, and my attitude. What in the world was I thinking? How did I think I could hit on my husband's attorney and get away with it? What if I started the come-on with Cody and he didn't respond like I thought he would, but instead told Shaun?

I was so glad that I took the extra moment to compose myself. I rethought my plan, realizing that trying to have a brief fling with Cody while Shaun was imprisoned wasn't such a good idea after all. The risks were too high. The consequences too great. God would forgive me, but Shaun would divorce me for even making an attempt to seduce his lawyer. He would probably try and take my babies away from me as well.

I left the bathroom with a no-nonsense-completely-business-demeanor and joined Shyanne and Cody in the living room where they settled.

"Well, I guess I'll let you two talk while I go upstairs and tend to the baby. It was nice seeing you again, Cody." Shyanne said and headed upstairs.

I sat in the chair opposite the sofa Cody sat on. If I had stuck to my original plan, I would have sat relatively close to him on the sofa. But I digressed. I was all about business now.

"Are you okay, Lindsay? Seems like every time I see you, you are off and running to the bathroom," Cody said jokingly. Then he gave me his award-winning smile. My resolve to be professional cracked, but just a bit.

Cody was just as beautiful as I remembered, probably more so considering I had not had sex in more than five months. He was semi-casually dressed in a pair of tan Dockers and cream colored Polo shirt. His hair looked a little longer and his skin perhaps a little darker than before. Cody was flat out dazzling. I closed my eyes and silently prayed that God would give me the strength not to make a fool of myself and risk my marriage for this man.

When I opened my eyes again, he was staring at me so intensely I simply lost my voice. I actually had to remind myself how to talk. It was as if I totally forgot I possessed the power of speech.

"I'm sorry I left like that, Cody. I felt like I had something on my face so I went in to check," I lied.

"I could have told you your face was perfect if you had only asked me."

Was he flirting with me or was I just imagining the sultriness I heard in his voice, hearing what I wanted to hear? A few more comments like that and all bets for a professional affiliation only were off.

"Thank you, Cody. You always say just the right thing."

"I only speak the truth, *Lindsay.*"

Okay. There went my imagination again. I could have sworn he put sensual emphasis on the way he said my name so I would realize he remembered the secret he and I shared in Shaun's presence. Help me, Lord.

"Uh . . . so you can help me with the FBI right?"

"Yes I can. As a mater of fact, all you have do is inform them that any questions they have should be directed to your attorney. I'll handle everything from there." That's exactly what Shaun said on the phone the other night. If that was indeed the case, why the need for this meeting?

Cody reached into his briefcase. He pulled out some documents and handed them to me. "These are the warranty deeds for your house, the car wash and the store. The dates of official ownership on all documents were established before you and Shaun were married."

I stood up and walked the short distance to the sofa to get the paperwork from Cody. After they were in my possession I sat down on the sofa next to Cody without thinking.

"The FBI should not ask you for them, but if they do, you will have them. Remember, don't give them anything or answer any questions unless I am with you."

I stared at Cody and read a lot more into his last few words than I'm sure he intended. Cody returned my stare with an unreadable expression as we fell into an awkward silence. I re-examined the paper in my hand to break the eye contact and tried to think of something to say.

"This all seems so simple, Cody. I guess I made it sound more urgent than necessary. You certainly didn't have to come over here for this. I could have picked these papers up in your office and saved you the trouble of the trip."

"Trust me, Lindsay, it was no trouble at all. It was actually my pleasure. I was grateful for the opportunity to see your lovely face again."

Okay that did it. I was convinced now that he was flirting.

Shyanne was right. The attraction *was* mutual. However, I still wanted to tread lightly. I wanted to avoid coming across like a cheap tramp by throwing myself at him. Cody needed to take the lead, but I figured a little nudging from me could not hurt. I gave Cody my most brilliant smile and placed my hand on his knee.

"You are so sweet, Mr. Vincini. I'm so glad you're my attorney. You're smart, you know your business, and you're so accommodating. What more can a woman ask for?"

I purposely left Shaun's name out of the equation. I wanted him to know that I felt he was my attorney now. Cody took the bait and ran with it.

Cody lifted the hand I had on his knee and began gently rubbing it between both his hands. He then lifted my hand to his lips for a light kiss.

"You are an amazingly beautiful lady, Lindsay, and at the risk of professional compromise, I would really love to take you to dinner some time soon. I promise I'll handle any personal interaction between us with the utmost discretion."

"I'm glad to hear that, Cody. In that case, I would love to have dinner with you."

My affirmative answer was rewarded with one of his devastating smiles, which caused me to get warm all over. I reminded myself to stay cool. I was a long way from the standard six-week waiting period after giving birth. But my objective was to have all of Mr. Vincini eventually.

Cody gathered his briefcase and stood to leave. I stood with him, walking him to the door. Just before he opened the door, he turned to me, grabbed both my hands, and gave me a tender peck on my cheek, then a more aggressive kiss on my lips.

"I'll call you later this evening to make arrangements for dinner. I'll talk to you then, beautiful." Then without a backward glance he was gone.

Chapter Twenty-Two

The plane began descending just as I found a comfortable position in my seat. I'm sure my seating companion was thoroughly tired of my fidgeting. For some reason I just could not relax. Who was I kidding? I knew exactly why I was so on edge. This would be the first time I had seen Shaun since I started my little fling with Cody. I was positive he would know I was up to no good with his attorney.

Cody and I had been on four dates in the last two weeks. Each one was just as marvelous as the previous. The time I was spending with Cody reminded me of how special things were when Shaun and I first started dating. We went to very exclusive restaurants for dinner. Whenever we would see a movie together, we drove twenty miles or more out of the way. Cody did this in an effort to live up to the promise of keeping things between us discreet. The only person aware of our liaison was Shyanne. She was totally in favor of our little secret rendezvous. Shyanne had never been big on commitment. She was especially displeased with mine for the past year considering whom I was committed to.

Last night the kids stayed with Mama since she knew I

had an early flight this morning, so I invited Cody over to watch television with me. He insisted on bringing a couple of movies with him. We stayed up past 2:00 A.M. watching *The Bodyguard* and *Pretty Woman*. This was the first time I had seen either movie. I found them both to be very romantic, which led to things getting pretty heated between Cody and me. The only thing that kept us from ending up in bed together was the fact that I was only two weeks into the standard six-week recovery after giving birth.

Cody had been the perfect gentleman, never pushing me into anything more physical than our kissing and heavy petting. As a matter of fact, I was usually the one who initiated any intimacy between us. He was patiently waiting for the time when we could explore each other fully.

I was amazed at how guilt free I have felt over this thing with Cody. Not once have I harbored any emotional remorse over cheating on my husband. It was my conclusion that this whole affair is all Shaun's fault. If he hadn't continually lied; if he had not cheated and fathered another child; if he had not continued to sell drugs, which led him to prison and away from his children and me, then it would be his arms that I lay in every night, not those of another man. I have earned some peace and happiness.

That was my rational response. My spiritual response was quite different. While I felt I owed Shaun no loyalty, I knew I owed God more. But I was hurt. I was in so much pain. It was so hard, too hard not to just follow my mind and enjoy the serenity I felt being with a handsome, intelligent, wealthy, attorney who found me beautiful, intelligent, and worthy of his time.

Besides, it was not as if I were going to end my marriage and be with Cody forever. This was just a here and now thing, something to take my mind off of everything I had been through in my relationship with Shaun.

Now would be the true test though. I wondered how little

guilt I would feel after facing Shaun in the prison visiting room, especially after having been kissed, fondled and caressed by another man just last night.

When I arrived at the prison I went through the normal routine of the degrading search, having them make sure I was on the visitor list and the lengthy wait. My wait was going to be a bit more tense than normal, however, because of a name I found signed on Shaun's visitor's page. Tawanda Jackson visited last week. I don't know Tawanda Jackson, but I was more than a little interested in finding out all about her.

I assumed the worst during my wait. Then I lectured myself on how much nerve I had considering what I was into with Cody. But darn it, I had been there and done that with Shaun. I was not going to stand for it again.

Shaun entered the visiting room about twenty minutes after I sat down, which gave me plenty of time to stew over the woman's name on his list. Before he could put his butt firmly in the chair I began questioning him.

"Who is Tawanda Jackson, Shaun?"

"Hello, wife. It is so nice to see you too. I have missed you so much since the last time we visited," Shaun said sarcastically.

I felt bad behind his reply. He was right. I didn't hug him, say hello, or update him on the kids.

"I'm sorry, honey. The kids and I are fine. Lil' Shaun's two-week check up was yesterday. He is as normal as he can be bodily, but when it comes to cuteness, he is off the charts." I smiled at Shaun to ease the tension I caused by my initial behavior, but it was still prevalent in my mind.

"That's all wonderful to hear. It is reports like those that keep me going in here. I keep my mind focused on the positive and count my blessings instead of stressing over the time I have to do. I can't wait to meet my son.

Something about Shaun had changed in just the six short weeks since I last saw him. Physically he was a little heavier. I assumed he must have been working out to help pass time. The new weight and muscles added to his beauty, but it was more than that. He seemed more subdued, calmer. I know we haven't spent much time talking today, but it was more than what he said or even how he said it. It was as if something was exuding from his soul.

Shaun pretended as if he never heard the question I asked about Tawanda Jackson, so there was no way he was going to be forthcoming with any information. I had to wait for the perfect opportunity to bring it up again. I decided to stick with the small talk for now.

"How are Sha'Ron and the rest of your family doing?"

"Sha'Ron is doing pretty well. He's growing like a weed and his grades are good. My being here is hard on him though. He's older than Shauntae, so he's aware of my absence and why I am in jail. But I make sure my mother brings him with her when she comes to visit. The last thing I want is for him to forget me or feel like I have abandoned him."

I was a little envious of the fact that Shaun wanted Sha'Ron to visit but not Shauntae. However, my understanding outweighed my jealousy. Sha'Ron is four years older than Shauntae.

"Has Uncle Bobby been here yet?" I figured if I could get him to keep talking about his visitors, I could bring up this Tawanda person.

"No. Uncle Bobby doesn't do the prison visitation thing, but I'm not mad at him. He just can't stand to see me locked down like this."

"Well, who is Tawanda Jackson, Shaun? I saw her name on your visitor's page. I assumed she was someone you know through your uncle or your work."

I could tell Shaun knew I was lying by the way he looked

at me. He shook his head slightly and took a moment before he answered me. I waited patiently versus doing my usual grilling and rushing.

"You know what, Lindsay, I was going to make up a story about Tawanda, but I think you're mature enough to handle the truth."

Oh my goodness! What in the world was he going to tell me? This sounded as if it were going to be painful. I braced myself for his revelation. For comfort, I armed myself with the knowledge that I had my own little thing going on just in case he was about to tell me he was cheating again.

"What is it now, Shaun?" I asked with as much attitude as I could muster.

"Tawanda works for me . . . on the outside and here on the inside."

He said that like I understood what he meant. I became angry, yet somewhat relieved. I was prepared for him to tell me she was another baby mama.

"What does that mean? How can she work for you inside?"

Shaun pulled my chair very close to his and hugged me. It was for appearances sake more so than the desire for actual contact. He needed me close because he was about to whisper what he wanted me to know.

"Tawanda brings me a supply of cocaine in here to sell."

"What?" My scream brought on the attention of the guards in the visiting room. One of them came to our table to question us.

"What's the problem over here, Taylor?" he asked.

"No problem. My wife wasn't happy with something I asked her, that's all," Shaun replied, then looked me in the eye, begging me to support his story.

"Ma'am, is everything okay over here?" security asked me directly.

"Yes, sir. Everything is fine. I apologize for my outburst. My husband just gave me a shock. I'm fine, honestly."

"Okay. Please try to keep it down. As a matter of fact, I'd like you two to separate your chairs." We complied with the guard's request, then he walked away. However, he kept his eye on us for quite some time afterward.

"Shaun, why are you doing this?" I asked in a calmer voice.

"Baby, I am just trying to keep my promise to you. I am doing this so we will be all set when I come home. I'm just putting things together, Lindsay."

This all sounded like the same old runaround he continuously gave me when he was on the street. Shaun always made it sound like he was doing what was best for our family. The real truth was he just had to be in control, and he loved the power that control gave him. While he was careful and effective at dealing drugs, he never thought rationally when it came to being a *drug dealer*; being the man. As intelligent as he was, the power of the streets made him neglect to use his intellect. If he did, he would see how dangerous this was.

"Shaun, what happens if you get caught? It isn't worth it, honey. We will be fine once you come home and get a regular job. I'll be working and we still have the businesses. We'll finally have a normal family life."

"Lindsay, trust me. I won't get caught. It's all worked out."

I wanted so badly to ask him how, but I knew he would never tell me. Especially here. He never gave me the details of his business.

"I don't want to come out and go to work for somebody else. Lindsay, I want to own my own businesses, businesses much bigger than the party store and the car wash. I want to be a billion dollar entrepreneur. Honey, it takes big money to make big money in this world. You and the kids deserve better than some weak sucker working nine to five or keeping track of stock and inventory at our little mom and pop corner store. I deserve better than that. I am too smart for that and you know it. No! I have to be in charge of my destiny and the well being of my family."

This time it was Shaun who got a little loud and the guards gave us their attention once again. They stayed in their seats, opting to stare at us, giving us warning to be careful.

Shaun and I both calmed down and looked at each other intently. Shaun grabbed my hands, hoping to communicate without speaking. He wanted me to know his business venture could not bring us any more trouble. There was something else in his eyes as well. It was that same something that I noticed earlier and couldn't put into words.

"Are you sure that's all Tawanda is to you?" Again that *look* surfaced, and for the first time since I had been here today, I began to feel guilty about my association with Cody. Was there some way Shaun could possibly know about us? Then the look was gone as quickly as it came.

"Baby, I promised you I would never do anything like that to you again. I meant it. She is just an employee. Someone willing to take a risk for the amount of money she's getting paid."

Shaun's eyes softened, and I chalked up my previous thoughts to paranoia. There was no way he could possibly know what I was doing on the outside. Cody and I have been very careful.

Shaun and I spent the rest of the visit just enjoying each other's company with no more talk of another woman or any more thoughts about my other man.

Chapter Twenty-Three

May 2004

Cody and I have been seeing each other for the past eighteen months. It's been so cool. Cody has been my substitute for my husband since Shaun has been in prison, less all the heartache I have endured with Shaun. My relationship with Cody is purely physical and psychological; there is nothing emotional about us. Neither of us is falling in love. He enjoys my companionship, and of course the sex; and I get to relive with him everything that was good about Shaun in the beginning of our relationship. The sex has been pretty good for me too.

Even in the midst of my adulterous affair, I have remained faithful to my church and Bible Study attendance. My relationship with Cody has continually caused me to have spiritual conflicts in my relationship with God. I know my affair is wrong in and of itself, but it feels so very right. I rationalize my affair by bargaining with God. I remind Him that this is just a temporary situation, and I will repent of my behavior as soon as Shaun comes home.

I have continued my schedule of seeing Shaun every three weeks or so. He is still none the wiser about his attorney and me. Ms. Tawanda also continues to visit him twice a month. Shaun reports that business is great, and everything is under control.

Cody and Shaun have many similarities. They're both drop dead gorgeous; I wouldn't be bothered with anything less. Only one year separates them in age. Cody is 31 and Shaun is 30. Both men are the two most intelligent people I know. They both make lots of money. And while Cody is an attorney with two college degrees, and Shaun is a convicted felon and a drug-dealer, they both made their fortunes in the same business. Ninety percent of Cody's clients are people just like Shaun.

Neither of my children has ever seen nor heard of Cody. I would never disrespect Shaun to that degree, nor would I want to confuse my children. Shyanne is still the only one aware of our relationship.

Cody called earlier this afternoon asking me to go to dinner tonight. He sweetened his invitation by telling me he had a few surprises he wanted to share with me. I was so excited that when he got here, I didn't bother waiting for him to come to my door to get me. I was out of the house before he had a chance to exit his car . . . a car, I might add, I had never before seen.

Cody had purchased a brand new convertible Mercedes Benz SL500 for himself. It was almost as beautiful as he. This, he said, was the first surprise. In my experience most people save the best for last. So I couldn't wait to find out what else he had in store. But if I have learned anything from my time with Shaun, it was the value of patience, so I held my tongue. The weather was still cool for May, so we drove with the top up on the Mercedes as we rode to Beverly Hills to have dinner at Cody's ritzy country club.

We dined here frequently, and the waitress sat us at our usual table. Because this was an exclusive club, Cody and I often received our share of stares from the older white members. Initially I was unnerved and angered by their bigotry. Cody told me the best way to handle them would be to simply ignore them; behave as if I had just as much right to be there as they did. Cody was right. The last thing I wanted to do was cuss one of them out and give credit to their preconceived opinion of 'us' being ignorant and uncontrollable.

We were halfway through our dinner when I just couldn't stand the suspense of the second surprise any longer.

"Okay, Cody. When are you going to tell me about the other wonderful surprise?"

"What other surprise, Lindsay?" I was amazed that he said that with a straight face. He looked like he was dead serious. This man had to be fierce in the courtroom.

"Don't play games with me, Mr. Vincini. I have waited long enough. I am a patient woman, but you are trying me," I said sternly. "Now please, please tell me about the other surprise."

Cody shook his head and blessed me with his smile. "You know, I have never been with anyone who makes me laugh and smile the way you do."

"Good. Now repay me by telling what the surprise is."

"Okay. You win. I just bought a summer home in Martha's Vineyard. I want us to drive up and spend the weekend together there. It's just a small cottage, but it was you I had in mind when I purchased it. It is you I want to share it with."

Cody eyes held a far away look, one I had never seen before. If I didn't know better, I would have sworn he was starting to get serious on me. As I concentrated on the look, the surprise slipped my mind. Cody brought me back to the time at hand.

"Did I say something wrong, Lindsay?"

"No, Cody. It's just that . . . well, for a second I thought maybe you were trying to take our friendship to another level."

Cody was a gifted attorney and a very smart man. He was smooth and his livelihood depended on his being convincing. He could effortlessly make me believe anything he said.

"Lindsay, we've been spending a tremendous amount of time with each other for the better part of a year and a half. It is only natural I have developed some strong feelings for you. However, I knew the situation with you when I came through the door. You're a married woman; a woman married to my client, so I know there are limits on how far we can go. But you describe what we have as a friendship. I think that's inaccurate. You have to know that we are more than friends. I may be at a loss to identify exactly how we should be classified, but the word friend does not do us justice."

I took a sip of my strawberry daiquiri and remained silent as I tried to process what Cody said. I was afraid to ask him to be more specific. The last thing I wanted to hear him say was he was in love with me. Yes. I did have feelings for Cody, but the only person I was in love with was my husband.

Cody recognized I was becoming uncomfortable with the conversation. He performed his signature move of grabbing both my hands in his and gently kissed each of them. He then looked intently into my eyes. I looked around to find the usual nosy bodies staring at us, but Cody ignored them and continued his spiel.

"Listen, beautiful. The last thing I wanted to do was make our relationship difficult for you. So far we have been able to enjoy each other's company to the fullest, never once having a single disagreement or moment of discord. With all that we have shared, how is it that I was supposed to keep myself from becoming a little more than infatuated with you?"

I opened my mouth to interject, but he cut me off by continuing to speak. "I know you belong to someone else. I have accepted it, but human nature has prevented me from being able to control my feelings for you. I realize, however, that you are more than likely going to return to your marriage in six months when Shaun comes home. I have accepted that as well. I just want to enjoy the rest of the time I have with you all to myself. Allow me to show you and share with you all the adoration I have developed for you. Enjoy the ride with me for the rest of the time it lasts. I promise when this coaster comes to its time restricted end, I'll get off, no strings attached."

Cody was so sincere that I had no choice but to believe he was serious about letting me walk away when Shaun came home. It was overwhelming that this brilliant, wealthy, fine attorney thought me worthy of such deep feelings and consideration, knowing I was married to someone else. I was floating on cloud nine, so I readily agreed to strap myself down and ride this puppy 'til the wheels fell off.

"That was so beautiful, Cody. Your offer of limited bliss is one I can't turn down. Yes. I'll go with you to your new cottage this weekend, and I'll stand with you until our hour glass runs empty."

We arrived at the cottage around 11:00 P.M. Thursday; two days after Cody made the initial invitation. The entire drive up was wonderful. We made stops in all the major cities between Michigan and Massachusetts. Cody bought me beautiful souvenirs from each state. It was an exciting sightseeing adventure. Until now, the only places I had ever visited were Las Vegas when Shaun and I got married, Walt Disney in Florida with Granny and K.J. when we were children, and the prison in West Virginia.

Shauntae and Lil' Shaun stayed with Mama and Grandma while they and Shaun believed I was on vacation with Shyanne.

I financed a vacation for Shyanne and our childhood friend, Sharay, to Miami, Florida as part of my alibi. Shaun was at first hesitant about me taking a vacation without him, but I convinced him that I truly deserved it after all the stress I had endured over the past several months.

Cody opened the door to let me in and look around while he retrieved our luggage from the car. He was right about the place being small, but it was very cozy and intimate. It was a small cape cod with three bedrooms; one on the first floor, the other two upstairs. There was a small living room with a fireplace, a kitchen complete with all the latest appliances, and a full bathroom with a separate tub and shower stall. There were no furnishings in either the living room or the downstairs bedroom.

Cody joined me just as I was about to head upstairs. We toured up there together. He showed me the upstairs bathroom first, which was much larger than the one downstairs. It too had a separate shower stall, but the tub doubled as a Jacuzzi.

We then viewed the smaller of the two bedrooms on this floor, which he would eventually use as an office. This room was unfurnished as well. He'd owned the place for less than two weeks, so he hadn't had time to shop and decorate.

The last room on our tour was the master bedroom. Now this room was fully furnished. It was complete with a beautiful, antique, king-sized cherry wood canopy bed. Two traditional styled Queen Anne chairs were covered in the same fabric and mint green color as the canopy. The bedroom set also included a matching dresser, mirror, and an armoire. This ensemble was breathtaking. There was a fireplace accented with shiny brass that matched the knobs and handles on the dresser and armoire. When did he have time to decorate this room?

As if reading my mind, Cody spoke. "This is the only room

I rushed to furnish. I figured we would be spending the majority of our time in here," he said with a devilish grin.

I smiled back. "I can't believe you're using me for my body, counselor. Such deplorable behavior from someone who is supposed to be an ethical public servant."

I immediately felt guilty for my comment. I began to think about how very unethical we were being. I'm a married woman cheating on my husband with his attorney. I am a Christian woman cheating on God with my adulterous behavior. Who was I to question Cody's ethics, even in jest?

My little guilt trip took me on a path that led away from our verbal foreplay, and the mood was broken for me. I could still see the lust in Cody's eyes, however, so I tried to diffuse the situation.

"Why don't you start unpacking, and I'll fix us something to eat," I suggested. "I'll unpack my things after our meal. I'm starving. The kitchen looked pretty well stocked, so I have to amend my previous statement. Both sex and food were on your mind when you furnished this place." I stepped around a disappointed attorney and headed down the stairs.

This was not the first time the pangs of guilt interrupted an interlude between me and Cody. Call me crazy, but I was still very much in love with my husband. I was sure that would never change. It was only natural for me to feel remorseful every now and then. My spirit was also in a constant tug of war with my conscious. I was combating two very different sources over one bad situation.

My guilt suddenly warped into more than just feeling bad for my cheating. I was starting to feel guilty about Cody's admission of his emotions spiraling into more than just those of an intimate friend. The last thing I wanted to do was hurt him after all this was said and done. I felt so selfish. Maybe I should just make this weekend the last hoorah for us, and call it quits after this.

Cody came downstairs after unpacking and showering just as I finished preparing our midnight snack. He looked so delicious in a pair of cream colored linen shorts and his bare chest exposed that I almost decided to do without the food and simply eat him. How was I ever going to give up all this beauty?

As I walked around the table, setting it for our meal, Cody came behind me and wrapped his strong golden arms around my upper body. He smelled as good as he looked, and my knees, along with my resolve to put an end to us, weakened.

"Cody, how am I supposed to feed us while you have me in a bear hug?" I said as I tried to regain control of the situation and my composure.

"Sweetheart, I have spent the better part of a year and a half with you. I think I know a little about you at this juncture. You are no hungrier for that little snack you prepared than I am. I saw the lust in your eyes as soon as I entered the kitchen. I also saw the hesitation and guilt in them when you fled the bedroom earlier."

My entire body tensed, and I dropped the plate with the sandwiches. Everything went clanging to the floor in a big mess. I was stunned speechless that Cody could read my emotions so well. I guess that was another similarity he shared with Shaun. I assumed that Shaun's perception was a result of the depth of my feelings for him. Was I really just a transparent fool who wore her expressions and emotions on her sleeve?

Cody turned me around and looked directly in my eyes as he spoke words that would forever be embedded in my heart.

"Lindsay, please don't be afraid of me and what I feel for you. All I'm offering you is nothing short of what you deserve. You are an intelligent, beautiful, sensitive, caring mother, friend, and even wife."

When Cody mentioned the word wife, I tensed again and lowered my head, but he was having none of that. He placed his soft hand under my chin and lifted my eyes to meet his.

"Guilt is a natural emotion because you love your husband. As I said, I know that, and I accept it. This may sound strange, but that is also part of why I'm crazy about you. You are a very kind and responsive woman, putting everyone else's happiness above your own. There are not many selfless people in this world, Lindsay. It is my pleasure and my honor to know you. I take great joy in knowing I'm giving to you a little bit of what you give everyone you know and love."

I fought with all my might to stop them, but it was a wasted effort. The tears that burned my eyes eventually tumbled onto my cheeks. I couldn't move. I could barely breathe. I just stood there staring at Cody's face, taking in his beautiful words and storing them away for a time when I might question my own worth.

Cody didn't bother responding anymore either. He simply separated the miniscule distance between us and kissed me with a passion so hot it melted my equilibrium. Had it not been for Cody holding onto my body, I would have fallen to the floor in the mess I created when I dropped the dishes.

Cody lifted my limp body into his arms and carried me up the stairs to the master bedroom, never once releasing me from his kiss. He made short work of discarding our clothing, and before I knew it, we were making love. Up until now, my physical relationship with Cody could simply be classified as sex. This time, however, was quite different. When Cody slipped into my body this time, it was as if he were searching for my soul.

And I let him find it.

Chapter Twenty-Four

The three days Cody and I spent at the cottage were three of the most wonderful days of my life. We went sailing on a rented sailboat, we rode in a jet ski, and I went horseback riding, all of which were firsts for me. We also did the customary shopping, dining out, and making love in every room of the cottage.

Cody got very creative on our last night there. He turned on the central air unit to a temperature that would make the small house comfortable enough to light the fireplaces in the bedroom and living room. Cody prepared a traditional Italian meal and we ate in front of the fireplace in the living room. Even the drive home was special and romantic as we stopped in the smaller cities we missed on our way up to the cottage. I will treasure those days forever.

I was floating on cloud nine until the moment we drove up to my house. Reality set in with a vengeance. I was back at home; the home I shared with my husband and children; the home where I was wife and mommy. The place where I was not the stress free woman who lay in the arms of a special type of man without a care in the world this weekend.

Cody parked the car in my driveway and got out to retrieve my luggage from the trunk. I sat in the car and watched him as he walked to the front door expecting me to follow and let us in. I couldn't, however. I just could not get out of the car. My legs were immobilized, and my mind was on stutter-stop. Suddenly, I started to hyperventilate. My whole body broke out into a cold sweat. I was terrified because I was oblivious to what was happening to me.

Cody returned to the car after seeing my distress. I was so out of it I was unable to unlock the door for him. He stepped around to the driver's side and came in from there.

"What's wrong, Lindsay? Baby, talk to me; tell me what's happening."

"I . . . don't . . . know . . . Cody." I choked out. I was sure I was about to die.

"I think you're having a panic attack. I need you to try and calm down. Take short breaths through your mouth and let them out slowly through your nose until your breathing returns to normal."

I followed Cody's advice, and after about forty-five seconds, my breath was a lot less shallow. Within a minute and a half I was able to fill my lungs with air and breathe normally. My vision cleared, and when I stared out the window, again looking at my house, I was able to do so without having a fit.

I was so relieved. Never before had I experienced anything like that. A panic attack. Lord knows I have had my share of reasons to have gone there before now. What was it about coming home today that set me off like that?

Cody was now standing at the passenger door holding it open for me. "Are you better, baby? Can you stand?"

"I think so," I replied as I exited the car.

As soon as I was steady on my feet, Cody grabbed me and gave me a very affectionate hug right in my front yard. To anyone that may have been looking, it would have been obvious it was more than a brotherly embrace. It was filled with passion, concern and an emotion that almost sent me back into fit mode . . . love.

It felt so good to be in his arms, experiencing the strong feelings he had for me, showing me how much my well being meant to him. For the past eighteen months I had known nothing but happiness and peacefulness with Cody. We never had any cross words for each other. Even though he was a successful attorney, he was never too busy for me. This man was wonderful in every way, yet I couldn't find room for him in my heart. He occupied my mind and my body, but every ounce of passionate love, the type of love a woman feels for a man and vice versa, belonged to Shaun, the man who had caused me more than the lion's share of hurt and pain. What was wrong with me?

I felt so guilty for not being able to return his feelings. I separated myself from Cody's embrace and headed toward my house without looking in his face. He followed me to the front door, standing on the porch waiting behind me as I opened the door. We both entered the foyer and stood there for a few awkward moments with him staring at me and me staring at the floor. Cody closed the distance between us and reached over to lift my chin so he could look in my eyes.

"Lindsay, how are we going to continue to see each other if every time we're together you let guilt and remorse make you sulk and feel sullen? Baby, I only want to see you happy. You're going to make me begin to feel guilty. As far as I'm concerned, I have nothing to apologize for."

Cody spoke as if we were both in the same boat in this relationship. I was becoming a little annoyed with his goodwill speeches and pep talks. By the time I finished my own speech, I was yelling.

"I guess it's easy for you to feel that way, Cody. You're not married. You have no one to be accountable to except yourself. You don't have children who are depending on you to hold their family together so they never have to feel abandoned. Friends and family waiting in the wings to say *I told you so* once your marriage falls apart. You go home after an evening or a weekend trip like this, and all you have to think about is how much sex and fun you had."

Cody looked at me as if I had grown another head. I knew my words were painful to hear, but my own remorse outweighed his bruised ego at the moment. I was being totally unfair and I knew it, but there was nothing I could do to stop myself. So I added fuel to the fire by continuing to berate him.

"Do you ever think about how you're betraying your client while you're sexing his wife? Don't you lawyers, like doctors, have to take some kind of oath regarding morality and ethics? Oh, but then again how can I expect you to be ethical when you defend drug dealers you know to be guilty? What in the world was I thinking?"

Cody took a step away from me, backing in the direction of my front door. He stopped just as he backed into the doorknob, staring at me for a long while; then he spoke.

"All I wanted to do was show you a different side of love. I wanted to show you that loving someone doesn't have to come with stress and heartache. I wasn't trying to get you to leave your marriage or your family. I just wanted to love you for the short time I had with you, show you some happiness. I just wanted to love you, Lindsay."

"But I don't love you, Cody. I love Shaun, my husband. I guess I will for the rest of my life, even as foolish as that may sound to someone as smart and rich and cultured as you are. I love him for better or worse, richer or poorer, in sickness and in health, 'til death do us part."

Cody said nothing else. He simply turned and exited the house, defeated and in complete silence. I stood in the foyer staring at the door until I heard his car start and leave my driveway. Then I fell to the floor in a crumpled heap, crying until my eyes had no more tears to give.

I had just finished putting my children to bed for the night when the phone rang. I knew it was Shaun. His calls usually came in right around 8:00 or 9:00 in the evening. Shaun had been moved to Milan Correctional Facility right here in Michigan since he only had five months left on his sentence. At Milan, Shaun was not allowed to make collect calls. Money had to be inserted directly into the pay phone he used. I answered the phone knowing it was him.

"Hello, my precious husband whom I love more than life itself."

"Hey! Right back at you. How are you this evening?"

"I'm fine, Shaun. How are you?"

"Sad because I'm missing you and the kids; happy because in only four months, seventeen days, twelve hours, and thirty minutes, I'll be back in your loving arms."

"Oh. Now I'm offended. You mean to tell me you don't have it calculated down to the exact second?" I joked.

Shaun and I exchanged small talk for a few more minutes, then he said something that caused me to choke momentarily. "Lindsay, have you talked to Cody lately?"

I removed the phone from my face so he wouldn't hear my reaction. At first I was too stunned to speak. When I could talk again, I began babbling.

"Cody? Why would I need to talk to Cody? What makes you ask about Cody . . . your attorney . . . all of a sudden? Why would he need to see or talk to me?"

I hadn't talked to Cody since he and I returned from Martha's Vineyard six weeks ago. I tried calling him two or three times the day after we returned, but I got his voicemail each time. After receiving no response to any of my messages, I got the *message*; Cody was through with me.

I tried composing myself while I waited for Shaun to answer my questions by doing the same deep breathing exercises I did when I had the anxiety attack. I was on my way to being normal until Shaun threw me for a loop again with his next statement.

"Cody came to see me the other day about some business matters. He told me he ran into you a short while ago and you didn't look too well. He said you looked stressed, tired. I made him promise to call and check on you, make sure you and the kids were okay."

I almost fainted dead right there on the spot. How dare Cody sarcastically play word games with Shaun about me? I told him how intuitive Shaun was.

I started panicking, wondering if Cody told Shaun anything or everything else because he was angry with me about our last encounter. I played it as cool as I could though. If Shaun was fishing for something from my lake, his rod was going to come up empty. I was not about to help him figure out anything, collaborate anything, or give him any hint that something happened between Cody and me. What is that saying that men have? *Deny! Deny! Deny! Lie 'til you die.*

"Well that is either a promise he didn't keep or I missed his call. I haven't heard from Cody since he helped me with that mess concerning the FBI. That was more than a year ago." It was time to get off this phone and out of this conversation before things got beyond my control.

"Shaun, I hate to cut our conversation short, but Lil' Shaun is calling for me. This is the second night in a row he's awakened after I have put him to bed. Last night it took me thirty minutes to get him to go back to sleep." Shaun hesitated a moment, as if he wanted to hold me a while longer, but then he relented

"All right, Lindsay. You go ahead and take care of my son. Tell him his daddy loves him. I'll call again in a few days."

Then he disconnected the line. No I love you or goodbye. Nothing. He just hung up.

Now I was really worried. I held the phone in my hands because I couldn't gather my thoughts enough to realize that I needed to hang it up. I started sweating, my stomach started churning, and before I knew it, I threw up all over my kitchen floor.

After my stomach was emptied, I stood there still clutching the phone with vomit all over the place. I looked at the phone in my hand, staring at it as if it were an animated object. I felt as if the telephone itself was the lone source of my present trauma. Like it was to blame for Shaun being in prison, for my husband's infidelity, for every tear I have cried since knowing Shaun, for my affair with Cody, and even for my vomiting just now.

I slid down into the mess I made on the floor, still holding onto the phone for dear life, knowing it was not responsible for any of the things I mentioned. Nor was it the phone's fault, I realized just before blacking out, that I was pregnant . . . again.

I finally awakened from my emotional meltdown, feeling no less troubled than before I passed out. I couldn't believe I had gone and gotten myself pregnant by Cody during our affair. Up until the time we went to the cottage in the Vineyard, we had been so very careful, using a condom each and every time we had sex. How could I have allowed myself to be so careless simply because we changed venues?

Unlike my first pregnancy, where I seesawed about my decision to abort, or my second pregnancy where I was adamant about carrying my child to full term, there was no doubt how I would handle this one. I made up my mind right then and there that Cody would never know about this baby. The only person I would tell was Shyanne. I would need her support and assistance going through the procedure. I would also need God's forgiveness.

"Dear, God. I'm here in another mess right now. I'm pregnant again, Lord, as if you didn't already know. But, Lord, you also have to understand that I cannot keep this child. It would ruin my marriage, my life, and possibly get Cody killed. Father, I know you don't agree with me, but I'm asking that you forgive me and give me a fresh start at life. I will never, Lord, ever fall into this type of pit again."

With that decided, I cleaned the mess I made on the floor, then went to the bathroom to clean myself. While I showered, I decided I needed to call Cody to find out exactly what he and Shaun discussed during their visit. I had to know if he acted vindictively by giving Shaun some sort of clue about our involvement. I didn't think it likely, but I wasn't willing to chance it. I just hoped Cody would answer when I called. Otherwise, I would have to stalk him at his office.

It was late in the evening so I took my chances on calling his home versus his cell or his office. God was with me so far because he answered on the second ring, acknowledging it was me from the caller ID.

"Hello, Lindsay. Long time no hear from. How are you?"

Hearing his voice for the first time in several weeks shook me somewhat. I was surprised by my reaction. I was certain that the little emotion I felt for Cody was out of my system. I found myself now wondering if I still felt a little something for him, or if what I thought was a *little* something was perhaps more. I bypassed those thoughts for now. I had to handle my business.

"Hello, Cody. It has been a while since we talked. I realize it's late, but I really needed to get some information from you."

"Sure. How can I help you?" he asked so casually.

I don't know what I expected, but I was startled by his

blasé attitude. I guess I thought he would either be begging to see me again or yelling at me for hurting him the way I did. This nonchalant demeanor was throwing me off. I pressed on, however. I needed to know the content of his and Shaun's conversation.

"This may be unorthodox considering you are still Shaun's attorney and your conversations are privileged, but I need you to tell me exactly what you told him when you last saw him."

"Oh! Wanting to know what your husband and I talked about during my visit is unorthodox." Cody chuckled. "You are truly funny, Lindsay Taylor."

Now I was a bit more comfortable. Call me a weirdo, but hearing a little animosity and sarcasm from Cody actually calmed my nerves a bit.

"I wasn't trying to amuse you, Cody. Shaun made me a little nervous when I talked to him this evening. To get straight to the point, I need to know if you in any way, shape, or form, let on about our affair?"

Cody became completely serious again as he stated, "Of course not. I would never do anything that would cause you any harm or heartache in your life. You know that, don't you?"

"Yes, Cody. For the most part I do, but like I said, Shaun made me uncomfortable when I spoke with him. Maybe I'm just dealing with my own guilt and paranoia."

"Well, to put your mind at ease, I'll tell you what was said between me and your husband. Shaun asked me to come up and help him with the paperwork for his release. He needed my legal advice on handling things regarding his transition between the prison, the halfway house, and coming home to you. It was an unusual request, but when my clients pay as well as your husband, I try my best to oblige them."

"Cody, Shaun said you told him you ran into me, and I didn't look good. Why would you tell him that?"

"I never said anything like that to him. He asked me if I

had seen or talked to you. I told him I called you once to see if you had any further problems from the FBI and that was that."

Okay somebody was lying. If I were a betting woman, I would put my money on Shaun because he had the history. But why would Shaun say something like that? What kind of game was he playing?

Cody interrupted my thoughts. "You have to know I have missed you, Lindsay. I thought it was best, however, to leave things alone after our last confrontation. We ended a little sooner than I hoped it would, but I knew the end was inevitable. Tell me you're okay though. Please tell me you have not been suffering with the broken heart that I have."

As usual, Cody's words were so full of compassion, caring, and love that I almost slipped and told him I was pregnant. I wanted and needed his love and his strength to get me through this. Yet, I didn't think it was fair to ask him to help me abort his child, so I held my tongue.

"I've missed you too, Cody, but you are right. Ending our relationship was the best thing to do." I knew he wanted me to say more, but I didn't want him to hear the misery in my voice.

"All right then, Mrs. Taylor. Perhaps we will meet again in another lifetime." And with that he hung up.

So much was going on inside my head. I was sorry about the pain I caused Cody. I was scared and angry with myself over the pregnancy and the impending termination. I was baffled over the lie Shaun told me about Cody and his reasons behind it. Filled with the heavy weight of confusion and stress, I did what I always did when things got too hard for me to figure them out alone. I called Shyanne.

It was now after midnight, and I knew Shyanne would be sleeping since it was a week night. But what were best friends for if not to wake them in the middle of the night with your crises? She answered on the first ring, knowing it was me.

"What do you want, heifer?"

"I'm pregnant again, Shy." There! That is what she gets for answering the phone with an attitude. I showed her.

"You better be playing, Lindsay."

Uh! Oh! I guess I took teaching her a lesson too far because now she was mad. She used my first name, and the only time she did that was when she was upset with me. Well, it was out there now. Since it was the truth, there was no need to retract it and try to say it any better. I just went with it and explained everything that transpired that evening. By the time I finished Shyanne was no longer angry with me, just disappointed, and it broke my heart.

"Nay, I cannot believe you keep doing these disastrous things to yourself. Being your best friend is what I imagined having a rebellious teenage child would be like. Every time I turn around it's something new and more damaging with you. Girl, you are wearing a sister thin, but as usual, I've got your back. Let's start with trying to figure out why Shaun would come at you like he did."

"Do you think he knows about me and Cody?"

"Well, that would be the first thing I would think, but how would he know for sure unless he was having you followed?"

"That is the same thing I thought. It doesn't seem plausible though, Shy. Shaun is so arrogant. He believes that I'm so totally devoted to him that I would never cheat on him. The only other explanation would be that someone he knows saw us together and it got back to him, but that, too, would be farfetched. Cody and I never hung out in the hood."

"All right, Nay. Let's just assume Shaun doesn't know for sure. What probably happened is Shaun said something about you to Cody, and he responded strangely or something without realizing it. That might have caused Shaun to get a little suspicious. You always said Shaun had ESP when it comes to you. He may just be a little insecure, so he tested you. Since you and Cody both told the same story, you passed the test with flying colors, and now Shaun is cool again."

That made perfect sense to me for two reasons: one, because it was logical, and two, because at this point I was willing to believe anything that gave support to the fact that Shaun didn't know about me and Cody.

"Okay. That takes care of my mental dilemma. Let's handle the emotional issue. What do I do about these feelings I still have for Cody?" I asked Shyanne.

"Nay, only you can answer that question. If it were up to me, I would say divorce the man behind bars and marry the man that passed the bar, but it's not my life or my marriage. You have to decide who you love more and who you want to be with. But I will say this. Unless you plan on having a real relationship with Cody, you should let him go. No more being with him just to make the time you spend waiting for your husband more bearable. Cody deserves better than that."

As stupid as it sounded and as dumb as I felt for feeling this way, I still loved Shaun more. I wanted to make my marriage work when he came home. We had too much history, good and bad, for me to let him go. Shaun was deeply imbedded in my soul. Cody only occupied a small space in my heart.

"I know you don't want to hear this, but I have to stick and stay with my husband, Shy. I guess that makes problem number three, the physical problem, solve itself. I have to have an abortion."

"Nay-Nay, it is not about what I want to hear. It's only about how you truly feel. Besides, I already knew who you were going to choose, so don't think your response surprised me. Just tell me when we are going to the clinic."

"Well, I need to go first thing in the morning to take an official pregnancy test, then I will make an appointment for the procedure."

"Okay. I'm going back to sleep now. Call me in the morning, and I'll go to the clinic with you. Do not call me anymore tonight, understand? I don't want to hear your voice again before 10:00 A.M. Goodnight!"

After Shyanne hung up, I mulled over our conversation. I kept going back to the part where she said I made her feel like my mother, and I was a teenager she always had to rescue and clean up after. Once again, she truly hurt my feelings. Once again, I had to agree that she was absolutely correct. When was I going to grow up?

One week later, I went through with one of the most juvenile decisions I have made since becoming an adult. I lay upon the sterile white table at the clinic to have the result of my irresponsibility and infidelity extracted from my body.

Before being brought to the procedure room, I sat in the waiting area with Shyanne and a bunch of young ladies, not one of them looking to be a day over twenty-one. I sat hearing some of them talk about how this was not their first visit here. They gave each other advice on the best way to get through the physically painful process.

After it was all over, I sat in the recovery room with Shyanne as she held my hand. Few words were spoken between us. Never once did she ask if it hurt. If she had, I would have told her that I couldn't remember. The only thing I could think about during the quick process was why nobody in the waiting area gave any advice on how to deal with the emotional scar that started to fester in my heart.

Chapter Twenty-Five

August 2006

"Lindsay, come here a minute, will you, baby?" Shaun yelled from the bottom of the steps. I came to the top of the stairs and gave Shaun an angry glare. He knew how much his yelling through the house irritated me.

"Shaun, will you please use the intercom system? Lil' Shaun has been beside himself today and has gotten on my last nerve. If you wake his bad behind up, you will have him with you the rest of the day."

"I apologize. I just wanted to let you know I'm on my way out. I'll be back in a few hours."

"Where are you going?"

"Don't ask questions you don't want answers to, Lindsay. I'll see you in a little while." He turned and walked out the door.

I flopped down on the top step and put my head in my hands, exasperated. Shaun had been out of prison for twenty-one months now. He spent the first six months in a halfway house. The entire time he has been out of jail, he has been back at his old occupation, selling drugs.

Since the day after Shaun was released into the custody of the halfway house, he has been back in business. He had some phony papers waiting for him when he got out, indicating he had a job. The papers gave the employer's name, address, and the hours he was to work. He used that time, of course, to do his real and true business. Shaun remained shrewd in handling his street business. He never once missed curfew, and whenever his parole officer checked up on him, everything always checked out.

I begged and pleaded with Shaun to just quit the business cold turkey, but he wasn't trying to hear any of that. He insisted he needed to make more money in order to legitimize successfully. To this day, I have no idea what additional business ventures he plans to pursue once he thinks he has enough money saved.

The time since Shaun has been out has been just as stressful as right before his incarceration. During his initial time at the halfway house, I would drive one hundred miles, fifty miles each way, to see him at various locations, but we spent very little time together. He never wanted me around his business. After the first month, I would make sure I was only there during the last hour before he was due back to the halfway house. We would have dinner together. It was awful for me seeing him on such a restrictive basis, but I never missed a day.

In the six months he was there, I can count on one hand the number of times we made love. Shaun was curt and distant with me. Still I made the trip every day, figuring it was just the stress of not being able to come to our home that made him so moody.

Things only improved slightly once he was released from the halfway house. The first few weeks were great. Shaun became reacquainted with his daughter, and he got to know his son. The children adored their daddy. Sha'Ron even began staying with us every weekend. Keva and Kevaun were still missing in action.

Shaun decided he wanted to make numerous updates and improvements to our home. For some reason he wanted a completely new look. He did a complete renovation of the whole house, including new furniture for the living room, dining room, and bedroom. I had very little say in his choices, but I let him have his way with minimum fuss. He installed a security monitoring system and we were able to view the entire property inside and out from his office, which was an addition he added to the house.

It took approximately ninety days before everything was completed to his satisfaction. Right after it was all finished, he started spending less and less time at home. I couldn't understand why he went to the trouble of doing the renovations, then not stay home to enjoy them.

Shaun and I fought constantly about his continued street hustling. I reminded him during every argument about the promise he made to quit when he got out of jail. He always countered my arguments with the fact that he also promised to provide for his children and me.

It was after one of these fights that I realized I had just as much cause to be angry with myself for not keeping the promises I made to myself. I never went back to school, and I never attempted to look for a job. I chose the easy road, deciding to spend my time being an adulteress and partying. Now here I am, still hopelessly in love with a drug dealer and stuck in an unhappy marriage. Sometimes I wondered if my current state of discontent was God's punishment for my affair.

My telephone started ringing just as my butt fell asleep from sitting on the hard stair. I stumbled up to answer it just before the voicemail picked up. It was Shyanne.

"Hey, Shy."

"Hey yourself, girlfriend. What's going on over in the Taylor household?"

"Nothing new. Same grief, just a different day."

"Maybe you need to get out of the house for a while. How about you and your best friend go on a shopping spree and spend some of that money your husband is so fond of making. We will go out and pick out a nice birthday outfit for you. Can you get your mother or Kevin to watch the kids for a while?"

"I'll call Kevin. I'm sure he would love to come over and sit with them. I'll meet you at your house after he gets here."

"It's a date."

I had been so upset with Shaun and his activities that I nearly forgot my thirtieth birthday was two weeks away. With the stress of these last four and a half years of my marriage, it felt more like I was turning fifty. I wondered if Shaun realized I had a big birthday coming. At least my best friend remembered. I could always depend on Shyanne when no one else was dependable. She was my own personal God-sent angel.

Kevin readily agreed to come over and play with his niece and nephew. I was very lucky to have him in my life. Kevin was a grown 27-year-old man, and I still called him my little brother. He was such a great person. Since his brief jail-house experience with Shaun a few years ago, Kevin had been a model citizen. He left the store right after he completed his degree and has been working as an executive with a major corporation, steadily moving up the corporate ladder.

Shyanne and I drove out to Somerset Mall in Troy. Somerset housed all the high fashion and department stores. Like Shyanne said, I planned on spending a great deal of the money that my drug-dealing husband was so fond of making.

I purchased a couple of great outfits for both Shyanne and

myself and a ton of things for the kids, mine and Sha'Ron, but my heart wasn't in it. Shyanne could tell. She suggested we take a break and get something to eat, so we stopped in a small café. As soon as the hostess seated us, Shyanne started her interrogation.

"Not that I don't already know, but tell me what has you so down in the dumps this evening."

"Of course you already know, so why bother asking."

Shyanne covered her face with both hands in an expression of frustration and exasperation, letting out a deep pinned up breath. "Nay, why do you stay with this man when all he does is make you miserable? Please don't give me that crap about you loving him or it's for your children. You deserve better for both you and your kids. What the Bible says in I Corinthians 6:4-8 is the kind of love you deserve. Those are the only scriptures I know by heart."

"You know what, Shy? I don't even know if I still love Shaun."

The look on Shyanne's face was priceless. Her mouth fell open, her eyes bulged from her head, and her hands flew to the sides of her face. She resembled the little boy from the movie *Home Alone* when he realized his family left him behind. It was almost comical, and if I were not so mad, I would have laughed.

Shyanne recovered from her little attack and said, "Again, I ask, Nay, why do you stay with him?"

"I don't know if I know why. He's hardly ever home, and when he is, we're constantly arguing, but for the life of me, I cannot bring myself to walk away. I guess I keep hoping one day he will walk through the door and say, 'Lindsay it's over. I finally did it. I am finally satisfied that I have enough money, and I quit selling drugs,' and I'll magically fall back in love with him. I just don't know, Shyanne." I covered my face with my hands and shook my head.

When the waitress appeared to take our order, I was too

distraught to speak, so Shyanne ordered for both of us. After the waitress left, Shyanne pried my hands from my face. Her face held so much compassion for me that I silently started to cry. The tears ran unchecked down my face. Shyanne held my hands and just let me cry. We acted as if we were the only two patrons in the restaurant. By the time the waitress reappeared with our food, I had gotten myself somewhat under control, and I wiped my face with a paper napkin.

"Well, it's obvious that you still love him, Nay, otherwise you would be out of there in a heartbeat. But I must say it is encouraging to not hear you say he is the center of your universe. That shows excellent progress to me. Just keep praying. And who knows, maybe that's what Shaun's planning to give you as a birthday present. He could very well waltz into your home on your birthday and announce that he is now a legitimate man, free and clear from all sales of illegal and illicit narcotics."

I knew Shyanne didn't actually believe a word of what she said, but I held out hope that perhaps my best friend was prophetic. Maybe that's exactly what Shaun was giving me for my birthday.

I neglected to voice my next thoughts because I knew Shyanne was tired of hearing it. But as God was my witness, if that was not my birthday present, my thirtieth would be the last birthday I would spend married to Shaun Robert Taylor.

I could not believe Shaun's cell phone was vibrating at 4:30 in the morning. When I looked at his nightstand, his cell phone was there, but it wasn't vibrating. The vibration was coming from the bottom of the bed where his pants lay. I was unaware that he even had a second phone. With the way he was sleeping through the noise one would have thought he was unaware as well.

I eased from the bed so I wouldn't wake him and went to answer the phone. By the time I got to it, the caller had hung up. I hated the thoughts running through my head, but who else other than a female would be inconsiderate enough to ring a married man this time of morning?

I retrieved the phone from his pants pocket, and I checked the number to make sure it was not a number I recognized like his mother's or his sister's. It was neither so, I took the phone downstairs to the kitchen to return the call.

I dialed the number with nervous anticipation, knowing that I was going to be none too happy no matter who answered the phone. Of course I was not wrong. The frantic person on the other line answered expecting the caller to be Shaun.

"Shaun, what took you so long to call me back? I have been ringing your phone for more than forty-five minutes."

"Who is this?" I asked

"Who is this?" the woman replied.

"This is Shaun's wife. Why are you so urgently calling my husband?"

"His wife! What's going on? Tawanda never said anything about Shaun being married. I'm going to kick that heifer's tail when I get back in that hospital room. She knows I'm a Christian woman and I don't want to be involved in no drama like this."

Tawanda! Now it was my turn to be shocked and wonder what was going on. Why were she and Tawanda at the hospital and who was I talking to now?" I guessed I needed to ask her that.

"Again I ask, who am I speaking with?"

"My name is Alberta. I'm Tawanda's mother. As far as I know Tawanda and Shaun have been going together for more than two years. Never once did my daughter tell me Shaun was married."

Two years! I guess their strictly business relationship

turned into something more when he got out of prison. Perhaps this was his way of rewarding her for all of her hard work. I was heartbroken but not surprised. Now was not the time to get into all of that.

"Ma'am, why is Tawanda in the hospital?"

"It's not Tawanda. It's their four-week-old daughter, Shauna. The baby started seizing, and we rushed her over here to Sinai-Grace . . ."

Ms. Alberta continued speaking, but I heard little else after she said 'their daughter.' I stood in my kitchen on shaky legs while my heart burst into a million pieces. Shaun had cheated on me again. Again he fathered another child while we were together. Then my mind switched gears. I started thinking about how I cheated on him and had gotten pregnant by Cody. Did I actually have the right to be angry with Shaun?

Ms. Alberta's voice trying to get my attention brought my mind back to the present. "Baby! Baby! Baby! Are you still there, young lady?"

"Yes, ma'am, I'm here. I'm sorry, but you have to understand that I'm a little stunned to hear that my husband has cheated on me again and has another baby by yet another woman."

"I can certainly understand that. Honey, I didn't mean no disrespect. I am shocked to find out Shaun has a wife. I wonder if Tawanda knows he is married. And what do you mean by yet another woman. Is this something Shaun has done to you before?"

I found myself ready to poor my bleeding heart out to this stranger; the mother of my husband's other woman; another baby mama, but I stopped myself short. I needed to get off this phone and sort through some things.

"It's not something I want to talk about right now, ma'am. Just tell me how the baby is, and I'll let Shaun know that you called."

"Tell Shaun that we have been here forty-five minutes, and they have the seizing under control. They're going to keep

Shauna here for a few more hours to make sure she doesn't have another one. She was born seven weeks premature and didn't weigh but three and a half pounds, so there were a lot of complications with her birth. They believe this may be a result of that. I'm real sorry about this whole mess, young lady. I just didn't know. I felt Shaun would want to know what was going on with the baby."

"It's okay, ma'am. I will wake Shaun up and tell him right now," I lied, then hung up the phone before she could say anything else.

Once I disconnected the call, I threw the phone across the room, smashing it against the far wall. I staggered into my living room and sat on the sofa feeling crazy and confused. My mind was whirling in a thousand different directions. I became nauseous, so I lay down on the sofa and stared up at the ceiling.

At least I knew this nausea was not the result of another pregnancy. When Shaun was released from prison and still at the halfway house, I told him I wanted to have my tubes tied. I explained that I was very satisfied with Shauntae and Lil' Shaun and that I didn't want to have any more children. He agreed without hesitation. Why wouldn't he when he had another egg donor at his disposal? After my abortion I knew I could never give birth again without feeling the over- whelming anguish of killing my child.

I lay in the disbelief of reliving the nightmare of finding out Shaun had another child, this time a daughter, by an- other woman. This clown now has five children by four dif- ferent women: Rhonda, Keva, myself, and now, Tawanda.

I must have drifted off to sleep while I lay on the sofa thinking about my husband's latest infidelity. The next thing I knew a fully dressed Shaun was standing over me with a big ole smile on his face.

"Happy birthday, sweet wife." With the mess I experi- enced earlier, I totally forgot it was my birthday.

I was so grateful that my mother offered to keep the kids for the weekend as part of my birthday present. I was about to go so far off on Mr. Taylor. How dare he stand there grinning like a Cheshire cat while I lay here with a broken heart? Knowing Shaun, he had some spectacular surprise planned for me. But the surprise was going to be on him. The only present I wanted from him was a divorce. I jumped from the couch and got right in Shaun's face.

"Happy birthday? What makes this birthday so happy, Shaun? Is it because today I found out I had a four-week-old stepdaughter? Wow, baby! Thanks for the marvelous birthday present."

Shaun backed away from me looking wild eyed and scared. I used his weakness to bolster my anger and confidence. I walked up to him and pushed him hard in his chest as I continued my tirade.

"What's the matter, Mr. Big Man, or should I call you Big Poppa? Or perhaps, Lil' Ole Man Who Lived in a Shoe. Had so many baby mamas he didn't know what to do!"

"How did you find out, Lindsay? Do you have my other phone?"

I ignored his questions and continued fussing. "I thought you said she was just a business associate. You said she only brought dope for you to sell while you were in prison. Isn't that the lie you told your wife?"

Suddenly Shaun's demeanor changed from that of the guilty husband to something different. He backed up a few steps and folded his arms across his chest. I felt like I was losing the upper hand so I tried to continue.

"What's the matter, sweet husband? Cat got your—" Shaun's cut me off with a hand in my face and a menacing grimace on his.

"You have got some nerve, you little whore," Shaun growled slowly in a low voice.

My mouth flew open and my eyes bulged from their sockets. I had no idea what gave Shaun the gall he now possessed. I was more furious now than I had ever before been in my life. Never had he called me out of my name like that. I went after him clawing for his face, but Shaun was quicker than I. He grabbed my swinging arms and pinned me with my hands pressed against my chest and my back pressed against his chest.

Shaun whispered in my ear. "How dare you give me the *'how can you do this to me speech'* when you were screwing my attorney the whole time I was in prison?"

Shaun pushed me away from him in disgust. I landed on my knees between the coffee table and the sofa.

I stayed there staring at the floor in total shock. How in the world did Shaun find out about Cody? How long had he known? I didn't have to wait long for answers because the next thing I knew he was standing over me screaming. "Get up!"

I complied because I was too terrified not to. I sat on the end of the sofa farthest away from Shaun, but he quickly erased the distance between us. He came and sat down next to me and got right in my face and grabbed my chin roughly.

"Who do you think you are? Or maybe I should I ask do you realize who I am? Did you really think I was going to go away for two years and not have someone out here watching you? I know all about your little rendezvous at the country club, your little out of town trips; everything. I know that you never let him spend the night here, and he has never been around my children. That was about the only smart thing you did during that time."

Shaun got up from the sofa and started pacing back and forth in front of me. I released the breath I wasn't aware I was holding while my body started trembling. I was shocked that he knew almost everything about Cody and me. He had yet to mention the abortion, but he was hardly through with me.

"I never said anything to you about your affair for one reason and one reason only. It was expected of you. You see,
there are rules to this game that you have no idea about.
When a baller gets time, he has to go in being realistic. There
is very little chance that your woman is going to remain one
hundred percent faithful, especially if you have wronged her
at any point. So I was prepared for your infidelity; I even expected it to be with Cody. Don't forget, Lindsay, I know you
better than you know yourself.

"You come at me this morning with all of your self-righteous
garbage knowing full well you had dirty hands yourself. You
are a trip, little girl."

I was unsure where I received the courage, but it was time
for me to fight back. There was no way he would get away
with feeling like I had wronged him as much as he had me. I
kept my position on the sofa and started speaking to him
very calmly.

"So who did you have following me, Shaun, your new
baby mama? You want to wipe away all of your dirt by using
my one indiscretion as the eraser, but I refuse to be that big
a fool for you ever again."

Even if I were willing to forgive him yet again for father-
ing another child and for still selling drugs, I knew I could
never live with him as long I knew he knew about Cody. Our
relationship, our marriage was a done deal, so there was no
use holding back anymore. I still, however, wanted to walk
away with the upper hand. I had to use my ace in the hole.
While I played my last card, I prayed that Shaun was in the
dark about my last pregnancy and couldn't use it as his
trump.

"Yes, Shaun, I had a relationship with Cody for two years,
just like the one you had with Keva for two years. Now I
know it has been a while since we have seen or heard from
the first wench that you cheated with, but I'm sure you still
remember her and the baby you fathered with her. Right?"

I knew I was playing it close, because even after all these years, Shaun was still salty about losing his son to who knows where. But I was a woman out of control. Discretion was not a word I cared for right now. So I pressed forward. I stood up now. Shaun and I faced each other in front of the sofa. I remained quiet for a few seconds, waiting to see if he would reveal that he knew about my abortion. When he remained silent, I took that to mean that he knew nothing.

I circled behind Shaun while he remained standing with his back to me. I pushed him slightly and continued talking.

"Now today, on my thirtieth birthday of all days, I find out that you again have not only cheated on me, but didn't have enough respect for me to at least wear a condom, and you have another baby. Yeah, Shaun. I cheated, but at least I made Cody wear a condom, and I didn't bring home any illegitimate babies."

Shaun turned around slowly and faced me again. The look in his eyes held immeasurable anger. He struggled, but he stayed composed. "How did you find out about Tawanda and the baby, Lindsay?"

The sound of his voice calling me by my first name now sickened me when it used to sound like poetry. The face that I once thought more beautiful than any I had ever seen now looked monstrous to me. The man I used to love more than I loved myself made me want to spit on him.

I struggled with my own composure because the anger I felt threatened to spill from my eyes. I refused to let Shaun ever see me shed another tear. So instead of crying, I let the anger pour from my mouth.

"Your baby's mama's mama called you at 4:30 this morning. I got the phone from your pocket and returned the call to find out that your daughter is in the hospital. I destroyed the phone after that."

Shaun exploded and was right back in my face now. "What? You mean to tell me you have known since 4:30 this

morning that my baby was in the hospital and your evil behind didn't tell me?"

I stood my ground and yelled back in his face. "Oh! I'm
supposed to be concerned about your little bastard child
being in the hospital, stupid? That baby could be dead for all
I care, Shaun." I screamed.

BAM! Shaun punched me in the face like I was a 220-
pound truck driver. Luckily I fell onto the sofa, but he was
on me instantly, striking me about the head and face over
and over again. I tried fighting back by flailing my arms and
kicking my legs to get him off me, but he was like a mad
man.

Once he stopped punching me, he put his hands around
my throat and started choking me. He pressed his hands
into my neck with what seemed like every ounce of strength
he had, yelling crazed profanities and spewing spit all over
me. I could no longer breathe. I was unable to make out
most of what he was saying. Eventually I blacked out.

Chapter Twenty-Six

When I awakened, my whole body was sore, but most of the pain radiated from my throat. Dried blood splattered the front of my nightgown. My head pounded as I tried to open my eyes. When I succeeded, Shaun was nowhere to be found.

I gingerly arose from the sofa to look at myself in the mirror on the foyer wall. I would have screamed if my throat had allowed it, but the only sound that escaped was a painful gasp. I looked like something from a science fiction movie. Two of my bottom teeth were missing and one of the top fronts was badly chipped. My head had lumps in every visible spot and my eyes were practically swollen shut. I could barely see myself. As horrible as my face looked, I almost wished I were totally blind.

I nervously explored the house to make sure Shaun was gone. He was. It looked as if the only thing he took with him was his cell phone. This made me believe he would return at some point. Therefore I wanted to leave. If and when he decided to come back, I didn't want to be there. Driving was out of the question because I could barely see. I was also dizzy after my tour of the house. I raced to the bathroom to vomit and it turned out to be one of the most painful experiences of my life. My throat burned and ached something terrible. I needed medical attention.

My first instinct should have been to call the paramedics and have them take me to the hospital, but instead I called Shyanne.

"Hey, birthday girl. I wasn't expecting to hear from you so early. I assumed you would have slept in since the kids were away. Has your husband given you your birthday present?"

This was my first attempt at speaking since my beating. I hardly got the words out of my mouth, but I did the best I could.

"Shy . . . I . . . need . . . to   go . . . to   the . . . hos . . . pi . . . tal."

"I can't hear you, Nay. What did you say?"

I painfully repeated what I said as loud as I could and prayed she understood me. I didn't have the strength to say it again.

"Oh my God, Nay! What's wrong? That's okay. Don't talk anymore. I'm on my way. You can tell me when I get there."

Shyanne was letting herself into my home about twenty minutes later with Kevin following about ten seconds behind her. I was upstairs in my bedroom after having taken a shower. I was painfully trying to dress myself so I could go to the hospital. I put on a pair of sweat pants and was struggling with getting the matching shirt over my head when Shyanne burst into the room.

"I called Kevin and told him to meet me here. I told him not to tell your mother until—" Shyanne screamed as I brought the shirt down over my head and Kevin, who apparently stood at the bottom of the steps, came running into the room as well.

Shyanne gently helped me to sit on the bed and she and

my brother examined my face and mouth. Silent tears streamed from Shyanne's eyes. Pure rage covered Kevin's features.

"Did Shaun do this to you?" Shyanne asked

I nodded my head in affirmation. She placed her arms around me, holding on very tightly. A little too tightly considering how badly my arms ached, but it was the best pain I had ever felt.

Kevin's reaction was the complete opposite of Shyanne's. While she was gentle, he became violent. He picked up the crystal clock from my nightstand and threw it across the room, smashing it into what seemed like a million tiny pieces. I had never seen my brother so angry. His wrath brought on a fresh flow of tears from me. Shyanne got up from the bed and went over to try to calm and console Kevin.

"Hey, little brother, I know you're mad right now. So am I, but we have to take care of Nay first. We will figure out how to deal with Shaun once we get her to the hospital and have her checked out, okay?"

Kevin nodded his head in agreement and he and Shyanne hugged.

I gave them the details that led to my birthday beat down as best I could on the way to the hospital. Shyanne sat in the backseat with me, and as I whispered to her, she repeated what I said to Kevin who drove. The more I struggled with my words, the angrier each of them became. Having known them both all of my life, it seems I was able to read their moods and emotions. It was ironically easy considering their feelings were one in the same at that moment. They were both seething enough to kill my husband with their bare hands.

The emergency waiting room was crowded as usual. It seemed as if all eyes were on me. I knew I looked a hideous mess and the stares from the patrons at the hospital confirmed it. I was so embarrassed. I felt as if everyone in that room knew my entire history with Shaun and they were all condemning me, thinking that I got what I deserved for staying with him as long as I did.

After an eternal wait, a doctor finally saw me. Most of my injuries were just ugly cuts and bruises. I received a few stitches in my mouth where the teeth were knocked out. The doctor said that my throat would probably be sore for a few days but no major damage was done.

After giving me my discharge instructions, the doctor told me he would have to contact the police and report my case as possible domestic violence. "It is our obligation to report anything that looks like a crime. I also suggest you go to the police yourself. No woman deserves to be beaten by her husband or anyone else. You deserve better."

The doctor spoke in a tone indicating that he believed this was a regular occurrence in my marriage. I neglected to dispute his thoughts. While this was the only time Shaun ever hit me, it was surely not the most abusive thing he had ever done to me. I nodded my understanding, and I thanked him for his help and concern.

We waited in the hospital room until the police arrived, and I told them my story. I then gave them Shaun's personal information, the type of car he drove, and the address to his mother's house, indicating that was where he could more than likely be found. After the police wrote up their report, I was allowed to leave the hospital.

Shyanne and Kevin silently drove me home. They wanted me to rest my throat, so I was not allowed to talk. The two of them were still stewing in their anger so speech was not high on their list of priorities either.

At my house, Shyanne helped me to get comfortable in my bedroom and Kevin went out to have my prescriptions for a pain killer and antibiotic filled. Shyanne fixed me a can of soup to coat my stomach for the medication. She orally fed me the soup and verbally fed my spirit with her words of comfort and encouragement.

"I know this has to be a very painful time for you. You just found out that your husband has a baby with yet another woman. He beat you, and you got to spend your thirtieth birthday in a hospital emergency room."

My best friend paused a moment in her speech to wipe the soup that dribbled onto my chin and pajama top. When she continued, I could see that her eyes were full. The water threatened to spill, but she continued.

"Nay, all of this has to make you feel absolutely horrible right now. But I want you to hear and believe this. God will walk you through this, and I promise I will be here with you for whatever it is you go through until Shaun is out of your life and out of your system."

The tears were now running from her eyes unchecked, and within seconds we were both crying enough to make a small puddle in my bedspread. Neither of us bothered to stop.

"God will help you learn to live without him. God will help you learn to deal with him for the sake of the children. God will nurse you back to complete emotional health and help you learn to be stronger as a result of this horrible relationship. He won't let you pity yourself, but He will help you dry your tears. In other words, God will be with you every step of the way. And I'll be here to act as His servant; no matter how sick you make me or how long it takes. God loves you, Lindsay Renee Tay . . . Westbrook. I love you too, and I have got your back."

We sat and cried until our wells ran dry. By the time Kevin came back with my prescriptions, we were both spent. We were two messy heaps, and Shyanne's eyes were almost as swollen as mine.

I figured I would start taking the antibiotic in the morning setting up an easy schedule for myself, but I took two of the pain pills right away. Before I knew it, I was on my way to Sleepy Land with Shyanne lying right next to me. Kevin left saying he was going home to let Mama know what happened and to help her with the kids.

It was several hours later when Kevin woke me up. I was sleeping so soundly I didn't realize Shyanne had left the bed. I assumed she had gone to let Kevin in the house, and she was still downstairs.

I lifted my head from my pillow to focus on Kevin's face. I could tell he was distraught and had been crying. When I looked closer I saw that there was a lot of blood on his shirt. I panicked, thinking Kevin went out looking for Shaun and the two of them got into a fight.

"Oh no, Kevin. Are you all right? What happened?" My throat still hurt so my voice was quite raspy, but I was able to speak better.

Kevin collapsed at the side of my bed, bawling. The only time I had heard Kevin cry like that was on the rare occasion he had gotten a whooping from Mama.

His passion confused me. I figured fighting Shaun would make him mad, but the anguish I heard in my little brother's tears was not from anger. My fear intensified.

"Something is wrong, Kevin. I can feel it. Please, Kevin, tell me what happened. Why are you crying like that?"

"Nay, I'm sorry. I'm so sorry. It was an accident, Nay. It was all one big mistake, and I am so sorry," Kevin screamed through his tears.

"It's okay, Kevin. Just calm down and tell me what happened." I spoke in a soothing voice as I tried to calm Kevin, but inside I was terrified. I knew I had to find out what he was talking about. Everything in my being told me I would never be the same once I knew what it was.

Kevin never changed the pitch of his voice. Through his

wails and tears he uttered the most crushing words I had ever heard in all my life.

"Shy is dead, Nay! They killed her! They shot her by mistake. She's dead, Nay! Shyanne is dead!!!"

I heard what Kevin said, but something must have snapped inside of me at that very moment. The pain and devastation that those words should have caused was not present. Instead what I felt was pure unadulterated anger. Just a few hours ago she promised me she would see me through this mess with Shaun and now her lying behind was dead.

Chapter Twenty-Seven

Today is going to be the most difficult, horrific, painful and tragic day of my life. If I ever have to endure a day worse than this, I won't survive it. There's no way I can go through anything more terrible than this and come out sane. Today is the day I bury my best friend.

It took an hour to get over the initial shock and anger when Kevin told me that Shyanne had been shot and killed. It was a full two days later before I stopped screaming and crying enough for him to tell me exactly how my best friend ended up dead.

Mama called a doctor friend from church to come by my house to give me a shot of something so that I could calm down. Mama was afraid I might do something horrible to myself, even if it were by accident. I completely trashed my house, throwing everything I could lift. I did all of this before I found out Shaun's connection to Shyanne's death.

On the day of my beating, Shyanne got a call from Kevin telling her that Shaun had been spotted at his mother's house. The two of them were determined to get their hands on Shaun for putting his hands on me. They neglected to inform me of their decision, but I was not surprised when Kevin told me about it either.

Kevin called someone he knew in Patricia's neighborhood to keep an eye out for Shaun. Once he got the call from his friend, Kevin called Shyanne and she left my house to pick him up at Mama's. When the angry duo arrived at Patricia's, they parked three houses away. Shaun was sitting in his mother's driveway with a female they assumed to be Tawanda. Shyanne was infuriated. She jumped from the car and quickly approached Shaun at his car.

Kevin said he tried talking to her so they could formulate some type of plan. He was positive that Shaun had a pistol, so he wanted to sneak up on him. However, Shyanne was so out of control she started after him on her own. Kevin followed her, and by the time he reached Shaun's car, Shyanne already had the driver's side door open pummeling Shaun with both her fists.

Kevin says the next events happened so fast he could not accurately recall them. He said Tawanda jumped from the car while he was trying to pull Shyanne away so he could get a piece of Shaun himself. Tawanda came at him clawing hard at his face. He had to let go of Shyanne so he could get her off of him. He and Tawanda somehow ended up tumbling in the grass just off the curb and the next thing he remembered was hearing about five or six gunshots.

Kevin untangled himself from Tawanda and got up to find Shyanne lying bloody, completely still in the street on the side of Shaun's car. Shaun was chasing behind the car that sped away, firing at it with his own gun.

Word on the street is that the hit was meant for Shaun over a drug deal gone bad. Shyanne's death was a simple case of right place, wrong time. If she hadn't gone after Shaun that evening for what he did to me, she would still be alive, and Shaun and Tawanda would probably be dead.

I felt so guilty. If it were not for me and my stupidity, my best friend would still be here with me. If I had only listened to her when she told me to leave Shaun so many times in the past, Shyanne would be alive. I don't care what Mama, Granny, Kevin or Shyanne's parents say; I am responsible for the murder of my sister, my friend, my comforter, and my protector. I hate myself for it.

I am not alone, however, on the list of people I hate and blame. Shaun is just as much at fault as I am. I hate him even more than I hate myself. Ever since the night of the shooting, I have prayed that the person or people who shot Shyanne find him soon and finish what they started. It is killing me that he is walking around breathing the same air that I am; air that Shyanne is no longer privy to.

The D.A.'s office contacted me yesterday to let me know they have issued a warrant for Shaun's arrest for a violation of his parole on both the domestic violence charge and being in possession of a handgun. I am hoping the killers get to him before the police do.

I haven't heard from Shaun since that infamous day. He has not returned to the house nor has he tried to see or contact the children. I assume he is held up somewhere with his new baby mama, hiding from either the police and/or the people who are trying to kill him.

I'm unsure why, but half of me expected his arrogant behind to show up here for the funeral. Thank goodness he didn't, because I'm sure that I, Mama, Kevin, nor Shyanne's parents, would have been able to hold on to our dignity. We needed to be as composed as possible to give Shyanne a proper homegoing service. If Shaun had shown his face, it would have been a popping right up here in this church.

Mama T and Mr. Kennedy wanted me to read the obituary for the service today, but I just couldn't do it. I felt unworthy of the honor of getting up in front of all Shyanne's friends and family since it was my fault she was dead. I would have never made it past the first word. The Kennedys kept assuring me they placed no blame on me, and I believed them. They understood my not wanting to read, however, and they let me off the hook. Our childhood friend, Sharay, did the honors.

At the time for the final viewing before they closed the casket, I was unable to move from my seat. Seeing her lying there when I first entered the church was almost more than I could bear. There was no way I was going to be able to do it again. Mama, Kevin, Shyanne's parents and grandparents went up to say their final goodbye. I stayed glued to my seat. Granny opted not to attend the services and to keep my kids instead. This was not how I wanted them to remember their godmother.

They all cried silently. Shyanne's parents held onto each other, both needing the other to stay on their feet. Once they all returned to their seats, the funeral directors lowered Shyanne's body deep into the casket and closed the lid. It was the final click as the top snapped shut that did me in. I rushed to the casket and threw my arms around it as far as they would go, screaming like a mad woman.

"Please, Shyanne, don't be dead! Get up! Please get up! I'm sorry. I am so sorry! I'll never go back, Shy, I promise! I'll never love him again! Just please don't be dead. God, please let her not be dead!"

I fell to the floor in a pitiful heap with my dress hiked up around my hips and my underwear exposed for all the church to see. Kevin and Mama came to my rescue, lifting me back to my seat. It seemed my little scene caused a domino effect, with everyone now relinquishing their pinned up grief. The wails and screams coming from all of us on the front pew were deafening.

After several minutes, the church nurses were able to comfort and calm us somewhat, and the service proceeded. I didn't hear most of what was said because I was so caught up in my misery. I only looked up from my lap once when I heard Sharay read my name from the obituary. "Her best friend and sister, Lindsay a.k.a. Nay-Nay," was what she said. The guilt threatened to suffocate me. How could I be her best friend when I was the one who got her killed?

Once the church service concluded, we headed outside to ride to the burial site. Kevin escorted me because I could barely walk on my own. From the sidewalk I heard a familiar voice call my name. I looked up to see Cody standing at the bottom of the steps. Kevin held me protectively and asked, "Isn't that Shaun's lawyer? What is he doing here?"

No one besides Shyanne, and of course Shaun, knew of our affair, so I understood Kevin's concern. "He's cool, Kevin. He, Shyanne and I remained friends after Shaun was locked up. He's probably just here to pay his respects. I'm going to go over and talk to him."

"Are you sure, Nay? Does he still work for Shaun? I mean, if he does, he could be up to something." I was certain that Shaun no longer retained Cody as his attorney after finding out I was sleeping with him.

"Trust me, Kevin. I'll be okay. I won't be long. I'll meet you all in the limo."

Kevin walked me down the stairs and delivered me to where Cody stood. Kevin nodded to Cody in greeting, then headed off to the waiting car.

Cody stared at me for a few moments. My face still held some of the bruising from the beating. I guess he was surprised to see me looking like this. I began explaining.

"I know I look a little crazy, but for my thirtieth birthday my wonderful husband gave me a merciless beating as a present."

"I heard all about it, Lindsay, and don't worry. You still look beautiful to me."

"That's sweet of you Cody." I gave him a smile with my temporary replacement teeth.

"I'm so sorry about what happened to Shyanne. I was here

for the entire service. It tore my heart out to see you grieving like that." I nodded my head in agreement. If I had opened my mouth to speak, I would have let loose with another dam of tears. I composed myself before speaking again.

"You said you heard all about it. How did you find out about the beating and the funeral?"

"It's a long story and I know you have to get going. If you don't mind, I would like to come by and give you all the details. Once you're settled this evening, give me a call." He handed me his card with his contact information on it. "It's all the same, but just in case you forgot.

"Okay. I'm staying at my mother's house right now, but you can come by there. I'll call you as soon as I can." I wanted to hug him, but I settled for touching and holding his hand, then I walked to the car where my family waited.

Cody was just as beautiful as the last time I saw him almost three years ago. If only I had left Shaun for Cody and let him love me as I knew he could, my best friend would still be alive.

Directly after the burial, most people went to Shyanne's parents' house to pay their final respects and have something to eat. I spent the majority of that time in Shyanne's old bedroom. Her parents hadn't made one adjustment to the space. It was still the same room that held all of our secrets, our hopes, and our dreams.

I lay down on Shyanne's bed, closed my eyes and inhaled, hoping to still catch a scent of her. I was not disappointed. I kept my eyes closed and the comfort of feeling close to her lulled me to sleep.

"Nay-Nay, I know you think it's all your fault that I am no longer alive, but it is not. Please don't let the guilt of my death eat you alive. I died doing exactly what I felt I had to do. If you just try to put things into perspective, you'll see that. If the situation were reversed, you would have done

the same thing and you know it. There is no way you would have not gone after the person who hurt me the way Shaun hurt you.

"You always knew I would die and kill for you. I knew the same was true of you. Don't be angry with yourself because I loved you that much. Live knowing that you loved me just as much.

Take care of yourself. Take care of my parents; be their daughter. Take care of my godchildren. Live, Nay, knowing that we will all be together again. I love you."

I bolted upright in the bed and looked around, expecting Shyanne to physically be in the room with me. I immediately realized it was the spirit of my best friend once again coming to comfort me.

"Thank you, Shyanne, for all the years we shared, for all the love you gave and for being there for me now, then and forever. I'll see you in heaven. God, take care of my angel for me . . ."

I arrived at Mama's around 9:00 P.M. and called Cody. He came by thirty minutes later. We went to the family room in the basement to talk. We got comfortable on the sofa, and Cody began to fill me in on everything he knew right away.

"When I saw you at the funeral earlier, I had a lot to tell you. Now so much more has happened since and I don't know where to begin."

"Try giving it to me a little at a time, starting with what you initially wanted to tell me at the church," I replied.

"Good idea. Remember I have a few clients who are in the same profession as your husband, so the news of the botched hit on his life and the subsequent death of Shyanne were all over the streets. Getting the information about her funeral was easy." Cody paused to make sure I was okay so far. I assured him I was fine and he continued.

"Along with the news that there was a hit on Shaun's life for a murder someone in his crew committed, I was also told that Shaun wanted me dead."

This time I was not so calm. First Shyanne and now Cody's life was in danger. My God! What kind of mess had I created? I threw my hands over my face and started shaking. Cody was as cool as a cucumber, however, not acting the least bit affected by the fact that Shaun had a hit on him. Cody reached out and gently rubbed my shoulder and continued to explain.

"When I initially heard about the hit on my life, I was surprised. I wondered why just now, after all this time. Shaun and I have had no contact since he has been out of prison. My source confirmed that Shaun issued the hit on my life the same day that Shyanne was killed. I was told that something evidently happened that day to cause Shaun to start behaving recklessly and violently."

I knew exactly what that something was. It was the argument that Shaun and I had before he beat me, where my affair with Cody was thrown in my face. Shaun must have wanted to take the anger he felt for me that day out on Cody too.

"Cody, what are you going to do?" I asked in fear for his safety.

"Don't worry, Lindsay; I'll be fine. That nonsense was quickly put to rest once Shaun was made to realize the great risk of retaliation. Remember, Shaun and I run in the same circles. I know some pretty ruthless people too."

I gazed up at him with a look of surprise, wondering if he were in any way responsible for the death of Shyanne. I mean, he may have sought to get Shaun before Shaun could get him. He obviously read my thoughts loud and clear because he quickly put my mind at ease.

"I swear, Lindsay, I had nothing to do with the people who

tried to kill Shaun. Like I said, his beef with me was put to rest. Trust me. However, the people who are responsible for Shyanne's death are still after him."

"Good. I hope they catch him, kill him, and feed him his testicles."

I surprised Cody with my words. He looked at me strangely at first, but he got over it quickly. He chuckled and finished telling me the rest of the story.

"Well, that may not be so easy, at least not tonight. Shaun found out about the warrants for his arrest. He went with his attorney to the D.A.'s office to turn himself in this afternoon. He will go before a judge tomorrow morning for arraignment."

"So he's in jail now?" I asked, feeling both a mixture of relief and grief.

"Until tomorrow morning, yes. The judge will probably give him bail, and he will be back on the street. What happens from there is anybody's guess."

Well, that was something for now. I looked up from my pondering to find Cody staring intently. I knew the moment I looked into his eyes he was still in love with me. And Cody being the man that he was had no problem verbalizing what I could already see.

"I have missed you so much, Lindsay. I have dealt with not being with you because I knew you belonged to someone else when we were together. So I took the lumps of losing you like a man and let you go. But seeing you here like this, your face swollen at his hands, your heart broken at the loss of your best friend, and your life in shambles right now, it pains me more than I can tell you. Somehow as ridiculous as it sounds, I feel responsible."

I gave Cody an incredulous look, admonishing him for blaming himself for any of the mess in my life. "How can you possibly feel responsible for any of this, Cody? All you did was be good to me. I blamed myself for a while, but Shyanne told me she wouldn't allow me to do that to myself. So I had to let that go. If there is any blame left to be handed out it belongs to Shaun. He lied to me continuously. Because I loved him like I was supposed to do, his lies cost me." I placed my hand over my heart hoping that the mere touch of my fingers would somehow ease the pain I felt there.

"As I said, I knew it wouldn't make sense to you and not everything in this life makes sense, Lindsay. I knew you were too good for Shaun, yet I let you go back to him. I didn't try to fight for you or convince you that you deserved better than him even if the better was not me. I feel like I let you down."

Cody gathered me in his arms as gently as a mother does her newborn child and held me as I cried my hundredth stream. I wet the front of his shirt with the moisture from my eyes and nose. He sat holding onto me, not the least bit phased that I was ruining his expensive clothing. How could I have let a man this strong out of my life in an effort to hold onto a weak little boy? Cody was right; life often times made no sense.

I knew beyond a shadow of a doubt that Cody would gladly take me back into his life if I offered myself to him even after all these years. I also knew that now was not the time. I had too much going on in my head and in my heart. I needed time to heal from everything. I needed to deal with and then get over the mistakes I made with Shaun before I could pursue another relationship. Cody deserved a whole woman. I was too battered and broken mentally, physically, emotionally, and even spiritually to be of any good to him. But I also knew that God was more than willing and prepared to put me back together, piece by piece.

I looked up from the mess I had made on Cody's shirt and gazed into his eyes. "Cody, you know I appreciate your coming here this evening to talk to me about the current state of affairs with Shaun. I'm even more grateful for all that you have said since. You are one in a million. This means you ought to have someone who is your equal. Right now I can't be that for you. I need time to recover from so many things. I need to heal without the complications of worrying about someone else's feelings. Do you understand what I'm trying to say?"

"Of course I do. I understand perfectly. Just know that I am here for you. Yes, I am in love with you, Lindsay, but I love you as a friend as well. I can be that for you. Okay?"

With all that said, I walked Cody to the door. I kissed him on the cheek, waited for him to get in his car and drive away. I held on to every word he said tonight, and for the first time in a long time, I felt a little peace.

Chapter Twenty-Eight

It has been a month since Shyanne's death, and this was the first time that I had returned to my house. The last time I was here, I tore up the place. I was now on a clean up mission.

My emotions had run the gamut over the death of my best friend and the end of my marriage. I had gone from being extremely depressed when I thought about Shyanne never again being here with me, to exceedingly joyful when I thought about the wonderful times we shared.

When I think of Shaun, I am sometimes filled with so much anger and rage that I curse God for not only creating him, but his parents and their parents and so on. Other times, like when I look at my babies, I am grateful that I knew him because I have them. I remember the love he used to lavish upon me and my heart breaks. I am so hurt because my dreams of sharing a life with him and raising our children together have been shattered.

As I cleaned my house, I started noticing little things that changed since I was last here. It became obvious that Shaun had been here at some point since the beating. I went upstairs to see if anything was missing. The only things I found gone were the photo album of Shauntae that I made for him on our fifth wedding anniversary, the pictures I sent him of Lil' Shaun while he was in prison, and his mink coat. It looked as if all of his clothing still hung in the closet.

On my way out of the bedroom I noticed a shiny object sticking out amongst the rumpled covers on the bed. I went to retrieve it and found it was a gun. The pistol was silver and seemingly polished to perfection. The darn thing was almost glowing.

I picked it up to find it was surprisingly light considering its size. I had never handled a gun before, so I was ignorant to anything regarding a pistol other than the simple point and shoot. I fiddled with it, making sure to keep my fingers away from the trigger. I certainly didn't want to shoot myself in the foot or worse. While examining the weapon, I discovered how to release the clip. There were about four bullets missing. I searched some more and figured out how to put the safety on so it wouldn't discharge automatically.

Since the gun had missing ammunition, I figured I would take it to the police and turn it in, letting them know it belonged to Shaun. This would perhaps give them something to use against him when he went back to court. I stuck the gun in my purse when I got back downstairs and left it there. I would go to the police station after I finished cleaning.

I was immersed in putting my house in order when the phone rang, startling me. I assumed it was Mama. She was the only person who knew I was there, so I neglected to check the caller ID. I answered the phone and almost fainted when I heard the voice on the other end.

"Hello, Lindsay." he said

I had not heard a word from Shaun since my birthday, the day he beat me. Hearing his voice now made my head spin instantly. I stopped breathing. I could not speak if my life depended on it.

"I know I caught you off guard, baby, and I apologize. I drove by about a half hour ago and saw your car in the driveway. I didn't want to come in and scare you half to death, so I kept going."

I couldn't believe it, but Shaun's voice was actually soothing in my ear. I tried to shake off the calming feeling, but it kept coming and the next thing I knew I was talking again.

"Thank you for your consideration, Shaun," I said more affectionately than I wanted to.

I stood in the middle of the kitchen floor having an internal war between my heart and my mind. My stupid heart was winning.

Shaun could always read my moods even through the phone lines, and today was no different. He took advantage of the tone in my voice.

"I know this sounds crazy to you, but I miss you so much. I'm sure you don't believe me, but it's true. You are my wife, Lindsay. You and the kids mean everything in the world to me."

After everything, and I do mean everything, Shaun had put me through, I could not believe my foolish heart was warming to him. My face became flushed and my sexually dormant body began to heat.

"You're right, Shaun, it does sound crazy. Even crazier is the fact I really miss you too. What is it? What kind of hold do you have over me that I could still love you like I do even with all that has happened?" The questions came out of my mouth, but I honestly didn't recognize my own voice.

"Lindsay, what we share is unexplainable. I have loved you from the first moment I laid eyes on you in the grocery store thirteen years ago. I think you felt the same way that same day. No matter how hard we try, we can't seem to shake what is to be our destiny."

I started crying and my mind clouded for a moment. It seemed that for so many years all I had done was cry. I cried because Shaun had hurt me. I cried because Shaun made me happy. I cried because Shaun made me flat out crazy.

That was it; the answer was right there. I was standing in the middle of my kitchen floor losing my mind, only I was conscious of the fact. No doctor was necessary to diagnose me as looney. I was at least coherent enough to establish it for myself.

The next words from my mouth surprised us both. "Where are you, Shaun? I need to see you."

"Are you sure you're ready for that, Lindsay? You've been through so much. Perhaps we should take this real slow and just settle with talking for a while first."

"No, Shaun. You don't understand. I need to see you as badly as I need air in my lungs. I need to wrap myself in your arms and have you slip yourself inside me so that we can become one again. Please, Shaun, don't deny me this. I feel like a junkie in desperate need of a fix. Your love is my drug. I have to see you, Shaun."

I spoke with an urgency in my voice that even I could not recognize. I was shaking like a leaf. If Shaun denied me the opportunity to see him, I felt as if I would collapse in the middle of the floor and die.

"All right, Lindsay. I'll come. Give me about an hour, and I'll meet you at the house."

"No, Shaun. I don't want you to come here. There are so many bad memories in this house. I can come to you. Where are you?"

Shaun told me he was leasing a townhouse in the complex we used to live in together before we got married. He gave me the address. I told him to give me a few hours. I wanted to get my hair done and make myself beautiful for him.

I called my hairdresser and was able to secure an emergency appointment. She had not seen me since Shyanne's funeral, and she knew my head was a mess. I also got my nails done. Then I went back to our house to shower and find something sexy to wear. By the time I was all dolled up, it was dark outside, which was just fine with me. The night-time gave the atmosphere the appropriate feel for the rejoining of my husband and me.

I arrived at the complex and had to search for Shaun's townhouse. It had been a while since I had been back there, so I got turned around a few times. When I finally found his place, I parked in front and sat outside to get myself together. I was so nervous. Something inside my soul told me that once I crossed Shaun's threshold, my life would forever be changed. That same something said that when I left this place again, that very change would be for the better.

I finally gathered my runaway nerves, listened to my inner voice, and exited the car. I approached the door and rang the bell. The door opened after only a few seconds and there stood Shaun with his devastatingly beautiful smile and equally beautiful face. He moved away so I could enter the house and I stepped inside. I was immediately struck by the scent of a familiar fragrance. I couldn't put my finger on exactly what it was, but I refused to dwell on it.

From where I stood the place looked completely furnished, which made me wonder how long Shaun had this place? But tonight was not about the past. It was not about being suspicious over anything he did before he called me today. It was only about starting from this moment and moving forward, rebuilding and strengthening the unbreakable emotional bond the two of us shared.

Shaun led me to the coral leather sectional that took up the majority of the living room and offered me a seat. I thought it a little amusing that Shaun would have this type of furniture in his living room because he always wanted leather furniture in our home. I was not fond of the look myself, thinking of it as bachelor pad furniture. But this piece was nice. It suited Shaun well.

We sat staring at each other nervously for a few seconds, then Shaun broke the ice by telling me what he felt was good news. "Lindsay, my mother gave me a letter she received from Keva. From the date on the letter, it seems that she has had it for more than three months, but neglected to give it to me. I questioned her about why she held on to it so long, and her simple answer was she forgot. I get the feeling—knowing my mother—that she probably wanted to make Keva sweat the same way Keva has made me sweat all these years. The letter said that she and Kevaun have been living in Atlanta for the past four years. She said she moved there and took Kevaun to get back at me for ending our relationship. Keva said she has since gotten married to a really nice guy. She said he was the one who convinced her to contact me. He explained to her how unfair she was being to Kevaun by keeping him away from me. My plan is to call Keva in just a little while. I wanted to share the good news with you first. I am very anxious to see my son again as soon as possible. I hope that I can convince Keva to let me come and visit him for a little while, then have him come here to visit with us for the Thanksgiving holiday."

Shaun seemed very excited about getting to finally see his son after all this time. Surprisingly, I felt nothing one way or the other. I was neither angry nor happy for Shaun. I guess I was still just nervous over seeing him for the first time in a month myself. But I still felt I should say something.

"That's great, Shaun. I know you're really happy about that," I said tensely.

I put my purse in my lap and fidgeted with the strap to give my hands something to do. Shaun observed my discomfort and took my hands in his, rubbing them both very gently. He then stood and motioned for me to do the same. Not wanting my purse to fall to the floor, I lifted it in my hands. Before I had a chance to put it down, Shaun grabbed me and held me very closely in a warm and sensual embrace. I wrapped my arms around his back while still holding my purse in my hands and held on as tight as I could.

As I hugged Shaun, I kept my eyes open and looked over his shoulder. On the end table at the side of the sectional was a copy of Shyanne's obituary. My body completely froze, but my mind started working overtime. The familiarity of the fragrance I smelled when I entered the house assaulted me again with renewed strength. What I smelled was Red Door, Shyanne's favorite perfume. Since it could not have been Shyanne wearing it, I knew the scent had to belong to Tawanda.

Shaun had not yet noticed the tension that now consumed my body. His silly behind just held onto me for dear life. He buried his face in my hair and inhaled its fresh from the salon aroma, something he always enjoyed doing. He then moved his lips to nuzzle my neck, something he knew I always enjoyed him doing. Finally he moved his mouth back to my ear and whispered very tenderly, "I love you, Lindsay."

By the time Shaun released me from his embrace, I had removed his pistol from my purse. I aimed the barrel straight at his heart. I undid the safety on the gun, not like the amateur who just learned how to engage it, but more like the seasoned murderer I was about to become.

Shaun still had not noticed the gun. He was staring so intently into my eyes, looking for the love that used to pour from them every time I looked at him. That is not what he found. The look of confusion on his face let me know he didn't find what he was searching for. Confusion turned to fear as he looked down to see the gun I held in my hand and Shaun's eyes widened in shock.

I pulled the trigger before he had a chance to react any further, and the force of the bullet from the nine millimeter sent him flying over the arm of the sofa, crashing onto the table that held my girl's face.

Shaun tried to force himself into a sitting position, but I stepped forward a few inches and fired the gun again, hitting him once more square in the chest. He collapsed and rolled onto the floor face first, leaving blood splattered on the table and Shyanne's image.

It was unnecessary to go closer to the body. I knew my husband was dead. I calmly placed the gun back in my purse and walked out the door.

When I got outside, nothing seemed disturbed; no one came out of his or her homes as if they had heard gunshots. As I got into my car and drove away, all seemed quite normal and peaceful

And for me it was.

Epilogue

Shaun's body was discovered two days later by his girl-friend, Tawanda, who convinced the police to kick down the door after she had not heard from him in more than forty-eight hours. She told the cops that the last time she saw him was 8:00 P.M. on the day I killed him, which was about thirty minutes before I arrived at his house. The low-down dirty dog.

The police tracked me down at my mother's house several hours after moving Shaun's body to the morgue and told me of his tragic death. They asked me to come down and make a positive identification, but I refused. I told them we were separated, and I just didn't want to do the I.D. I told them to let his new girlfriend do it.

Tawanda told the police all about the contract that was on Shaun's life by the rival drug dealers. That war is where they focused their investigation, at least until I shot Rhonda at Shaun's funeral with the same gun. I was arrested at the scene and taken into custody.

My children were brought in separately and my mother was allowed to pick them up from the police station. One of the officers at the station was cool. He gave my mother the message that I needed her to contact Cody, my attorney. After that I exercised my right to remain silent until I saw Cody's face.

By the time Cody arrived at the station, the police had matched the bullets from Rhonda's body to the bullets from the nine millimeter I used to kill Shaun. Thankfully there were no other bodies linked to the gun. The following day I was arraigned and charged with two counts of second degree murder. I pleaded not guilty and bail was set at half-million dollars cash. Cody posted it without blinking an eye.

After hearing my entire story coupled with Cody's fancy lawyer talk, the D.A. pleaded my case down to second degree manslaughter. I accepted the plea and the judge sentenced me to a term of two to five years in a minimum-security women's prison.

I often think about the day I killed Shaun. I realize I probably could have gotten away with a temporary insanity plea. I honestly believe my mind snapped when Shaun called the house that day. In my deranged grief-stricken, heart-broken subconscious, I started plotting the murder of my husband from the time I heard his voice on the telephone.

My brain made my heart feel all those emotions I spoke to Shaun about on the phone so I would go to him and put an end to the chance that I would ever let him back in my life. I promised Shyanne I would never love him again and that was a promise my subconscious planned on keeping, even if my outer emotions betrayed me. I have never shared these thoughts with anyone, not even my fiancé.

Since my incarceration, Cody has served as executor of my estate, and with my permission, sold all the things that were in my name while I was married to Shaun; the house, the businesses, the car, all of my jewelry; everything. The money has been divided up five ways and placed in a trust for each of Shaun's children.

Cody has been so supportive over these two years. He and my mother get along famously and she has allowed him to get acquainted with my children. Four weeks from today, two weeks after I walk out of here, we will be married in a small private ceremony at his cottage, or should I say our cottage in Martha's Vineyard. Cody and my mother both wanted a more traditional ceremony with all the fixings. Not having Shyanne to serve as my maid of honor put a damper on going that route.

During my first week here at the prison, I met a woman named Darlene who has truly been a Godsend. Darlene is an older woman who is also serving time for second-degree manslaughter in the death of her husband, who she killed after suffering over twenty years of physical and mental abuse. Darlene has taken me under her wings and reintroduced me to Jesus Christ. She and I have Bible Study daily, and I am learning to once again follow Jesus' road map on the road to earnestly living a Christian life.

For the duration of my life with Shaun, I have gone back and forth in my Christian walk. Before I came to prison I assessed that all of the horrible things that happened in my life were a result of God's direct punishment for my straying away from Him. Darlene, however, has made me view things differently. Darlene says that Jesus' death on the cross eradicated that kind of punishment from God. She told me that my pain and misery were directly caused by me and my own actions. God gives us choices, and I chose to follow my own way versus the will of God for my life. God didn't cause the misery in my life, He simply allowed me to follow my own course, which detoured me away from God's purposes for my life.

Darlene has shown me that I made Shaun's love my true god and I left Jesus in the background, only calling on Him when things got rough as a result of my choices. But now, with Darlene's help, I have learned how to put God first by making Him the leader of my life. I now seek Him in all my decisions instead of just a back-up solution. This is the key to living a richer more fulfilling life.

When I came to prison, I walked in wearing Shaun's murder as a badge of honor. I felt I had avenged the death of Shyanne and somehow made right all the wrong Shaun had done to me. Darlene taught me, however, that I needed to humble myself and seek forgiveness for the sins of killing Shaun and Rhonda. Not only had I broken God's commandment, I didn't realize that killing them neither erased the hurt done to me nor had it brought Shyanne back. Dealing with Shaun was God's job.

What I needed was to let go of the hurt, anger and hate and free myself of the demons that caused me to make the mistake of letting someone other than God rule my life. God's love is real and unconditional, full of grace and mercy. It is compassionate and always right. I now know that as long as I depend on God to give me everything I need, He would send me the man that will love me forever as He has given men the instruction to do. And my God has not let me down with my Cody.

Cody, too, has decided to turn his life over to God and to live for Him. We both understand that if we ask for forgiveness for our adulteress affair, God will forgive us and prosper our marriage. The Bible has taught us that God has a way of turning what the devil meant for evil around for good and to God's glory. As stated in II Corinthians 5:17: *Therefore if any man be in Christ, he is a new creature; old things are passed away; behold all things are become new.*

I am now a new and better person because I have come to realize that I am a true child of God, deserving love, respect, compassion, honesty, and every good thing in this life.

I am so thankful to Darlene for opening her heart and her arms to me, showing me the only way to a better life for myself, my children and everyone that I love. And while Darlene is the vessel that He chose to deliver His message, all my love, honor, praise and worship belongs to God.

The Bible states in Job 36:11: *If they obey and serve Him, they shall spend their days in prosperity and their years in pleasures.* I have had enough sorrow behind trying to do it my way. I am now more than ready to try it God's way. Amen!

READING GROUP QUESTIONS FOR DISCUSSION

1. Who is your favorite character in *His Woman, His Wife, His Widow*? Why?

2. Who is your least favorite character in *His Woman, His Wife, His Widow*? Why?

3. Did you think Shaun was too old for Lindsay at the beginning of their relationship?

4. After getting into the book and meeting Shyanne, did you go back and check for her name at Shaun's funeral in the prologue?

5. Do you believe that Lindsay and Shyanne's friendship was realistic? Would you be willing to die for your best friend? Do you blame Lindsay for Shyanne's death?

6. Considering that Lindsay and Shaun were not married when Keva started dating Shaun, did Keva have a right to be upset with them? Do you blame Lindsay for Keva taking Kevaun and disappearing?

7. Do you believe Shaun was telling the truth when he initially told Lindsay that Tawanda was no more than an employee? If so, do you believe that it was Lindsay's affair with Cody that pushed him into a relationship with Tawanda?

8. Describe your feelings about Lindsay and Cody's affair and subsequent marriage. How do you feel about Lindsay aborting the baby she conceived with Cody while they were having their affair? Do you think she should have told Cody about the baby in the beginning? What about after they became a couple while she was in prison?

9. Knowing that Shaun would eventually die, were you surprised that Lindsay was the one who killed him?

10. Lindsay killed Shaun, then approximately one week later, she killed Rhonda. After reading the final chapter, did you think about the fact that Sha'Ron, who is now fourteen years old, lost both his parents at the hands of his stepmother? Given the environment in which this young man was raised, do you think there is a possibility that he may retaliate when Lindsay is released from prison?

11. Is there any part of the book that you would re-write? If yes, which part?

BIO

Janice Jones is a native of Detroit, Michigan, but currently lives in Phoenix, Arizona. She is the mother of two sons, Jerrick and Derrick Parker, and grandmother to Jevon Jerrick Parker.

A self-proclaimed avid reader, Janice's deep appreciation for the written word began at the age of seventeen when she was introduced to *The Burning Bed*, by Francine Hughes. However, her passion for writing came sometime later in life when she began crafting poetry.

After attending church for the better part of her life, Janice fully accepted Christ as her Lord and Savior in May of 1999. Approximately one year later, she heard the voice of God instructing her to write her first fictional novel, *His Woman, His Wife, His Widow*. Obediently, but slowly, she did.

Her first published work, *Still Standing*, is a true-to-life spiritual testimonial of how God brought her through every harrowing hurtful, and horrific experience of her life. It was released in 2006 after much encouragement from Sabrina Adams, Publisher and CEO of Zoe Life Publishing. Janice has recently completed her second nonfiction project entitled *Beyond the Drama*, which is a follow-up to *Still Standing*.

Janice Jones a member of First Institutional Baptist Church under the leadership of Dr. Warren H. Stewart, Sr. As a member of F.I.B.C., she works with the Women's Ministry and

Ms. Jessie's Place, the church campus bookstore and coffee house. During her time in Detroit, she was led and directed by two dynamic pastors: Dr. Nathan A. Proché of Tree of Life Missionary Baptist Church and Dr. Wilma R. Johnson of New Prospect Missionary Baptist Church.

Urban Christian His Glory Book Club!

Established January 2007, **UC His Glory Book Club** is another way by which to introduce to the literary world, Urban Book's much-anticipated new imprint, **Urban Christian** and its authors. We are an online book club supporting Urban Christian authors by purchasing, reading and providing written reviews of the authors' books that are read. *UC His Glory* welcomes both men and women of the literary world who have a passion for reading Christian based fiction.

UC His Glory is the brainchild of Joylynn Jossel, Author and Executive Editor of Urban Christian and Kendra Norman-Bellamy, Copy Editor for Urban Christian. The book club will provide support, positive feedback, encouragement and a forum whereby members can openly discuss and review the literary works of Urban Christian authors. In the future, we anticipate broadening our spectrum of services to include: online author chats, author spotlights, interviews with your favorite Urban Christian author(s), special online groups for *UC His Glory Book Club* members, ability to post reviews on the website and amazon.com, membership ID cards, *UC His Glory* Yahoo Group and much more.

Even though there will be no membership fees attached to becoming a member of *UC His Glory Book Club*, we do expect our members to be active, committed and to follow the guidelines of the Book Club.

UC His Glory members pledge to:

- Follow the guidelines of *UC His Glory Book Club*.
- Provide input, opinions, and reviews that build up, rather than tear down.
- Commit to purchasing, reading and discussing featured book(s) of the month.
- Agree not to miss more than three consecutive online monthly meetings.
- Respect the Christian beliefs of *UC His Glory Book Club*.
- Believe that Jesus is the Christ, Son of the Living God

We look forward to the online fellowship.

Many Blessings to You!

Shelia E Lipsey
President
UC His Glory Book Club

**Visit the official Urban Christian Book Club website at *www.uchisglorybookclub.net*